PRAISE FOR

Liquid Lies

"Martine delivers an ingenious plot filled with plenty of unexpected twists."
—*Chicago Tribune*

"With her debut novel *Liquid Lies*, Hanna Martine is poised to make a huge splash with her hot, steamy tale."
—*RT Book Reviews*

"I found the plot new and different and it kept me reading into the wee hours of the morning!" —*Kindles & Wine*

"*Liquid Lies* is an intriguing beginning and I wonder what will happens next in this alternate world."
—*Romance Junkies*

Long Shot

HANNA MARTINE

B
BERKLEY SENSATION, NEW YORK

THE BERKLEY PUBLISHING GROUP
Published by the Penguin Group
Penguin Group (USA) LLC
375 Hudson Street, New York, New York 10014

USA • Canada • UK • Ireland • Australia • New Zealand • India • South Africa • China

penguin.com

A Penguin Random House Company

LONG SHOT

A Berkley Sensation Book / published by arrangement with the author

Berkley Sensation Books are published by The Berkley Publishing Group.
BERKLEY SENSATION® is a registered trademark of Penguin Group (USA) LLC.
The "B" design is a trademark of Penguin Group (USA) LLC.

For information, address: The Berkley Publishing Group,
a division of Penguin Group (USA) LLC,
375 Hudson Street, New York, New York 10014.

ISBN: 978-0-425-26751-6

PUBLISHING HISTORY
Berkley Sensation mass-market edition / October 2013

PRINTED IN THE UNITED STATES OF AMERICA

10 9 8 7 6 5 4 3 2

Cover art by Claudio Marinesco.
Cover design by Rita Frangie.
Interior text design by Kelly Lipovich.

For anyone who has ever been reunited.

Acknowledgments

This book never would have been born if it weren't for the extraordinary plotting power of Erin Knightley, Heather Snow, and Eliza Evans. What a magical plotting session that was!

Additional heartfelt thanks to my beta readers, Lynne Hartzer, Clara Kensie, and Erica O'Rourke, who helped me with the fine-tuning.

A hearty chuckle to Chuck Wendig, who likely thought he'd never be thanked in a romance novel, for the awesomely bad joke Leith tells in chapter twenty-two.

I did a large amount of research using the websites of the North American Scottish Games Athletics (www.nasgaweb.com) and Scottish Heavy Athletics (www.scottishheavyathletics.com). They are terrific sources of information, particularly the NASGA web forums.

Thanks to my agent, Roberta Brown, who didn't blink when I told her I wanted to write contemporary romance with kilts, and to my editor, Cindy Hwang, who took yet another chance on me.

Chapter

1

*J*en Haverhurst swerved onto the gravel shoulder of Route 6 and braked the rental car with a jolt. Just out the passenger window, on the other side of a fence that didn't quite look sturdy enough to contain them, Loughlin's Highland cattle swung their giant horns and orange, hairy heads toward her. It seemed as though they remembered her and weren't exactly happy she'd returned.

She'd had the whole drive up to New Hampshire from New York City to come to grips with the fact she was going back to Gleann, but it didn't really hit her until the last stretch of empty rural route spun her around the mountains, spit her into the familiar green valley, and she came face to face with those damned beasts.

Beyond their gently rolling field, across a cracked, weed-filled parking lot, rose the sparkling silver and vacant Hemmertex headquarters, which had just started construction her last summer in Gleann and now stood like a scar among the trees.

Directly ahead, tucked into the last bend in the road before the town proper, sat a familiar, tilted produce stand.

That's where Leith had parked his dad's boat of a 1969

Cadillac convertible that summer night ten years ago. The moon had been a sliver, the stars each their own atmosphere. And Leith had given her the first orgasm that wasn't from her own hand.

Jen punched up the weak air conditioner on that hot early-June day and whipped out her phone, pressing the single button to connect her to her office. She needed a dose of her real world. Fast.

Her assistant picked up. "Gretchen, it's me."

"Oh, good. You're alive. Didn't get eaten by a bear or anything?"

"No bear. A cow, maybe." One of the Highland cattle had wandered closer to the fence and eyed her, warning her off its turf. "But yeah, I'm here."

And here she was. Back in Gleann, New Hampshire, after all this time.

Jen stuck the Bluetooth earpiece into place and slowly pulled back onto Route 6, following its curve down the hill and into town. "What'd I miss today?"

Gretchen started talking, but Jen inadvertently drifted off, her mind following the narrow, meandering town streets she'd gotten to know so well after spending nearly every summer here growing up. Though it was clear Hemmertex had been gone for a while, no one had replaced the sign welcoming people into the small downtown: *Gleann, a wee bit of Scotland in America. Home to Hemmertex Corporation.* Sad.

Once upon a time, the Scottish immigrants who'd settled the valley knew how to pronounce *Gleann* with a proper brogue, but the name had since been American-bastardized to "Gleen." As an eight-year-old new to town, Jen had needed a good month to get used to it.

She instinctively knew the way to the Thistle, the Tudor-style B&B once owned by Aunt Bev. Jen parked in front of it, under the low, heavy branches of a tree, but couldn't bring herself to get out of the car.

Down the block, past the playground, she glimpsed the stumpy Stone Pub with its gorgeous thatched roof, its faded sign still swinging out over the sidewalk. She and Leith had waited tables there during her last summer here. He'd purposely brushed up against her one shift, sparking a quick transition from old friends to sneaky, desperate teenaged lovers.

Gretchen let out a singsong whistle. "Yoo-hoo. Jen."

Jen shook her head. "Sorry. What was that?"

"I asked if I can switch a few things around for the Umberto Rollins cocktail party. The table pattern doesn't quite work, I don't think. And I question some of the menu choices for the type of attendee."

Work snapped Jen away from the past and back into the present. "No, no. Don't change a thing. Everything is all taken care of. This is the same annual party they throw for their employees, and I had to make do with a drastically reduced budget this year. They've approved everything. All you have to do is see it through and take care of hiccups."

"All right. If you say so." But Jen could hear the reluctance in her assistant's voice.

"Gretchen, I'm serious. They're very particular and traditional. They trust me, they trust Bauer Events. Just follow my directions for Rollins and then we'll tackle the Fashion Week party when I'm back in the office in two weeks."

"I thought it was three."

"Nah." She peered out the side window, at the ivy creeping up the side of the B&B she'd once considered home. "This should be a piece of cake. In and out."

"Tim is okay with you taking vacation now?"

"Vacation time is stacked up and Rollins is set. It's all good."

At least that's what her boss, Tim Bauer, had told her two days ago when she'd proposed her last-minute leave. She'd worked her ass off for him for six years, almost single-handedly tripled his client list, and snagged a prestigious fashion house account.

He'd strongly hinted that he was considering her for a partnership in his company. As her mentor he'd given her opportunities she'd always dreamed of having. There was a chance he'd even send her to London to be a part of his branch over there, and if that's what it took to get to the top, she would volunteer to swim across the Atlantic.

She deserved a partnership. She *needed* it.

Once it was hers, she could finally kill the heel-biting fear of mediocrity that had chased her all the way from Iowa.

"I still can't believe you left the city to go watch guys in skirts throw heavy stuff around."

Jen suppressed a laugh. "They're called the Highland Games. Gleann needs them."

And Gleann, her life's savior, needed *Jen*.

Someone, a familiar shape, moved behind the curtain in the front room of the B&B. "Listen," Jen told Gretchen, "I gotta go, but call me if you need me. For anything. I'll check in from time to time."

"You're on vacation."

"Oh, honey. In this business, you're never really on vacation. Nor do I ever want to be."

She disconnected and stared out at the hushed, empty streets of Gleann. Reaching over to the passenger seat, she lugged her giant purse across the center console. It hit the car horn hard, sending a loud and nasal blast echoing up and down the curving streets. In New York, a single horn meant nothing. Here, it was a day's excitement.

So much for a quiet arrival.

The front door to the Thistle flew open and Aimee Haverhurst bounded out, her hair, as dark as Jen's but much longer, streaming behind her. Jen stepped out of the car, hoisted her bag higher onto her shoulder, and headed for the taller and eleven-month-older sister she hadn't seen in three years.

Jen's foot struck something and she toppled forward, all balance and grace and professionalism gone.

Aimee lunged, catching Jen and hauling her to her feet. "Whoa. You okay there?"

Jen righted herself and frowned at the slab of cracked concrete poking up from the sidewalk. "That wasn't there before."

Aimee gave a little laugh, but there was familiar strain in the sound. Her sister looked incredibly different without all the makeup of her youth. She looked . . . grown up.

That wasn't the only thing that had changed. Jen eyed the tree in the bed and breakfast's fenced front yard, the one whose boughs now hung over the street. "That thing's enormous now."

Aimee winced. "Did you expect the place to stay the same? Waiting for you to show up again after ten years?"

Maybe not to that extreme, but the distance between northern New Hampshire and New York City had stopped time in Jen's mind.

Unexpectedly, Aimee pulled her into the tightest hug they'd ever exchanged. Or maybe that was just distance and time again, pushing them together instead of pulling them apart, as had been happening between them for so long.

"I'm so glad you're here," Aimee said into her hair, in that serious, pleading way Jen remembered well. The one that usually preceded Jen scraping Aimee out of one of her messes. Only this time, the mess Jen had been called in to fix wasn't Aimee's. "Thank you. Thank you for helping us."

Jen awkwardly patted her sister's back then stepped away. "I said I'd *try*. Even I can't guarantee how it'll all turn out."

Aimee nodded. "I know." But there was hurt and worry behind her green eyes, the same shade as Jen's. They had different fathers, but both physically took after their mom.

If Jen didn't succeed here, if she couldn't fix and put on the local Highland Games, and keep the Scottish Society from dissolving all support, there was a chance Aimee could lose the B&B. The town could lose a lot more. The games were pretty much all it had left.

Jen glanced at the Thistle. "Where's Ainsley?"

Aimee rolled her eyes as she smiled. "A friend's. Who's a boy. I don't know how I feel about that."

"She's what? Ten?"

"Oh, God. Nine. Please don't make her older than she already is."

When Jen had been ten, she'd been great friends with a certain boy. It had been wonderful—and then not so wonderful— but she wouldn't bring that up to Aimee now.

Her twenty-nine-year-old sister had a nine-year-old daughter. Wow. There went time again, churning up dust as it zoomed past.

"Come on." Aimee took her arm with a small smile. "I'll show you your room."

It was a small guest room in the front of the B&B. Not the room Jen had slept in all those summers ago, from age eight to eighteen, but she remembered it well: frilly and soft and pale. She dropped her bags outside the connected bathroom, took a few minutes to run her hands over the pillows and curtains that screamed of Aunt Bev's influence, and went back downstairs. She could hear Aimee clanking around in the kitchen.

"What are you doing?" Jen asked, stepping into the kitchen that hadn't changed at all, with its shiny red refrigerator and everything.

"Cooking."

"You don't have to do that."

"Sure, I do. You're a guest."

A guest. Right. A guest in the house that had once been the only place she'd considered home. But then, she'd been the one to go away to college and leave it all behind. *She'd* been the one constantly working when Bev was sick, and then out of the country working on an incentive event during the funeral. Bev had left the place to Aimee, a fact that still stabbed Jen's heart with a dull knife laced with guilt.

Jen pushed a smile onto her face and tried to make a joke. "It's lunchtime. Your sign says Breakfast."

Aimee pressed her palms to the countertop. "Please, Jen. Let me do this."

Jen got it. She'd spent her life taking care of her older, crazier sister, and now Aimee had something to prove.

"Okay," Jen said, lowering herself into a familiar wood chair around the heavy kitchen table. She fingered the watermelon-shaped placemats. "So I, uh, saw that sign out on Route 6."

Aimee slid a cutting board onto the counter. One dark eyebrow twitched. "Which one was that?"

Jen hated the way she felt her neck heat up. "You know."

"Ohhhhhh. That one." Aimee craned her neck to peek at the clock. "Wow, only twenty minutes."

"For what?"

"For you to mention him."

Jen supposed it had to have taken coming back here to finally ask Aimee about Leith, considering neither of the sisters had brought up his name in ten years. "They put up that huge sign?" Jen asked. "Just for him?"

Aimee took out a roast from the refrigerator and started to carve thin slices from it. It looked like she actually knew what she was doing, and Jen tried not to gape. This being the sister who'd once needed Jen to boil water for mac and cheese.

"It was a big deal then," Aimee said, "a local who wasn't a pro winning the athletics in the games so many years in a row. And after his football season and those state track championships and all . . . It's a small town. He's a bit of a celebrity."

"Huh." Jen had forgotten about the football and track. She'd only come to Gleann in the summer, so she'd never seen him do those things. But she had watched him turn the caber and throw the hammer and toss the sheaf, and do all the other heavy athletic events in the games.

"He doesn't compete anymore," Aimee said, "but they still love him like he won the Olympics or something."

"I'd say. That sign was like a shrine. An effigy shy of a temple."

Aimee gave her a weird smile and started to assemble sandwiches.

Jen gazed out the window, into the backyard that sloped down to the creek. Old images of Leith came back to her, and she felt more than a little dirty picturing his eighteen-year-old body, big even back then, moving on top of her in the back of that Cadillac. How cliche to have lost it to each other in the backseat of a car.

How wonderful to have lost it to him.

Aimee ducked into the pantry, her muffled voice floating out from inside. "You should ask him to compete again."

Jen felt like she'd tripped over something, and she was still sitting down. "Wait. What?"

"You know. Get him to come out of retirement or something. DeeDee tried before she took off, but it didn't work. I bet the town would love it."

Suddenly her chest felt tight. "You mean he's still here?"

Aimee tipped down a bag of pretzels from the top shelf. "Sure. He owns a landscape business, though word is he's hurting, like everyone else, now that Hemmertex is gone."

But he was still here. Oh, God, Leith was still in Gleann. Jen didn't feel guilty for leaving him ten years ago—it was what her life and dreams had demanded of her—but the possibility of seeing him again . . . "Why didn't you tell me?"

Aimee shot her a hard look that was *way* too familiar. "Because everyday news about Gleann hasn't interested you in a decade. Until you learned it was dying."

Jen swallowed and dropped her head in the face of the truth.

She'd chosen to keep her memories as just that: particles of the past drifting around in her mind. They weren't allowed to affect her life in New York. She couldn't afford to move backward, not even an inch. To live in the past was equal to stagnancy and laziness, and that, to Jen, was a fate worse than death.

It meant she was no better than her mom.

Jen lifted her eyes to the backyard again. Leith had once kissed her under the giant maple tree, up against its trunk that leaned over the creek. That particular event had led to sex on a blanket, with a tree root gouging into her back. How could something she hadn't thought about in so long now feel so fresh?

"Has he ever, um, said anything? To you? About me?"

"How old are you again?" Aimee shoved a plated sandwich in front of her. "No, he hasn't. When we run into each other, it's smiles and small talk. You remember how he was, like nothing could ever faze him. He's like a walking good mood."

A little piece of Jen's heart crumbled off and knocked around inside her chest. She'd managed to faze him all right, the night before she'd left Gleann for good and he'd begged her to stay. Told her he loved her with his soul in his eyes. But what was she supposed to do? Sacrifice college and career, and risk suffering the drunken, aimless, bitter lifestyle of her mom?

"So he doesn't know I'm here?"

Aimee shook her head. "No one does except the mayor and me. What if you'd said no, Jen? We didn't want to get our hopes up and then be denied." A pregnant pause. "I've had enough disappointment."

I, not *we*. Jen knew Aimee wasn't talking about today as much as her and Ainsley's disastrous visit to New York three years ago. It had coincided with the same week the fashion house had called, and Jen had had to drop everything to secure the prestigious new client, including entertaining her sister and niece. Without their reason for visiting, Aimee and Ainsley had left the city.

Aimee took a bite of sandwich and talked with her mouth full. "When's your meeting with the mayor?"

Jen flicked on her phone to check the time. "About ten minutes."

Which, if she remembered correctly, gave her about six minutes to eat, since it took four minutes to walk to Town Hall. They ate in silence, Aimee's past disappointment hovering around them. Then Jen fixed her hair and makeup, grabbed her purse with her trusty laptop, and headed for the front door.

A hard wave of memory slammed into her. This moment felt like all those other summers, leaving for job after job after job, her college-fund bank account growing with every hour worked. It was as though ten years hadn't passed. Even the feel of the front door's oblong brass knob brought back memories. She'd drown in them if she wasn't careful, and she'd only been in Gleann for an hour.

She opened the door, the scent of thyme and rosemary wafting in. The herb garden, surrounding little metal breakfast tables, was new. She couldn't, for the life of her, picture Aimee having planted that, but apparently she had.

"Jen."

She turned around to find Aimee standing in the hallway, at the foot of the narrow, creaking staircase leading up to the guest rooms, her eyes filled with emotion.

"I want you to know that I feel bad asking, for taking you away from the city."

"Don't. It's no biggie. Came at the perfect time." Jen's eyes swept over the foyer and she smiled. "Anything for this place. Anything for you."

She hadn't told Aimee about the impending partnership or the risk she'd taken coming here at this particular time in the year. There was no point. She'd been taking care of Aimee her whole life. Back when they were growing up, it had been a responsibility Jen had assumed with drive and determination. Now she accepted it with bittersweetness, but still with love.

Aimee blurted out, "I'm older. I should've been taking care of you, instead of the other way around. And here you are again."

The first time Aimee had said anything of the sort, and it struck Jen like a bell. She covered it with a smile, as reassuring as she could make it. "It's okay. I'm going to do what I can," she said, and then headed downtown.

Gleann legend claimed that its founders had used Celtic magic to transport a chunk of old Scotland into this out-of-the-way valley in the new world, from its stone-facade shops crowding the narrow sidewalks, to the meandering paths of its streets. The Stone Pub stood at the center, beckoning everyone under its thatched roof. Jen had always found this place magical, despite no truth to the legend. Even as a doubtful eight-year-old, the first glimpse of Gleann had set her at ease.

Now, however, the place was practically deserted. She remembered buckets of bright flowers spilling from window boxes and street lamps, and the shop that had once sold granny sweaters and wool pants. All gone. Kathleen's Kafe, with its row of six-paned windows, still stood though, and that made her sigh with some measure of relief.

The ice cream parlor where she'd scooped out orders one summer had long since closed, but she could see that at the building's last use, it had been a scrapbooking store. The Picture This sign still hung over the door. A faded poster was taped inside the window, one corner curling back, proclaiming: *Gleann's Great Highland Games! Don't Miss It!*

Looking around town, she realized it was the *only* mention of the games anywhere, and the thing was supposed to happen in two weeks. It matched what Aimee had told her over the phone, that the games had faded into an annual event with very little enthusiasm and dwindling participation, yet the town clung to it out of tradition. If this was the kind of hill she'd have to scale while here, she was in deep shit. But then, that's what she excelled at: climbing her way out of that deep shit and putting on the best events any amount of money could buy, in any amount of time, no matter how short.

Then she looked closer at the poster.

Leith. His brown hair longer than when she'd last seen him, wet and clinging to his forehead and cheek. His rugged face contorted in exertion, his body even bigger and more muscular than she remembered. He clutched a hammer in his great fists, thick arms sweeping the thing high around his head. The hammer wasn't an actual hammer at all, but a large metal ball on the end of a long handle. The thrower twisted it around his body several times, then released it backward over one shoulder.

In the picture, Leith looked powerful and focused. Badass. And he wore a kilt.

Good God, a kilt.

She'd seen him wear his family's tartan before, back in high school when the whole town had turned out for the annual games. But a kilt on a boy was a much different thing than a kilt on a man. In the photo the wind had kicked up the hem, displaying the hard lines of his thigh muscles set in a wide stance. Black kilt hose—knee socks, she'd once called them and had been quickly corrected by Leith's dad—showed off bowling balls for calves.

None of the men in New York were *that* kind of gorgeous.

The pseudoshrine out on Route 6 declared he'd last won the heavy athletics competition five years ago, the same date on the poster, which would age him in that photo at twenty-three. What did Leith look like now? Seeing how much he'd improved from age eighteen to twenty-three, the curve for hotness progression over time indicated he should be approaching godhood right about now, at twenty-eight.

Her phone blared a warning heralding the time, and at first she didn't recognize the sound. She was never late. Ever. She hurried down the street, past the half-filled Kafe, to the small brick house that served as Town Hall. Ringing the doorbell to the locked front door, she couldn't help but feel like an underappreciated teenager all over again—as though she'd accomplished nothing in the past decade and had nothing to show for herself. It was an odd feeling and one she annoyingly couldn't attribute, until the door finally opened and a silver-haired woman in braids, jeans, and a gigantic Syracuse T-shirt frowned down at her.

That expression Jen remembered with painful clarity.

"Hi, Mrs. McCurdy." Jen pasted on a smile.

Mrs. McCurdy, Jen's old manager at the ice cream parlor and also a former steady dog-walking client, looked Jen over with awkward appraisal. The mayor stepped back and opened the door wider, her fleshy arm jiggling. "Here. Let me show you the mess you've inherited."

Jen took a deep breath. "Um, great. Thank you, Mrs. McCurdy. It's great to see you, too."

"It's Mayor Sue now," the other woman threw over her shoulder as she headed down the hall.

"You . . . you want me to call you that?"

"Everyone else does."

"I'm glad Aimee called me," Jen said. "I would hate to see the games die."

"Well, you agreed to work for free and Aimee said you know what you're doing."

The thing was, Jen knew Sue must have had some form of confidence in her, otherwise why would the older woman have continued to hire her in the past, job after job, summer after summer? Still, would it have killed her to say, just once, "Nice job, Jen. Thanks so much"?

Sue turned in to what must have been a bedroom at one time, but was now a tiny corner conference room with a giant box fan whipping warm air around. A laptop sat on the table. Sue hooked loose strands of wiry hair behind each ear and spun the laptop around so its screen was visible.

Jen bent over and squinted at the spreadsheet, specifically at the tiny number in the bottom right rectangle. "That's what's left? Where'd DeeDee run off to again?"

"France, we're told." Sue snorted, and Jen wasn't sure if the disgust came from the fact that the longtime organizer of the Highland Games had run off with a sizable chunk of the town's money, or that she'd run away to a place that wasn't Scotland with a man who didn't have a drop of Scottish blood in him.

Jen wasn't remotely Scottish either, which might have accounted for some of Sue's snobbery over the years. In Gleann, there were the descendants of the original founders . . . and everyone else. Sue McCurdy was the former. Years ago, the joke had been that Aimee and Jen Haverhurst were Irish twins in a Scottish town. Also, there was the fact that Aimee had been a hellion during her summers here, and Jen had had to skip out of work on more than one occasion to bail her out. Maybe Sue had never gotten over that joke or Jen's sister-related absences.

Jen tapped the spreadsheet on the screen. The amount left in the games' account wouldn't even have covered her fee back in the city, but she wasn't here for the money. A part of her got way too excited at this challenge. It was, quite simply, a matter of pride. Aimee's income, Aunt Bev's legacy, and Jen's own childhood memories were at stake.

"I read that the other games across the state are doing amazingly well."

Sue narrowed her eyes. "Did your research, did you?"

"Always."

Sue nodded, braids swinging. "They get bigger every year, more commercial, more notoriety, pro athletes. We get smaller. The society doesn't like giving resources to something that doesn't even really compete. But we have more history. Better atmosphere."

Jen hadn't been to the other games, but she nodded with Sue's assessment about Gleann's. It was too bad, however, that they seemed to have lost that history.

"Think you can do it?" Sue crossed her arms under her generous boobs. The *Syracuse* printed on the front looked like *yracus*.

Jen pulled her hair back into a ponytail and took a seat. "I think so. Yes."

Sue frowned at her before leaving, as though she'd had hundreds of other event planners lined up around the block to take this gig for free, and Jen still had to prove herself.

The thing was, she *would* prove herself. To Aimee, who'd been so clearly disappointed in Jen's absence the past decade. To dear Aunt Bev, whose love and encouragement had brought her to Gleann and changed her life for the better. To Leith, who'd been so hurt and angry when she'd left. And to her mom, who'd laughed when Jen said she wanted to go to college.

Jen spent the next two hours flipping through old files and memorizing spreadsheets, committing totals and rearranging numbers in her head. There were very few resources, even less money, and practically no organization or innovation. No wonder the society was about to pull out. The timeline to pull this thing off—and to make it better than in years past—would be extremely tough. She couldn't turn the games into the grand affair she'd like to, but there were lots of small, special things she could add to or improve in the time allotted that would make a nice difference.

She needed to take inventory. She needed to contact vendors and perhaps wrangle some short-notice sponsors. She needed to learn how the hell to run a heavy athletic competition or get someone to do it for her, and, in looking at the scant number of entrants, attract more athletes. She needed—

Her phone rang. Aimee.

"Hel—"

Screeching and sobbing filled her ear.

"Calm down, Aim, I can't hear a thing you're saying."

"Oh my God, the whole place, Jen!" There was splashing and squishing in the background. "The toilet or the bathtub or something up in your room. Something must have burst. Water everywhere. Totally flooded." A sob, a sniffle. "It's dripping through the floorboards, into the main room downstairs. Oh my God! I don't know what to do!"

Despite her earlier vow to give this thing her all for the next two weeks, Jen's first instinct at hearing Aimee's panic was to run. To swim like hell far, far away from her sister's mess. Why the hell was her sister calling *her* now? Ah, of course. Because Jen was here, and when Jen was here, she took care of things.

All her clothes and toiletries were in that room, sitting right outside the bathroom. Probably floating down the hall by now. Crap.

She ground fingers into her temple. "Maybe you should, I don't know, turn off the water at the source and then call a plumber?"

"What? No." More crying, more splashing.

"Why the hell not?"

"Because I can't call *him*." It came out like *hiiiiiiim*, and Jen finally got it. Aimee had probably slept with whoever *hiiiiiiim* was and they hadn't moved past the After-Sex Awkwardness.

Lovely. Jen Haverhurst to the rescue.

"Just hold on, Aim. Be there in a second. Can you at least find the water shutoff?"

"Okay. Yes. I think so."

Jen hung up and sighed. She pushed back from the table and poked her head out of the conference room door. "Mrs. McCurdy?"—because she could never, ever bring herself to call her Mayor Sue—"Know of any places in town I can rent? Like, today?"

Chapter

2

Leith MacDougall stacked three bags of topsoil, shoved his hands under the bottom one, and heaved all three into the back of his white pickup truck. On the other side of the barn, his phone jumped and buzzed from where it sat on the empty potting bench. He let it go to voicemail. There was a shitload of packing up and consolidating to do before he closed down this location and handed the keys back to Loughlin, the property owner. Wasn't like it would be a new client calling anyway.

Chris, his lone remaining employee, entered through the big sliding door, pushing an empty wheelbarrow. The younger guy eyed how much Leith had cleared out in fifteen minutes. "Wow. Motivated?"

"You could say that."

Leith lifted the bottom of his already-soaked T-shirt to wipe his sweaty face. His muscles ached, but that's what he loved most about his business. Planning and designing the landscapes fed his brain and gave him a deep sense of accomplishment, but it was the digging and planting and grunt work that really made his blood buzz. The physical stuff always got him going, and over the past year, he hadn't gotten nearly enough of it.

Was he referring to landscaping or sex? Sadly, either one applied.

The phone stopped ringing.

"Heard this morning at the Kafe they're still going through with the games this year even though DeeDee took off," Chris said, crossing the vast, empty floor. "Rumor has it Mayor Sue found some sucker to take over, last minute."

Leith reached for the last two bags of soil. "Good for them."

God, the barn was so empty. The only things left were his worktables and the shiny sign hanging on the far wall, an indulgence he'd splurged on when business had been so good he could afford such a thing. *MacDougall Landscape Design. Gleann, New Hampshire.*

Chris popped up the wheelbarrow and turned it upside down in the truck bed. "You're not even going to stick around for it?"

Leith swiveled the final soil bags so they'd fit nicely. "Why would I?"

Chris took out a rubber band and tied back his hair. "Dunno. Curiosity? Tradition? DeeDee said my band could play." He was trying to come across as nonchalant but failed miserably.

Like so many others living here, Chris had been born in Gleann, would probably die here. At nineteen, he hadn't gone to college, not that that had been an option for the kid who'd barely made it out of high school. He'd had a rough go, made some shitty mistakes with drugs and booze, gotten in some serious trouble, and then Leith had given him a chance at employment. Turned out that chance had been exactly what Chris needed to straighten out his life, and Leith did fear what might happen to the guy when he left.

There came that old guilt, rising up to bite him again.

Leith didn't answer Chris. The games he'd once loved and excelled at had turned into a sad, sorry event showcasing how sad and sorry this town had become. He'd stayed for so long out of a loyalty that seemed to be part of your blood if you grew up here, and because when Hemmertex had been here he'd been swimming in money, but now he needed to move on. Correction: he was *dying* to move on.

Of course, the second he let himself think that, his da's voice rattled through his mind—*Don't turn your back on the people who need you, boy*—and Leith was right back where he started.

"Sorry, man," Leith finally replied. "I'm supposed to head over the state line that weekend. Checking out a possible new location in Vermont."

Chris hung his head. "Oh. Yeah."

The landscape business should have been enough to keep Leith here, but it wasn't. Not any longer. He'd started his business right as the rich people had arrived, and he'd made his own killing. But the whole valley had been slowly dying since the last Hemmertex executive locked up his giant vacant house on the outskirts of town almost two years ago. No one to design for anymore. Local maintenance was no longer going to cut it—not for his bills, and not for his dreams.

Family could have kept him in town, but with Da gone three years now, he was alone.

His phone started ringing again. He realized he hadn't heard a beep earlier to indicate a voicemail had gone through. Maybe it *was* a client. A shrubbery emergency or something. Hell, he might take anything at this point; the finish line of his reserve funds was in painful sight. He jogged across the barn and grabbed the phone.

"'Lo?"

"Mr. Lindsay, my name is Jen Haverhurst. I'm told your property at 738 Maple Avenue is available for rent."

The connection must have been pretty crappy, out here in the "suburbs" of his tiny hometown, because he could have sworn the fast-talking woman had claimed to be Jen Haverhurst.

"Mr. Lindsay, are you there?"

It was Jen, all right. Same flat Midwestern accent. Same barely contained impatience, same determination.

His ass sank onto the tipped-down hatch of his pickup. Why the hell did she think he was Mr. Lindsay? Oh, yeah. Because he owned that house now, along with two others on that block. More empty properties dragging Gleann into the murky depths. Whoever kept track of the rental listings must have updated his contact phone but not the name. And if the listing still had Mildred's husband's name, the records hadn't been touched in the twenty years before that.

Jen.

Last he'd heard from Bev Haverhurst before she died, Jen's job was putting on big parties and events in New York City.

Wait . . . was *she* the "sucker" Mayor Sue had dragged in to help pull off the games on short notice? Why on earth would someone like Jen agree to attach herself to a sinking ship?

And why hadn't she called him when she got back? That's right. Ten years ago she'd taken off like a flash and never looked back, not even to see how damaged he'd been by the force and speed of her wheels. He'd long since given up imagining her returning, but, pathetically, never stopped hoping.

He wasn't about to let this surprise phone call be their reunion. No, it had to be better than that, and, honestly, he wasn't *quite* ready to face her.

He pushed off the truck and turned his back to Chris. "Yeah," Leith said into the phone, pitching his voice lower. "I'm here."

"Is the property still available? I'm looking for immediate move-in."

"Immediate." Now he didn't have to concentrate on disguising his voice. It dropped all on its own, along with his stomach. She was *here*. "It's available."

"Great. I'm looking for a short-term stay. Two weeks. It's furnished, right?"

Two weeks, up through the games. So she definitely was the sucker.

"Yes," he said.

"And it has a working washer and dryer?"

"Sure." Truthfully, he had no idea if the things worked. Two months ago, after the shocking inheritance, he'd taken a quick tour of 738 and then locked the place up tight, overwhelmed.

God, her voice. Despite his reservations, despite all the bad feelings returning and mixing with the good ones that he'd never completely let go of, the sound of her was starting to make him dizzy. Excited. What did she look like now?

"Can you knock two hundred off the rate?"

"Two hundred?" he gasped. It was already cheap as dirt, priced to be used. And Jen lived in New York, where she probably paid ten million dollars a month on rent anyway. But then, she'd always been the haggler. Had always wanted things done on her terms.

Which was why the two of them hadn't lasted.

A little bit of that excitement died as he remembered how

they'd ended, that sharp, hard conclusion to something that had been really fucking good.

He could use her cash, though. "Fifty off," he countered.

"One fifty."

"One hundred."

"Done."

He scrubbed a hand over his itchy, stubbled chin, his body starting to hum. It felt too good, playing like this with her again, even if it was one-sided. Back in the day, when they'd been the best of summer friends, they'd spent many nights playing innocent pranks on the townspeople.

She exhaled, and just that little sound, leaking through the cell phone waves, sent him hurtling back in time to when they'd last spoken—also on the phone, only far less civil. Ten years should have been enough to dull the hurt and fill in the ache. Surprisingly, it wasn't.

"Great," she said. "Like I said, I'm looking to get settled in tonight. Will that be a problem?"

"Ah, no." He straightened and swiveled back to Chris, snapping his fingers. "I won't be around but I'll have someone leave a key and rental agreement under the mat."

Chris pointed to his own chest and mouthed, "Me?"

Leith nodded. He was due to scout locations in Mount Caleb, two hours south, this afternoon. A new corridor of strip malls was going up over there. That usually meant progress, housing starts. New construction always meant new landscaping.

"Under the mat." She chuckled. "Of course." *How quaint*, her tone said, and he gritted his teeth.

"I don't know if you have a car," he added, "but you can't use the garage. A, uh, local is using it for storage."

"Oh. That's okay, I suppose. Thank you so much, Mr. Lindsay." In her pause he heard the distinct sound of fingers on a laptop. He suddenly remembered how sweet she could be, how genuine, when she wasn't running you over with her severe drive. "You can reach me at this number if you need me."

He pulled the phone away from his ear, saved her number, and tapped it off. Stared at the phone as though it were her face.

She hadn't faded for him, over time. Why would she, when every corner and crevice of Gleann had something to remind him of her?

First sex. First love.

"Who was that?" Chris came over. "Yo, Dougall. Who was that? A ghost?"

You could say that, he thought.

Fuck. Jen Haverhurst. Back in Gleann. Staying at 738 Maple.

Right next door to him.

*I*t was approaching ten o'clock by the time Leith turned the pickup onto Maple Avenue back in Gleann, and he almost put his face through the windshield, he braked so hard. A compact black rental car was parked under the carport of 738 and the kitchen light glowed between the drape of the brown curtains. One month he'd been living in the two-bedroom cottage at 740, and he'd gotten used to not having a neighbor.

He also thought he'd gotten used to not having Jen in his life.

He'd tried to get out of Mount Caleb faster, but the real estate broker had sprung several more properties on him, and there'd been a terrible four-car pileup blocking both lanes of Route 6 coming back. He'd been hoping to get back and surprise Jen, though he hadn't gotten much further than that in his head. What exactly did he want to do? Just walk up and knock on the door? Pretend to run into her on the street?

Slowly he pulled into the 740 driveway, absently noting the bushes along the front walk needed a prune. Mildred used to pay him to do that. Now that she was dead, she paid him in three headaches in house form and probably thought she'd done him a favor. Old people were like that, thinking you wanted to keep their stuff forever and ever. He wondered if he'd be like that eventually.

He pulled his truck into the garage and got out, careful to shut his door with minimal sound. There was a chance she'd turned off the air-conditioning and opened the windows; it was a perfect night for that. The light from 738's kitchen window angled across 740's postage-stamp backyard. The soft, yellow rectangle froze him. He stood right in the center of it, willing Jen to come into view. Wondering what he'd do if she did. Clearly she was awake; a shadow moved inside. Should he just walk over there? No, he decided with a tight shake of his head.

She'd been in town a whole day, and she hadn't made any attempt to see him.

Then, there she was. She sauntered into the kitchen, holding a giant mug of something steaming and blew gently across the top. She wore these dark-rimmed glasses that screamed Bad Librarian. So weird how he remembered that her eyesight was for shit. Her hair looked darker and it was piled in a giant mess on top of her head. A sensory memory struck and nearly leveled him: how thick her hair had felt. Setting the mug down on the kitchen table, she leaned forward on her hands, peering at the glowing screen of a laptop.

Was she . . . ? *Jesus.*

No bra. A little black top with dental floss for straps. Black underwear that covered her tight ass, but just barely. And a whole mess of skin, the sight of which made his mouth dry up and his palms tingle with the urge to touch.

Ten years apart from whom he'd once thought was the love of his life, almost six months since he'd had anything remotely resembling sex, and this was his re-introduction to the female species. He told himself that seeing anyone of the opposite sex wandering around like that after his length of forced abstinence would inspire such an epic hard-on, but the truth was . . . she looked incredible.

Then he realized that it was more than just the way she looked. Seeing Jen again, here and close, was like being swept through a time warp. His brain flipped back through all the summers they'd been joined at the hip. Back when they used to play kickball in the park, when they'd played all those good-natured pranks together. When they'd spent evenings sitting with Da on his front porch, listening to his childhood stories of Scotland. Back when they'd laughed so easily, and talked about anything and everything.

Then came that summer before she left for college. Right from the start he'd known it was the last summer she'd make it to Gleann. Mix that up with the fact that he'd been almost nineteen, raging with hormones, and she'd showed up right after high school graduation looking like sin. They'd resumed their friendship as easily as any of the previous nine summers, but he'd felt the change inside him so suddenly and so acutely it was like she'd reached inside his mind and thrown a switch.

When they'd waited tables together one night at the Stone, he'd very intentionally brushed up against her. He remembered her response so clearly: the slow way she turned around, the perfect circles of those incredible green eyes, the slack-jawed look of surprise. He'd grinned at her, knowing. As soon as their shift was done, he'd pushed her against the outside wall of the pub and kissed her.

And continued to do so every summer night thereafter.

So by the time they'd wedged themselves into the backseat of his old man's '69 Cadillac DeVille convertible and, shaking, they'd stripped each other and gone through three condoms in one night, he was pretty sure he was in love with her.

Then she'd left.

Back in the kitchen of 738 Maple, Jen pushed away from the table, the lean muscles in her arms flexing. She started to pace between the table and refrigerator. Her lips moved soundlessly as she talked to herself. She gestured with her hands, ticking something off on her fingers.

She was curvier now, fuller everywhere, but still fit. Definitely more of a woman. She yawned, stretching with arms overhead.

He reached down, adjusted himself through his jeans.

He realized that a little bit of the old anger still rattled around inside him. Also, even more surprisingly, some pain. Which angered him even more. He was an adult. He was over her. He'd been over her for ten years. Okay, maybe nine. But they'd been eighteen and, when he thought about it, they really hadn't been ready to be together long-term.

Besides, he hadn't exactly turned priest after her departure. And he was pretty sure she'd forgotten about him soon after their last phone call, when she'd told him she loved him back, one month and a thousand miles too late.

Of course that was the moment his phone chose to go off, the ring clanging across the yard, the sound so loud it could have reached the moon. He fumbled with taking it out of his pocket, his thumb missing the mute button. The phone kept ringing. Jen froze where she stood in the middle of the kitchen like she might have heard, but then she started talking to herself again and he knew she hadn't.

Still, he quickly ducked out of the light and dove for the

back door, which he never locked. Nothing of his inside to steal anyway. In the mudroom, he flipped on the weak bulb over the basement stairs.

He glanced at the number on the phone before answering and tried not to get his hopes up. "MacDougall."

"I still think you should answer with a Scottish brogue," chuckled the woman on the other end.

"I would, if I had one," he replied.

"Bah, just fake it. No American would ever know."

Leith smiled, thinking he could probably pull out a brogue if he thought about Da hard enough, but just the idea made his chest ache.

"What can I do for you, Rory?" She'd been one of his favorite clients before her Hemmertex president husband had moved the headquarters to Connecticut and changed the valley forever.

"Sorry to call so late, but I just got back from this boring office party where I heard a wicked rumor that you were leaving Gleann and going to set up your business elsewhere."

He moved through the darkened house to the little TV room in the front with the window overlooking Jen's rental. He kept the light off, and collapsed into the pink velour recliner with the lace doily armrest covers.

"You heard right," he told Rory.

"Then I'm calling to beg you to come work for us again." Now he heard the slight slur of drink in her voice. "Hal's bought the most ridiculous house in Stamford and I hate all the landscapers. You'd be my very own, just like I always wanted. Well, at least until word got out. Then I suppose I'd be forced to share you."

At least Rory was open and lighthearted about her flirting. Mildred had just peeked at him from behind her curtains. And Rory was completely devoted to Hal, who teased Leith mercilessly about being the underage gardener of his wife's fantasies.

And now Rory Carriage wanted him to start work in Stamford, one of the more competitive areas in the country, to say the least. But if he could get an "in" using her . . . It was the first lead he'd had in over a year, and it really didn't get any better than this one.

He scooted to the edge of the recliner and switched the

phone to the other ear so he could twist toward the window and watch Jen's shadow pace.

"What do you need?" he asked Rory.

"Oh, honey, don't ask me such open-ended questions." She laughed. "Everything. I've got three acres, a concrete hole for a pool, and a gazebo from 1983. The gardens were laid by the most boring designers ever. *I* could have done what they did. I need you and your big bulldozer. Don't say no."

Three acres. He started to sweat from the excitement. Three acres, from scratch, in a whole new area he could immerse himself in researching. Brand new inspiration.

"Sounds promising." He kept his tone level. She'd called him and begged, which meant he could probably get away with a little jump in price, when all along he'd been preparing to cut back. He stood up, the recliner groaning and snapping back into position.

"I'm heading out tomorrow for one of Hal's conferences; I don't even know what it's for. We'll be home Monday. Any chance you can get here first thing? I want everything done before Candy's wedding in September."

Monday. Stamford was a five-hour drive. He'd get up in the middle of the night if he had to.

"Monday it is," he told Rory, then got her new address and hung up.

Fucking A. Exactly the kick start he needed at exactly the right time.

Jen's kitchen light went out. A few moments later, the dim chandelier over the staircase blinked on, followed by a warm glow in one of the upstairs bedrooms.

Yeah. Exactly the right time.

Because even though Jen had come back after all these years, she'd leave again. And this time, so would he.

He stood there in the musty dark of Mildred's old house, staring up at Jen's window. She reappeared, and it stopped the breath in his throat. Her gorgeous body backlit, her hair now down around her shoulders, she yanked the curtains closed. A second later, the lamp went out.

Leith ground his forehead into the window, knowing he was about to have a completely unsatisfactory few minutes with his right hand.

Chapter

3

*A*imee hadn't slept with Gleann's sole plumber just once. A single occurrence might actually have made things easier to handle. No, apparently they were an ongoing thing. And in this case, "ongoing" meant "dramatic" and "exceedingly strange."

Jen stood in the middle of the Thistle's front sitting room, her sister hovering in the kitchen doorway and Owen, the handsome, middle-aged man with the gigantic metal toolbox, inspecting the buckled drywall on the walls and ceiling.

"I need to cut into this so I can get to the pipes and see what caused the burst." Owen was cool as could be, but Aimee was watching him with her arms crossed.

Aimee said to Jen, "Ask him how long until it's all done. New pipes. New walls and painting and everything."

Owen's eyebrows shot into his forehead.

Jen rolled her eyes. "Seriously? He's right here."

Ainsley flounced into the room, her sandy blond ponytail swinging, her oversized, crooked teeth chomping into an apple. She took one look at her mom and Owen, and heaved a sigh worthy of a guilt-loving grandma. "Are you guys fighting again? Hi, Owen."

Owen turned from where he was running fingers down bubbled, soggy wallpaper. "Hey, you. If your mom wants to play games, tell her I said hi, and that I'm sorry."

"What'd you do now?" Jen thought Ainsley said around a mouthful of apple.

Owen smiled. An affectionate dad's smile. He wasn't Ainsley's dad, but he was someone's, that was for sure. "Nothing I can tell you."

"Ew." Ainsley came over to Jen and gave her a quick hug.

Owen chuckled in a way that said he'd been teasing.

Ainsley seemed shockingly comfortable with the sudden reappearance of her aunt, considering how badly Jen had left them high and dry during their first and only New York City visit. Nine-year-old Ainsley didn't care what happened three years ago, but Aimee would never forget. And really, could Jen blame her?

Last night Jen and Aimee had taken the girl to the Stone for fish and chips since the B&B's water was still off, and Jen had desperately grabbed for something to talk about. But Ainsley, apparently a seasoned pro and a social natural, had it all pegged. She'd chattered on in a way that reminded Jen so much of Aimee at that age, all opinion and I-don't-care-what-you-think. Her favorite topic was these two older girls she seemed to emulate—someone named Lacey, and another she just called T.

Jen turned to her sister. "You have insurance, right? Money to cover repairs?"

Owen pulled out a long, narrow saw from his toolbox. "Aimee, I'll only charge you for materials, as usual."

Aimee ignored him and looked at Jen with worried, glassy eyes. "I've got a little put away, and insurance will cover some of it. But I need the income from during the games. The Scottish Society president is staying here and I'm fully booked. The rooms have to be perfect. Can you ask Owen when he'll be done?"

"Maybe he'd be done quicker," Jen noted, "if you didn't play these games. What is going on here anyway?"

Ainsley laughed. Owen added wryly, "Yeah, I'd kinda like to know, too."

Aimee worried her lip and suddenly looked sheepish. "Old habits," she mumbled. Just as Jen had figured.

"I don't have time for this, Aim. I'll let you explain that

comment to Owen." Jen pressed a hand to her forehead. "You brought me here for another reason and I have to take care of that."

"Taking care of that" involved getting out to the fairgrounds and seeing firsthand all the supplies and tents and signage stored there. She also needed to do a location assessment, make sure she agreed with the layout and found the grounds suitable.

"Aimee," Owen said with a chuckle, "tell your sister it was nice to finally meet her."

"Jen," Aimee said wearily, "Owen says good-bye."

Brother.

Owen whipped around to face Aimee. "Ha!" His wide grin made the silver in his cheek stubble shine. Aimee had always gone for older guys. So had mom. Two peas in a pod, those two, and usually not in the best ways. "Gotcha. You're talking to me now."

Aimee's oval face went splotchy red and she glanced up at Jen in embarrassment. She kicked at a baseboard. "Oh, hell."

As Owen started to cross to Aimee, his intent plastered all over his expression, Jen threw up her hands. "I'm out of here. You guys figure . . . this . . . out." She headed for the front door.

"What was *that* all about?" she heard Owen say to her sister.

"I'm sorry," Aimee replied.

"So am I," he said, and there the talking ended.

It had heated up a good ten degrees since Jen had been delayed by Aimee's retreat into her seventeen-year-old dependent self. Jen was already sweating through her wrap dress and her feet felt like they were swimming in her heels, but this was still work and she refused to dress down, even if she did sort of feel like she was playing a part while she was here. Besides, they were the only articles of clothing she'd managed to clean and get dry after yesterday's waterlogging. The rest of her belongings were strung up all over the rental house on Maple. She didn't trust that ancient dryer not to cook her delicates down to a size zero, which she definitely wasn't.

Halfway to her car, Jen heard footsteps behind her. She turned to find Ainsley on the flagstone path, squinting up at her, the sun shrinking the pupils in her bright blue eyes to tiny specks. Aimee said her daughter looked exactly like the thirty-year-old guy who'd gotten Aimee pregnant at nineteen and then took off as soon as he got the news. Jen had just started college then, with Aimee stuck back in Iowa, so Jen had never known the guy. But Ainsley definitely didn't take after her mom, and Jen wondered how long it had taken Aimee to get used to the everyday reminder of the asshole.

"They'll be okay, you know," Ainsley said, shaking her head. "They fight sometimes, but then it's all good."

Jen hid a smile. "So you like Owen? Is he good to your mom?"

"Sure, yeah. It's only when he's with the guys too much that Mom gets upset. That's probably what that was about in there." She looked at her dirty fingernails. "And sometimes things with Melissa don't let them see each other."

"Who's Melissa?"

"His wife."

"Wait . . . what?"

A serious, stomach-dropping worry swept through Jen. *Two peas in a pod.* How could Aimee *do* that, get involved with a married guy, especially after all the crap they'd had to deal with as kids?

She closed her eyes and mouth and breathed carefully through her nose. *One problem at a time.* Technically, it was Aimee's problem, but when had Aimee's issues ever only been her own?

She opened her eyes to find Ainsley tossing the apple core into the herb garden. "Melissa and Owen are still married and they live in the same house. That big old white one over on Catalpa?"

Jen ground the heel of a hand into her eye socket. "And Aimee *knows* this?"

"Oh, yeah."

"What about Melissa?"

"Oh, she knows, too."

Jen thought she might be sick.

"T and Lacey say it's no big deal," Ainsley said. "So do I."

Those girls again. "And who are they exactly?"

"Owen and Melissa's kids. Relax, Aunt Jen." The girl actually put a hand on Jen's arm and gave this little bat of her eyelashes that screamed *Aimee.* "They're getting divorced. It

just hasn't happened yet. Or maybe it won't. I don't know."
Then she shrugged and the kid was back. "Whatever."

Whatever was right. Jen started to laugh. She couldn't help
it. "Alrighty then. My sister is dating a not-yet-divorced guy
who still lives with his wife. Hey, where are you going?"

Ainsley turned from where she'd been heading down the
sidewalk, away from downtown. "To Bryan's. He got a slingshot
yesterday."

As Ainsley walked away, Jen turned to look through the big
front window of the Thistle, where she—and anyone else walking by—could plainly see Owen the still-married-but-*whatever*
plumber and her sister making out. What the hell was going
on here?

Jen couldn't help but flash back to so many days of her
youth. To the embarrassing, awful, public scenes she'd been
forced to witness—and sometimes break up—between her
mom and the random women who seemed to know Frank, the
live-in boyfriend who wasn't Jen's or Aimee's dad, all too well.

No time for that, she reminded herself with a shake of the head.
Now she was working, and the past was the past. First, she had to
run back to the rental house and switch out her shoes for something
more appropriate to traipsing around fairgrounds.

But when she pulled up to 738 Maple, there was a huge
white pickup truck consuming the driveway. *MacDougall
Landscape Design* was stenciled in green on the sides.

Jen sat there clutching the steering wheel and closed her
eyes. It wasn't that she didn't want to see Leith—she did; she
really did—she just wasn't ready. She hadn't prepared herself.
Hadn't thought it all through, as she was so good at doing. For
a small, sleepy town, everything was happening so incredibly
fast.

Maybe if she opened her eyes slowly, her mind would admit
it had played a trick on her and he wouldn't actually be here
right now. She opened them. The truck stared back at her.

And then, there was Leith MacDougall sauntering out of
the open garage. He lifted his thick arm to wipe the side of his
sweaty face on the shoulder of his stained white T-shirt. The
old poster tacked to the vacant store window downtown hadn't
done him justice. That kilt had hidden the true power of his

thighs, but the dirty jeans he wore now showed them off like trophies. He was at least thirty pounds bigger than in high school, maybe more. Not 'roided out or disgustingly cut, but firm. Unmistakably strong.

Why was seeing him like this affecting her so much? It had been a high school thing, before either of them could even define the word *mature*. Nothing more.

Reaching over the side of his truck bed for something unseen, he froze. Turned his head. Saw her sitting there in the car.

Suddenly she couldn't breathe. Just sat there like a dumbass staring at him through the passenger-side window. Maybe in New York she could've gotten away with hitting the gas and peeling away. She could've lost herself in the traffic and there'd have been a good chance she'd never run across him again. But here?

She'd never been a coward her whole life, and she wasn't about to start now.

Opening the car door, she swung her legs out and stood, turning to face him. She smoothed her dress that didn't need smoothing, then lifted a hand in greeting. He was wearing thick working gloves, and he slowly tugged them off, finger by finger. Then he pulled one of those dark blue handkerchiefs with the white swirls out of his back pocket—the kind she remembered his dad always used to have—and wiped his hands on it.

She started toward him. He didn't move.

"You were right, Leith. I do love you." Her palm went damp around the phone.

He didn't say anything for a long time, but she could hear him breathing and it sounded labored. "Why the fuck are you calling to tell me this now, when you're half a country away?"

"Because." She swallowed, and it hurt. "I thought you'd like to know."

"Well, you're wrong. I don't want to know. Not now."

Jen almost stumbled on the ragged asphalt of the driveway. That had been so long ago, when they'd been kids. And he was sort of smiling at her now. Sort of. Maybe he'd forgotten the crappy way she'd ended it. Maybe it didn't matter anymore. They were both adults.

"Hey, you," she said, throwing on a smile of her own.

His brown hair had gotten lighter at the ends. A bonus—at

least from her point of view—from working outside. It curled around his neck and ears in a way that might have looked like an overdue haircut on any other guy.

He stuffed the handkerchief back into his pocket. "So you're really here."

She stopped, the heel of one shoe clacking loudly. "You don't look all that surprised."

He glanced over her shoulder, down Maple where it dipped and curved around in front of the elementary school. "Small town." His eyes drifted back. She'd forgotten how intense they were. How he always looked people in the eye. It was that personal attention, that charm, she remembered, that drew people to him. "I *was* surprised. Yesterday."

"Ah. Yeah." She nodded at the sidewalk. "It was a crazy day. To be fair, I had no idea you still lived here until I got into town. And then I was pulled in a million different directions."

He just looked at her. How did he manage to stand so quietly when such violent tremors were rocketing through her body? She'd always been a fidgety person. Always had to move, to think about her next step—where to go, what to do, what to say. Standing there under this scrutiny, wearing this strange uncertainty, she had no idea where to channel her energy.

Leith was as still as his image on that poster. She knew what he was thinking: *You never asked Aimee about me?* But then, she also knew that he'd never once asked Aimee about her, so really, weren't they even?

All kinds of awkward floated in the air, mixing with the midday June heat and the fine mist coming from the sprinkler in the yard of the small brick house next to 738.

He ambled to the back end of the truck, closer to her, his fingers trailing over a taillight. "So you're here to save the games?"

Of course he would know why she was here.

"Small town," they said at the same time. It cracked some of the tension, but didn't break through completely. Her purse strap dug into her shoulder.

"I'm going to try to," she told him. "Aimee called me, what, only three days ago? She begged. I had an opening in my schedule. Here I am."

"An opening in your schedule," he said, his voice flat as a

board, as though he didn't quite understand. "So this is what you do now? Plan . . . things?"

"Yes. All kinds of . . . things." She smiled, proud. "I'm pretty good at it, too."

He drew a deep breath, nodding. It seemed to relax him some. "Then I'm happy for you, that you got what you wanted. I really am."

She looked at his truck, the one he couldn't stop touching. Not much was bigger than him, but that white thing on wheels was a *beast*. "And you're a landscaper? Like what you did in high school?"

The moment it came out of her mouth she knew she'd gotten it wrong, that she'd sounded dumb. She winced.

One corner of his mouth twitched. "I'm a landscape architect."

"Of course. Right." Who was this stupid, nervous woman who'd taken over her mouth? And why did he seem so calm?

She peered around Leith's body to the open garage door of 738, where she could see all sorts of lawn equipment inside. Shovels and ride-on mowers. One of those small diggers. Piles of topsoil and mulch bags. A drafting table turned on its side.

"When I rented this place," she said, "the owner said a local was using the garage."

"I guess I'm that local."

"Why here? In a garage?"

He sat on the bumper. It was so high that even with his height—six-three, as she recalled; an inch taller in those thick boots—he barely had to bend to park his ass on the edge. The truck sank. "I'm closing down my business in Gleann. Going somewhere else. Had to find short-term storage."

"I saw that Hemmertex closed. It makes sense for you to move then. Follow the clients."

He eyed her for a moment and she focused on not squirming. "Exactly."

The next seconds were interminable. With him perched on the bumper, and her still in her four-inch sandals, they were eye to eye. Somehow, at some time, she'd edged closer. They were now maybe four feet apart.

She tried to seem as at ease as he did, but this was, perhaps, the most awkward conversation ever. "So we're all caught up now?"

He pressed his lips together, like he was trying to stifle a smile. "Guess so."

"Who needs Facebook, right?"

He just stared.

"Okay," she said. "I can't stand it anymore. Would it be weird to hug you?"

His answer came fast. "I wouldn't."

Hers came even faster. "Right. Sorry."

"I mean, I'm pretty disgusting. And you look . . ." At last he dropped his eyes, shaking his head. The first hint he was somewhat affected by her reappearance. When he looked up beneath his lashes, she saw a very old pain, resurrected. "Wow, you look really great, Jen."

The breath she drew refused to come easily. "So do you."

"I'm in love with you, Jen. Don't go to Texas. If you do, I know I'll never see you again."

She buried her face in her hands. "You just think *you're in love with me. And who says we'll never see each other again?"*

He never answered that. He just said, "I do *love you. And I know that you love me, too."*

"God, Leith. That's such a big word. Why would you say this, put me in this position, the night before I leave?"

He pushed to his feet, towering over where she sat on the blanket in the middle of the fairgrounds. "Because it's *the night before you leave," he said. "And I don't want to be without you."*

Leith kicked his legs out farther, his weight jouncing the truck. He cracked his neck, and more memories came back to her. How he used to do that when he was nervous.

She stretched for something neutral to say, because it was clear their past had been shoved off the table.

"So what do you know about this Mr. Lindsay?" she blurted out. "I don't remember him from before."

Leith loosely crossed his arms over his middle. "Not much. I think he, uh, lives on the other side of you, in that blue house. Why?"

She leaned forward and lowered her voice. "I think he's a

bit of a pervert." She reached into her purse and handed Leith the piece of paper she'd found taped to her front door that morning.

Leith took it after a strange pause. *"Dear Ms. Haverhurst,"* he read out loud, breaking into an immediate smile. *"Would you kindly remember to close your drapes in the evening?"*

She snatched it back. "It's not funny. Should I be worried?"

He laughed. "Were you walking around naked or something?"

"No. Never mind."

The glint in his eye was so much like the old Leith, the one who'd been hers.

"What are you doing now?" he asked. "Going upstairs to tease an old man again?"

"No." She could always talk about work in a steady voice. "I need to get over to the fairgrounds and check out the space and the equipment they have in storage."

He gave her a long, slow look from her face down to her feet. She couldn't help but feel exposed. She couldn't help but like it.

"Got any better shoes?" he asked.

"Yeah, some flat ones upstairs. I hope they're dry."

"Dry? Were you fly-fishing in them?"

Why did his humor make her heart hurt? "I was supposed to stay at the Thistle but a water pipe burst and"—she waved a hand—"here I am."

"Ah," he said, as if the whole world made sense now. He ran a hand through his hair, distributing some of the sweat gathering at the roots, making it slick and gleaming. "Owen over there now?"

"You know about that, too?"

"Everyone does. Been going on for about a year now."

"What is *that* all about? I wasn't about to ask Ainsley, and I really don't know how to deal with it."

He shrugged in much the same way Ainsley had. "Word is he and Melissa have been talking divorce, but just haven't gotten around to it."

"Listen to you. You're like one of those women who used to do crosswords at the Kafe every Sunday."

He flashed her a grin, ignoring her comment and continuing about Owen and Melissa. "They fight less now that Owen has

Aimee, believe it or not. The whole town is thankful for that. I guess Melissa's loaded? Maybe they're still working it all out; I don't know. Melissa's with some guy over in Westbury."

"Wow."

Jen dropped the subject there. She'd never told Leith about her mom's issues with Frank. Actually, she'd never told Leith anything about her terrible life back in Iowa. There'd been too much shame back then, and whenever she'd come to Gleann she'd wanted to forget. Here, she could be someone else.

"So." He rubbed his thighs with the heels of his hands. "You, uh, want some company at the fairgrounds? I'll give you a tour."

Leith threw his long legs over the front seats and fell into the back. They were both laughing so hard, Jen could barely see through her tears. "Why don't you come on back here?" he said, running a hand in a circle over the Cadillac's white leather seats. "I'll give you a tour."

Jen blinked, the memory overlapping with reality. But Leith was just looking at her as though he didn't recognize his old words, what they'd started that night. Chances were, he didn't.

Workwise, she didn't need him or his "tour." She knew the way, and the fairgrounds lay just on the other side of the trees lining the backyards of the Maple houses. Personally, she . . . well, she didn't know exactly *what* she wanted from him, just that now that she'd seen him again, she didn't want to walk away yet.

"Sure," she replied, and tried not to read into the way his chin lifted or the way his massive chest expanded. "Let me go up and grab those shoes."

He nodded. Though she didn't turn around, she could feel him watching her, even through the brick walls of the house as she climbed the stairs and threw on the ballet flats that were now just slightly damp. When she came back down, Leith was still leaning against the truck, arms across his chest.

He gestured to her purse. "You carry that suitcase everywhere?"

"It's got my laptop in it. So, yes."

He grunted. "Mind if I go back to my place so I can take a shower first?"

His place? This was moving too fast again, but she wasn't about to let her minor panic show. "Not at all."

He went around to the driver's side door and nudged his chin toward the passenger seat. "Get in."

"I can't believe your dad is letting you drive his car when you just got your license last week."

"He's not." Leith waggled his eyebrows. "Get in."

So she did. Both back then—before he'd been grounded for a week for taking out the Cadillac without his dad's permission—and today.

She clicked on the seatbelt, settled in. He threw the huge truck in reverse, backed out of her driveway with more speed than necessary, swerved the vehicle around, made a huge arc, and aimed it . . . right into the driveway of 740 Maple.

The truck stopped with a screech. He put it into park and whipped out the key. She sat there, mouth agape, looking first out the window at the tiny brick house with the metal window awnings, and then back at Leith.

With one arm crossed behind her seat back, he gave her the slowest, sexiest grin she'd ever seen. "Hey, neighbor."

Chapter

4

*T*he look on Jen's face was absolutely priceless as she sat in his passenger seat and hugged that gigantic green bag to her chest. She looked like she'd been lured into a stranger's windowless van with the promise of candy. Leith threw back his head and laughed.

"Relax," he said. "You can wait here. I'll just be a minute."

But it took him a few moments to actually pull the door handle and swing his legs out, because he'd been sitting next to her for about 3.6 seconds, and he didn't want to move away quite yet.

Shower. Yep. That's what he needed to wash away the sur-reality of this whole situation.

He left her there in his truck, with those bright green eyes he'd almost forgotten about impossibly wide, and her mouth slack and open, ready to . . . say something. He'd probably get it when he returned to the truck; Jen had never been one to back down from saying anything she wanted to say.

He jogged into Mildred's house and took the stairs two at a time, stripping off his grimy shirt as he went. He kicked his boots and socks and jeans into a pile in the hallway, and ducked

into the cramped bathroom that looked like a bushel of peaches
had exploded inside it. The shower curtain was frilly and dusty,
but the water that hit his chest was refreshingly, wonderfully
cold on such a hot, strange day.

Jen Haverhurst was outside. Sitting in his truck.

Jesus.

Watching her walk toward him on the driveway, the way
her legs moved under that dress . . . He'd never seen her wear
high heels before. When they'd been together it'd been all
shorts and flip-flops and sneakers. She'd smelled of sunscreen
and sweet girl sweat after a long day waiting tables. Whenever
they made out or had sex, the ChapStick on her lips would
transfer to his, and he would spend half the night lying in his
bed, rolling his lips together to bring back the flavor.

Today—even though he'd glimpsed her half-naked through
the window last night—she looked exactly as he'd expected,
and yet entirely different. Better.

But the truth was, he had no idea what sort of person she'd
become. Likewise, she couldn't claim to know him anymore,
either.

How much had he changed, when it came down to it? How
much could he have been *allowed* to change, given the fences
that had been erected around his life in this valley? The thought
threatened to level him as he pulled on a clean T-shirt and
jeans, and shoved his feet back into his mud-caked boots.

The second he opened the truck cab door, she started in on
him, just as he'd predicted. "You *live* here? Right next to the
house I'm renting? How the hell did that happen?"

He slid behind the wheel, averting his face so she couldn't
see his shit-eating grin. Then he turned to her and shrugged.
"Fate is weird."

She tucked a glossy piece of dark hair behind her ear and
stared back at him with that wide-eyed look of hers. "Is that
what this is? Fate?"

He had one hand on the wheel. The other, holding the truck
key, froze halfway to the ignition. It was just a split second—a
flicker of a fly's wings—but there it was. *That.* That shuddering,
overpowering, nameless *thing* that had overcome him one night
a thousand summers ago. That *thing* about her that had flipped
his brain from, "Hey, I can't wait to tell my best friend Jen

about that," to "Wow, Jen is amazing and gorgeous and you want to be a lot more than just her friend."

With a hard, sharp shake of his head, he cranked the key and the truck rumbled to life. He said, as he backed out of the driveway so he wouldn't have to look at her, "I don't know what this is."

Jen settled deeper into the seat. "I thought I heard someone pull in here last night."

"Yeah, I was out of town until late." *And then I saw you, half-naked. God help me, I can't get it out of my mind. Change the subject.* "So how much do you remember about the games?"

"Oh, gosh," she said to the window as she watched the rounded hills and thick trees of Gleann pass by. "Bits and pieces. Nothing about the organization or anything, nothing that I need to know now, of course. But I remember the pipes and drums, that sound echoing everywhere. I remember the pretend sword fights and sneaking beers with you after sophomore year. I remember people in lawn chairs watching little girls in tartan dancing on a stage. But most of all I remember sitting at your dad's feet watching the heavy athletics. He explained all the events to me. I wish I remembered all the details."

Leith nodded and found it difficult for the tightness in his chest.

"I'm scared to ask, but . . . your dad?"

He cleared his throat. "Died. Three years ago. The old guy held on five years more than they gave him."

"I'm so sorry."

He was so glad he was driving so he wouldn't have to see her face. Wouldn't have to witness what would surely be the kind of pity that made him want to gouge out his own eyes.

"I've gone through all the stages," he told the road with a practiced and perfected shrug. "Anger, denial, all that jazz."

The truth was, if Gleann reminded Leith of Jen, Gleann *was* Da. The fact that Da wasn't here anymore gave Leith perhaps the biggest reason to get the hell out, but it also packed him with some pretty terrifying guilt for up and leaving a place that had embraced him so completely. A place that Da had chosen to love as much as his homeland.

"Okay," Jen said. "That's good. He was such an amazing man. I remember that everyone loved him."

He blew out a breath and turned into the fairgrounds, which

were nothing more than a large, undulating field butting up against Loughlin's cattle pasture. A row of barns, also owned by Loughlin—because what in Gleann didn't the old farmer own?—lined the back side of the grounds, and it was there that Leith aimed his truck, gritting his teeth at every hole in the field his big white baby found.

"How have the games changed since I've been here?" Jen asked in such a sunny manner he knew she was trying to turn the tide of the conversation away from his father. For some reason it made him feel worse, so he flashed her a smile and draped one forearm over the top of the wheel.

"Couldn't really tell you," he said over the rattle of the truck. "Haven't been in a couple of years. I mean, I heard stuff, but I don't compete anymore."

"Aha," she said in a way that told him she already knew that. "Why not?"

"No time, once my business took off. Summer is the busy season." He parked by the largest barn, which the city rented from Loughlin to store everything for the games.

"You look like you work out, like you could still throw."

He turned to her sharply and her gaze skittered away from his arms.

"Maybe," he said with an amused quirk to his mouth, not indicating which statement he was addressing.

She blushed, and at first he didn't recognize it, since it was so unusual for her. "Aimee said you won the overall three years in a row while I was at college."

His eyes flicked up to the rearview mirror, to the expanse of field spreading within that small rectangle. He could still hear everything Jen had described in her memories, but underneath that, even stronger in his senses, came the sound of the laughter and ball-busting between competitors, his longtime throwing buddies. He could still feel the power and exhilaration as his muscles worked and threw the various heavy implements. And if he turned his head just so, he could still see Da, sitting on the edge of the athletic field border, Jen at his ankles.

"I did," he said, then he parked and got out of the truck.

Jen slid out after a second or two, having to use the running board to step down. "Let me ask you, did you ever throw at the bigger games across the state?"

"For a couple of years. Much tougher competition, took me away from work too much. The AD's a good friend of mine."

"AD?"

"Athletic Director. Handles all the heavy events at each games."

"Ah." She hoisted that giant purse higher up on her shoulder and turned in a circle, her lips together, assessing.

Not for the first time, he saw what she was seeing: an oddly shaped patch of semiflat land, riddled with holes and dirt patches and weeds, dotted with outbuildings that maybe at one time might have been handsome stables for 4-H livestock shows or other events that might have drawn crowds from all over New England. Now they tilted to one side or another, their wood walls weathered, creeping vines covering any sort of character.

He pointed to the biggest barn. "This is where they keep all the stuff for the games. The tents and tables, the big castle and stuff."

She turned to him, eyebrow lifted. "I'm sorry. Castle?"

He wiped at the corner of his mouth and glanced away. "Eight or nine years ago DeeDee made this huge fake castle. It looked like a kid's art project. I think it was supposed to give authenticity or something."

Jen looked horrified, covering her mouth with a hand, then recovered quickly. "Did the attendees like it?"

"Maybe the first year."

"And then?"

"Then it turned into a cartoon, and the non-local attendees all but ran across state."

"See? You did know how it's changed."

"Maybe a bit."

She dug into her bag, her whole arm disappearing, and pulled out a small key ring. "Let's go take a look."

After it was unlocked, he lugged open the barn door on dry and screeching rails. She set down her expensive-looking purse right there in the dirt and edged deeper into the barn. Leith followed, popping open a stubborn crate or moving the bigger ones when she couldn't do it herself and asked for his help.

She was talking to herself, as he'd spied her doing last night through the kitchen window. She was utterly absorbed, her hands moving like she was conversing with a colleague. There was something endearing about it, but something also equally frustrating, because she wasn't back in some office in New York. She was in a barn. In Gleann. With him. And though he wasn't expecting a laughfest or the immediate comfort they'd had ten years ago, he didn't think he'd be on her pay-no-mind list.

She was perusing the back corner when she made a sound of surprise.

"What is it?" he called.

"Come take a look."

He wove around disorganized piles of, well, crap to join her in the corner. There, tucked between some crates, was a dirty blanket, filthy pillow, a red baseball cap with a partially unraveled potato chip logo, and an empty pack of cigarettes.

"Homeless person?" she asked.

He shrugged. "Maybe." The valley did have a few.

She wandered back to her purse and pulled out a slim, light laptop, plopping it down on a nearby crate. He liked the way she curled her hair behind her ear and tilted her head so it wouldn't hang in her face. He liked how the movement exposed her neck. He even liked her animated expressions as her fingers flew across the keyboard.

Singularly focused, that was Jen. And right now, her focus wasn't anywhere near him. Not that he'd expected it to be.

He leaned his back against the barn door and turned his head to look out at the field again. That ragged expanse of grass and gravel cupped many of his memories in its dips and rises, but perhaps none as strong as Jen's last night in Gleann. It had been a cloudy, hot night, and they'd spread a blanket right there in the center, where no house or town lights reached. Just them.

"Can I come say goodbye before I leave tomorrow?"

Her words struck his back as he stomped across the fairgrounds, the Cadillac parked crookedly on the other side of the gate.

"Don't bother," he shouted into the darkness. "Sounds like you're taking care of that tonight."

Maybe that's why he'd never been able to give his heart away to anyone else over the past ten years: because it was still here where Jen had smacked it down, and every time someone walked or drove across the field, they ground it deeper into the dirt.

Since he'd steered her through the fairground gates, she hadn't even looked in the direction of that scene. Not even a single glance. He sure as hell wasn't going to be the one to bring it up. Once upon a time he'd been the one to start everything, and look how they'd ended up. Besides, did it even matter anymore?

Leaving the laptop as though she'd heard his thoughts, she walked past him out of the barn. She stood staring out at the empty fairgrounds for what seemed like an hour. His heart picked up its rhythm. He couldn't see her face and he was dying to see her reaction, to watch the memories come back to her, but he didn't want to seem obvious.

When she turned around with her brow wrinkled, her breath hitched as though she was preparing to say something. He pushed away from the door, expectant.

Instead, she circled around him, heading in the opposite direction of that fateful patch of grass. She peered around the corner of the barn, to where a narrow drive shot past the splintered, angled posts of Loughlin's cattle pasture and emptied into the vast, empty parking lot surrounding the vacant Hemmertex building.

She turned back around, her eyes as brilliant as the grass. "What do you know about the Hemmertex land over there?"

"What do you mean?"

"Does Loughlin own that, too?"

He looked over at Loughlin's rotting fences and decaying properties. "No, he sold that parcel. I know the company who owns it now; it's not Hemmertex."

"You do?"

"Um, yeah." He cringed. "Don't be influenced by what you see now, but I did all that landscaping."

Her eyes popped wide and he caught a faint smile as she turned back around to survey the work he'd done—and that had since gone to weed and overgrowth—years and years ago. Sweeping lawns surrounded the building. The CEO had once thrown company picnics there. Leith had constructed a small amphitheater near the cafeteria door, where on some Fridays there had been musicians. Chris had played his fiddle there once or twice.

"I'm good," he felt the need to add. "Better than corporate, better than that. Go take a look at some of the huge homes up in the hills, if you want."

He told himself that the slow, sly smile she threw him over her shoulder had no heat in it. None whatsoever.

"I believe you," she said. "Can you get me contact info for the Hemmertex landowners?"

He'd have to dig out his computer from storage. "Yeah, I think so. Why?"

As she turned back around, her appearance—the shoulders-back confidence, the stunning, mature beauty—sent a blast of such powerful desire through him, he actually took a step back.

"Because I want to move the games over there," she said.

Leith hissed through his teeth and shook his head. "Gleann doesn't do so well with change."

She shrugged in a manner that said she was used to getting her way. "They're going to have to, if they don't want to lose this."

"You sure about that?"

"Positive. Change is good. Change is the answer."

A hundred different confrontations sprouted in his mind. He pictured Jen holding one of those fake swords DeeDee loved so much and standing in the center of Gleann fighting off angry townspeople, Mayor Sue wielding a pitchfork.

She advanced toward him predatorily. "Are you expensive?"

He coughed. "Excuse me?"

"Landscaping. Maintenance."

He ran a palm down his scruff and eyed the land in the distance, where his carefully selected shrubs and native grasses now resembled an old trailer park off I-93. "I used to charge a pretty penny. Back when I could."

"Give me a ballpark figure. For cleaning all that up back there."

He lowered his chin, trapped her eyes with his. "You want to hire me?"

There it was again. That glint of something *more* on her face. That hint that beneath her professional facade, there was an actual woman who remembered what had happened between them, and who, quite possibly, was still affected by it.

"Maybe." Her eyebrow twitched. "If the price is right."

He rattled off a number. She haggled it down, of course.

He'd already started low and he didn't care. Chris could do most of the work while he was running around scouting new locations, and he could pitch in when he felt the need to get on top of a mower or wave around a Weedwacker. It was income. Then he could pay Chris, who needed it far more than Leith did.

Jen gave him a blazing smile that had him picturing her in her underwear and glasses again. That made him back away, because what she was getting out of this situation was entirely different from what he was, and he hated how uneven it felt. *Again.* He was never balanced around her.

He ambled back to the barn. "So we done here?"

"I wasn't aware there was a 'we,'" she said, "but yes."

Of course there wasn't a "we." He did *not* look over at the center of the field.

Tapping on her computer, she went right back to work, her fingers blurry, her delicious bottom lip caught between her teeth. The sight of her drew him forward until he looked over her shoulder at the screen.

The open document was titled "Changes." Other programs made a patchwork of the screen—spreadsheets and graphs and a website or two. She moved between them with lightning speed. Then, suddenly, she snapped the laptop shut, shoved it into her purse, and straightened. She jumped when she finally realized how close Leith had gotten. She swallowed, glanced down his body and back up to find his eyes again. Selfishly, he was more than a little happy he'd managed to disarm her. Or maybe it was he who was unarmed and defenseless, because the urge to push her against the crates and kiss her suddenly overtook him.

"Um." She held her purse strap in a death grip. "I have to head over to Town Hall now."

"Meeting with Mayor Sue?" He still didn't move, even though he blocked the door.

"I refuse to call her that. That woman made my life miserable five summers running. It's bad enough she's my boss again."

"Miserable? Really?" He didn't remember that, didn't remember Jen ever being affected by criticism or bad air. It was strange for him to hear, when he thought he'd known her so well.

Jen blew a piece of hair off her forehead. "She's predisposed to hate anything I do. I'm always running uphill with her. I'm surprised she let me do this."

"*Let* you? They're not paying you?"

"No. I took vacation."

Dumbfounded, Leith cocked his head and planted his hands on his hips. The girl had worked at least two jobs every summer she'd been here. She'd checked her bank balance nearly every day. All she'd ever talked about was being someone, being a success. Work, work, work. What else didn't he know about her? What else had he gotten wrong?

"So why *are* you doing this?" he asked, voice soft. "Really. This doesn't . . . seem like you."

Her facial features tensed. "You can't say that."

He had to look away because the urge to *want* to know her was building and building, and he wasn't sure if he should let it. "You're absolutely right."

She cleared her throat but said nothing.

"So." He stepped closer, even though there was scant space left for him to erase. A little cloud of dust rose between them where he'd scuffed the dirt with his boot. She had to tilt her head back to look at him, and he tried not to remember that this was exactly how she'd looked with her back against the Stone Pub wall the night of their first kiss. "Is this who you are now? Is this what you do? Save small town festivals?"

"No." She licked her lips, and the way she stared into his eyes had him feeling eighteen all over again. "Just this one."

Chapter

5

"Leith MacDougall, what a surprise!" Evidently Sue McCurdy did know how to smile, and it was when the town's celebrity was in touching distance. Today's Syracuse T-shirt was navy blue, and the age-inappropriate hairstyle was pigtails sticking out from just behind her ears. The mayor stood in the open door of Town Hall, beaming right over Jen's head at the big man at her back. "To what do I owe this pleasure?"

Leith moved to Jen's side, crowding her on the small front stoop, their arms touching briefly. "Just dropping off Jen," he said.

Sue blinked at Leith, then shifted a confused glance to Jen, as though seeing her for the first time. Jen understood. Leith somehow managed to consume the atmosphere and draw eyes wherever he went. If he were a true celebrity, his pockets would be full of women's underwear. Dimly, Jen wondered if he'd ever found the pair of hers they'd lost in the dark woods one night a long time ago.

Jen wished Leith would leave. Not because she wanted to be rid of him, but because she needed to exhale. From the second he'd turned his giant truck into the fairgrounds and the sun had hit that quiet spot in the center of the field where he'd told her he loved her, she'd been holding her breath. There was a great pain in her chest because of it.

Appropriately, the picnic blanket that night had been red plaid, not his family tartan or anything, but appropriately Scottish looking. The evening had started sad, with the two of them knowing she was leaving, and ended in catastrophe.

Only a few minutes earlier, as she'd stood outside the barn, she'd been relieved Leith couldn't see her face, because she was sure there was no color in it. She'd wanted to clamp her hands over her ears. That stupid spot on the grass had beat like a diseased heart: loud, erratic, deadly. She'd turned back around, and the sight of him—older, bigger, longer hair—had nearly brought up ten-year-old tears from where she'd shoved them deep inside.

He was so nonchalant, so frustratingly cool. Maybe he'd buried his memories of that night the way she'd buried her tears. Nothing ever fazed him, Aimee had said, but how could even he not be affected by the fact that they were standing in almost the exact place they'd said good-bye?

Maybe he'd finally forgiven her. Maybe he hated her and was doing a damn fine job of covering it up.

That second thought made her want to throw up.

"Thought I'd come say hi, too," Leith said to Sue, "and to let you know Chris'll be taking over your yard when I'm gone."

"Are you helping Jen?" Sue asked Leith, her eyes brightening. "Because that would be just fantastic."

The smile he gave Sue was pure gold. "Wish I could, Mayor Sue."

The mayor leaned forward conspiratorially. "But you're going to throw, right? Your last hurrah before you leave us for good?" Leith was laughing in a genial, polite way until Sue added in a syrupy voice, "It's what your father would have wanted; I'm sure of it."

Maybe Sue didn't notice, but Jen did—that little hiccup in Leith's laugh, the slight narrowing of his eyes. Then those were gone, leaving Jen to wonder if she'd actually seen them.

"I'm sure he would have," Leith slowly replied, "but I just haven't been training like I should. Out of practice, you know. Besides, I'll be gone by then. The Carriages—you remember them? Rory and Hal, the Hemmertex president? Anyway, Rory called me out to Stamford to redesign their entire property. I'll be going back and forth until I find permanent digs down there."

Now it was Jen's turn to blink. Not that he owed her any information of the sort, and not that they'd really talked about anything other than the Highland Games in the past, oh, hour or so since they'd reconnected, but she was still shocked to hear it. Leith MacDougall was really up and leaving Gleann. It wasn't just talk.

Sue stood back, a girly pout pushing her bottom lip forward, and sighed.

"So," Leith said to Jen after an awkward pause. "You good here? Or you want me to stick around in town and take you back when you're done?"

Jen shook her head. It was only a fifteen-minute walk back to Maple, nothing by New York City standards, but that wasn't why she said no. "I want to go see Aimee when I'm through here. Thanks, though."

"'Kay." He touched Sue's arm in good-bye, but didn't reach for Jen. Just gave her a weird, tight-lipped grin, eyebrows raised, and then bounded back down the steps.

She didn't exhale until his rumbling truck made a U-turn and headed up toward Maple. He didn't once look back.

"So what can I do for you?" Sue's arms folded under those boobs, and she glared down at Jen with a look she knew all too well. Like Jen was seventeen again and she'd given the mayor's three Yorkies the wrong food at the wrong time of day.

Guess what? She wasn't seventeen anymore, and she wasn't doing this for Sue. Above everything, Jen was a professional. "I have a bunch of questions for you before I give my recommendations to the city council. Do you have time?"

Sue flattened her back to the wall to allow Jen to pass, but Jen still inadvertently brushed against that chest.

"He's leaving, you know," Sue said as she turned into her office at the front of Town Hall. "It would be kind of stupid to start something with him again. I remember how you two were back in the day."

Jen froze in the doorway of the cramped office, flabbergasted and unable to speak for several moments. Sue flicked annoyed eyes at the windows, as if Jen didn't already know she was talking about Leith.

"Thanks for the advice, Sue, but nothing is starting up between us again." Jen sat in the lone chair opposite the mayor's saccharine statue of three Yorkie puppies. Tugging her laptop out of her purse, she muttered under her breath, "Glad you noticed, too. That's not creepy at all."

*D*usk fell fast over Gleann, and then suddenly it was full-on night, someone somewhere having flipped a switch to send the world into black. Jen had forgotten that about this area, how there weren't miles of lights in all directions eating up the darkness. She'd forgotten that she liked it.

Jen let herself in the front door of the Thistle. The interior was shadowy dim except for a pale glow filtering through the giant sheets of plastic marking off the stripped-to-the-studs front room. The soft light came from the kitchen, but the B&B was so quiet, Jen assumed Ainsley and Aimee must be in their apartment above the garage and had just forgotten to turn off the lights. Then she heard Aimee's low voice drift out from the kitchen.

"Aim?" Jen called quietly as she tiptoed down the hallway. For all she knew, Owen could be back there with her sister, putting on a show for the deer in the backyard.

No man's voice followed Aimee's, just silence. Still, Jen peeked carefully around the corner, one eye scrunched shut, for fear of what she might see. But Aimee was merely sitting at the country table, head in one hand, the other pressing the phone to her ear. She was nodding and saying "Uh-huh, uh-huh. I'll ask Jen."

"Hey," Jen whispered, and knocked lightly on the door frame to catch Aimee's attention.

Aimee startled, her head snapping up. Her face turned chalk white. Her wide, terrified eyes belonged to someone who'd been caught with a bloody knife. She pulled the phone away from her mouth and stared at it like it was the murder weapon and she hadn't realized the horror of what she'd just done.

Jen had no idea what was going on, but her stomach dropped. She eased into the kitchen, whose light suddenly didn't feel so soft, and pressed both hands into the back of the chair opposite her sister. "Everything okay?" she mouthed.

She could hear a garbled woman's voice inside the phone, but no distinct words.

Aimee licked her lips and said into the receiver, "I have to go. Talk to you later."

She hung up, her hand shaking.

"What's going on?" Jen nodded at the phone. "What are you going to ask me?"

The back screen door opened and Ainsley pounded into the kitchen in her tiger-striped pajamas. The garage wasn't attached to the Thistle and you had to cross the backyard to get from the apartment to the inn. "Okay, Mom, it's nine. My turn to talk. Oh, hey, Aunt Jen."

"Hey, Sleepy McGee."

Aimee rose from her chair and was turning toward her daughter when Ainsley saw the silent phone on the table. "You already hung up? Crap. I wanted to tell Grandma about Bryan's slingshot."

"Watch your language," Aimee said in a dull voice that lacked authority.

"Grandma?" Jen squeaked. No way. Couldn't be . . . "Not Mom. You weren't talking to Mom. Were you?"

Aimee brushed her dark bangs off her forehead and took forever to answer. At least she looked Jen in the eye when she did so. "Yes," her sister said, with a forced strength cut by a clearing of her throat. "Yes, I was."

Jen still wasn't sure she'd heard correctly. She looked to Ainsley for a second opinion, but the girl seemed as confused as Jen felt.

"What's going on?" Ainsley asked, her big blue eyes darting between her mom and her aunt.

"Ainsley, could you go back to your room?" Aimee asked quietly.

"Can I take your phone? Call her back?"

"No."

"But—"

"*Now.*"

Ainsley left, but not before Jen saw the disappointment smeared over that young face. What on earth was going on?

"Ainsley wanted to know her grandma," Aimee said before Jen could ask. "And I thought it couldn't hurt to try."

Oh, Jesus. "Seriously?" Jen fell into a chair. "How long has this been going on?"

"A few years now. After we left you in New York. It started slow, a phone call every couple of months, just so they could connect, you know?"

"And now?"

"And now"—Aimee pulled out the chair she'd vacated and sat, lifting pained eyes to Jen—"It's a weekly thing. Mom and Ainsley . . . they talk a lot."

Jen just stared, the explanation difficult to process. Did Aimee even remember all the shit Mom had put them through? Didn't they have the same memories, the same hurt, even if they didn't have the same father?

"You know Ainsley," Aimee said with an artificial laugh. "She can talk to anyone, be friends with anyone. But she wanted a grandparent, and Mom was the only one I could give her."

In a terrible way, Jen understood. Whatever Mom had inflicted upon her and Aimee growing up, the woman was half a country away. And Ainsley wasn't Aimee or Jen.

"It sounded like you talk to her, too," Jen said, and Aimee nodded. Jen ground fingers into her temples. "So does she know what you're doing with Owen?"

Aimee sat up straighter. "That's none of your business, Jen. Owen is mine and I know what I'm doing."

"Are you forgetting what Frank did to Mom? All those women around town, flaunting themselves in front of her? All those scenes? Do you remember bailing her out of jail for attacking that one who came to the house? Owen isn't divorced. I heard he's still living with his wife. You don't think this sounds horribly familiar?"

Aimee thrust out a hand. "Stop. There is nothing to be 'fixed' with Owen and me. You don't know the whole story and, honestly, it's none of your business. Stay out of it."

Jen wondered if Aimee kept any vodka in the freezer.

"She's different now." Aimee laid her hands flat on the table. "She really is."

Jen highly doubted that. The woman had just gotten worse

every year her girls had aged. "You were talking about me. She knows I'm here?"

Aimee swallowed. "Yes. She wanted to talk to you."

Jen froze, her body welded to the chair. "She said that? In those words?"

"Well . . . no."

A strangled laugh escaped Jen's throat. "Of course not. Was she drunk?"

Aimee's cheeks flushed. It was clear she wanted to say something, then gave a little shake of her head. Heavy silence weighted down the air between them. The kitchen was fogged with tension. Aunt Bev's grandfather clock chimed the incorrect time out in the hall.

"It's been ten years, Jen. You have no idea what she'll say now—"

"I don't have to know! She slurred enough the day I left for Austin. That I was ungrateful. That I was abandoning her. That I thought I was all high and mighty, but that I really wasn't worth anything. Those are the kinds of words that stick."

Aimee nodded sadly at the table. "I see."

It was then Jen finally noticed the smell of cookies and the timer on the stovetop counting down the final seconds of baking. Just another normal evening for Aimee. A normal, weekly evening. The buzzer went off and Aimee rose to pull out the tray of chocolate chip.

"What did she want you to ask me? I heard you, before I came in."

Aimee shoved a spatula under each cookie and slid them one by one onto a cooling rack before answering, her back still to Jen, "She wanted to know if you were planning on sending a check this month."

So now Aimee knew. Jen fought against the urge to scream in frustration. To kick a chair halfway across the room. To stomp out of the house. "See? She hasn't changed at all."

"Jen." Aimee finally turned around, hands braced behind her on the counter edge. "That's not the point. You've been sending her money?"

Jen shook her head, but not in denial.

"If you're so worried she's still drunk all the time, if you hate her that much . . . why?"

Salty, stinging tears filled Jen's eyes. The day had finally caught up with her—first facing Leith and his indifference, then clawing her way uphill with Sue, now this.

She calmly rose. "If you're going to play the 'that's none of your business' card, then here's me, playing mine."

Chapter

6

*L*eith had his bare feet kicked up on the rickety coffee table
with the angel inlays and the chipped legs, TV muted and
tuned to the Red Sox game he wasn't even watching. Ten
o'clock at night and Jen still wasn't back. He knew this because
he'd positioned the pink velour recliner to perfectly view her
driveway and side door.

The security light over 738's porch flicked on as Jen
appeared, walking slowly, head bent, that damned purse dragging one shoulder down. She carried a brown takeout bag from
the Stone in the opposite hand.

He sank deeper into the recliner and nudged back a corner
of the lace curtain. It could have been the harsh glare of the
motion-sensor light, but there was a pale haggardness to her
face. If he didn't know that she always managed to hold herself
together no matter the situation, he might have named it
sadness.

No, never that on her. A trick of the light then. But it made
him think of earlier that day, when he'd doubted how well
he actually knew her.

She must have spent a long time with Aimee to have come
back so late. He wondered if it was difficult for her, to have

been called back to Gleann to work, only to spend so little time with her sister. But then, the two of them had never been all that close. Aimee had run with the partying crowd every summer, with Jen often having to rescue her from shit situations or drive her home after she'd drank too much. Jen and Leith's jokes on the townspeople had been harmless, but Aimee's antics—vandalism, a pot bust—rarely left people smiling, least of all Jen.

Being closer to Jen, Leith had always held Aimee at arm's length. Then one summer, while Jen had been off at college, Aimee had reappeared in Gleann holding a baby. Bev Haverhurst took her in without question. Aimee mellowed, grew up. Gleann was a good mother that way; if anything, Leith knew that. Then Bev died, leaving the Thistle to her older niece.

Outside, Jen reached the side door. *Showtime.*

Leith sat back, hand over his grinning mouth. Maybe Jen refused to acknowledge their romantic past, but he would love for her to remember their friendship, how fun it used to be.

She struggled to take out her keys while balancing everything else, then finally managed to wiggle the key into the testy lock. Then she saw it. The takeout bag slid to the ground as she plucked the folded piece of paper taped to the door.

He shouldn't be laughing. Really, he shouldn't be. Except that it was too damn funny. Even when she pressed the piece of paper to her chest and crept around the front of 738 to peer over at the empty blue house she thought belonged to Mr. Lindsay, he was laughing.

The Jen he knew was getting ready to march over to that house and pound on the door, intending to shove the note in the old man's face and tell him to back off. Then the jig would be up, Leith would head outside to meet her and reveal himself, and they'd have a good laugh. So when she turned to look over at Mildred's house instead, he flattened himself against the back of the recliner, out of sight.

Seconds later, someone rattled his back metal screen door. *What the—*

He pushed to his feet, checked to make sure his fly was up, that he didn't reek. He stood in front of the foggy antique mirror hanging crookedly in the narrow hallway and ran a hand through his hair.

For the life of him, he couldn't fully wipe the grin off his face. So when he opened the back door, one foot propped on the single step leading up into the kitchen, he was sure he looked like the proverbial cat who ate the canary.

Jen sighed when she saw him. Actually sighed.

Hello, canary.

"Holy crap, Leith. Look what that pervert left me now!"

She shoved the note in his face, and even though he didn't have to read it to know what it said, he scanned his own chicken scratch anyway.

"Ms. Haverhurst," he read, unable to hide his smirk, *"Would you mind not hanging your clothing and unmentionables around the house in plain view of anyone walking along the sidewalk?"*

Leith laughed as he lowered the paper, but Jen's arms were clamped over her chest as though she were naked and he were Mr. Lindsay. Which he was, technically . . . and which she wasn't, unfortunately.

"I'm a little freaked out," she said. "You tell me. Should I be? Should I move? What's this guy like?"

Leg still hiked up on the step, one arm braced on the railing, he asked, "So why's your underwear hanging around the house?"

"Because I don't trust that old dryer not to fry it! And that shouldn't matter. Is he peeking in my windows?"

"Well, they're actually *his* windows."

She pressed fingers to her mouth. The law of fluorescent lightbulbs said her skin and eyes shouldn't look so beautiful under their glare, but she'd never been one to follow those kinds of rules.

"Do you think he's actually gone inside the house? Do you think he's actually, you know, *touched* my stuff?" Her whole body did this exaggerated shiver as her hands dropped. "Why are you laughing? This isn't funny at all."

But he couldn't stop. He just laughed and laughed, pinching the bridge of his nose. "Relax, Jen."

"Don't tell me to relax—"

"I wrote those notes."

"Don't tell me—wait. *You?*"

His foot dropped off the step and he leaned a hip against the basement railing. "Yep."

Body frozen in a midrant pose, only her eyes shifted back
and forth. "You. You're Mr. Lindsay?"

He recognized the start of Jen's anger. The gathering of her
lips, the careful swipe of her tongue between them as she
ordered her words.

"Before you start"—he held up a hand—"I freaked out when
you called me out of the blue the other day. I had no idea you'd
come back here. I heard your voice on the phone, you thought I
was Mr. Lindsay, I ran with it." Her shoulders dropped, her giant
purse sliding with a jerk to the crook of her elbow. His other
hand came up, warding off the verbal blow he could feel coming.
He was shoring up his house, nailing boards to the windows in
preparation for the hurricane. "I'm sorry. I thought it would buy
me some time to deal with you suddenly reappearing. Thought
it'd be funny for a bit; you know, since we used to play all those
tricks on people together back in the day. Didn't know you'd get
so bothered."

"A strange man leaving notes on my door. You didn't think
it would bother me."

He ran a hand around the back of his neck and looked at
the linoleum floor with the decades-old line of wear leading
from the door to the stairs. "I didn't think. I'm sorry." Chin
down, he looked up at her.

She broke. Her smile was the sun lasering through the swirling clouds, dissipating the storm.

"Jesus Christ, Leith!" She breathed like she'd just sprinted
across the fairgrounds. The takeout bag dropped to the floor. But
she was smiling. And laughing. "There's no one out here! The
thought of some creepy old guy looking through my window?"

Hand to his chest, he said, "I'm sorry. I really am." He let
himself have another chuckle, but this one not at her expense.
"Want me to walk you back to your place? You know, in case
any old men are lurking about?"

"Well, no. There's underwear strung all around."

"Like I said, want me to walk you back to your place?"

He hadn't meant to flirt. Really. It caught both of them by
surprise, their smiles fading, the laughter petering out. In the
crappy foyer light, their gazes caught and held. The house felt
too small, her proximity too close and yet not nearly close
enough.

"I, uh . . ." she began, then cleared her throat as her eyes drifted away, over his shoulder. The moment her expression changed, from awkward—but also eager?—attraction, to one of bewilderment, he knew she'd spotted Mildred's kitchen. He shifted his body to try to block her view, but it was useless.

"Okay, I may have underwear hanging from a clothesline across the living room," Jen said, "but at least I don't have shelves of Precious Moments and painted wooden hearts on my kitchen wall."

Dropping her purse to the linoleum, she pushed past him and jumped up the one step into the kitchen. He sighed, waiting for it.

"Leith." She stood in the center of the pink braided rug and turned in a circle, amusement plastered all over her face as she took in the elderly horror. He deserved her laughter. "I never pegged you as a pink kitchen sort of guy."

He had to run with it, though he was loathing where her next line of questioning was heading. "Isn't it more of a mauve?"

She guffawed. "Did you just move in or something?"

"Or something." He shut the back door and joined her in the small kitchen.

"Is this your *grandma's* house?"

"No." Strangely, he felt a little defensive, and reached out to straighten a faded and burned pot holder hanging from a hook above the stovetop. "It was Mildred's."

"Who's Mildred?"

"Mildred Lindsay."

Jen nodded slowly. "Ah, okay. I get it. I think."

"Her husband died, oh, I don't know, thirty years ago? She lived alone here, but Horace Lindsay's name was still on three houses—this one, yours, and the *empty* one on the other side."

She laughed low and graced him with a smile that said she'd forgiven him.

"May I?" She gestured down the darkened hall toward the front room. He shrugged. None of the stuff inside was his, and she wasn't laughing at the house anymore.

Leith followed Jen deeper into Mildred's home. She turned into the formal living room that looked out over the street. Leith leaned in the doorway, watching as she turned on a lamp with a fringed shade. The room was filled with knickknacks—porcelain figurines and blown glass vases in pale colors and framed Victorian prints—that meant absolutely nothing to him, and which he'd been viewing as a hindrance these past few months. But Jen spent time looking at each one, giving them a fragile, sad, forgotten meaning he'd been purposely avoiding.

She turned from a glass-enclosed bookcase near the window. "So why are *you* here?"

The lamplight hit her in a way that turned her dress into a translucent suggestion. She was still wearing that pale gray one from this morning, the one that seemed to wrap around the best parts of her body. Thanks to the fuzzy light from behind, he could see her shape: the subtle dent of her waist, the round curve of her hips, the slope of her inner thighs.

Though he'd seen her last night wearing a lot less, there was something terribly intimate about her appearance now—especially in the way she regarded him, head tilted, eyes gone soft.

He cleared his throat and angled his body to stare at a crack in the well-worn hardwood floor. "Mildred left all her stuff to me. The three houses. Everything inside. A bit of money."

Jen trailed her fingers over a secretary desk. "Why to you?"

He shrugged.

"Did you know her well?"

"No. Not really."

"But you must have made an impression."

"I said I don't really know why."

"No, you didn't. You just shrugged." Her expression turned sly, teasing. "Did you buy her groceries or something?"

"No."

"Date her granddaughter?"

"No grandkids."

Jen came forward, moving out of the tormenting lamplight, thank God. He was momentarily blindsided by the memory of how she'd looked the night of their first kiss. Her face turned up to him, him towering over her, she'd looked delicate and beautiful and trusting. And also scared.

Much as she seemed just now.

Jen, true to character, somehow covered all that up with a hand on her hip and a playful squint. "So you must have cut her lawn."

He shoved his hands in his pockets, feeling like he was ten. "Yeah, I did."

She swallowed a smile and went to the window, leaning over to pull aside the curtain. That smooth, clingy, gray fabric settled into the crack of her ass, and he had to look away again.

"Wow," she said, examining the plainest, smallest front yard on the block, "you must have done a *spectacular* job."

"I also talked to her. I think I might have been the only person who did."

She swiveled to him, green eyes giant, dark hair swishing around her shoulders. "Oh my God, she had a crush on you!"

There was the Jen he remembered, the Jen he'd once loved. The one who knew how to be fun and giggly and teasing when she stopped moving or working for a minute or two. That, more than anything, made him turn around and head back into the kitchen. There was beer in the fridge somewhere.

"You're nuts," he said, opening the door and hearing the satisfying clink of brown bottles along the side shelf.

Jen followed him. Of course she followed. She was laughing now and her voice hit all sorts of wonderful high notes. "I bet she watched you out that big picture window and just . . . pined."

Thinking about Mildred spying on him while sitting in that rocking chair was plain weird, but he knew that's exactly what she'd done. He'd caught her once. Maybe twice.

"She watched youuuuu," Jen sang, "and she thought"—here's where she adopted a really bad old lady's voice—" 'That man is so fine. Maybe if I leave him everything I own he'll sleep with me in the afterlife.' "

He snatched two beers from the fridge door and swiveled around, finger pointing around the neck of the bottle. "That's disgusting."

Jen showed no signs of stopping laughing. A wave of emotion hit him as they fell back into their old camaraderie as though time had never happened, and he hid it by taking a half-bottle swig of beer.

She kept going. "And when you took your shirt off—"

"Hey, I don't *ever* take off my shirt when I work."

She stopped, scrunched up her face. "Really? I bet you'd get double the work in half the time. Seriously."

"I'm not in high school. I'm a business person."

God, he loved her smile. All diamonds and joy. But it faded a bit as she said, "I know you are."

Another gulp of lager. He held out the unopened bottle. "You want this one?"

She eyed the brown bottle, her eyes shifting back up to him. He had no idea what she was thinking, taking such a long time to answer. It was a beer, not a shot of Jäger.

"No, thanks. I'm presenting to the city council tomorrow afternoon."

If he didn't know better, he'd say she looked nervous. "Good. More for me. I need it."

She fingered the edge of the tiny breakfast table, and for a moment he was scared it was an indication she was getting ready to head out, to walk away again. Even though she was just next door, it felt painfully far. Too soon to separate after what had broken and been reformed during this strange little conversation.

She didn't leave. Instead she scanned the kitchen again, but this time in no joking manner. "You didn't really answer me before. Why are you here in Mildred's house?" There was a soft, filtered tone to her voice. "And don't say because you inherited it."

He scratched at the back of his neck then cracked it. "Okay."

"I mean, you had to have lived somewhere before here. Did you have a house?"

He finished the beer, setting a new personal record. "Nah. Never owned a place of my own in Gleann, believe it or not. Been holding out for when I find the perfect house so I can do it up right. I want to work on it, create it, from the inside out." He glanced out the dark kitchen window to the town he couldn't see. "I guess I know all the houses in the valley and none of them are mine."

"Huh." A little smile tugged at one edge of her mouth. "So where did you live before here? And why'd you move out?"

He leaned his ass against the counter and cracked open the second beer. "Because I knew I had to get out of here months ago and things happened real fast. Right around the time Mildred died, Chris Weir, the last guy I have on my payroll, needed to get out of his place because things had gone south with his roommates. He's trying to get out from a bad crowd. Anyway, I sublet my duplex to him, and moved in here because it was the smallest of the three houses and I knew I wouldn't be here long. I packed all my shit and divided it between the three garages until I can settle elsewhere." The second beer tasted even better than the first. "It's a good transition, I think, to getting out of here. Living here now will make it easier when I won't have a Gleann address."

She cocked her head. "Is it hard now? You make it seem like it's so easy for you to take off."

Shit. He waved the bottle. "No, no. It's all good. I meant financially."

She was nodding, but in a careful way that said she didn't quite know whether to believe him. Thankfully, she didn't press the subject. "Do you feel bad for leaving? I mean, I can totally understand you going when the clients have dried up, but this place needs businesses."

"Do I feel bad? Yep. Every day." He also felt pretty crappy about the idea of staying, but he didn't say that.

"Isn't it weird, though? Living in this house that so clearly isn't yours? Being here when she isn't?"

Leith scratched at his face. His five-o'clock shadow usually came in around three, and it was past ten. "At this point, it's hard to say what's weird or what isn't. I'm living in limbo. There's weird on all sides."

He was trying to make a joke, but realized, as soon as he said it, that he was a big fucking liar. He knew *exactly* what was weird, and that was having Jen Haverhurst standing within arm's reach in the old-lady kitchen that wasn't his.

The bottle at his lips, he regarded her as coolly as possible. "Sure you don't want that beer?"

"I'm sure." But her voice didn't sound so steady.

Time to change the subject. "How'd the meeting with Sue go?"

With a hiss through her teeth, she grimaced. "Dunno. I asked her a bunch of things, tried to be cagey about possible changes, since you said she'd put up defenses if I asked too much right away, but I think she saw right through me."

"Probably, knowing Mayor Sue."

"She wants the same-old, same-old, but I can make the

games *better*. I know I can. Think she'll sway the council against me, shoot me down before I get my points across?"

"I don't know."

"Fuck."

Though she wasn't talking about the physical act, the idea of doing *that*, with her, zoomed in with blood-pounding strength and threatened to replace all sane thought. He drank.

There were things he could do to try to ease her mind, to make her job easier. To help her.

"Want to have breakfast with me tomorrow?" he asked.

Because he was a guy, his mind scrolled through all the events that might come before a man asked a woman to breakfast. But also, because he was a gentleman raised by a fine Scottish man who'd taught him to respect women, he tried to push them aside.

"Yeah, I can do that," she said.

"Great. The Kafe at eight?"

She nodded and then started toward the door. Then she stopped and looked at him strangely, as though she'd seen something on his face, when he was usually so careful about not betraying his thoughts. "What are you thinking about?" she asked.

"Kissing you."

The truth just fell out, like one of his two-hundred-seventy-pound throwing buddies had come over and whacked him on the back, expelling the words from his mouth. He wouldn't back down, though. He'd own that statement like he owned four unwanted houses in Gleann.

She drew the tiniest of breaths, holding perfectly still. "Like . . . now?"

Well, yes, but she looked so scared he couldn't bring himself to admit it. Another casual gulp of beer. "Actually, I was thinking about our first."

Her thick, dark eyelashes fluttered as she dipped her chin, and he considered that maybe she'd been thinking about that night, too. Or maybe one of the sixty other nights that summer they'd grabbed each other whenever time and circumstance allowed.

She surprised the hell out of him by saying, "It's hard to walk past the Stone and not think about it."

No shit. He'd had to see that thatched-roof reminder every day for the past ten years. The place where he'd first tasted Jen's mouth, that kiss in all its messy, frantic, hormonal glory, could do him a giant favor by leaving him alone for a day or two.

So she'd talk about their beginning but not remotely acknowledge their end?

He considered taking this further by finally breaking and being the one to bring it up, then realized it would be like slamming a bulldozer through the wall. Their interaction tonight had been so easy, so warm. So like two adults who still—maybe, hopefully—felt some sort of attraction or affection toward one another.

He put down the beer and grabbed the back of a chair with both hands, leaning into it. It let out a giant groan under his weight. He should be thankful for their distance, because the way she breathed now, with deep movements of her chest, her head tilted back slightly on her neck, brought to mind images of surrender.

She ran a hand up and down one bare arm, and even though it was warm in the small summer kitchen, her skin pebbled.

"I have to go. My food's probably ice-cold and I have work to do before bed." She mimed typing.

He let her turn and descend the step into the foyer, his body aching to follow. She picked up her purse and peeked at him over her shoulder, her shiny dark hair hiding a green eye. Those things were powerful, brilliant enough to stun with just one.

There. A flash of remembrance. A second of desire. She hadn't forgotten, hadn't pushed it away.

His own brand of desire came back from the past, shooting straight through the years, intensifying as it spun and grew. It slammed into him. Any other woman he'd dated over the past decade didn't even register. He and Jen though, they had an anchor that was pretty impossible to dig out of the sand.

He couldn't help himself. "I lied, Jen. I was thinking about kissing you right now. Still am."

He watched the shiver pass through her, could see it even across the room. *Good.*

And then *he* was across the room, his legs eating up the kitchen floor in three strides. Hands on her hips, the feel of that dress in his palms, he lightly pressed her against the back door.

She didn't protest, didn't stiffen, and if that wasn't a sign, he didn't know what was. Her body was warm and giving along his.

His head lowered, her mouth three inches away. Then two. Then . . .

It was short and gentle, the brush of his lips against hers. But the promise, the heat . . .

He pulled back with a restraint he'd never known himself capable of. Straightening, he looked down at her dazed face.

"What do you want, Leith?" she whispered.

He knew her question was bigger than this moment, that she was referring to the fact that her presence here—and his, too—was temporary, at best.

"Right now"—he gave her waist a squeeze—"I'm pretty sure I want you. Beyond that, I don't know." Then he pushed back fully, putting charged air between them. "Still want to have breakfast with me?"

Only he wasn't talking about just eating. He meant everything that came before.

"Yes," she breathed. A heated mingling of stares, and then she opened the door and was gone.

Chapter

7

*J*en hauled open the glass door to Kathleen's Kafe the next morning at precisely 7:59. It was one of the only buildings in town that had been renovated and updated, and that had been sometime in the seventies. Though hideous, the faux-wood veneer booths and tables, and the brown vinyl cushion covers felt like a warm blanket around her shoulders. The walls were covered with sagging shelves packed with tchotchkes: T-shirts and mugs from valley-area high school events, stuffed animals coated in a layer of dust, photos of people long dead but still smiling. She wondered if the hash browns were still as crispy as she remembered.

The place was nearly full, which gave Jen heart. It was the most number of people she'd seen in one spot while in Gleann, and if they still supported this place and its local flavor, it gave her hope for her version of the games.

As she entered, a bell over the door chimed. Eerily, as one, every patron in the diner looked up or craned their necks to see who'd come in. Every patron, that is, except for Leith, who sat sideways on one of those attached, swinging stools at the long, low breakfast bar, his back to her. He didn't turn around, but he shifted on his seat—a slight squaring of his shoulders, an inch adjustment of his boot on the floor—which told her he was well aware she'd come in.

Last night she'd stumbled across Mildred Lindsay's lawn, somehow found her way into her rented house, and stood in front of the air-conditioning window unit. It had taken her a good hour to get to work after that, those sixty minutes needed to thoroughly burn away the panty-melting sensory recollection of the tease of his mouth. Their connection had been combustible, undeniable, but she, like him, had no idea what to do with it. She didn't know what she wanted either, though the buzz zooming through her body said she pretty much wanted him inside her.

With an inward groan and a squeeze of her eyelids, she willed the desire gone. Or at least toned down. Being this close to him wasn't ever going to make it go away entirely.

She stood next to the stack of local, out-of-date valley newspapers by the door, and watched the rest of the patrons watch her with varying degrees of interest. She smiled back, to no one in particular, but it felt shaky and forced, and her own awkwardness shocked the hell out of her.

A woman with brilliant red hair sitting with two young teenagers absorbed in their phones studied Jen for a moment, but then returned to her magazine. Sue McCurdy and another woman, maybe in her fifties, sat in the booth farthest from the door. By their spread of newspapers and crumb-filled breakfast plates, it looked like they'd been sitting there awhile. Maybe for the past thirty years. Sue gave Jen a small lift of the hand, but the other woman peered at Jen suspiciously like Jen was here to bulldoze the entire town.

At the breakfast bar, the guy sitting next to Leith was younger, with long brown hair pulled back in a messy ponytail. The younger guy was shoveling French toast into his mouth while Leith talked. Leith clutched a coffee mug in one hand and drew something invisible on the counter between them.

Behind her, the Kafe door opened, the bell above making a strangled *ping*. Someone needed to get out the oil and screwdriver.

"Aunt Jen?"

Jen turned, the girl's voice causing an instant smile. "Hey there. Having some breakfast?"

"Yeah." Ainsley scooped a wad of bubble gum out of her cheek and slapped it into a wrapper. She shoved it into one shorts pocket while pulling a twenty out of another. "I told Mom I'm buying today."

Jen swept a hand over Ainsley's unbrushed hair. "Where'd you get that, Moneybags McGee?"

"She's a little you," Aimee said, and Jen finally looked up at her sister standing several feet away. Their argument from last night still pushed them apart; Jen could feel it as solidly as the hot summer air coming through the open door. Aimee's green eyes shimmered with a coat of tears that she quickly blinked away. "She does odd jobs around town and sometimes helps me out at the Thistle. Yesterday Gary Ashdown had her pulling weeds and unpacking his groceries."

"I used to pull weeds, too," Jen told Ainsley.

"You did?" Ainsley gasped. "Maybe that means someday *I'll* get to live in New York. Oh, look! T and Lacey are here!"

Ainsley shoved past Jen, dissolving any hope Jen had of quizzing her niece about her aspirations. The nine-year-old darted across the Kafe, running her fingers through her hair as she approached the table in the back with the red-haired woman and the two teenagers.

The red-haired woman. Melissa.

Jen turned, wide-eyed and worried, to Aimee. Jen held her breath, waiting for either Aimee or Melissa to explode into a scene worthy of a Mexican soap opera.

But Aimee just watched her daughter talking with the girls belonging to her still-married lover, and said an unexpected thing: "Maybe she will."

Jen shook her head to clear it, to try to follow Aimee's train of thought. "Maybe she'll what?"

Aimee's ear tilted toward one shoulder. "Maybe Ainsley will get to New York. She's more like you than me anyway." She sighed. "I often wonder how a kid created out of such ugliness managed to turn out so completely opposite."

"Would you hate that," Jen asked, "if Ainsley eventually went to the city?"

Aimee thought about that, still watching the scene over at the table that had Jen digging her fingernails into her palms in gruesome anticipation. "No. I mean, the place isn't for me, but

I think you and I both know that just because we're born to certain people doesn't mean we're automatically like them."

Jen couldn't help adding, "You were exactly like Mom once."

"And I fight that battle every day. You don't think I do?"

Jen bit the inside of her cheek.

Aimee said, "I'm sorry for not telling you about the phone calls."

Jen rolled her eyes. "No, you're not. You would've kept on hiding them from me if I hadn't walked in."

"Maybe you should call her. Talk to her yourself. Then you'd see—"

"Nope." Jen's hair swished across her cheeks as she shook her head. "Can't do it yet, Aim."

"Then don't get all pissy because I am."

"I *am* mad. I'm mad you're talking to the woman who almost ruined both our lives."

"She was the only other adult left in our family, because you clearly weren't."

Jen distinctly felt the bite of those words.

"What's worse?" Aimee asked. "A grandma with a shitty track record as a mom actually paying attention to and loving my little girl? Or the sister who was a better mom to me blowing off my little girl for most of her life, including one specific weekend in New York City?"

Jen nodded, understanding. "I'm sorry for that. I really am. I'm hoping that by being here now, I can try to make it up to you and her."

Aimee didn't look all that convinced. "I'm not like Mom anymore. I'm not even the same Aimee you knew and took care of."

Jen raised an eyebrow. "Really? Because the other day with the water pipe—"

Aimee winced. "It was so weird. It was like the second you came back I reverted. And you always know what to do. I'm not really like that. Not anymore."

"Then show me, Aim."

Her sister drew herself up. "Okay. I will." A glance across the Kafe. "I better go. Ainsley's starting to give me the pancake stink-eye." Then she let out a rueful laugh. "Another way she's like you. She gets mean when she's hungry."

Jen saw that Ainsley had slid into the booth behind Sue's.

"Okay," said Jen. "I'd join you, but—"

"Leith," Aimee filled in, with a tiny smile that cracked some of the tension. "I see him. And he sees you, too."

Jen could feel Leith's eyes on her, but she was watching Aimee cut to Ainsley's booth and grinding her teeth against a potential mess with Melissa. Several of the other diners were whispering and pointing, too, their disapproval clear. Jen cringed. She was waiting for Melissa to jump up, flip the table to its side, and reach for Aimee's throat, nails bared.

Jen expected this, because it was an exact scene she'd once broken up between Mom and some woman named Janet, who'd been Frank's flavor of the week. Funny, she hadn't thought about that day in such a long time. Now the visuals of the past and present overlapped, so much so that when Melissa looked up and gave Aimee a polite but aloof smile, Jen saw Melissa letting out a snarl, sharpening her fangs. Preparing to attack.

Jen was already three steps toward her sister, ready to step in, when her name cut across the Kafe.

"Jen."

She startled, stopped, and looked over at Leith who was waving her over. A glance back at Aimee saw that her sister waved to Melissa, then slid into the booth with Ainsley.

"Jen, I want you to meet someone." Leith swiveled on the stool, his hard, massive thighs taking up the whole seat, his grin aimed only at her. She joined him.

"This is Chris." Leith gestured to the ponytail guy who held a forkful of French toast. "Chris works for me. Plays a mean fiddle in the band DeeDee hired for the games."

There was a watchfulness to Leith's expression. He seemed to be looking for something on her face. Then she realized what he'd done, calling her over here just as she was about to charge into a battle that didn't exist. He'd spared her a scene. He'd saved her from embarrassing herself and Aimee, when Sue McCurdy and a good chunk of the town sat in the same room.

A long time ago, he'd witnessed some good fights between

the sisters. He'd been there for Jen when she'd had to rescue Aimee from more than one mess.

Jen drew a deep breath, cleansing herself of the past. "Hi," she said to Chris, offering him a genuine smile. "Great to meet you." Out of the corner of her eye, she noticed Leith's shoulders relax.

Chris was chewing, nodding, but there was a wide-eyed worry in the way he stared at her. After he swallowed, he said, "We still get to play at the games. Don't we?"

Jen gave him an exaggerated look of appraisal and pretended to consider it. "Have a digital file you can send me?"

Chris wiped his hands on his jeans, leaving smears of powdered sugar. "Oh, absolutely." She gave him her email address and he practically jumped from his seat. "I'll get that to you right now. I promise you, there won't be any issues with the guys. Then I'll get to Mayor Sue's yard. That okay, Dougall?"

"Issues with the guys?" she asked Leith when Chris had gone.

"Remember I said he had problems with one of his roommates? That guy's also the drummer. Alcohol problem he's trying to kick. I don't know if it's working, though." Leith picked up his coffee cup and said into it, "So what other Scottish folk rock band do you know that could possibly play here on such short notice?"

She steepled her fingers. "Oh, I have resources you couldn't possibly know about." Then, seriously, with a wave of her hand, "I'll take Chris at his word that things will work out."

He gave her that slow, sexy grin. "You shouldn't tease a man like that."

"Says the guy who taped false stalker notes to my door."

"Hey, Lindsay wasn't a stalker. He was just . . . interested."

She leaned down and she could smell his shampoo. "Who exactly teased whom?"

His eyes flicked up over the top of his mug, and in them she saw the same desire from last night.

"Sit down." He pivoted to face the bar. "I'll buy you hash browns. I remember you liked them here."

"Ooooh, are they still the same?"

He pointed to the silver-haired man at the burners, who was

cooking so furiously and fast that little pieces of food flew everywhere. Jen recognized him and grinned. A middle-aged man wearing an apron, jeans, and checkered shirt came over to take their order, and the icy glare he threw at Leith was unmistakable.

"What was that about?" she asked Leith under her breath as the server shuffled off. "The only person within a twenty-mile radius who doesn't worship at the feet of Leith MacDougall?"

Leith pressed his lips together and nodded. "Used to work for me. Had to let him go, along with two other full-time guys. Chris is the only one I have left."

"Oh." That had to have been hard for him. She was about to ask him more about it, when he turned and lifted a muscled arm to an older couple who'd just entered the Kafe. They came over, wearing the looks of delight she'd come to associate with being recognized and acknowledged by Leith.

The man looked older than the woman by twenty years, and she already had a pure-white bob and a face lined with distinguished wrinkles.

"Rob," Leith said, "do you remember Jen Haverhurst? Used to come here every summer and stay with Bev at the Thistle. She and I stole the lawn furniture from in front of your hardware store that one year."

An uncomfortable laugh erupted from Jen's throat. While their harmless little pranks weren't unknown, she just didn't feel like reminding people of that side of her at this particular point in time.

"Ahhh," Rob said in a hoarse voice, narrowing rheumy eyes on her. "That was you, huh. Remember you set the furniture back up in the middle of the high school football field."

"And then we put it all back," Jen added, throwing a disbelieving look at Leith, who looked ready to burst into laughter any second now.

"And now you're back to run the games?" Rob asked skeptically.

Jen folded her hands and tried to look as professional as an admitted thief could. "Just for this year, yes."

Leith touched the older woman's shoulder. "And this is Bobbie, Rob's wife."

As Bobbie shook Jen's hand, Rob pinched his wife's butt. He said, "We met online."

"How nice," Jen said, not knowing how to take that.

"Yeah," Leith said with a waggle of his eyebrows. "Bobbie's a bit of an . . . Internet celebrity."

Please, please don't let that mean what they're making it out to mean.

"You two need to stop doing that," Bobbie said, slapping Leith's arm. "You're giving people heart attacks."

"She's got one of the biggest followings of any scrapbooking website," Leith amended.

Jen let out a relieved laugh. "Scrapbooking. Oh! There used to be a store across the street."

A pained, regretful look crossed Rob's face while Bobbie swished the air with one graceful hand. "I should've known it wouldn't work," the older woman said. "It was always a dream to own my own store. I thought the online success would translate to a physical presence in my lovely new town, but it didn't."

"I'm sorry," Jen said, and meant it.

"My belly says we need to go," Rob said abruptly, and then the couple—*please don't let their last name be Roberts*—left, hand in age-spotted hand.

As Jen and Leith turned back to the counter, the disgruntled former employee slid their plates in front of them. Jen eyed hers skeptically, wondering if he'd spit in it, but Leith shoved his fork into a mound of scrambled eggs and took the biggest bite she'd ever seen.

"The Roberts are good people to know." He washed down the gigantic bite with a swig of orange juice.

"No way. That's really their last name?"

"Heh, no. It's just what everyone calls them."

They talked and ate, with nearly everyone in the Kafe either coming up to Leith or him calling them over to their spot on the bar. At one point, a woman dressed in a pristine, belted dress and sunglasses the size of her face came in. Leith said she was Irene, married to a Hemmertex manager who'd chosen to retire rather than relocate out of New Hampshire, and one of Leith's few remaining lawn maintenance clients.

By the time Jen's belly was distended with perfect hash

browns and homemade bread slathered with honey, Leith must have introduced—or reintroduced—her to half the town.

Sue McCurdy and her breakfast companion watched all the exchanges, and as Jen rose to leave, Sue's friend gave Jen a slow nod that might have actually bordered on approval.

Chapter

8

Jen and Leith left the Kafe together, exiting into a brilliant morning. Sun sparkled through the thick tree boughs that draped themselves over the main street, their massive trunks tucked behind the old buildings. Jen squinted, imagining the storefronts filled with merchandise, their signs lit, and tourists ambling up and down the sidewalks. It filled her with such purpose, with such hope, that she smiled.

Leith stood next to her at the corner, hands in his back pockets. An unspoken, comfortable companionship laced them together. She tried to recall feeling this way ten years ago, but they'd been different people then, all nerves and excitement, completely oblivious to anything beyond that day, that moment.

A car slowly rolled past; the driver, a man with two children whom Leith had introduced her to, honked politely and called out a farewell, adding a "Good luck with the games" to Jen. She'd been here three days now and no one had wished her that.

Then it hit her, what Leith had just done.

She turned to him. "Thank you."

He shrugged and threw her a sideways grin. "Not exactly the first date I'd have normally picked, but the eggs were good."

"That's not what I meant." She touched him without thinking, her fingers sliding around the firm warmth of his forearm. There was power under that skin, as well as a generosity and a kind soul that she'd thought she understood, but really had only just begun to uncover. It made her heart hurt, to wonder about the man he'd become, to think about what she'd once given up.

Regret was the ugliest feeling in the world.

He winked, gently tugging his arm from her grip. "Don't know what you're talking about." He started to cross the street in loping strides. "If they start to see you as the Jen that knows this place, that cares about it, and not just a big-city girl swooping in to shake up their town and then leave, they'll listen. They may not push back so hard. And they'll definitely come to the games to see what you've done, when so many of them haven't gone in years."

"Who was the woman sitting with Sue?"

"Vera Kirkpatrick. Town council. She was watching you the whole time."

"Thank you," she said again, which was answered by yet another one of his shrugs. She couldn't decide if he really was denying his actions, or if he honestly thought they were no big deal.

The Kafe door pinged across the street and she watched Aimee and Ainsley exit and head in the opposite direction, toward the Thistle.

"You raised her right, little sis." Behind her, so close, Leith's voice had gone deep and soft. "The years here have been good to Aimee. You can see that, right?"

Her sister and niece disappeared around the two-pump gas station, their heads bent together, talking.

"Yes," Jen replied. "But—" She cut herself off. She understood what he was saying with a few carefully placed words: that Aimee was an adult and could take care of herself. But Jen also knew Aimee forward and back. With that woman, there was a wild tornado inside, constantly trying to get out. And when it busted free, take cover.

Jen drew a deep, deep breath, loving the scent of this place, how she could almost smell the nearby lake between the breezes. If she remembered correctly, the central park was just over that little stone footbridge spanning the creek, beyond those thick hedgerows. She pointed. "Does the park still look the same?"

"Uh." His small laugh sounded strangely uncomfortable. "Yeah. Sorta."

Well, now she had to look. "You coming?"

He twisted to glance back at his truck, taking up half the small parking lot just behind the Kafe. "Don't you have, you know, work to do?" He gestured to the bulge of her phone in her pocket. The thing was, for once, blissfully silent.

"Let me think." And she did. The best events captured the perfect atmosphere and reflected the host's personality and vision. Sure, so far she'd reorganized what she could, balanced the budget, and made new plans to present to the city council, but there was still something missing. Something she couldn't quite put her finger on.

Crossing the footbridge was like crossing over a line in time. Leith's feet dragged. They both stopped to gaze over the side to where they'd once had a contest to see who could land the most number of pebbles on that flat, wide rock twenty feet out.

"I totally won that day," she murmured.

He laughed. "Not how I remember it."

She waved a hand in front of his face. "Your mind is muddied by all the other girls you brought here to throw rocks. I only have that one day, and it's still crystal clear." She tapped her temple with two fingers. "I kicked your ass."

Stepping off the bridge, she turned into the park. Still exactly how she remembered it, with the gravel path following the stream, circling around the gazebo where bands had sometimes played on summer nights, and ending at the playground near the edge of the trees. There was, however, one big addition.

"Hold on . . . what is this?" She left the path and crossed the grass. Behind her, Leith groaned.

In the center of the open space, a caber—an implement thrown during the Highland Games made of a tree trunk carved into a round pole nineteen or so feet long—had been tilted onto two iron cradles, displayed for all to see. For people to set up their picnic blankets around, for kids to slam into when playing Freeze Tag. A little plaque nailed to a post declared *Leith Mac-Dougall, Gleann Highland Games All-Around Champion*.

The first time Aunt Bev had taken her to the Highland Games and Jen had watched these huge men throwing the cabers, she'd laughed and hadn't understood the point. Then she'd met Leith and had gone to the games the subsequent years with him and his father, where Mr. MacDougall had explained the rules of throwing a caber. The athlete held the narrower end of the caber while balancing the rest straight up in the air, then he took off on a run, flipped the giant pole end over end, and hoped the thing landed at twelve o'clock in relation to his body. Once she understood the heavy athletics' rules and history, she'd loved them.

"Where'd they get the caber?" she asked.

When she turned around, Leith was staring off into the trees, face all scrunched up and looking supremely—gloriously—uncomfortable. So something did faze him, and it was this kind of attention.

"It was mine," he said, looking everywhere but at Jen. "Well, it was Da's. When I stopped competing I didn't know what to do with it, and Chris took it and gave it to Mayor Sue. She had this built."

"Well, I can understand that," she said in mock seriousness. "I mean, the huge billboard out on 6 wasn't nearly enough."

"You can stop now."

"Do people come here to, like, lay flowers and stuff?"

"No, really. Stop." He was desperately trying not to smile, and failing, which pleased her immensely. Because behind his eyes she saw something else—some old pain she couldn't begin to name. She remembered what he'd admitted last night: that he felt bad, every day, for leaving Gleann. But there was more to it; she could tell. He fought it, glossed over it, and she realized she was dying to know what it was. Dying to help him through it.

She walked down the length of the caber, trailing fingers over the wood, then came back on the other side. Leith ambled toward her with those mountains for shoulders and tree trunks for legs, all set against the delicate, lovely backdrop of Gleann. She was struck by how strongly he'd become part of this landscape. His father, too. The two MacDougall men, as big a part of Gleann as Loughlin's orange cattle or Kathleen's horrid cafe decor. And, from what Jen remembered, completely inseparable.

With a hard pang, she realized she missed Mr. MacDougall greatly. During the games, he'd given colorful, delightful commentary on the competitors and their form, and in between, he'd woven in stories from back home in Scotland. Later, she and Leith would sit with him on his front porch, turning the stiff pages of his old photo albums, listening to tales of his best throwing days in Fort William, near where he'd grown up.

Those photos had been her first true exposure to a culture that wasn't American. She'd been enraptured. She'd been enthralled by Mr. MacDougall's accent, dulled by decades spent in his new country.

"All kidding aside," she told Leith, "you should be proud."

"I am. I really am. But my wins were just the Gleann games, so small compared to others all over the country. And in the amateur division, not even pro. I don't know why they make such a big deal out of it."

She looked at him, astounded. "It's not small to them. It's their world. And you're a huge part of it. You and your dad." She spread her hands wide on the wood. "You're theirs."

And you were once mine.

The thought was so potent, so powerful, she feared she'd said it out loud. The look on Leith's face said maybe she had. Or that he shared the same thought.

He placed his palms on the outside of her hands, his thumbs grazing her pinkies. The pinch of his eyebrows worried her.

"What is it?" She pressed closer, the caber the only thing separating their bodies.

"It's just"—he looked up, right into her eyes—"when you say things like that, I'm even more conflicted about leaving."

She gave him a tiny, close-lipped smile of apology. "That's not what I meant to do."

"I know. The thoughts are already there. Some things just bring them to the surface."

They stood there in near silence, the only sounds the gentle splash of the stream and a single car negotiating the curve up from the small glen where Leith's childhood house used to be. Thinking about that house, and the two men who used to live there, made her think of something. A crazy-good idea.

"I'm about to ask you to do something," she said. "Something for the games."

He was already shaking his head, his words overlapping hers. "I'm not throwing."

She showed him her palms. "I get that. I mean, I don't *really* get it, but I understand you don't want to compete. Instead . . . would you consider being my athletic director?"

Stepping back, his hands slid off the caber. He didn't look spooked, just surprised.

He took out that blue handkerchief—the one that reminded her so much of his dad—and wiped his hands even though they weren't dirty. "I wasn't planning on being in Gleann that weekend. The job in Connecticut has the potential to be huge; I may have to work."

"It's one day, Leith. Well, two if you count the opening party the night before. Just one day to give back to Gleann before you head out for good. Come on. Please. I need the help. I have no idea what I'm doing when it comes to the athletic events, and with so many other changes I want to make, I'm sure I'll be needed elsewhere."

He slowly turned his head, scanning Gleann from one corner to the next, his longer hair curling around his ears. It might have been the sexiest he'd ever looked to her.

"There's this buddy of mine, Duncan Ferguson. We used to throw together, and he's still really active in the circuit. He lives just across the lake in Westbury. He might even have already signed up to compete here anyway. I'm sure he could help you out."

"But—"

"I can't give my promise, Jen." There was such earnestness in his voice, such belief in his expression. "I make promises, I keep them. I wouldn't want to say I'd do it and then let everyone down." He glanced toward town, then back to her. "And I wouldn't want to let you down."

She could have prepped for a week straight on how that one sentence would make her feel, and she still would have stammered. She still would have felt the stumble of her heart. "I understand."

He nodded once, in that way men learned in some sort of existential Guy School. "I'll get you Duncan's number."

"Thanks."

That word closed a chapter in their conversation. With a tap to the caber, he wandered off toward the playground equipment. The ladder and slide and play structure were faded and weathered. Exactly how she remembered them, but sadder. When he changed subjects and asked, "Hey, do you remember the last time we were here?" she wasn't a bit surprised.

His lopsided smile said, *Aw, yeah. Something dirty happened up there and I was a part of it.*

She loved that look.

"I do," she said, inching closer. "I also remember the first time."

This was where they'd met, after all. She and Aimee had walked to this park their second day ever in Gleann. She'd been eight, Aimee nine. Leith had been playing here with another boy who'd moved away shortly thereafter. The four of them had quickly fallen into that easy, you're-my-best-playground-friend thing. Except that the next time she and Leith had met, they'd resumed that companionship while Aimee couldn't have cared less.

He leaned against the slide. "You do? Because you're not acting like it."

So this was it. They were finally going to talk about the past. She was surprised he was the one to bring it up, too, because he'd been so aloof. But last night had shifted something between them, cracked some walls, broke apart some dams.

She stepped into the wood chips surrounding the play structure. "*I'm* the one not acting like it?"

His head snapped back with an incredulous expression. "You walked up that driveway like your last summer here didn't exist. You ignored everything that happened between us at the fairgrounds."

It took her a few seconds to swallow, because the truth felt like a giant horse pill coated in sawdust. "I could say the exact same thing about you, you know."

He threw out his arms. "I live here. Stood on the side of the road as you drove off, exhaust in my face. Of course I remember. I remember everything. Every. Little. Detail."

"Okay." She licked her lips and flicked her gaze to the awning over the slide tower. "You want to know what happened up there? What I remember? It was the first time you put your hand up my shirt. The first time *any* guy did. There were fireworks, too. Somewhere across the lake, someone was lighting off bottle rockets. And since it was before the first night we actually had sex, it was the greatest night of my life."

He inhaled. Exhaled. Did them both again. He looked supremely satisfied . . . and also terribly frustrated. So was she.

She kicked at some wood chips, rearranged them with her toe. "I didn't plan for this, you know. Seeing you again." *Feeling things.* "I wasn't . . . looking for anything."

For a second he looked amused, then she realized it was sarcasm. "Oh no?"

"No."

"That's bullshit, Jen." But he smiled as he said it, shook his head at the ground, pieces of golden-brown hair falling over his forehead. "Somewhere deep down you knew I'd still be here. Somewhere deep down you hoped for it."

She didn't know which struck her harder: his confidence or his candor. At first she was indignant, ready to battle him, to deny all he'd just claimed. The way he stared at her said *Bring it. I'll defend myself.* But the power of the desire to sink her hands into his hair and yank his mouth to hers was so strong that her fingertips tingled. Fighting him and his words was pointless.

It was quite possible he knew her better than she knew herself. Maybe he always had. The thought was overwhelming.

"I don't know if I'm ready to talk about it yet." Was that *her* voice, shaking like that?

"It." He was toneless. "'It' meaning what happened to us ten years ago? Or 'it' meaning what's happening between us now?"

Denying the latter would be stupid; there was definitely something going on between them in the present day. Sure, it had begun when they were younger, but this yearning, this connection had aged too well. It was too delicious and she couldn't stop drinking it.

But to tell him about her past now, to explain why she'd come to Gleann in the first place and then left so abruptly, meant talking about Mom. Her confrontation with Aimee last night and the sudden reappearance of their mother had left Jen too raw.

She knew there was a direct line drawn between the end of her and Leith's relationship and what she'd never told him, but she wasn't that eighteen-year-old. The reasons shouldn't matter today.

"I'm not ignoring the old us, Leith. I promise. What we had, what happened, is here between us, no matter what we say. It will always be here, whether we talk about it directly or not."

What exactly did he want out of this conversation? To pick up where they'd left off? To start something new? Didn't he realize that both were impossible, even if they were desirable?

"I'm not quite sure what you want me to say," she said. "Are you looking for a complete rehash of my last summer here? You want to relive the night I left, or our last phone call? Because I don't. The memories are strong enough, thank you very much, and we're different people now." She glanced up to the slide tower. "Or are you looking for another make-out session up there?"

"That last one would be nice." He went to the seesaw, set a massive boot on it, and sent the opposite end flying up. "You know what? I'm not exactly sure. I guess I just didn't want you to pretend we never existed."

"I'm not pretending. Not at all. I'm compartmentalizing. I thought you were the one pretending."

"Maybe I was. But not anymore."

In that moment, she realized that since they'd entered the park, she'd completely forgotten the true reason for her coming back to Gleann. Leith had consumed her thoughts, even for this short time. That scared her. Too many people—Aimee and Aunt Bev's memory most of all—were relying on her to do good work here. She only ever did her best; nothing less was acceptable. And these were only the first few days of what she knew would be a massive amount of work.

Her phone rang and she pulled it out of her pocket. Gretchen.

"Ah, there it is," Leith said wryly. "I was wondering if you'd had it surgically removed."

"Hey, Gretchen," she answered, throwing Leith a perturbed look. She moved away from the playground to talk to her assistant.

"How's it going out there in the boonies?" Gretchen asked when they were done talking about preliminary items regarding Fashion Week.

"Fine. I feel like I'm still missing a few pieces, but they'll come together."

Right as she said it, she noticed Leith slowly walking down the length of his old caber, hands in his pockets, his profile set to the town. After Jen went back to the city, this was how she'd remember seeing him, as much a part of the town as his dad.

Mr. MacDougall. That was it.

"Gretchen, I gotta run." She clicked off the phone and shoved it back into her pocket, then crossed to Leith.

He watched her approach, his shoulders less tense and his eyes warm. The sun hit him, bringing out the gold streaks in his hair, and she forced her voice to be steady in the presence of a man whose looks she'd correctly pinned as approaching godhood. "Hey. Have a question for you."

"Shoot." He smiled in the same relaxed way she'd once known—and loved—well.

She rubbed her hands together. "Remember those old photo albums your dad had? The ones from back in Scotland, showing all those games he competed in?"

The smile faltered. "Yeeeaaah."

"You wouldn't happen to still have them, would you?"

She wasn't mistaken; he'd paled a bit. "I . . . think so."

"I was wondering if I could look through them, get some ideas for here. You know, to ramp up the authenticity and get away from DeeDee's fake castle."

"That's a good idea, actually." He took a deep breath. Paused. "Sure. You can take a look at them."

"Oh, great. Thanks. Are they packed into one of Mildred's garages?"

"No, they're, ah"—He began to stroke a finger down each side of his face, over and over again—"all at the house."

"Which one of the three?"

He turned then to gaze across the park and down the narrow lane that swooped into the lowest part of Gleann, where Leith's childhood home stood.

"Not Mildred's house." His voice turned distant. "Da's house."

Not *my house*. Not *our house.*

"Oh. You never mentioned you still had it." She wondered

why he wasn't living there instead of in a strange old lady's time warp.

"Yeah. I do." He cleared his throat. "Why don't we run back to Mildred's and I'll get the house key for you. You can let yourself into Da's, take what you need."

"Are you sure now's a good time?"

"Now's great, actually. But I'll have to drop you off, if that's okay. I think I might head out of town earlier than I'd originally planned. Get down to Connecticut with plenty of time before I meet with Rory tomorrow morning."

"All right," she said, but he was already walking away, and she knew something was up.

Chapter

9

"**Y**eah, sorry I can't go in with you," Leith told her as she sat next to him in his truck. He jabbed up the air conditioner, even though the cab was already Frigidaire cold. "I gotta get on the road if I want to make it to Stamford by tonight and find a motel."

When he'd gone inside 740 Maple to grab the key to his father's house, he'd also come out with a packed bag.

"It's okay," Jen said, while wondering who the hell this pale, fidgety guy was sitting next to her. "Tell me where the photo albums are again?"

He squinted through the windshield at the brick two-bedroom, one-car ranch house plunked at the foot of a steep hill. "Da kept all the stuff like that in the den. In the big hutch along the wall. Bottom shelves. Here." He flipped open the glove compartment and took out a huge flashlight, slapping it in her palm. "You might need this."

"Why?"

"No power."

She opened her door and gracelessly finagled her way to the ground. One hand on the door handle, she peered back inside the truck. But Leith wasn't looking at her. The house had him entranced.

"Thanks," she said.

"Sure." A stiff nod of the head.

"When will you be back?" As if she had any right to know, or any claim on him.

"Not sure."

Alrighty then.

His thigh twitched and flexed, preparing to lift off the brake. She took the signal and shut the door. It was barely latched before he pulled away, tires grinding in the gravel driveway. When he hit the asphalt, he gunned it back up the hill, on his way out of Gleann. She watched him go until the truck was no more than an obnoxious lumbering sound filtering through the trees. When silence fell, she turned to the only house in this quiet, lovely part of the valley.

The house she had once thought of as heaven now seemed dark and sad. It looked almost exactly the same—the same row of wind chimes dangling from the eaves, whose sound was a glorious, calming memory; the same patio furniture sitting on the giant slab of concrete serving as a front porch—but the melancholy surrounding it was ghostly.

Upon closer look, the furniture she'd sat on for so many summer nights, holding a glass of lemonade—and later a sneaked beer poured into a coffee mug—was terribly weathered. She wondered why Leith even bothered to keep it out. The concrete slab was cracked and uneven, and several sets of wind chimes were missing pieces and hung crookedly.

But the yard . . . the yard and the front flower gardens and the raised vegetable boxes were lush and lovely. Tended with care. Like a grave.

The grass had been mown in perfect diagonals, the bushes neatly trimmed. The produce was magazine perfect. She remembered that when Mr. MacDougall was alive, he'd spent hours in his yard, tinkering and digging and planting and pruning, Leith always by his side.

It made sense to her then that Leith had become what he had: a landscape architect to honor his upbringing and to satisfy his own soul. He'd kept up his old house as a memorial. But . . . why, if he didn't live here? There was no For Sale sign anywhere, and this place hadn't been listed on potential rentals when she'd looked through them at Sue's just the other day.

Jen negotiated the slim flagstone walk, noting the way the flowers and shrubs perfectly draped over the edges, beautiful and artistic. They gave atmosphere to the wonderful memories made here, the ones outside of the evenings looking through photo albums or playing Scrabble at the kitchen table.

This house was where she'd first learned what a true family should be like.

Aunt Bev had brought Jen and Aimee to Gleann with the sole purpose of giving them time away from their mom, Bev's own sister, but it had taken a few awkward years for Jen to warm up to the aunt who was essentially a stranger. She was, after all, related to her mother. But Leith and his dad had lived outside of Jen's wicked experiences, and she'd clung to that. She'd clung to *them*.

A real family, she discovered, had nothing to do with the number of people involved, or the titles of the family members, or even if they were blood related. It was about interaction. Support. Jokes. Generosity. Teaching. Respect. Everything Mr. MacDougall had passed on to his son.

She couldn't help it; she smiled as she pushed the key into the front door lock. It took a good effort to slam it home, and turning it to the left required even more power. She pushed open the door with a wobbly jerk, as it finally came free from the ill-fitting frame.

That emptiness she'd sensed outside instantly transformed into a heaviness that settled on her shoulders and dug into her soul.

Daylight spilled from the front door into the tiny, cramped den, but even that was quickly swallowed up and she could barely see. The heavy curtains in the front window were drawn, but the shadows and silhouettes told her that every piece of MacDougall furniture was placed exactly where she remembered. The couch beneath the window, the hutch against the wall to the right, the TV in the corner, the pass-through window to the kitchen straight ahead.

A musty scent assaulted her nose and made it tickle. She went to the window and yanked back the curtain. A cloud of dust rained down and she waved it back, peering through the particle-riddled air into the lightened room. As the air cleared some, she could see where her footsteps had left prints on the dusty, matted carpet. No others accompanied it; no one had walked through this room in a really long time. The layer of dust covering every surface was so thick it would take twenty vacuums to suck it all up. The air-conditioning hadn't been turned on in ages; the smell could attest to that.

All of the knickknacks she remembered in foggy images were still there, sitting and waiting for use or attention. She passed through the den and into the tiny kitchen that had never been able to fit more than one MacDougall male at a time. The yellow plastic clock still hung next to the refrigerator, stuck on 7:56, and the waffle maker still leaned against the microwave, all coated with a gray film.

The floor groaned as she left the kitchen, walked past the hutch, and went down the hall toward the bedrooms. Mr. MacDougall's bedroom faced the backyard that sloped severely up toward town. She recalled him saying once that he liked how dark and cool it got in there in the evenings. Leith's was the room facing front, which had made it convenient for him to sneak in through the window when she and he had been out past curfew.

She went first into Mr. MacDougall's room, cracking the door and flinching at the awful, dry squeal of the hinges. The room was darker than midnight. By habit she flicked the light switch, but nothing came on. She remembered the flashlight hanging loose in her hand and shot the powerful beam into the room.

The bed was made, the dresser neat. Mr. MacDougall's gray wool cap sat on the corner edge, waiting for him to come in and put it on. Jen had rarely seen him without it.

A lovely cane with a brass tip tilted against the wall near the door. When she'd watched the games with him, he'd held that cane between his legs with both hairy-knuckled hands.

Shaking a little, she closed the door and turned to the opposite side of the hallway. The sight of Leith's bedroom door—just the door—made her smile. Whenever she and Leith had been in his room, they'd been required to leave the door open. Mr. MacDougall would then sit on the couch, less than thirty feet away, and pretend not to be listening.

That's because the one time they'd closed the door, they'd gotten caught with Leith on top of her, making out like they would die the next day. His dad had put a quick and embarrassing end to any more of that kind of private time in his household.

Now she opened Leith's bedroom door, prepared to see the room inside just like all the others: left exactly as her memory recalled. And it was, with the queen bed against the far wall, its dark green comforter now pilled and completely dusted over, the big dresser close to the door, its legs making huge divots in the old carpet. In high school, Leith had kept his discus and shot put trophies and medals lined perfectly on a set of shelves next to the closet. They were still there, arranged biggest to smallest, their luster now dulled.

The one thing different was the walls. She vaguely remembered plaid wallpaper, but it was no longer visible. Framed photos covered the walls from ceiling to baseboard, and she stepped deeper into the room for a closer look.

Almost every single one of them was of Leith and his "da," arms slung around each other's shoulders, identical grins facing the camera. At the Highland Games, at high school football games, camping at the state park, gardening . . . at all stages of Leith's life. Just the two of them, inseparable.

This place was a fraction of the size of that great, obnoxious billboard out on Route 6, and not as odd as a displayed caber and a plaque, but this small, crowded room held a world more heart. She knew that once Leith had moved out, Mr. MacDougall had hung this visual display of pride and joy.

She let the flashlight fall on the largest picture near the door. An 8x10, it showed Mr. MacDougall in his gray cap, big arm clamped around Leith's neck, pulling in tight his only child, a gigantic smile on his wrinkled face. Leith wore a kilt, his face and T-shirt damp from his having recently thrown. Jen recognized the old games grounds in Gleann. It was the only photo in the room in which Leith's grin looked strained. A date had been scrawled in ballpoint in the bottom corner—the year *after* Leith had last been all-around champion.

Jen suddenly felt guilty for being in there. She backed out, closing the door against the very personal nature of the place, and leaned against the wall. Leith had let her into the house to get the photo albums, nothing more. Yet . . . he had to have known she'd take a look around—that she'd see what she'd just seen—and realize the extent of his grief. The grief he'd been hiding so well for three years. He had to have known she'd realize he'd been lying about getting over losing his dad. That he still felt lost.

He trusted her enough to show her this, trusted her with his pain. Hell, maybe he *wanted* to show her. Maybe this was his way of asking for help.

Or maybe, to him, this had been a necessary casualty. Maybe his only intention had been to help her do her job with the games—like he had back in the Kafe with the townspeople—and he'd cut himself open to do it. He'd taken an invisible knife, carved out his despair and heartbreak, and displayed it. For her.

Muscles didn't have anything to do with strength. If she could, she would absorb his pain and relieve him of all that pressure of putting on a good, healed face for everyone.

She pushed off the wall and went back to the hutch in the den. Sunlight streamed in the front window now, the air clear of dust, so she easily found the latch and opened the hutch doors. Inside, the shelves were stacked with disorganized photo albums that might have made Bobbie "Roberts" twitch.

Jen ran her fingers down the spines of the thick, relatively new albums, the ones from the last thirty years, the ones dedicated to Leith's life. Placed on its own shelf was one labeled "Margaux MacDougall," and if ever a single, earthly item gave off a saintly vibe, it was that. Though Jen had never seen a picture of Leith's mom, who'd died when he was just a baby, cracking open that album seemed far too personal, far too invasive.

She touched the albums near the bottom, where Leith had said the ones she was looking for would be. *No, no, no, no.* Ah, *there.*

The documentation of the elder MacDougall's life in Scotland was in big, thick treasuries made of actual leather. The two burgundy covers had cracked and dried at the edges, their spines brittle. They didn't have labels and they didn't need them.

Because the concrete porch was where Mr. MacDougall had showed her and Leith these books long ago, that was where she took them now. Blinking hard in the bright sunlight, she gingerly sat on the rickety wood bench, hoping it wouldn't splinter and crack under her weight. It held, and she flipped open the first album.

Pages and pages of mustard-yellow photos and paper, of blurred, black-and-white children running around Highland meadows, dark skies billowing overhead. She could have stayed there all day, flipping through the past of a man she dearly missed, but there was a purpose to this, and unfortunately it wasn't nostalgia.

The second album was almost entirely dedicated to Mr. MacDougall's teens and early twenties, namely, his throwing days in the old country. Nibbled-edge fliers for the Fort William and Dufftown and Aberdeen Highland Games, their words typed on, yes, a typewriter. Line drawings of heavily muscled athletes wielding competition stones and cabers and hammers. Competitors' listings, with MacDougall's name circled in pencil. Ribbons of all places stuffed into the cracks, their adhesive long since gone. Swatches of tartans, their clans unknown to her. A single pressed flower.

Photos upon photos of a young MacDougall: throwing, smiling, posing with other men in kilts, standing at attention as the massed bands strolled past.

Jen studied each photo with an eagle eye, calling back to mind Mr. MacDougall's accented voice as he'd told each scene's story—and even more stories from off-camera. She paid attention to the backgrounds, to the setting and atmosphere. She picked out details and let her mind trail off to brainstorm possibilities. Setting the album to the side, she took out her laptop and let her fingers fly, recording all her random, scattered ideas. She'd make sense of the lists later.

A million new pieces clicked into place. Her brain buzzed with the possibilities.

Gleann had been trying to compete with the bigger, more well-known games across the state, going for showy but ending up cartoonish and laughable. She lifted her face to the sun and pictured the beautiful town of Gleann, built by Scottish hands and inhabited by people with deep roots. That's what their games had lost: that link to their history. The fearless *Scottishness* of the event.

She was going to get that back, and she held the key to success in her hands.

Chapter

10

*F*ive hours on the road, and Leith's eyelids felt coated in lead and sandpaper. He entered the lake valley just as the sun lifted itself above the eastern horizon and painted the hills that hid Gleann from the rest of the world.

He'd spent almost three nights down in Connecticut. Two full days of walking around the Carriage's new estate with Rory, taking measurements and soil samples, sketching, and tossing ideas back and forth with her, then back to his motel at night to fire up the computer design programs he hadn't used in months. This job was everything he'd wanted and more. Dream landscape with incredible topsoil, dream client who wanted to give him his freedom, new dream location. The adrenaline rising out of the potential—out of what could possibly signal his future—pumped through his system.

Early yesterday evening, when he'd started a new computer file outlining what kind of equipment he'd need to transport down from Gleann and in what order, and then had made lists of potential plants and supplies, he thought of Jen and her mosaic of windows always open on her laptop.

He'd expected to hear from her while he was gone. Hell, he'd expected to get a phone call an hour after he'd left her at that mausoleum of a house, once she saw what he'd been purposely forgetting. He could almost hear the questions, the concern, the disbelief. But the call never came.

Maybe she'd just gone in, grabbed the photo albums she wanted and then left. *Ha!* This was Jen, and he highly doubted that. She'd probably inventoried the whole place and had drawn up a schematic and schedule over what needed to be done to get the place cleaned out and sold. And that was okay, he told himself. He knew what he'd opened himself up to, and he'd deal with it when he got back. Maybe, he thought with a twinge, it was exactly what he needed.

Or maybe he could just leave the house shut tight and continue to pay Chris to take care of the yard.

The day of Da's memorial, after Leith had illegally spread his ashes in various spots around Gleann and the valley, he'd locked up his childhood home and hadn't opened it since. The following month Chris had come around to tell Leith the yard was beginning to look like shit, so Leith had sucked up the grief and drove down to the house, waving off Chris's offer to help. At first he'd only meant to mow and clean up the overgrowth, but as soon as he started working, he roped off new flowerbeds and dug out the old vegetable garden. He'd stopped when it got too dark to see, and only then did he step back, hand on the shovel, and felt Da all around him.

That work—the kind of work they used to do together, before the pain had got to be too much for all that bending and Da had taken to sitting on the front porch and ordering his son around the yard—had kept Leith tethered to the warm memories of his father without drowning in them. Which was what would happen should he go inside that house again. It was easy to not feel sorrow when his body didn't stop moving. It was helpful in keeping the sadness and loss at bay when he could step back and see the immediate fruits of his efforts—the kind of results Da would have loved.

Why was it necessary to go back into that house anyway? Why risk getting mowed down by an absence when he could stay outside and bask in the good memories? So he'd kept the door locked and had remained satisfied in his ability to keep his grief and acceptance at bay.

That is, until Jen had wanted to go inside, and he was

reminded of all that he'd shut away. All that he'd never addressed. He'd sat there in his truck in the driveway, and it seemed like the house was ready to burst at its seams from all that he'd shoved inside and let fester over the past three years. No one could see those ghosts but him.

Except now Jen knew they existed. Now she would know that leaving Gleann was a lot more difficult than he'd been letting on, but that staying would be even worse.

He slowed his truck as Route 6 narrowed through the dramatic cut into the mountains, sheer, jagged cliffs rising three stories on both sides. The road curved here like a roller coaster, and when it spit him out into sloping, open land overlooking the valley lake, he knew he was five miles from Gleann. But something felt off. The sky was cloudless, the sun near blinding, and yet the valley looked dull, the water matte when it should have sparkled. To the east, where Gleann's rooftops and lone stone church steeple poked between the trees, it looked like an extremely localized storm had focused on the town. Then he realized: That was no storm. It was a fire.

Pedal to the floor, he prayed his truck would stay on all four wheels as he sped around the curves toward the thick plumes of black smoke rising from what he guessed to be Hemmertex. The glass walls of the headquarters were obscured; he couldn't see if that was indeed where the fire was centralized.

He drove until he could physically drive no more. Half the town of Gleann had filled up both lanes of Route 6, people clustered together in tight, murmuring groups, making no room to let him through. The other half of the town was lined up along the shoulder and against Loughlin's cattle fence, staring across the fields and into the fairgrounds . . . where the barn serving as storage for the Highland Games was little more than a charred skeleton, its rib bones pointing angrily toward the sky.

"*Shhhhit,*" Leith said, throwing the truck in park and shutting it off. He got out, leaving the thing blocking the right lane. No one was going anywhere for quite a while. He pushed through the crowd, for once no one paying him any mind. He found an open spot on the fence and stared at the destruction.

Fire trucks from the larger community of Westbury, across the lake, had circled the blackened barn. All the water from putting out the fire had turned the fairgrounds into a mud pit, and violent tire tracks cross-hatched the grass. The air stung Leith's lungs. Around him people coughed and held handkerchiefs and their shirtsleeves over their noses and mouths, but no one went home. Why would they? This was the most exciting thing to happen in Gleann in a hell of a long time, and misery and speculation would be conversation fodder for decades to come.

Though ninety percent of the stuff in that barn had seen its best days years ago, and the other ten percent was cheesy crap and as far from the Highland Games Da had described from back home, it was still Gleann's, and they'd need it. *Jen* would need it to do what she'd come here to do.

As though his thinking of Jen had called her into the collective consciousness, he heard two women whispering behind him.

"Do you think she burned it down on purpose?" the first woman said.

"Maybe. Vera told Annabelle who told my Jack that she wants to change everything. And I mean everything."

The first woman made a sound of disgust. "Don't know why Sue brought her in. We could've just taken over, had it ourselves, the way we like it."

Leith almost laughed. Jen burn down a barn? And yeah, the town probably could all gather in the middle of the destroyed fairgrounds and play some pipes and stuff, but the Scottish Society would pull support, no one who lived outside Gleann's borders would attend, and then they'd be just a bunch of people standing around doing watered-down events that once upon a time had actually meant something. Jen wanted something bigger and better and she would work her ass off for that. To her, burning down a barn would be an insult to her prowess. To her, it would be taking the easy way out.

Where was she anyway? The fire was out and the firemen were picking through the smoking wreckage, but no one was dissipating. He had to say, despite his belief she had nothing to do with it, it would definitely look bad for her if she were the only person *not* here.

He rounded on the gossiping women. "That's the stupidest thing I've ever heard. Jen's here to help." He got the reaction he was looking for: fish mouths and huge, shocked eyes.

"But . . . but, look at her," the first woman said, nudging her chin to the south, "sitting down over there, on her computer and phone, not even caring what's going on."

"And she's not even doing anything to stop that trashy sister from coming between Owen and Melissa . . ."

That's when Leith turned away. Let them say dumb, meaningless things.

There was a shift in the crowd, and then he saw her.

Jen had plopped down in the grass on the very edge of the gapers, her back to a fence post—and also the burned scene—her laptop open over her crossed legs, her phone pressed between ear and shoulder. Talking and typing simultaneously. In her pajamas and mismatched flip-flops. Her hair wound messily around a rubber band, and her glasses framed dark smudges underneath her makeup-less eyes.

He recognized the two lines between the dark arch of her eyebrows; he'd seen them in the barn that no longer existed, when she'd switched into severe work mode and nothing else existed but the task at hand.

Goddamn it. He'd missed her.

He'd felt it as he'd pulled away from Da's house three days ago, that sickly twist in his stomach as he'd glanced into the rearview mirror and saw her standing in his driveway. He'd sensed something nagging at him as he'd driven south in search of his new life. Something that told him maybe he'd just driven away from a pretty big part of himself that had nothing to do with Da's house or his business or Mildred's properties.

He wasn't supposed to miss her. Not after only a few days. He'd already gone through that need and separation once before, a long time ago, and with Jen both were especially potent. He wasn't doing that again. Nope.

Yet as he sifted through the people he'd known all his life, drawing closer and closer to where she sat, all he could imagine was kicking aside that laptop and phone, dragging her up by the shoulders, pinning her to that leaning fence post, and kissing the hell out of her. Then, after he caught his breath, he'd apologize for driving off the way he had, and kiss her all over again.

He stopped just beyond her flip-flops. The townspeople had given her a wide berth, though he saw Mayor Sue lingering nearby, the bright orange of today's Syracuse gear proclaiming her presence.

Jen was typing furiously while saying "Uh-huh, uh-huh, uh-huh," into the phone. He just stood there watching, wondering what exactly she was doing.

"Oh, that's great to hear. Thanks so much. I'd say I owe you, but it seems like we're even now." Then she laughed, said good-bye, and dropped the phone from her ear.

He cleared his throat. It took her a moment to look up, but when she did, something inside his chest did this uncomfortable flip because those facial lines of concentration and problem solving disappeared. Just vanished.

"Hey!" She saved whatever it was she was working on, shut the laptop, and scrambled to her feet. "When did you get back?"

He gestured down the hill, over the heads of the crowd, to where his truck was parked jauntily in the road. "Just pulled in now."

"Silly me. Should've heard that thing coming. I've been a bit busy."

He threw a look of regret at the barn. "Hate to say it, but you look way too pleased. The people are talking."

She grinned, but he got the feeling she was reining in her true pleasure. As she leaned closer, he saw how sleepy she was, even underneath the projected alertness. "Because everything's taken care of," she whispered.

"See, now even I'm starting to see you with matches and a crazed smile."

"No, no." She waved the hand that still held her phone. "I mean that I've fixed things. Hemmertex landowners have agreed to let us rent their land, and I've called in a few favors. New tents, new tables, new signage, they're all on their way." She wiggled the phone, then playfully hit him in the shoulder with it. "And you make fun of me for having it on me all the time. This thing is going to save the games, you know. I need to go tell Sue."

Jen walked off, leaving him in a sort of wondrous daze. He watched her gesture excitedly to Sue, who just looked squinty-eyed back at the woman who was telling her that she had it all under control, that everything would be all right. Sue merely nodded. Jen never faltered.

He wanted to walk right over to those two women who'd bashed and speculated about Jen and set them straight, tell them all about what Jen had just done. How she'd probably been dragged from her bed before the sun—a hysterical phone call from Sue, most likely—and had been working her ass off for hours to fix it all for the benefit of people she barely knew and who didn't appreciate it.

Except that Jen would probably hate that. She'd want her actions to speak louder than any of his words could possibly do. She'd want to prove herself. So he just stepped back and watched.

Watched as Jen turned away from explaining to Sue, and finally let her frustration show at still not being able to get a positive reaction from the mayor. Only Leith could see Jen's face, the tightening of her lips, the pained squint of those jewel eyes. Only Leith saw her hold a hand to her stomach as though she might be sick.

As Jen bent over to gather her computer and purse from where it sat in the grass, the movement of bright orange caught his eye. Mayor Sue was on the move, weaving in and out of her people like a chieftain after a particularly intense and bloody battle. She was rubbing the backs of some people, patting children on the head, and clasping hands with others. Nothing too unusual for the woman who loved Gleann perhaps most of all, except for the fact that he could read Jen's name on Sue's lips. And when the mayor gestured to Jen, there was satisfaction on her face. A little bit of surprise. Perhaps even . . . pride. Sue was many things, but inauthentic wasn't one of them. She was just slightly prickly and sometimes difficult to please.

He considered pointing out to Jen that it seemed she had impressed Sue, but then Sue turned around and the moment was gone. He knew Jen would never believe it had happened.

"So, what now?" he asked as Jen straightened.

She jammed fingers into her hair, unknowingly snagging some of it free from the rubber band and making it even messier. There were a few sun-damage freckles sprinkled on her shoulders; he didn't know if they'd appeared in the past ten years or if they'd always been there and he'd just never noticed.

"Now?" She glanced sheepishly at her pajamas and flip-flops. "Coffee. And likely clothes."

"What about sleep? Your eyes are closing."

She looked at him as though he'd suggested giving the State of the Union in clown makeup and a feather boa. "But that's what the coffee is for."

When she started to eye him in a serious way, he knew her quick-firing brain had switched from thinking about the smoking barn to how they'd parted three days ago. He knew this because her expression softened with exactly the kind of pity he'd wanted to avoid.

"Well"—he took off his Red Sox baseball cap, scrubbed through his hair, and then repositioned the cap—"I've been driving since midnight so I'm gonna hit the sack."

"Okay." The pity disappeared, which shocked him. She'd always been good at picking up hints, but not necessarily as good at heeding them if they didn't fit into the direction she wanted to go. "Talk to you later?"

He knew what she meant by "talking," and he still nodded, because he'd knowingly thrown wide open the door into his mind and allowed her to take a good long look inside.

Now that Sue had made the rounds with her reassurances, the flashing lights on the fire trucks had been turned off, and the big hoses were spraying down the last of the barn ash, the townspeople started to dissipate. He wouldn't have to mow anyone down to get his truck back to 740 Maple.

Jen called his name when he was halfway to his truck. He turned around. "Yeah?"

"Thank you for the albums. They helped. A lot. I don't know if I would've been able to get all this done this morning if I hadn't seen them."

Her smile was so warm that it melted a bit of his fear over having let her inside the house.

"Good to hear it," he said, and finally escaped to the safety of his truck.

Chapter

11

*L*eith watched Duncan Ferguson do a killer hang power snatch with a massively weighted bar. After heaving the bar from its resting place on the mat, then jumping into a squat and thrusting the bar high over his head for the second time, Duncan let the bar drop. The guy with the shaved dome and neck rolls blew out breaths in big puffs and stepped back, looking incredibly pleased with himself, as he should be. That was some serious weight.

"Shit, man," Leith said from where he sat on the edge of the incline press, shaking his head in a half laugh. "You're in sick shape. Want to come over here and spot me on this twenty-pounder?"

Duncan ran a towel around the back of his thick neck. "Only 'cause I kept it up. Why'd you stop training?"

Leith consistently worked out, but he wasn't following the insane lifting regimen he used to and that Duncan still subscribed to. Duncan was shorter than him, but thicker and more compact. Back in the day, Leith spanked him on the field, consistently out-threw him. Looking at Duncan today, Leith was pretty sure Duncan would wipe the grass with him. All right, he'd admit it. It bothered him. It bothered him a lot. He'd thought that competitive edge had died when he'd stopped throwing—had tried to convince himself it no longer existed, at least—but it was still there, burning just under the surface. A low pulse of a whisper that said, *You can take him.*

Leith just shrugged. "You pro yet?"

"Nah. Still amateur class A. Some great competition out there. Pushes me, you know?"

Leith rose, loving how his thighs felt tight, his arms a little shaky. Using the weights he kept in Mildred's garage didn't match an honest workout with someone stronger.

"Hey, thanks for the call this morning." Duncan held out his hand and Leith slapped it, turning it into a hearty handshake. "Good to hear from you. Been a while."

"Yeah. Sorry about that."

Duncan held up his taped fingers. "'S'okay, man, I understand. Sorry to hear about your dad. I know that sounds shitty a few years after the fact."

Leith waved off his friend, as he'd gotten so good at doing.

Duncan began to pick off the tape, unwinding the battered pieces in long white ribbons. "You really not going to throw this year? I bet you'd do well. Still have the strength for the most part. The form comes back to you. Muscle memory. All you need is a little refresher." He shot Leith a good-natured grin. "And it's just Gleann. It's not like it's the New Hampshire games."

Leith understood, but the little jab niggled at him. It was *just Gleann.* He knew if Jen had heard Duncan say that, it would have lit a firecracker under her ass.

"I hear you're going to be AD for Gleann?" Leith whipped off his wet T-shirt and traded it for a dry one, then pulled on light warm-up pants over his shorts.

Tape gone and stuffed in the garbage, Duncan started to take apart the weight bar, sliding off the clamps and lifting the circular weights onto their stands. The guy had a pretty sweet setup here in his basement in Westbury, across the lake from Gleann. Complete with rubbery, sweaty guy smell and everything. Leith had always wanted his own gym. When he found his house, his *perfect* house, there'd be a room just like this.

"Yeah," Duncan answered his earlier question. "Should be a piece of cake. A bit surprised they called me, though. You gave them my name?"

Leith nodded as he picked up Duncan's bar and tilted it against the wall. "Hope you didn't mind. Jen seemed pretty desperate for the help."

"So you know her?"

Leith ignored Duncan's side-eyed look.

"We go way back. She used to spend every summer in Gleann from when she was about, oh, eight or so. Been friends forever."

"Aha. She was, um, intense."

Leith had to laugh. "You could say that. You didn't try to say no to her, did you?"

"'Try' is the operative word there. I did try to pass it off on you, but she said you'd already turned it down."

Leith stuffed his weight-lifting gloves in his gym bag and slung it over his shoulder. His stomach rumbled. After a good workout, he wanted to eat a house. And drink a whole six-pack of beer.

"Fuck, I was supposed to call her back earlier today," Duncan said.

At first Leith doubted Jen would have noticed, being buried under the fire nonsense, but this was Jen they were talking about. If she needed to get a hold of Duncan, she'd probably call at ten p.m. if need be.

"Want to go back across the lake and meet her?" Leith asked. "Maybe I can drag her away from that computer and phone of hers for an hour and we can all go grab a burger and a beer."

Duncan glanced at the clock on the wall, which showed 6:23.

"She needs more allies," Leith added.

A small smile quirked Duncan's mouth.

"What?" Leith said.

Duncan's eyebrows arched into his forehead. "Nothing, nothing."

He let Duncan shower and they climbed into Leith's truck, pulling out of the historical neighborhood lining the lakefront and rolling through the downtown. While not bustling by any means, it didn't look like it had lain down on its deathbed like Gleann.

"No way," Leith said, jerking the wheel to the right and

swerving into an empty parking spot in front of an all-season Christmas shop.

"What the—" Duncan began, as Leith threw the truck into park.

There, coming out of the Christmas shop, was Jen, wearing some sort of short, yellow, swishy dress and high heels, and holding a box of papers.

Duncan chuckled, following Leith's stare out the windshield. "Damn. I might have caused a five-car pileup for that, too."

"That's Jen," Leith said, his gym shoes already hitting the pavement. Duncan followed him onto the sidewalk.

Leith called to her, and she turned, all movielike, with the wind pushing her hair over her shoulders, her dress clinging to her legs. The moment of surprise as she realized who he was was priceless. They walked toward each other.

"What are you doing here?" he asked.

"Might ask you the same thing."

He pointed to Duncan, who raised a hand. "This is Duncan. Your AD. I was just bringing him across the lake to meet you."

Immediately she assumed her "business stance," that thing she did—probably unconsciously—when her body went into this straight line and her neck stretched, lifting her head higher. She smiled, however, and it was still genuine. That's how she got you, Leith thought. She may be all business, but she wasn't fake. Her presence pulled you in. You couldn't help but be affected by how much she cared. You couldn't help but be ensnared by her intelligence.

She thrust a hand at Duncan, and even though Leith had never shaken her hand in a business manner, he could tell she had a good, strong grip.

"I did the recruiting you asked for," Duncan told her. "Made a ton of phone calls and got a bunch of guys from all over New England to come to Gleann at the last minute. Not any pros, but they'll throw, and I'll make damn sure they have a killer time. I may owe some sexual favors after this."

She sighed in thanks. "So great to hear. The roster was so thin before."

Leith gestured to the box she carried. "What's all that?"

She grinned. "A little recruiting of my own. Ads for

Westbury-to-Gleann bus service across the lake during the games, so no one has to drive drunk or worry about parking."

"Huh," Leith said, staring at her. And staring. He couldn't look away. Had to be her brain. Yeah, that was it.

"So were you just hanging out here?" she asked him.

"Came over to see Duncan. Haven't touched base in a while."

"He's just using me for my gym," Duncan said.

Jen took in Leith's grubby T-shirt and workout pants. "Thought you said you weren't training."

"I'm not. It was just a workout."

"But he should be," Duncan added.

"That's what I say!" Jen said.

"Well. Um." Duncan coughed. "It was great to meet you, Jen. I'll be in touch with an equipment report, and you call me if you need anything."

Leith turned to him. "Thought we were going to grab a beer."

"Yeah, you know. I'll let you two go. Just remembered some shit I have to take care of. Don't worry about a ride; I'll walk back."

Then the big guy with the shaved head was gone, jogging back down the street toward his house as though he hadn't just kicked his own ass in the gym.

"So," Leith said to Jen. "What do you say? A pint at the Stone?"

*D*espite telling himself not to—despite the fact that he'd been going to the Stone since birth and knew exactly what to look out for—Leith still clonked his forehead on the ceiling crossbeam dividing the dining room from the bar.

"Mother—" He pressed the heel of one hand to the smarting place, and ducked even farther down to make it into the bar without losing his head at the neck. Had the Stone shrunk since he'd last been in here? Maybe. He hadn't come in since, what, before Memorial Day? As he made his way through the crowded, chunky-legged tables to the bar at the back of the room, he wondered why he hadn't dropped by. He wondered if, subconsciously, he'd slowly been severing all his ties to the valley.

Da had never brought him back to Scotland—too expensive—but the old man had loved the Stone as much as he loved anything in Gleann. Cozy, cramped, warm. Not a TV in sight. People you knew, always a conversation at hand. The whole place had maintained a remarkably authentic feel without succumbing to the kitsch DeeDee had embraced for the games. The menu remained basic and hearty, the beers pulled from great brass taps lined up on the bar, the nook by the cold fireplace prepared for folk musicians that used to play every Sunday afternoon, but had since stopped when half the band had died from old age. It was another world in here—a world Leith already missed.

He lowered himself onto a stool, his back to the bar, and waited for Jen to arrive.

She'd had to finish up her promotion stuff over in Westbury, and then had to do a bunch of other things she was wonderfully cagey in mentioning. He loved how excited she was getting, how she was planning this big to-do right under all their noses, and it was starting to make him feel guilty for not being able to be there, when he hadn't felt anything of the sort since Da's death.

Meanwhile, he'd gone back to Mildred's, showered and changed, and ate an appetizer of a frozen pizza. It was full-size but one of those thin-crust ones, so it didn't completely fill his appetite.

When Jen walked in, the incongruous digital clock sitting on top of the cash register glowed 8:05. She wore tight jeans with perfect hems, a tank top with straining seams, and flip-flops. The outfit itself was far from flashy, but she drew the eye of everyone in the Stone.

And Leith himself, of course, who was virtually knocked over by the way her hips glided side to side as she skirted around the tables. It was that sway that had smacked him upside the head that one night in this very same room, ten years ago. The movement that had changed everything.

Now, tonight, it struck him dumb and motionless, so when she finally reached him and said something or other in greeting, he said, "Great. And you?"

She wrinkled her nose in a way that reminded him of a particular nine-year-old girl who lived here in town. "I asked how long you'd been here."

The constricted barroom suddenly shrank even more. "Oh. Uh, ten or so minutes." As she threw him a sly, knowing look, his hands felt empty. "I need a beer."

"Me, too," she said. "Where's Rafe?"

Leith pointed to the round table in the darkest corner, where Rafe, the Stone's aging owner, and the farmer Loughlin sat hunched over pints. Leith raised an arm to catch Rafe's attention. "Two red ales. Two fish and chips," Leith said when the old guy caught sight of him and gave him a nod of acknowledgement.

"Two fish and chips," called a hoarse Rafe in the general direction of the kitchen.

"Two fish and chips!" came the shouted, unseen response from beyond the swinging doors.

Then, to Leith, Rafe waved toward the bar. "Get 'em yerself. You know where they're at."

Leith slid off the stool under Jen's amusement. "Wow," she said. "They just open up the whole town for you, don't they?"

"I pay for it." Stopping shoulder to shoulder with her, he added. "And I'll pay for yours, too."

In the corner, Rafe was talking with his gnarled hands. Loughlin was listening, but staring at Jen as though he really did think she'd burned down his barn. It didn't help when Jen's phone went off and, by the sound of the one-sided conversation, it was the Hemmertex landowners, settling the new location bid.

Leith went behind the bar and pulled down two thick glasses, then filled them with his favorite ale.

"You know," Jen said to him, pocketing her phone. "The last time the two of us were in here together, we weren't even old enough to drink."

He glanced up at her, but her eyes were sweeping through the dim interior.

"We've never had drinks together. Isn't that weird? It's so . . . adult." She sighed deeply. "I love it here. It's like another world."

Those words, echoing the exact same thought he'd had earlier, caused him to massively overflow one glass. The cold beer poured over his hand and he shook it off.

"Hurry up with those beers," she said. "I'll meet you at the dartboard."

He looked up in surprise, but she was already moving toward the black, white, and red circle mounted between the brick fireplace and a giant Scottish flag. An old white line had been drawn on the floor, but a few tables stood between that and the board, and she began to shove the tables to the side.

"Is it okay if we play, Rafe?" she called over to their old boss.

The owner gave her the same do-whatever-you-like-I'm-busy wave he'd given Leith, and in return she gifted him a brilliant smile.

When Jen was done clearing the area, Leith handed her the beer. "Darts, huh?"

She shrugged. "Are you scared?"

"Should I be? You look very serious."

"Oh, I am. You can throw around the big stuff. Let me handle the little things."

She opened the wood flaps on the scoreboard and took out the small piece of chalk resting inside. Some kid had scribbled a pair of dragons on the scoreboard—after he'd had his mac and cheese, by the looks of the orange handprint on the side—and Jen used a towel to wipe the slate clean. She wrote *Dougall* on the left and *Haverhurst* on the right.

Removing a handful of darts from a small basket nailed to the wall, she inspected the tips, handed him three, and kept three for herself.

"You know how to score without electronic bells and whistles?" he asked.

She threw him a look somewhere between pissed off and exasperated. "Please." She pointed to the white line. "Get over there, big boy. You're about to go down."

"Do I hear a challenge, Haverhurst?"

She flicked the flights of her darts. "Yep."

"Stakes?"

She said, "Loser has to do anything the winner wants. Until midnight tonight."

The grin that spread slowly across her face said that she'd walked into the Stone with the stakes already in mind. Why was he surprised? She never did anything without a plan. Only this time *he* was her plan, and it unhinged something in him. Solidified something else. He was scared, but that good kind of scared, the kind that made him all excited and tended to get him hard when he least expected it.

Immediately he zeroed in on her mouth. *Anything?* "You already know what you want me to do, don't you?"

She nodded. "Absolutely."

He stepped closer, because if there was one thing he never backed down from, it was a challenge he was sure and desperate to win. As expected, she didn't back away, didn't even have the decency to appear off balance. He had to get to her, to move inside her brain, throw her off.

"Good." Leaning down, he whispered in her ear. "Because I know what I want from you, too."

Abruptly, he stepped back, turned toward the board and aimed. "Closest to bull's-eye starts off. Three-oh-one?"

She drew a breath that sounded beautifully ragged. "I prefer cricket."

He bobbled his head side to side, pretending to consider. "All right."

With a barely disguised smile, she lined up, aimed, and threw. It dug in at the narrowest part of sixteen. She brushed past him as she made room for him to throw—her ass grazing his thighs, much in the same way they'd touched that first night way back when, when everything had changed.

If she thought that was going to distract him enough to throw badly, she was sorely mistaken. But he'd let her keep trying *that* if she felt it was doing some good.

He hit twenty, two inches from bull's-eye.

Jen took his place and hit a triple seventeen and a fifteen. Ouch. But two more turns each, and he had the slight edge. The woman was going down. And "going down" would just be the beginning.

A wide shadow blocked his light, and he turned, ready to give her fake hell for trying to throw him, but it wasn't Jen's shadow. Owen had left his table and come over.

Leith watched the plumber, who had always been a confident guy, look a little unsure about going up to the sister of the woman he was sleeping with.

"Hey," Owen said to Jen. Clutching his baseball cap in both hands, he nodded at Leith.

"Hi, Owen," she said, then glanced pointedly over his shoulder at the group of men he'd left sitting at the table, rubbing their bellies. "Out with the guys tonight?"

He let out an uneasy laugh. "Yeah. Aimee's cool with it this time."

That seemed to relax Jen, for some reason. "Okay."

"Listen"—he edged closer—"I just wanted to say thanks for helping Aimee out. And for all you're doing." Jen's mouth opened. "There's a rumor going around you pretty much saved the games today?"

Jen nodded demurely then took a sip of her beer.

Owen gave her a tight-lipped smile. "I don't know if anyone else will actually say it, but they're glad you're here. Especially after what they saw today."

"Thank you."

"Everyone knows in their hearts that you didn't set that fire. You changed people's minds today, even if they don't know it yet. I just wanted you to hear that."

Then he was gone, back to gather his buddies and head out, probably over to the sports bar in Westbury with the TVs and noise and sensory overload.

Jen watched him go, and Leith waited for the gloating. It never came. Instead this strange look passed over her face— sort of dreamy, a tiny kick of a smile. Happiness, if he had to name it. Then it was gone with an invisible wipe as she swiveled to him. "My throw," she said.

Damn it. She closed out fifteen.

"So."

The tone in her voice filled him with dread. There was a question coming, dragging down that single word. This was why he'd suggested Duncan coming with them earlier, to act as some sort of a buffer so he wouldn't have to address the thing with Da's house. He wasn't ready. Not yet.

"Yeah?" He set his toe on the line and aimed.

She waited for him to throw and then asked, "How was Connecticut?"

"Great. Really great. Want another beer?" When she nodded, he ambled around the bar, making a show of motioning to Rafe that he was taking two more. He marked off the tally by the cash register.

"It's scary, you know," he said, when he saw she was watching him, waiting for him to go on. He held the pint glass with one hand, the brass pull with the other. "To start over somewhere else. I mean, completely start over. I've never been so scared in my whole life."

That had just fallen out, and when he glanced up, he saw Jen watching him with complete understanding. "Sometimes," she said, "being scared is the best thing for you."

He nodded at the head on the ale rising up over the lip of the glass. "It's a challenge. I've never had a challenge before." *That* was a strange realization. "Wow. No, I haven't."

"Tell me about you after I left for college." She'd switched her darts to one hand and leaned into a chair, all her focus on him.

"That's what I'm talking about. You left. Hemmertex opened later that year. The next two years I exploded with lawn maintenance jobs. Enough to buy equipment and hire help. Then I realized that I had just enough interest and talent to start suggesting landscape changes, but I didn't know enough about the actual land and the plants, so the next summer I went after my associate online. The first class, the first book I cracked open, I knew I'd found it, what I was meant to be. All those days with Da in the yard, and me staying in the valley, it all clicked. I had the knowledge. The focus. I didn't even have to go after clients; they came to me. I was booked solid. And now . . ."

"And now you're going to start something even better."

It was still scary as fuck, but she was absolutely right. Connecticut would change him, and he couldn't wait.

When he came around the bar and handed her the beer, she asked, "Why didn't you go out and look for it?"

"'It'?"

She sipped. "What you needed."

Of course she would say that. She, who had left everything behind to go after her own "it."

He put down his glass, a little more forcefully than intended, and red ale splashed to the wood. "Because of Da," he answered, then turned his back on her to throw.

The muffled *thunk* of the darts hitting the board, *one two three*, released the sharp, sudden tension that had built inside him. He exhaled, pleased at closing out twenty.

He knew she was waiting for him to expand, to explain. His

reason for staying in Gleann was Da, and he'd leave it at that, until the words felt comfortable on his tongue.

"I have to go back," he told her. "To Connecticut."

"When?" There was a telltale sag to her shoulders, a little hitch in her voice. Her disappointment made his chest expand with something other than breath.

"Not sure. Soon, though. I can do some work here, some design and planning, but I'll need to be on-site more and more. Definitely need to find an apartment and arrange transport and storage of my equipment."

"Right. Absolutely," she replied, way too quickly. "Hey, did you know there's an actual town in Connecticut called Scotland?"

Then she threw, hitting two bull's-eyes to win the game.

"Two out of three," he offered, and she clinked his glass in agreement.

Four more beers on his side—because you only got better the more you drank, is what Da always said—and no more on hers, he won the second game.

Then she won the third.

"Fuck." He stood two feet from the dartboard, hands on hips, glaring at where the metal tip of her dart had juuuust slipped inside the triple sixteen for the win. He was just buzzed enough to turn and give her a wildly, purposely flirtatious smile. "So what do you want from me? I'm all yours."

The look in her eyes said it wasn't kissing, but then again, he could be wrong.

Please, please be wrong.

"Come with me."

Then she reached out and took his hand, and it tripped a live wire in his system. That strange, simple touch. His fingers closed tightly around hers, like a reflex. Like one of those patient, silent plants that sat open, waiting for food to wander in, and when it did, the plant closed around it. Never letting go until that unsuspecting creature was inside the plant forever, part of its being.

He held on to her, feeling the little roots she didn't know she'd planted burrow under his skin. He'd lost and had no idea what she wanted from him, but he followed willingly. She was giggling in a way that suggested she'd either reverted back to childhood or that she was drunk—which he knew she wasn't, not on two beers—or that she was about to make him do something horribly embarrassing.

She dragged him down the street and across the little bridge into the park with the gazebo and the playground and the . . . Oh shit.

Releasing his hand, she opened her arms and spun around to him. "You and me, Leith MacDougall, are going to relocate this caber."

Relocating is what they'd used to call their teenage habit of taking things from someone's yard and placing them somewhere else in town. Never destructive, never malicious, always got a laugh.

He eyed her. "Where?"

The exaggerated way she shrugged and rolled her eyes toward the sky in a faux-innocent way scared the crap out of him. In a good way.

"What do you have up your sleeve?" he asked.

"Just get over there and pick up that heavy end." She gestured to the thicker part of the caber, the tip that first struck the ground after it was thrown.

"This is vandalism, you know," he said as he unclamped the metal ring holding the caber.

"Yeah, and you're the one who taught me how to do it and laugh about it."

He had, hadn't he? All those years ago, he'd been the one to suggest taking the Thistle's outdoor furniture and relocating it to the parking lot of the market. Bev hadn't been happy, but after the town had got a good chuckle and Leith and Jen had moved all the furniture back, he'd caught Bev smiling.

Jen had a bit of trouble getting the narrowed end of the caber down from the metal cradle, having to push up onto her tiptoes. Once she steadied it in her hands, her tongue stuck out in concentration, there was such a fantastic glimmer in her eyes, all he could do was stare.

"I never get to do this anymore," she said.

"Do what?"

"Have fun."

She said it all casual in the way you might say, "Have a sandwich."

He saw it then: an emptiness that decorated the edges of her soul. A sadness that he couldn't remember having seen before. Maybe with age her resolve to hide it had cracked. Or maybe it was him. Maybe it was that part of her he thought he knew, but didn't.

The way she clutched the caber twisted her tank top. The moonlight settled into the lines of her arm and chest muscles, and made her dark hair gleam in a way that seemed almost magical. Moonlight had always been her friend.

Moonlight and a sky full of stars, sprayed over the open top of a Cadillac.

He cleared his throat, trying to clear his head in the process. "So now what, genius?"

She nudged her chin back toward town, the sparkle returning. When she smiled, there was the tiniest of crinkles along one side of her nose. "To your truck."

"Seriously?"

"Seriously."

He blew out a breath, but he could feel his smile getting bigger and bigger. "Lead the way."

So she did. Together they balanced the caber between them, jostling its weight, shifting between their hands, bursting into laughter as they tried to negotiate the nineteen-foot stick around the park hedgerows, then laughing so hard they had to rest when a car full of people rolled down the street, their eyes wide and fingers pointed.

Finally they managed to hobble and wobble the thing to where he'd parallel parked his truck in front of the closed and dark gas station.

"My God," she said as he shifted the caber to one shoulder. "It's huge."

"What is?" He lofted his end over the side of the truck bed, making the thing bounce. "My truck? Or my caber?"

She let out a really unfeminine snort that did decidedly masculine things to his body. "Get up in there and hold the thing. I'm driving."

"No. No. No one drives my truck except me."

"You had, like, six beers."

"And I'm two hundred and forty pounds."

She patted the side of the truck. "I can't hold that over the cab. Get up in there and hold it while I drive. I'll go slow and careful. I promise."

"This is eight million kinds of illegal, you know, driving around with big stuff not strapped down."

She made a dramatic glance up and down the empty streets, then peered down the long stretch of Route 6, where there were no lights. No cars. "Who's going to see? And besides, you're *Leith MacDougall*. Come on, big guy. Pretty soon you'll be in Connecticut and you won't be able to go five miles over the limit before you're thrown in the slammer. Enjoy your freedom, my friend."

Though he rolled his eyes, he hopped up into the cab and gripped the caber, swinging it up so the narrow tip rested on the truck cab and the thicker end was wedged well into a corner. He crouched, holding the whole thing in place. "Where to now, boss? Where are we relocating this thing?"

He didn't like the way she smiled at him, so full of secrets. "Keys?"

After a slight pause, he dug into his pocket and tossed them down to her.

"Just up the road," she said. "Hemmertex. You're going to throw that big stick for me."

Chapter

12

*H*e wasn't going to throw. There was no doubt about that. Yet he crouched in the back of his truck as the thing thundered under his boots, going where Jen was driving him. Because he'd lost the silly darts game? Partly. Because he didn't want to let her go tonight? Most definitely.

The caber was tilted up and over his head, his fingers latched around it from underneath. Funny how the weight and length of a caber could differ from place to place, competition to competition, but the feel of the wood was so similar.

Jen kept her word and drove like an old lady on the way to church. She flicked on the brights as she pulled off Route 6 and headed down the long drive onto Hemmertex land. She crossed the empty parking lot on a diagonal, angling for the large lawn on the northeast side of the building. She killed the engine but kept the headlights blaring into the darkness.

He stood as she exited the cab, and he felt like a giant looking down at her upturned face.

"The athletics field is going to be just beyond that line of bushes. I need to know if it's big enough."

"Isn't that Duncan's job as AD?"

She grinned. "Duncan isn't here."

"We couldn't do this tomorrow?"

"No time. Booked solid pretty much every minute of daylight from now until the games. I need you tonight, Dougall."

There was something else in those words, something he'd been looking for, dying to hear. Just yesterday she would have looked away after having said something like that. Just yesterday she would have glossed over it, pretended she hadn't inserted a hidden meaning. Ignored her own intentions, her own desires.

But right then, she seemed to remember very well how he'd kissed her.

"So." She planted a hand on the back hatch. "Go on out there, throw the thing and tell me if I have enough room."

She was damn sure she had enough room. In fact, he could pretty much bet that she'd already been out there with measuring tape and survey equipment and a GPS system to ensure the place was absolutely perfect. She was just playing with him, thinking she was lightening the mood, trying to get him to smile after all the sadness she'd seen inside Da's house.

They'd had an incredible evening; every second, every laugh, every word nudged them close together. He wasn't about to let the big giant elephant wedge itself between them. He'd talk her out of throwing. He'd distract her by what they both wanted.

Putting one hand on the side of the truck, he launched himself over, landing heavily on the cracked asphalt. Straightening, he saw her catch her breath. Saw the way her eyes had gone a bit glossy, a bit lost. *Good.* He felt pulled toward her from deep inside, as though the very essence of him, down to his molecules, was calling to her, and she was answering.

"Wow," she whispered. Or maybe it was more like an exhale, with a curse unknowingly tagged on.

"What?"

She threw an exasperated hand at his chest. "No one should look as good as you do in a green plaid shirt. It's a ridiculous thing to wear. I mean, really."

Suddenly it was his most favorite shirt in the whole world. "I can't throw, Jen."

"Sure you can." She reached over and flipped open the truck hatch. The caber, having been braced by the hatch, slid out.

"Jesus!" Leith lunged, caught the stick just before it hit the ground. "Watch the truck!"

"Sorry, sorry." She helped him get it out and laid it on the grass just inside the yellow circle made by the headlights.

He moved to the back of the truck, forcing her to follow.

"You're not actually thinking about welching on the bet, are you?"

He turned around, mid-eye-roll, to find her much, much closer than he expected. There was a soundless *bang* inside his mind and a virtual lurch of his heart as he looked down at her and found himself caught between two worlds.

The thing was, for the last ten years, all he'd had of her was the past. An eighteen-year-old Jen owned the images and memories that had remained in his mind, and they carried such mixed messages. Most good. Some sour.

He realized something profound. It felt better to be with her today than it had back then, *because* of the time spent apart. Because of who they'd become during those years. Because of who they were today.

"I'm not welching," he said, suddenly finding it difficult to swallow. "I haven't been—"

"Don't even say you haven't been working out."

"I was going to say training, which is an entirely different thing. And I'm not warmed up at all."

"So get warmed up."

The invitation couldn't have been more intentional, more sexy. Just looking at her mouth fed his brain some pretty wicked pictures—ones sprouted from memories of what she'd once felt like, and enhanced by a man's experience and exposure. And ones from just a few days ago, when he'd teased himself with her lips. The things he wanted to do to her . . . the things he wanted her to do to him . . .

But.

This had all happened once before. He'd pursued her, caught her, and in the end she'd slipped free, run off. Only this time he was under no assumption that she would stay. After all, neither would he. So why did he still want more? He knew the dangers, the stakes, and yet he wanted to be more to her than someone reappearing out of the past. He wanted her to be more than that to him, but there was no way, in this universe, that that could happen.

Fuck it.

He grabbed her. Just shoved his hand around her waist, pulled her to him with a not-so-tender yank, and wrapped his other arm around her body, fingers splayed between her shoulder blades. He waited for her to protest, to push away, to say something that would contradict her earlier invitation, but then he felt the pressure of her arms around his neck, and it wasn't gentle at all.

Despite the speed of the embrace, the clinging desperation of it all, the kiss happened slowly. It took forever to reach her mouth, and he savored every millisecond.

The other night against his back door, that hadn't been a true kiss. This, *this*, was their first kiss.

He thought "first" kiss because it was, in fact, entirely new. A first kiss with this new woman he somehow knew so well. It was the strangest feeling in the world. And also the most wonderful, the most natural. All his other first kisses—yes, even with her that night outside the Stone—had been precursors to true emotion, driven solely by a teenager's throbbing need. But this time, the emotions were already there. Already strong. His head felt light, spinning. His arms tightened on their own, needing no prodding from his brain. Tilting his head, he deepened the kiss.

Holy hell, her mouth. He couldn't exactly recall her taste from all those years ago, but it didn't matter because it was now all new. Jen. Here. Now. The taste on his tongue was exquisite—fine and sweet and rich. They were perfectly in tune, on the same beat, sharing the same need as the pressure and intensity of the kiss evolved into something almost painfully hard and teasingly soft.

In the back of his mind he was sure he'd kissed other women in the past ten years, positive that he'd slept with some of them, too, but the feel of Jen in his arms, in his mouth, erased all that. There were no others. He couldn't recall a single moment in time when she wasn't wrapped around him. Couldn't remember a single one of those bad dates and relationships with unsuitable women.

Her fingers curled into his hair. She'd never been able to do that before, and it caused waves of sensation to ripple across his scalp. She gripped him like he was about to dissolve, but that couldn't have been further from the truth. He wasn't going anywhere.

He was, however, losing it. Fast. The fact that she'd angled her body, turning him so his back hit the lowered hatch, and then essentially started to climb him, didn't help. If there was anything he needed right now, it was control.

In a swift movement, their mouths never releasing, he flipped her so her back was the one against the truck. There was a moment's pause, a simple stillness of her mouth that either spoke of shock or dislike, but he didn't care. He sank down, knees bent, and nudged her legs apart so that he could fit himself against her body. As he expected, it was the perfect puzzle piece, the one you search for on that table of a thousand tiny others.

He thought he might have made some sort of sound, because he could feel his throat vibrate, but he couldn't hear himself over the way her presence rang in his mind. And maybe he was moving, too, but his body seemed to be following the direction of his heart. Blood thumped in raging rhythms in his dick, and his movements were loose and uncontrolled.

Then she started to move. The slow undulations of her hips, perfectly angling the sweet warmth of her body against his hard-on, suddenly made him intensely aware of himself and his needs. As well as their past and lack of any future.

He wrenched his mouth away, desperate to breathe. Desperate to take hold of reality again. His forehead dropped to the curve of her neck, and he thought the whole world might shake with the force of his heartbeat. Her hands slid from his head, over his shoulders, to rest on his chest. Her cheek felt so warm against his ear.

"Jesus, Jen . . ."

He meant to take a break, to get a handle on himself, he really did. But there was hot, soft skin less than an inch from his lips. His tongue darted out, and it was just that little taste that got him going again. Pushing a hand into the hair that felt as smooth and dark and luxurious as it looked, he tilted her head to an angle he liked and gave himself the exquisite treat of her neck. At first she offered no resistance, and images of how else he could arrange her—on her back, on her knees, on her belly—flashed in smoky, sexy moving pictures behind his eyelids.

Then she pushed him off her, his mouth releasing, and his face was in her small hands. Her mouth was swollen, her eyes clear with wide-eyed wonder.

"I think I missed you," she said. Then she gave a little shake of her head as if to clear it and even in the very dim light, he could tell she'd reddened. She hadn't meant to say that; the admission had sneaked out under cover of desire, and he loved it.

"You think?" he teased. With a nudge of his chin, he indicated the big, open back of his pickup truck. "I want to see you up there."

She glanced dubiously over her shoulder. "Are you forgetting the last time we tried to do it in the back of a truck? We woke up the whole town with the squeaking."

He ran a loving hand over the taillight. "Aw, that was the old truck with the bad suspension and the rusty fender. This baby's practically brand new. Made for me in every way."

She rolled her eyes, but it was with a smile.

"Come on. Get on in." Then, leaning over to brush her lips with words, he added, "Promise the only thing that'll be making noise up there is you."

The way she drew back no more than a centimeter, the way her breath gave a little hiccup, had him shaking with anticipation. If lust had an image, it was her face at that moment. Her body felt so warm and free, but there was still an underlying tension, issuing a challenge he was more than willing to take up. He wanted to explore her new curves with his eyes and mouth and hands. He was dying to know how his larger body would fit into hers.

Maybe it reeked of caveman, but there was something about being that much bigger than her. Something incredibly appealing about having such a delicate, gorgeous thing all to himself, to protect and take care of. Something undeniably humbling about having that small, lovely woman want to take him into her body.

Wrapping his hands around her waist, he lifted her up without any sort of warning, her perfect little ass dropping onto the hatch. She let out a little yelp of surprise, and there was no mistaking the glare in her eye over that one. She looked ready to hop down and then climb back up, just to say it had been on her terms. Fingers splayed over her thighs, he held her in place and smiled up at her.

At last she answered him with a kiss, and a long, lingering lick of her tongue. He groaned and she pulled back with a wicked twist to her lips, just as he was about to go in for something deeper and harder. Hands next to her butt, she scooted back, out of his reach. Looking at him with sparkling anticipation, her face framed between her bent and raised knees, the picture of her made him go completely brain-dead.

She moved farther back. "It's hard up here."

He chuckled. "Yep. It certainly is."

"Walked right into that one."

"You sure did. There's a blanket in that metal box by the cab."

Bad suggestion. Bad, bad suggestion. The second she rolled over onto her knees and started crawling for the silver corrugated box in which he kept some essential tools, his mouth started watering. Her ass swayed as she moved, calling to him. He hopped up, the truck lurching violently but, keeping him true to his word, with no awful squeaky protests.

Jen had one hand on the box and was ready to open it. He couldn't help himself. He reached out and wrapped a hand around the front of her thigh, dragging her away from the box and closer to him.

"What are you doing?" she said as he pulled her back and turned her over. She was trying to look pissed off but wasn't succeeding. "The blanket—"

"Fuck the blanket."

After a pause filled with obvious consideration, she grinned up at him as he hovered over her body. She was spread out below him, her hair falling into the ridges of the truck bed. *His* truck bed.

She said, "But your knees—"

"I'll live."

He started to shake, could feel the little tremors shooting through his limbs. Something tickled his waist, and he looked down his body to see her fingers dipping under the drape of his shirt to curl around the waist of his jeans. He sucked in a breath, and then he didn't know if she was pulling him down or if he'd covered her all on his own, but she was under him.

Finally. Again.

Then she was arching up, her tits rising to meet his chest in that tiny tank top. His hands found her hair again. They dug in, held on. Shifting one knee, then the other, inside hers, he slowly pushed her legs outward and settled in. For a moment he worried about his weight, so much more than hers, but then she did that little roll with her hips again, a wordless synonym for *more*.

He kissed and kissed her, never wanting to stop and purposely not thinking about when it would.

"Remember how good we were?" he murmured against her mouth. "I barely touched you and you came. God, I remember that."

Ever since then, he'd been trying to figure out why no other woman had been like that for him. Because it was Jen? Or him and Jen together? Or youth mixed with new experiences and enthusiasm?

She released a little moan, then said mischievously, "As I recall, the same went for you."

He had to laugh, pulling back a little to run his tongue over his bottom lip. "I'm not eighteen anymore. I can last longer."

She raised a single eyebrow, something he'd never been able to do. "Care to test that out?"

He searched her bright face, saying "Oh my God," under his breath. He wasn't sure what the oath meant exactly. Disbelief? Pleasure? Awe? Then, louder, he said, "You first. Just like old times."

She'd barely nodded when he pushed up her tank top and slid his hands around to unclasp her bra. Looking into her eyes, his palms grazed her ribs as they moved around to her front. When his fingers scraped at her nipples, she sucked in a breath. When he filled his hands with her breasts, all soft firmness, his lungs nearly shattered.

He pushed her breasts together, his mouth dragging through their deep crease, then he freed one and sucked her nipple, the little bit of hardness like candy on his tongue. Shifting to her side, he kept his mouth where it was and spread his hand over the smooth, tight skin of her belly, fingers teasing just under her jeans snap.

Heat everywhere, coursing through him, being fed into her. The whole night felt ready to explode.

He released her nipple and moved to her collarbone, just to see how it tasted. Underneath his hand, he sensed her quivering, felt her hips curling up in a silent beg.

"Can I touch you?" He dipped his hand lower.

"Yes," she said, the *S* dragged out in a hiss.

Pop went the snap, *zzzt* went the zipper, and then his hand was down her pants, in the most secret part of her that was so wet he almost didn't believe it. His composure fractured and he shuddered.

"Oh, God," they said at exactly the same time.

Then he began to touch her, slowly first, in light circles. It was all coming back to him, how she'd once liked the slow tease and then the quick buildup to a really intense orgasm. Back then, he'd done this with an almost-crazed glee. It was better now, with this adult understanding of her body, this adult patience, this adult pleasure.

Back then, making her come with his hand—and pumping away inside her until he came, too—was all he'd known how to do. But that was back then.

Abruptly he stopped, rose up to his elbow and gazed down at her panting, flushed, and frustrated face.

"Why'd you stop?" she asked.

"I want to go down on you."

A lovely little surprise shimmered across her face. "We've never done that."

"No." He smiled. "Too nervous before."

"And now?"

"Nervous as fuck, but I want it so bad I can't think straight."

She looked around at his truck, then up at the stars. "It's not how I really imagined it, how I'd planned it in my head."

He ignored the fact that she'd done her share of fantasizing and replied with a grin, "Don't care. It's happening." He wasn't giving in to any of her little control issues right now.

The kiss he gave her was deliberately sweet. "There's lots we haven't done, Jen. As far as I'm concerned, it's all new, from here on out."

How long the "on out" part would last, he didn't know. But he'd sure as hell enjoy each step of the journey. Slowly, feeling her stare weigh heavily on him, he moved back between her legs and kneeled. Sliding both hands under her ass, which she graciously lifted, he grabbed the back of her jeans and pulled them down. Her underwear came, too, and he was dimly aware that it was some kind of dark-colored G-string. Then her clothing didn't matter, because her pants were trapped at her knees and she was bared to him, scraps of clothing dangling around her intensely gorgeous body.

He stared down at her, at the pink, damp flesh the teasing light showed him. He had to close his mouth because he could feel himself salivate. He'd seen her before, but never like this. Hands on either side of her hips, he came down, kissing first just below her belly button. She let out a sigh and then he heard her head hit the truck bed. He slowly kissed his way down, savoring her taste and scent.

A great burst of light filled the truck bed, then disappeared. Jen's eyes were closed, her head tilted far back, but his were wide open, taking it all in. The headlights, approaching from the rear, swept a long, too-brilliant path over them, and he let out a snarl of frustration. This was not happening.

"Shit." His forehead dropped to that amazing place between her hip bones.

"What?" Jen lifted her head. "Oh, *God*!"

Now it wasn't just headlights hitting the truck, it was a bona fide spotlight, filling the whole area like noon sun. Jen bolted upright and scrambled backward on hands and knees, stopping only when her back hit the long metal box, making her wince.

Behind them, a car door opened and closed. Leith moved right in front of Jen, using his body to throw her nakedness in shadow. She frantically redid her bra and smoothed down her tank top, but it was still crooked, and a bit of lace peeked over the top. He reached out and tucked the lace back in. Leaning back, she yanked up her underwear and then her jeans, and he let out a gravelly sigh of pained regret to see her clothed again.

"Damn it, Olsen," Leith growled over his shoulder. "Mind giving us some privacy so Jen here can get decent?"

Jen glared at him as she drew up her zipper, but the footsteps coming up behind them did stop. Good. Leith wouldn't have to kick a cop's ass.

"What?" Leith whispered to her. "Not like he didn't know

what we were doing anyway. He would've kept coming if I hadn't said anything."

Covered now, but still pretty disheveled, she came to her knees and peered around his body. With a great eye roll, she said, "We did *not* just get busted by the cops."

Her hair was a messy drape covering one of her jeweled eyes, and Leith reached out and nudged it aside. "Yeah. I'm sorry to say that we did."

"Don't laugh."

"Who's laughing? Believe me, there's nothing funny about being cockblocked by the sheriff."

With Jen all put together, the two of them clambered off the truck, into the spotlight beaming off the top of the sheriff's green-and-white car. Hands stuffed into her back jeans pockets, Jen directly faced Olsen without any outward embarrassment.

Sheriff Olsen looked more annoyed than pissed off, his chin nearly disappearing into the bulge of his neck. "Got a call about two people carrying a caber through town, and making an awful lot of noise doing it. So I went to the park and saw that that one was gone. You wouldn't know anything about that, would you?" He looked right at the caber lying in the truck's headlights.

Leith scratched at his neck. "No?"

"We're going to put it back," Jen said.

Olsen sighed. "This is private property."

Jen pushed forward. "Oh, I'm renting the land for the games. Technically it's mine—well, Gleann's—for the next two weeks."

"I heard," Olsen said. "I like the new location. Better than the old one. That barn blaze might've been a blessing in disguise."

The sheriff was watching Jen intently, but Jen, to her credit, just rolled her eyes in the face of the not-so-subtle intimation that she'd had something to do with the fire.

"That's why I brought Leith out here, Sheriff"—she patted Leith's arm—"to help me figure out the new layout. To determine if the athletic field is big enough."

Olsen pursed his lips and nodded dramatically. "Makes perfect sense. At midnight."

"Actually," Jen added, "Leith lost a bet. He's supposed to throw for me."

Olsen's eyebrows shot into his forehead as he looked at Leith with renewed interest. He crossed his thick arms over his even thicker chest. They'd gone to school together, with Olsen three grades ahead. He'd always been on the portly side.

"That so?" the sheriff said. He shifted his weight back and forth. "Tell you what, Dougall. You throw that thing right now, show me you still got it, and I'll let this theft and vandalism thing pass. And you've got to put it back in the park."

Jen was staring at him with that lovely smeared mouth and big eyes, enjoying this way too much.

Tell you what, he wanted to tell Olsen. *Why don't I take the damn stick back to the park right now and I can pick up where I left off with Jen?*

Leith glared at the sheriff. "You serious?"

Olsen clapped his hands once. "Absolutely."

Leith turned his head to look at the caber. He could do this. Just one throw. It didn't even have to be good. No one was around. No audience to impress. No competition. No personal records to reach for.

No Da.

"Going into next week without a police record would be really, really great." Jen smiled.

Leith turned, heading over to the caber. As Olsen got back in his car and swung it around so its headlights and spotlight mixed with that coming from Leith's truck, Leith dragged the caber farther into the field.

He stood next to it, staring at it for a moment before circling his arms and bending his torso, warming himself up, stretching. He cracked his neck. Then he went to the thicker end, picked it up, and walked forward, pushing it up so it balanced on the narrower tip. Years later and the motion came back to him easily. Too easily. He set the long, heavy weight against his shoulder, laced his fingers tight around the front of the wood, and glanced up.

Olsen stood to the side of his cruiser, his shape a thick shadow against the night. But Jen stood right in front of a headlight, her body outlined perfectly. He couldn't see her face.

"You throwing or not, Dougall?" she called. Hearing his nickname, spoken in her voice, calmed him a bit.

He gave the two onlookers his back, swiveling around the stick so that when he picked up the thing, he could run in the opposite direction. On the grass before him stretched the long, long shadow of his own body, the great caber looking like it was shooting out of his shoulder, fading far in the distance.

Memories came back to him with a jolt. Good memories. Training with Duncan. The days in the sun. The good-natured ribbing between competitors, and sometimes back and forth with the audience. The applause and cheers. The tinny, echoing sound of the announcer's voice reverberating across the field, calling each throw.

Fingers laced, he crouched a few inches, adjusted the caber's weight against his body. Then he slid his hands down a good foot, repositioning.

Oh, man, he'd missed this. There was an energy to it, to lifting the heavy stuff and heaving it with all your power. It was cathartic in a strange way, to use everything you had to flip this great object far away from your body and up in the air. You could put anything you wanted into that huge thing. Any bad issues or arguments or frustrations. As long as you kept your focus. As long as you kept your form.

Another crouch, feet planted, thighs strong. The caber pressed harder against his shoulder in the increasingly difficult angle, its thick end thrust into the sky. He shimmied his hands even lower.

In that moment, he'd forgotten why he'd stopped competing, especially because he'd once loved it so much. The reasons were there, somewhere in the dimness just beyond the headlights, but he couldn't see them. Couldn't make them out.

He lowered himself into the deepest position, knees bent far, and let the caber fit nice and snug against his neck and shoulder. He inserted his fingers underneath the narrow end, the grass and dirt cool against his knuckles. He was ready. He would do this. All he had to do was straighten his legs, find his center and capture balance, take off on his run, then throw.

It's been a while, boy. You can do it. You've always been able to do it.

Da's brogue, wheeling down from heaven, caused Leith to

sag and break form. The caber tilted and Leith caught it, brought it back.

Da wasn't speaking to him. It was all in his head, Leith knew. Then Da's low chuckle, skewed and endearing from where his lips had always been curled around that pipe, sailed over the field and twined around Leith's body.

I've never left ye, his old man said.

Yes. You did. You were all I had, and you left.

At the very edge of Leith's periphery, he could see Da scooting forward on the edge of that old aluminum lawn chair with the woven, green-striped seat. He could see the twinkle in Da's eyes just under the brim of his gray cap, and the confident nod—the same nod he'd given Leith before every football game or track meet or Highland Games.

Quit your excuses and throw. Like I taught ye.

But the last time I did this, Leith thought, *I lost. And then you were gone.*

The following silence spurred him, making him realize he was imagining this whole exchange. He was stupid for holding on to the grief and loss for so long. With a great heave upward, his heels digging into the soil, his thighs powering to stand, he lifted the caber, the thick end straight up.

It's all right, boy. You've got it. You've got it.

Leith didn't have it.

The smell of the grass, the hollow memory of last time he'd thrown—after Da's illness had shattered his concentration and Leith'd had the worst competitive day of his life—Da's voice and image coming back to him after three years gone . . .

The caber wobbled in his grip. Fell forward. No running, no throwing. Just limped out of his hands to land with a *thump* on the lawn.

"Hey, what happened?" called Olsen.

Leith gathered himself, plastered on his perfected nonchalance and carefree grin, and turned around. He walked toward the vehicles with wrists held out in invisible handcuffs. "Arrest me if you want, Olsen. Don't have it in me tonight."

The sheriff took off his hat and ran a hand over that shiny head. "Looked like you had it to me. And I was looking forward to telling everyone tomorrow I saw you throw."

"Mind if I leave the caber there and come back for it

tomorrow, when I can strap it down properly?" At that last
word, he threw a teasing look at Jen, who was gazing back at
him in a very non-teasing way. He didn't like that look. It was
too inquisitive, but in a way that said she'd already figured out
way too much. She had, after all, been in Da's house.

Olsen blew out his cheeks. "I suppose."

"Come on," he told Jen. "I'll take you home."

On the short drive around the fairgrounds, he rolled down
all the windows and let the breeze sweep through the truck cab.
Jen didn't say or ask anything. Neither did he. He wasn't sure
whose silence disturbed him more.

When he pulled into the driveway at 740 Maple, Da's voice
was still rattling around in his head. Jen inhaled as though
preparing to say something Big and Important, but just ended
up saying, "Good night."

"Good night." He risked a glance at her, but there was that
knowing look again, and it made him feel naked and flayed.
Pinching the bridge of his nose, he looked out the windshield
at the garage.

"See you tomorrow?" The note of hope in her voice
reminded him of how well they'd fit together earlier that night.
It was too much to think about just then: the confusion of his
feelings for her layered over Da.

"Yep. Sure." He didn't fool himself into thinking she'd
bought it.

The next morning before sunrise, he went back to Hemmertex, roped down the caber to his truck, and brought it back
to the park. Then he tossed a duffel stuffed with several days'
worth of clothes in the passenger seat, veered the truck out onto
Route 6, and headed south to Connecticut, too many memories
and emotions biting at his heels.

Chapter

13

*J*en sat alone at a central table in the Kafe, her laptop open to its multitude of windows, the cooling plate of hash browns and sausages and grilled tomatoes regretfully pushed to the back corner. The never-empty mug of coffee, however, sat within easy reach.

"Yep. Yep," she was saying into the phone tucked between her ear and shoulder. "It's on the G drive, Gretchen. I'm logged in remotely; I'm looking right at it. Invitation list for Fashion Week."

Across the Kafe, Vera the city councilwoman looked up from where she was reading the newspaper, wearing a little frown of concern. Jen threw her a reassuring smile.

"Ah, okay. Found it," Gretchen said on the other end of the line. Then, with a sigh, "The label is a little misleading, don't you think?"

"The label is fine. Don't make any changes to that list without running it by Tim. Anything new on Rollins? Anything I should know?"

"Nope. How's it going there?"

Jen glanced at the rental contracts that had just come through from the Hemmertex building landowners. Based on the trillion ideas she'd gotten from Mr. MacDougall's scrap-books, she had a bunch of new aspects to price out and fit into an electronic presentation before she met with the entire city council. Then later, based on whatever the council told her, she had a conference call with the Scottish Society. She should be focused on that. She shouldn't have to be checking in with Gretchen or worrying about Vera's eavesdropping.

She shouldn't be thinking about Leith. Except that there seemed to be little space left in her brain whenever he invaded it, and after last night that frequency had increased by, oh, a thousand.

Ending the call with Gretchen, Jen sat back in her chair and stared at the computer screen, which had blurred into squares of meaningless color. The coffee mug was barely warm when she wrapped her fingers around it, so she gestured to Kathleen for more. She had to remember to tip big.

The Kafe was filled with people she recognized from the other morning along Loughlin's fence. The only person she'd met besides Vera was Bobbie, who occupied the booth nearest the door. The older woman had her own laptop open and she was making changes to her website.

The bell over the door gave its strangled ring, and Owen and Melissa and T and Lacey came in. The girls chattered, and they all sat down and ordered without looking at the menu. Owen said something and Melissa laughed. Vera narrow-eyed them with drawn lips. They seemed . . . together.

Shame and embarrassment forced Jen's eyes to her lap. Despite Aimee's reassurances, and Owen coming up to her last night at the Stone in an obvious attempt to win her over, Jen knew her sister was making a colossal mistake.

If Leith were here, maybe he could talk Jen down again.

It always circled back to him, didn't it? And now he was gone.

Before sunrise that morning, she'd been awakened by the deep grumble of his obnoxious truck as it pulled out of 740's driveway and rolled down the otherwise hushed street. She'd thought he was leaving for a day of maintenance rounds with Chris, but on her way into the Kafe, she'd passed Chris, who was exiting, and he'd told her Leith had taken off again for Connecticut.

She wasn't fooled, even if Leith was doing a damn fine job

of fooling himself. He hadn't sped out of Gleann because the new client in Connecticut needed him later that day; just last night he'd hedged on when exactly he'd have to go back. No, something had freaked him out. It had started the day he'd brought her to his dad's tomb of a house, and crescendoed as he'd tried to throw the caber. The look on his face—a strained mask of false well-being slapped over a debilitating pain—had been more than a shock to her. It made her feel awful for telling him to throw the thing, but how was she to know that something that had once brought him such satisfaction now poked at open wounds?

Up until that moment, last night had been pretty damn perfect.

She'd been a virgin all over again. Every experience with a man she'd had outside of him in the past decade had been annihilated by that kiss up against his truck. Absolutely destroyed by the feel of Leith's body on top of hers.

She'd like to have claimed that she'd forgotten how well he kissed, or how big and gentle his hands were, and how much of her skin they covered at once. But the truth was, whatever nuggets of him she'd stored away were nothing—*nothing*—compared to what he'd done to her last night. Everything—the sensations he'd actually given her and the even more sinful ones he promised with his eyes and words—far, far surpassed her memories. Left them choking in the dust, actually.

Usually she knew exactly what she wanted in bed. Usually she got it, because she was used to getting her way and wasn't shy about voicing it. There was no use sugarcoating her desires, not when there were things to get done. She liked a lot of kissing and foreplay, a good long fuck to work herself up, and then some really intense clit work to give her an orgasm. Wham bam, thank you, sir.

Yet she hadn't said a thing to Leith last night. She'd let him practically throw her around that truck, her map to pleasure flying and flapping out the open window. At first she'd protested because the thought of not knowing exactly what would happen and how her body would react scared the crap out of her. But in the end, she'd loved it. That might have scared her most of all.

His mouth had *almost* touched her where she'd craved it.

He'd *almost* dragged his tongue through where she'd gotten swollen and wet. And because that was her favorite act, and because he was Leith, she would have come nearly instantly. Just the thought of it now, the intense dream of what had *almost* happened, shot a thrilling shiver through her entire body, which she had to disguise by shifting on her Kafe chair and reaching for her coffee. The black liquid made ripples against the cream-colored porcelain and she stared at them, trying to turn her mind to purer thoughts.

This man was doing strange things to her head. He was making her think of the past, of whom and what she'd had to let go when she'd walked away from here. She didn't like that feeling, that whispering question of *What if?* There was no room in her life for regret. She'd already overcome so much, and her goals and dreams still rose before her, a mountain she was still in the midst of climbing. To return to the past would be like falling off the cliff face without a rope. To return to the past would mean she'd hit the rocks at the bottom, and land at the feet of her mom, who would laugh and tell her she'd known all along that Jen would fall.

But he was Leith, and the man he was now was far more potent and exhilarating and alluring than his past self.

She wanted him. Maybe she even needed him.

"I see the caber was put back."

The hard screech of a chair against the floor jolted Jen from her thoughts. The mug slipped from her fingers and dropped an inch or so to the table, sloshing muddy coffee over the side and onto some papers. Opposite, Sheriff Olsen angled a chair to the side and sat down without asking permission, one forearm leaning in to touch the rim of her breakfast plate. He wasn't leering or smirking, but with a shudder she wondered how much of her body he'd seen last night.

"It was?" she asked. When Olsen nodded, she realized Leith must have hauled the thing back to the park before leaving for Connecticut, when the sun had barely lit the sky. Olsen tapped his pinky and forefinger in quick succession on the table.

"You're looking at me like you think I burned down the barn." The concept was so preposterous, she didn't think a joke would hurt.

"Did you?" He rested his other hand on his round belly.

Did he really think she did it? She swallowed and looked as serious as possible. "No."

He let her sweat for a good ten seconds before shaking his head. "I believe you. We're looking at other suspects."

"When I was in there the other day, I saw a blanket and things that looked like someone had been sleeping there. Or at least smoking some cigarettes."

"Mind if I have someone call you later for the details?"

"Sure."

Since Olsen didn't seem to be going anywhere, she asked, "So what's a Swede doing in this valley? I'm surprised they didn't stop you at the gates and turn you back around."

He snorted, then wiped his nose on her napkin. "Wouldn't they have stopped you, too, then?"

"Yeah, but I'm 'aunt-ed in,' so to speak."

Aunt Bev had married a Gleann Scot, though she'd never taken his name, and her husband had opened the Thistle. She'd taken over the B&B after his death. Her aunt had once said that because she'd stayed on in Gleann and showed such love for the Thistle and what her husband had built. the native community had gradually—although possibly never completely—accepted her.

"I'm half-Scottish," Olsen said, his fingers curling over his gut and giving it a good jiggle. "The meatier half."

After that, the sheriff didn't seem so much like he'd come over here to interrogate her. "The caber was my idea," she said. "So if you need to write anyone up, it should be me, not Leith."

Olsen waved the hand sporting a tarnished wedding ring. "You don't need to worry about that." He threw a nervous look around the Kafe, clearly anxious about what might happen to him if he ever dared arrest Saint Leith MacDougall for anything, including jaywalking.

"Are you two friends?" she asked.

He gestured to Kathleen for some coffee. "Isn't everyone friends with Dougall?"

If that wasn't the truth.

"We've hung out some over the years," Olsen added. "Less since his business took off. Hardly at all since Hemmertex left."

"You sounded excited about seeing him throw last night. Did you used to watch him at the games?"

"Yeah, of course. Thanks, Kathleen." He sipped his newly delivered coffee. "Then he stopped winning so he stopped competing. Football, track, the games—he was great at everything. Four years ago he had a piss-poor showing. The shine of his star was gone. So he stopped."

Jen leaned back in her chair and gazed out the window where Kathleen had gone out to water the hanging flowerpots with a big green watering can. Drops leaked from the bottoms of the pots and splashed against the glass. Olsen's assessment of Leith didn't seem right. Maybe part of Leith's troubles was the fear of failure—anyone who'd been at the top of their field and then stumbled downward would feel the ache of losing—but that wasn't entirely what she'd witnessed last night.

"When did Mr. MacDougall die again?"

Olsen scrunched up his face. "Three years ago? It was winter, as I recall."

That made more sense. Leith had thrown badly one summer, then his dad had died that winter. If her math was right, Hemmertex closed and his business dried up barely six months later. Too many layers of loss, stacked upon each other, pressing him down.

Her nose tickled in sensory memory of all the dust in Mr. MacDougall's home. Though Leith claimed to have healed from his father's death, he hadn't. He'd mistaken recovery for just *pretending* to recover. He thought that leaving Gleann and moving away actually meant he was moving *on*.

Maybe the town was fooled, falling for his numerous excuses—"I have to work." "I'll be out of town." "I'm not interested in competing anymore."—but Jen saw his denial for the big ol' Band-Aid that it was.

If Aimee were inside her head, her sister would be telling her to butt the hell out of Leith's business. Except that he'd let her into his dad's house and inserted himself back into her life and, yes, her heart. He didn't honestly expect her to turn her back on that, did he?

Maybe he did, since she'd been the one to walk away ten years ago.

"Well." Olsen gave the table a slap and stood. "I just wanted to let you know the caber was taken care of, in case you hadn't heard. See you around."

He wandered over to the back booth, which had already been set with two newspapers side by side.

Jen needed to work someplace else. Someplace that didn't scream *Leith!* around every corner. Yeah, right. Like that place existed anywhere in a ten-mile radius. Maybe Aimee would let her camp out at the kitchen table in the apartment above the Thistle's garage. She gathered up her papers, shut down her laptop, and grabbed a cold sausage with her fingers, eating it in three bites. After paying her bill, she was on her way out when Bobbie glanced up and their eyes met. It would be awkward to just walk out without saying anything; that's how Gleann worked. Jen went over and greeted her.

"Are you looking for company?" Bobbie asked politely, with a pointed look over at Jen's mostly uneaten breakfast. "Sometimes it's easier to eat with someone across the table."

Is that why Jen barely ate? Because she was alone all the time?

"Thanks, but I'm heading over to the Thistle." Jen gestured to the bright-green and orange website pulled up on Bobbie's laptop and smiled. "I checked out your site. It's excellently done."

Bobbie looked delightfully surprised at that, sitting back against the booth cushion. "Thank you. Although, forgive me if I'm wrong, but you don't seem like the type of person who's into crafts and scrapbooking."

Jen chuckled. "Nothing to forgive. You're right. But it doesn't mean I can't appreciate a great business model and terrific design. You do it all yourself?"

"Yes. I was an interior designer for years in Boston, and when I retired I turned from the big picture to the small details."

"I saw you have a huge online following. Almost half a million between social media and your blog? That's really incredible. I mean, do you know that? Do you realize that most Internet entrepreneurs would kill for those numbers?"

Bobbie's smile shifted from polite to genuine, widening as she bowed her head. "I do. But don't sound so surprised. You're starting to give me a complex."

"I'm not surprised. I'm impressed as hell. There's a million blogs and sites out there that just talk, talk, talk, but you've managed to create a pretty tight-knit community."

At that, Bobbie's smile faltered. She turned her head to the window. Across the street, a few doors down, stood the empty storefront that had once housed her shop. Jen had removed the old poster of Leith in order to put up her own newly designed promotions, but she'd rolled up the old one and brought it back to Mildred's, intending to throw it away. Someday. When she got around to it.

The old Picture This sign swayed over the sidewalk, its color faded. Even the vines trailing up the stone facade looked a little forlorn.

"So why did my store fail?" Bobbie asked, almost to herself. She laced her fingers on the tabletop. "I thought the big virtual community would translate to something like a pilgrimage here, where I could talk to people one-on-one and work on projects. It wasn't about money; I've got plenty of that. I really wanted to help out Gleann, too. I love Rob, but when I came here, I fell in love with this place almost as hard. So much character and history. Too much to be lost."

Suddenly Jen's fingers itched to get to a keyboard and translate all the words and tangents and ideas that were pinging around in her brain. A single concept could do that sometimes. A bare kernel of a notion or intention.

"I think you had the right motives," Jen said, "about the pilgrimage. I'm just not sure that a single store was the answer. It wasn't enough." It would take a lot to make Gleann enough, too, but she left that part out.

"So what would you suggest?" Bobbie let out a soft, short laugh that others might have taken as snobbishness, but that Jen understood as a quiet challenge, from one smart woman to another. It was something she'd seen often on the face of Tim Bauer when she'd brought him a new concept and he would say, "Okay, lay it all out, get me the numbers, and then show me you can do it." It was a look Jen relished, that charge to prove her worth, her acumen.

"Let me get back to you." A warm glow bloomed in Jen's chest, spreading out through her body, coming alive with possibility. She beamed at Bobbie. "I have an idea. Or fifteen."

Only when she reached the gate of the Thistle and stopped short, looking up at the sweep of Tudor eaves, did she realize that back in the Kafe talking to Bobbie, she hadn't thought of Iowa or her mom once.

Chapter

14

*L*eith had been back in Connecticut for two days, since Friday. He hadn't exactly told Chris the truth when he'd fled Gleann last Thursday. Before Connecticut, he'd meandered through Vermont, checking out the location he'd been considering before Rory Carriage's call had come through. It didn't feel like he belonged in Vermont, maybe because it was too similar to Gleann, or because it didn't have the energy and potential that Stamford had. Or maybe because Vermont was simply too far away from New York City.

Here, in Connecticut, the city—Jen's home—was a bridge away. A highway drive. A train ride.

He leaned against the driver's side door of his truck in the motel parking lot, holding his phone and staring to the southeast.

Duncan called then, gloating about how much he'd bench-pressed earlier that day. He sounded slightly drunk.

"You working okay with Jen?" Leith asked him.

There might have been a little laugh in Duncan's voice; it was hard to tell over the mobile line. "Jen. How did I know you'd bring her up? Yeah, she's all right. A bit intense, but really smart. Really organized. Not bad to look at, either. I think everyone in the valley is breathing a little easier this weekend, though."

Leith's stomach did a little flip. "Why?"

"I guess she went back to the city for a few days to take care of some things. Supposed to be back on Monday. You still driving around New England looking for new roots?"

He pushed away from his truck. "The city. As in New York?"

"No. Phoenix. Of course New York."

Jen had texted him once Thursday afternoon, after she'd likely heard he'd taken off. *Just wanted to make sure you're OK*, it had said. What a shit he was, to not have at least told her himself that he'd gone.

M OK, he'd texted back. *Sorry I left. Promise I'll call later.*

"Dougall?"

"What? Sorry, man. I gotta run. I'll give you a ring when I get back."

The second Duncan disconnected, Leith called Jen. His leg bounced as he waited for her to pick up—because she never let that thing go to voice mail—the thick sole of his work boots *thump thump thump*ing on the pavement.

"Hey there." She sounded a little out of breath, like she'd scrambled to pick up. It made his heart jump. In a good way. "Are you back in Gleann?"

"Wouldn't you know that, if you were there, too?"

"I'm not. I'm in New York for the weekend to take care of a few things."

"I know. That's why I called. I'm still in Connecticut. I want to see you. If I hopped on a train, would you go out with me tonight?"

All this was happening incredibly fast. He hadn't known this was what he wanted to do when he'd called, just that the thought of her being so close to him, away from Gleann, was alluring beyond words, and a chance he didn't want to miss.

"You mean like a date?"

He was bounding up the outdoor steps to the crappy motel room, tugging his dingy T-shirt out of his jeans to get ready for a shower. "Exactly like a date."

"What do you have in mind?"

He unlocked the motel room door and toed off his boots. "Don't care. You pick. I don't know the city that well."

"All right. You trust me?"

Going still, he caught his reflection in the generic mirror and noticed he was smiling. "Implicitly," he said, and meant it.

"Good." He glanced at a schedule and told her which train he'd arrive on, then she gave him instructions where to take a cab to meet her. Even though he was going to see her shortly, he didn't want to get off the phone, and he wasn't a big phone talker at all. She said good-bye and he hated it.

"Wait. Jen?"

"Yeah?"

"I just want you to know, that if it wasn't highly illegal, I would have killed Olsen for interrupting us the other night."

She exhaled in a way that had him picturing her lips in a beautiful *O*. "See you in a few hours."

Leith grabbed a cab outside of Grand Central and had a harrowing ride south to the corner in SoHo where Jen had told him to meet her. Even if he hadn't recognized her dark hair or the way her black-and-white dress wrapped itself around that body, he'd know her by her posture—by the way she paced back and forth on a small section of sidewalk outside the little bistro with the wicker outdoor furniture, her phone plastered to her ear. He slid the driver money and unfolded himself from the cab. Just then, Jen pivoted and saw him.

He liked the way she met his eyes and smiled. And he really liked how his appearance caused her to stutter midsentence. *She* didn't seem to like that so much, however, and turned her back on him to keep talking.

She wasn't yelling at whoever was on the other line, but her shoulders hunched with tension and she made curt gestures with her free hand. That's when he realized she wasn't carrying her gigantic purse. He had no idea what she was discussing in such strained terms—something to do with minimum guarantees and hard-balled negotiations with regard to tables and chairs—but when she hung up, he was a little scared of her.

It turned him on in a crazy, weird way.

"Ouch," he said as she came up to him. "Hate to be that person. Everything okay?"

She blinked and then looked in confusion down at her phone. "Oh, that? That was nothing." She flashed him a smile that was pure sunlight. "Hi. You're here. In my city."

Her city. Of course that's how she'd see it. The odd part was, just a week ago he might have felt uncomfortable hearing that and might have assumed she was deliberately putting space between them. But now that he was, indeed, standing here on a SoHo street with her consuming his vision, there was nothing uncomfortable about her words. It *was* her city, and he'd wanted to see her here, in her element. He wanted to know what her life had become after she'd left him. And before he'd found her again.

"I am," he said, then asked, only half jokingly, "So is this a pretty typical Sunday for you?"

She pursed her lips and nodded. "Yeah, a little quieter than during the week."

Wow, all right. "Well, I'm really glad you—"

Her phone went off again. She gave him an apologetic glance and looked at the screen. "Sorry, I have to take this."

Of course she did. She turned away, finger pressed against the ear without the phone.

"Hi! Yes, thanks so much for calling me back on a weekend. Uh-huh. Uh-huh." She listened for a long time, then spun back with a whirl and locked excited eyes with him. Looking the complete opposite of the business tiger he'd just witnessed, she bounced up and down on the balls of her high-heeled feet. "Okay, great. Thank you. That's such wonderful news. Email me the paperwork, I'll discuss it with my client, and then I'll see if we have a deal."

When she tapped off the phone she looked ready to burst.

"What was that all about?" he asked.

"I"—she took a deep breath and looked incredibly pleased with herself—"am setting up a craft convention for Bobbie, to bring her fans and followers together. That was the real estate company that owns the Hemmertex building. They are willing to rent it to Bobbie next winter."

"So . . . did Bobbie ask you to do this?" He knew her answer before she gave it.

"Not exactly. But! The option will be there if she wants it—and she will once I sell it to her. She wants to do more with her business since her store failed, and I know she wants to support Gleann. So I had this idea about turning Gleann into a destination convention area for small groups. You know, opening the valley up to a new kind of tourism. We could start with Bobbie's craft convention, really give it a fantastic kickoff."

He blinked slowly, shocked at himself for being so shocked by her initiative. "We?"

"Yeah. Maybe we could convince the Hemmertex landowners to convert the building into something that could host events all year-round. It would bring businesses back to the downtown. Open up more B&Bs and inns, maybe some motels out on Route 6. Increase usage of the lake. That kind of thing."

There was an odd sensation in his heart, pride and frustration duking it out. "You're talking like you'd handle it all. You called Bobbie your client before she even knows what you're doing." He opened his arms. "You live here. In New York. You have a job that can't even leave you alone on a Sunday. Remember?"

The shine of her excitement faded, but just a tinge. "Of course I do. But this is the sort of push that Gleann needs, only they didn't know they needed it. Bobbie will be ecstatic. Hell, I bet even Sue might crack a smile over the potential."

Of course, Leith thought. Set off a bomb and then walk away while the shrapnel rained down. Jen was really, really good at that.

Except that he felt in his heart that she was right. This could be a wonderful thing for Gleann, perhaps exactly the spark it needed. Maybe not to set off a bomb, but brilliant fireworks that would umbrella the whole valley and make it come back to life. And that had come from Jen Haverhurst, who didn't even live there.

Still, he was a realist. He had Da to thank for that. "But what if all that doesn't work? What if Bobbie goes through with her thing and it fails, or no other events come? What if—"

She looked honestly perplexed as she laid her hand on his bare forearm, just below where he'd rolled up the sleeve of his button-down shirt. No green plaid this time.

"I never thought you to be the kind of person to worry," she said in a quiet, calm voice that didn't seem like her at all. Then she stepped closer, so deep inside his space she had to lift her chin to look him in the eye. She searched his face for a long moment, and he wondered what she was looking for. She reached up and placed her hand on his cheek, and said something cryptic. "I never thought you to be the kind of person to think about failure."

There was an intuitiveness to her words that crawled down his spine with cold, sticky feet, and he pushed deeper into her touch to try to ignore it. It worked, because it only made him even more aware of her, of where they'd left off last time they'd seen each other, the last time they'd touched.

"I'm not thinking about failure." He bent down as close to her face as possible without taking her mouth. "I'm thinking about getting our date started."

A slow, rewarding smile. "Good. Is this place okay?"

"Perfect." He looked nowhere but in her eyes. "I have one condition, though. A challenge, actually."

"Oh?"

With a long look down at the unusually small purse she had draped over her shoulder, he said, "I see you're not shackled to your laptop today, which is good, but I want no phone. For two hours. No phone; just me."

That little wrinkle appeared alongside her nose and her eyes danced. He could practically see her thoughts driving back and forth across her brain, and he was pretty sure she'd deny him.

"All right," she said. "Deal. But I want to change our date venue, then."

He grew suspicious. "Why?"

She pressed a hand to her fine chest in mock indignation. "You make an ultimatum and then question my agreement? I'm agreeing to the no phone thing, remember?"

No wonder she usually got whatever she wanted. She could be demanding when she needed to be, charming when she had to be, and utterly personable and magnetic . . . well, pretty much all the time.

"Good point." He shrugged. "Like I said, I don't care where we go. As long as it's with you."

She turned to the side and offered him her arm. "So come on then. Let me show you one of my favorite places in New York."

* * *

"You know, a shot and a beer at a corner pub would've been just fine," Leith joked as he held open the hefty wood door to the Amber Lounge and let Jen go in ahead of him.

The door closed behind them, shutting out the warm summer evening and throwing them into the dim, air-conditioned lounge decorated in cream leather, substantial bookcases filled with backlit glassware, and plush carpets done in modern swirls of color.

Jen squinted up at him. "Is that where you would've taken me if the choice had been yours?"

He recognized the question as curiosity, not judgment. "No. But I called you on a whim, so I hadn't really given it much thought." He would now, though.

The gorgeous hostess came up to them from where she'd been straightening chairs by the low tables nearest the shuttered windows. She wore a not-so-gorgeous expression. "Two?" she asked in a bored voice, heaving out an encyclopedia-sized menu from the side of the hostess stand.

"Yes," Jen replied. "And could you tell Shea that Jen Haverhurst is here?"

The hostess nodded, then led them to a pair of deep, cream-colored leather chairs set facing a short table with a stone top. Leith sank into the chair that seemed to have been made for his size. Jen perched on the edge of hers, legs crossed at the ankle, perfect posture.

He let his eyes drift around the intimate lounge. Though he was an outdoor guy by inclination, he was trained in a visual art and could appreciate the fine design that straddled the line between modern and masculine, posh and welcoming. The elegantly painted sign out front had said the place had just opened ten minutes ago, so there were only two other patrons: guys in suits, one still wearing his plastic convention badge. They sat on the tall, cushioned chairs at the back bar, talking loudly.

"Is this place okay?" Jen asked.

Leith looked back at her and adopted an exaggerated Southern accent. "Yep. I think the country boy will do just fine in this here fancy place." As she laughed, he opened the tome of a menu and glanced at the side tabs dividing the pages. "Whis-key, eh?"

"You like?"

There must have been a thousand drinks listed, all liquids in various shades of brown or gold, and his mouth salivated as he ran his eyes over the exuberant descriptions.

"How are you, Jen?"

Leith looked up from the menu to see a tall, whisper-thin woman with white-blond hair pulled back in a severe ponytail extending her hand toward Jen. Jen came to her feet and firmly shook the woman's hand.

"Shea, great to see you. I want you to meet a friend of mine. Leith MacDougall, this is Shea Montgomery, whiskey expert and owner of the Amber."

Impressed, Leith rose and took Shea's hand, her grip strong, her eye contact no-nonsense. "Never met an expert before."

Shea gave him a deep, professional nod then turned to Jen. "Great launch at the Juniper Imports event last spring. I was very impressed with what you did for them. What can I do for you tonight?"

Jen kept her smile restrained, but Leith noticed by the gleam of her eyes how deeply the compliment had affected her. "Wellllll," Jen said, "the first thing you can do is help my Scottish friend here find a whiskey or two to his liking, and then I'm here to call in a favor."

One corner of Shea's mouth stretched for her ear. "Of course. Single malt?" She leaned over to flip through the menu to a specific page he guessed she could find in her sleep. Shea dragged her finger down listings labeled Speyside, spouting a few facts and brief tasting notes about certain ones. They all sounded fantastic, but they were all jumbling in his head.

At last he held up a gentle hand. "I think you're mistak-ing me for a half Scot who knows what the hell he likes to drink. My old man drank Famous Grouse every evening. I'm pretty sure anything you want to give me will be better than I'm used to."

Shea straightened, and he was having the hardest time read-ing her expression. One moment it looked like relief, another it looked like skepticism. Odd.

"Get him something excellent," Jen told Shea. "Something special. And bring me one of the same."

"Carte blanche. I like it," Shea said. "Do you have time to talk now? I have a private tasting for some conventioneers and I still need to get the back room set up."

Jen steered Shea toward the hostess stand. Someone turned on music, and a slow, sexy beat drifted from unseen speakers. Leith sat back and watched the two women speak, their words swallowed by the music. After only a few minutes, Shea headed behind the bar to bend over and reach into hidden cupboards. The obnoxious jerks at the bar blatantly checked out her ass and nudged each other, making not-so-quiet comments about what they saw.

Jen returned to his little table in their isolated corner. Only this time, she didn't sit professionally on the cushion edge. She collapsed into the chair, arms draped over the sides, a giant grin lighting her face.

"What was that about?" he asked.

"You've never heard of this place?" When he shook his head, she went on. "Shea's one of the most well-known experts on Scotch whiskey in the world. Turn on any TV special about whiskey, and she'll have been interviewed. She's on a first-name basis with pretty much every distiller in Scotland. She probably has the big liquor conglomerates on speed-dial."

"Or the other way around." Leith watched Shea open a bottle with very little of the good stuff left. "Wow. And she owed you a favor?"

"She wasn't my client at the Juniper Imports showcase, but I pretty much saved her ass that night when none of her booth arrived. Now she's going to do my whiskey tent at the Highland Games."

"The . . . *Gleann's* Highland Games?"

Jen leaned back, looking wonderfully sure of herself. As well she should be.

"Fuck, Jen. That's incredible. What a draw."

"I know. I'm starting heavy promo tomorrow all over the valley. Gleann isn't going to compete with the bigger, more commercial games across New Hampshire. So I'm going smaller and more intimate, but with elevated experiences. I thought of it when I saw your dad's scrapbooks, how whiskey was so prevalent in the old games. Big, local tents. Huge bottles as prizes to the competitors."

He loved how she glowed just then, knowing she'd done well. But even as he grinned in pride, he shook his head because he wasn't sure where anything else in her life fit in. Now or ever. "Even on a date, you can't not work."

"Hey, you're the one who said no phone. I wanted to bring you here, and I wanted to talk to Shea. Two birds, one stone."

"I did say that." The wonderful woman would always be working, always aiming for something. Leith gripped the armrests, fingers digging into the soft leather. "I wish I could be there," he said to himself, but of course she heard.

She leaned her elbows on her knees, her focus switched solely to him. Her tone turned soft and serious. "Why won't you be there, Leith? For real. Don't give me the work excuse. That might work on the rest of Gleann, but not me. Not anymore."

Shea, bless her, returned holding two spectacularly heavy-footed tumblers with a finger of shimmering brown whiskey in each. She set them down on the stone table with a musical *chink*. He reached for his without pause, lifted it to his nose.

"Thanks," Leith told Shea. "I hear you'll be in Gleann next week. It's my hometown. But I should warn you that no one there knows anything about whiskey."

Shea smiled in a way he could now classify as genuine, and he wondered what test of hers he'd passed. "Great to know there'll be a familiar face. Doesn't matter if no one knows whiskey. Nine times out of ten those people are more fun to talk to than the people who *think* they know a lot. I love teaching. And I do love to talk." Someone out of sight caught her eye and she acknowledged them. "I'll see you next week then. Enjoy the whiskey."

"Nice deflection," Jen said to him after Shea had gone. He'd known she'd been watching him the whole time. "You didn't answer my question."

He took his first sip, passing the lovely liquid over his tongue to bite on it with his back teeth. Heaven in a glass.

"Why are you helping Gleann?" he gently fired back. "For real? I asked you once before, in the barn. You want to talk about deflection?"

As she lifted her glass to her lips, she never removed her eyes from his.

"I mean," he said, because he knew she was buying time and he wanted to get in all that he could, "I've only seen how you live here in the city for about an hour now, and I can tell you get energy from it. You carry that to Gleann, yeah, but a little, non-paying gig like our games shouldn't mean anything to you. Not after you left."

Glass still in front of her mouth, she lifted one finger from its curved surface and pointed at him. "But they mean something to you."

She knew him. Only one other person knew him better, and he was gone. Leith stared into his swirl of whiskey. "Of course they do. They're some of my best memories." He lifted his eyes to trap her gaze. "Along with you."

She didn't respond with words—and he didn't expect her to. There it was, that hot, intense shock widening her eyes and making her mouth go soft. Then she looked toward the bar where the two suits had now become five and the noise had increased exponentially. Setting her glass on the armrest of her chair, she said, "It's my best memory, too."

"The games? Didn't you used to think they were a little hokey—"

"No." Her finger made a slow circle around the rim of the glass. "Not the games. I meant Gleann. I'm doing this for Gleann because that place means everything to me. I'm not sure if I realized the depth of that until I went back."

She started to play with her hair, plucking at the back pieces and rearranging it around her face and ear. Her glance at him—*holy shit*—was fleeting and wet, like she was holding back tears. Never had he seen her that way.

"Did you ever wonder why I was in Gleann every summer?"

That confused him. "No. Should I have? Bev just always said her nieces were coming and left it at that." He leaned forward, placing his glass on the table. "You never let on there was any reason more."

Her voice drifted distant. "I was really good at that, wasn't I?"

She had been. She really had been . . . up until the day she'd come back and he'd finally been grown-up enough to notice there was something more. "Jen, whatever you want to tell me, whatever you feel like you have to say, I'll listen. You know that."

The impending tears disappeared, just like that. She sat up, her posture rigid. She took a deep breath. "Going to New Hampshire every year wasn't my choice. At least, not at first. Aunt Bev brought us there, insisted on it and paid for it. Anything to get us out of Iowa. She couldn't stand the thought of us growing up in her sister's home with my mom's asshole boyfriend any more than we could stand to be there."

Leith's stomach dropped. The whiskey in his hand was easily the most expensive he'd ever had, and the thought of tipping it down his throat made him nauseous.

"Did he . . ." Oh God, he couldn't get it out. "Did he . . . do something to you? To Aimee?"

She laughed, loud and short and harsh. "No. He didn't do anything to us. Neither did my mom. And that was the thing. They didn't do anything, period. They sat on their asses, with a bottle in one hand and the other held out for a government check. They'd follow me around the house, drunk, calling me names and screaming that I thought I was God's gift. They called me ugly and nerdy and so many other names I've blocked out." Jen took a pretty big gulp of her drink and didn't even wince. "But no, there wasn't any sort of physical abuse, nothing Bev ever reported to the police or called social services about. I think she was scared we'd be put somewhere where she really couldn't help us."

He sat perfectly still, only partly aware that more people had started filing into the lounge, scared that if he moved a muscle Jen would realize she was telling him her secrets.

She finished her whiskey and frowned into the empty glass. "I've always believed in helping others out if I had the means to do it. I don't know, that part has always been in me, even when I was really young. But my mom . . . my mom made every excuse in the book. She sat around, waiting for handouts and hating the fact that I wanted to do more with my life. Hating that I wasn't like her. There was no pride, only jealousy, and the fact I was making her look bad, calling out her own faults. So she tried to call out mine even louder."

So it wasn't the boyfriend so much as the mom. No wonder Jen had never spoken of her.

"Or she just made them up," he offered.

"The sad part was, I didn't understand how bad it was until Bev brought us here that first summer. From that year on—I was, what, eight?—I realized the toxic world my mom had created in that house. And I vowed to do everything in my power to get the hell away from her. To not be her in any way. To be her complete opposite. Aunt Bev helped me. She saw what I was doing and felt responsible for me. Then I felt responsible for Aimee."

"That's why you took all those jobs every year," he said, piecing it together. "But not Aimee. She was pretty crazy when she was here."

Jen nodded sadly. "She didn't want to come. While I was saving every penny for college, I knew Aimee was going to end up like Mom. I tried to change that, but she never listened."

"Bullshit."

That got a big response, a nice emotional glare. Good.

"Excuse me?" she said.

"Aimee would've stayed in Iowa if it weren't for you, for your example."

"But she ran away and got pregnant."

"And now she has Ainsley. Who is amazing."

Jen blinked at him. Once. Twice. "She really is, isn't she?"

He let all that soak in. Jen was the kind of person who needed tangible proof for everything, but she was missing the biggest evidence right in front of her. That Aimee had an incredible daughter and had inherited a business that might go under through absolutely no fault of her own.

"Do you see," Jen asked, "why I'm such a control freak about her? It's killing me she won't talk to me about Owen."

"Because she and Owen have it under control. And she wouldn't have that kind of control if it weren't for all that crap you and she went through. Didn't we go through this in the park?"

At great length Jen nodded, but he wasn't convinced it was in agreement. She let out a long breath, like she'd heaved something invisible off her back and now had full range of and control over her diaphragm again. "So," she said in a hollow tone. "Yeah. Now you know that Gleann was pretty much the only good thing in my life for a really long time. And you . . . you were a huge part of that."

The old anger and frustration he'd once felt toward her seemed like it had happened to someone else. Those particular emotions were no longer hammering against his heart and mind, but her words, combined with the recollection of their last incredible summer, sliced open an old wound.

He had to ask. "If it was so wonderful, if Gleann changed you and healed you, and then we found something really powerful together, why did you leave? Why didn't you consider going to school here?"

She closed her eyes, and he couldn't recall a time she'd ever done that.

"We have to talk about it," he said, when she still didn't say anything. "We've been dancing around it for days now. I mean, I know we never made any promises to each other, but can you finally tell me why you left?"

When she opened her eyes, they were dry but sad. "It was only ever about college. About creating my own future. Somewhere *else*. But then you came along and, you're right, we found something together. It scared me so much, that I was even considering staying. But the thought of picking my place in the world before I ever got to see the whole thing, before I ever knew what I could become . . . The thought of staying in—"

"A small town."

She swallowed. "Yes. I suppose that was part of it. Gleann's so different from where I came from in Iowa, but it was still sheltered. The whole idea was to *not* become my mom, and to do that I had to go bigger. I had to move up and away."

He stretched his arms over the back of the chair, pressed his head into the cushion, and stared up at the ceiling beams. "I wish you'd told me that back then. I wish you would've just said, 'Leith, I have a shitty mom and a shitty home and I have to get as far away from that as possible.'"

"But it was still too close to me then. I didn't want anyone in Gleann to find out. The whole point was to pretend I was someone else and then literally become another person. Someone stronger."

He pulled his head off the cushion. "You are stronger. I can see it. So can everyone else."

And he hated himself for being selfish, for wanting her to stay with him all those years ago when she otherwise would have missed the opportunity to become this incredible, giving, talented person. To evolve.

I really did love you, he wanted to tell her. *And I can see myself doing it all over again.*

"I really did love you."

The words cut through the growing noise in the lounge. It took several shakes of his head for him to realize that it was Jen who'd said them. It was Jen who had somehow heard his thoughts and repeated them back, simply because he'd wanted her to.

She was smiling and moving to the very edge of her chair cushion. Knees pressed together, legs angled to the side, she leaned over the table, closer to him. There was such aching beauty to her. It made every place she was in feel smaller, with her perpetually in the center.

"In my young, inexperienced way," she said, extremely matter-of-factly, "I loved you. You probably don't want to hear that now, do you? You didn't want to hear it back then, and I didn't blame you."

His turn to scoot to the edge of the chair, only his legs bracketed the small table as he pressed his elbows to his thighs and leaned in. Their whiskey glasses now stared up at them from where they touched on the table. Hers was empty; his was not.

"I do want to hear it," he said. "Thank you." He was very glad she didn't say *you're welcome*. That politeness might have undone him. There was a sharp-edged need for her corkscrewing its way through his body. Hearing those two courteous words, on top of knowing what she'd gone through and that her feelings for him had once been real, and layered over what had nearly happened the other night . . . he was like a grenade, all primed and ready to go and just waiting for someone to pull out his pin. Waiting for her.

It was more than desire, more than sex. He had to make that clear to her, because he didn't think he could be with her naked if there wasn't going to be more when they were clothed. She needed to know how he felt and what he wanted. And what he wanted exactly, he just now realized.

"After you left," he said, touching his fingertips together, "I had a string of really awful relationships, most never longer than a few months." Carefully he watched her face, the way her jaw tightened and her eyelashes twitched in a barely discernible blink. "At the time I didn't realize what I was doing, but I'm pretty sure I was purposely choosing the wrong girls. Deep down I knew that those things would never last, because none of them would ever compare to you."

The last time he'd said something similar, Jen had sprinted in the opposite direction. But that corkscrew was turning tighter and tighter, and the pressure inside him was ready to burst. He had to get this all out, had to ease the weight bearing down on him.

Her shoulders dropped, the deep V-neck of her dress tightening across her chest, making him hard. He ignored it. He needed more than that. He needed her.

"Now that I've seen you again, now that I know our chemistry wasn't faked, I know we can be good together again, Jen. Hell, we could be fucking fantastic. I'm pretty sure, all those years ago when I was picking the wrong women, my mind was holding out hope that you'd come back. It knew something I didn't. Go figure."

"Leith—"

He didn't want to hear any protests, didn't want her going through any of those lists she loved so much in her mind. Not yet. "Just hear me out, okay?" She nodded, and he began to tick off reasons on his fingers. "We can laugh about anything without embarrassment. We respect each other. We know each other's past. We talk incredibly easily. I want to tell you things, Jen. So, so many things. We are both smart and business-minded, and we each have drive and dreams." Honesty ran through his blood and bones and muscles, the most powerful of which was his tongue and lips. He couldn't stop. He didn't want to.

"And look at you"—he waved a hand at her—"you drive me goddamn insane, you're so beautiful. Ah, fuck it, Jen; I'm just going to say it. I want to be with you. I want to try to make it work again. You're in New York. I'll be in Connecticut. I want to try, Jen. I have to try. I have to have you."

And there it was. He'd done it again. He may as well have slit open his chest, carved out his heart, and slapped it on the table between the whiskey glasses.

The longest pause in the world followed, and he had no idea how to fill it. When she slowly rose to her feet, the smooth fabric of her dress pulling snugly around her legs, he had an awful, sickly vision of her leaving again.

Then her eyes turned to green flame, like something magical, and the corners of her delicious mouth ticked up, and he did a mental fist pump.

"I know that look," he murmured, catching her infectious smile and finally allowing himself to feel the pound of blood in his erection. Let himself ride the desire without reins.

"Oh, you do, do you?" The lounge had gotten loud, but somehow he still heard her.

He slid all the way back in the chair and lifted his face to hers. "I do. You're going to kiss me." He glanced down at his lap. "And you're going to come over here to do it."

Chapter

15

*H*is statement pulled Jen toward him with a tender insis-
tence. Her gaze dropped to his lap, where he was sporting
a mighty proud hard-on. "I am?" she asked.

"Yes. You're going to kiss the hell out of me, and I can't
fucking wait."

He wore the barest hint of a smile, but it was full of cocky
assurance. And his eyes . . . oh, man, his eyes. Sparkling circles
the color of their drinks, hard and penetrating, bored into her.
She hated being told what to do, but he knew—he *knew*—that
for him she was putty.

Their gazes connected and held, tightening an invisible
chain between them that not even his giant-ass truck could
drive through. He licked his lips. Flashback to that tongue
working her nipples and trailing down her belly. Flashback to
the shivers he'd drawn on her skin before Olsen had shown up.

A hot burst of desire radiated out from between her legs,
knocking her knees out, making her instantly wet. The delicate
friction of her thong rubbed in such a powerful way that it
seemed impossible to hide, like she was broadcasting her desire
to everyone in the lounge. She let herself peek around. The two

of them were tucked into an intimate corner. No one was watching. No one cared. Except Leith.

He settled deeper into the armchair, pressing his shoulders against the leather and widening his legs.

"Get on," he said with a grin.

"You're so crude."

"No. I'm honest."

She loved that honesty. Always had. As she stepped between his legs, she wanted to lick the knowing look off his face. Placing her hands on his armrests and letting her hair swing forward, just shy of brushing his cheeks, she slid one knee between his hip and the soft leather. Without breaking their mutual stare, his hand dropped off the armrest and his fingers curled around the back of her leg. The jersey of her favorite dress, the one that fit her just right, bunched in his palm. There was possession in that grip. Possession and need. Pressing one hand on his shoulder, his muscles tense and warm under his shirt, she slid her other knee around his opposite hip.

"Come 'ere," he murmured, but she was already going. Already leaning down, her mouth covering his the same moment her ass dropped and she straddled him. Clung to him with every limb. The whiskey made their kiss spicy, their tongues entwining in slow surges.

This was Leith MacDougall she was kissing. *Leith.* Though the feel of him burned her everywhere, his presence undeniable, she still couldn't believe that he'd been returned to her after how she'd treated him. She couldn't believe that they were together at all. It defied logistics or chance.

This was Leith MacDougall she wanted now more than food or water, and the depth of that need scared her . . . and fueled her.

With a low groan that made his chest vibrate, his hands spread across her back and tugged her closer. She collapsed onto him, arms wrapped around his neck, the weight of her body sinking them deeper into the chair.

Leith. This was *Leith.* How did this happen? *Again?* The wonder of it all made her head so very light.

Then his hands were in her hair, tilting her head so he could kiss her in new ways, with new strokes. He demanded a deeper kiss, and there was absolutely no resistance left in her.

Underneath, his thighs flexed, pushed up against her, shifting her. The wrap of her dress parted over her legs. With a sharp, surprising sensation, he settled her against his hardened cock, the bulge and rigid line of his zipper hitting her right where she wanted him most. This was borderline obsession. If she didn't get him inside her *right fucking now* she'd die.

In the back of her mind she knew they were making out like drunken twenty-year-olds in a public place—a shadowy corner of a dim bar, but a public place nonetheless—but she just didn't care. It was so very unlike her, and it was fantastically, deliriously freeing.

Close by, someone cleared his throat. The sound made her drag her mouth away from Leith's—the sting of her lips and tongue aching with loss—and she looked up to see a group of men assuming the big chairs at the next table over. They weren't looking directly at Jen and Leith, but their eyebrows were raised and they smirked at each other.

Public place. Right.

Embarrassed, Jen pushed off Leith and scrambled to her feet. He was looking up at her with a deeply furrowed brow, like her absence pained him. Like he didn't know what to do with what raged inside him. His fingers dug into the armrests.

He was still the Leith she'd known since she was a kid, but the emotions shooting through her and driving her body to such extreme need were anything but childish.

The other night, back in Gleann, they'd been physically attached to the past: shooting darts in the pub they used to work in, strolling down the streets they'd walked hundreds of times, kicking through the grass of the central park they knew so well. That night, it had been nearly impossible to separate their past selves from all the stuff that had happened to them since. It had created this big jumble of memories and feelings, old images mixing together with the current, and she had had no idea how to parse them out. She had had no idea what to feel or how to react, and for someone who had so carefully planned her life, it had been more than disconcerting.

But here, in New York City, they were Leith and Jen. Two distinct people. Adults. Drowning in desire. She touched his lips, loving how she made them fall open, how she'd made them all wet.

Someone else cleared her throat and Jen turned slightly to see Shea setting their bill in an upright V on the table. The lounge owner didn't look at them as she sauntered away to attend to the new gentlemen customers who grinned giddily up at her.

Leith scooted to the edge of his chair, the creak of the leather giving away his movements. Jen looked down to see his legs encasing hers. Her thighs quivered, her head swam. His hand came up to curve around her waist—a gentle pressure, the slightest of squeezes. The question implicit.

"Yes." She nodded vehemently. "My place."

That almost-pained look returned, deep grooves gouging into his forehead, only this time, he sighed in clear relief. As his chest pumped, he smiled up at her. She felt herself sway and she reached for his steadying shoulder.

"You okay?" he asked. "Something affecting you?"

She should have known the vulnerability wouldn't last. At least his teasing broke the spell enough that she could open the bill and see she owed Shea close to ninety dollars. Leith didn't touch Jen as she waited for the hostess to run her card through. He didn't touch her as they exited the Amber and not as they stood on the curb, hailing a cab.

Only when they'd fallen into the white taxi that smelled faintly of patchouli did he reach across the seat for her. He touched her first on her knee, running his finger over the hem of her dress, nudging it higher with patient little jerks. Then, in one swift movement, he slid his hand under the jersey and up. All the way up.

Jen rolled her head toward him on the cracked vinyl headrest, but he was staring at where his fingers had found the slick, swollen place underneath her dress.

"What are you trying to do to me?" she whispered, attempting to weasel out of the touch, with the cabbie less than two feet away and all. And the fact that they were in the back of an NYC cab.

He held her tight as his eyes flipped up to hers. "Not 'trying' to do anything. I just do." Then his mouth found her ear, his whisper filling her head. "And I'm going to do you."

Maybe not the most romantic thing to say, but she didn't care. Not now. Not when her entire existence had spiraled down to her clit and the emptiness she was dying for him to fill. The dirty, honest words made her eyes shut, and she was a little horrified by the sound of surrender that escaped her throat. So un-Jen-like.

There were four other people in the elevator on the ride up to the twenty-first floor of her building in the Village. Leith wedged himself into the back corner and pulled Jen into him. His huge forearms wrapped around her shoulders, cradling her gently. It was strangely intimate, there in a metal box being shot into the sky. Her head fit perfectly against the firmness of his chest. The top, inward curve of her ass pressed against the erection that hadn't died, just felt even more imposing, if that was possible. The need to kiss him made her shake from withdrawal. Could this elevator go any slower?

The other people got off on the twelfth and twentieth floors. The second the last person stepped off, the intimate embrace ended. Leith flipped Jen around to get at her mouth, but she'd already tilted her face up and was going in. They kissed like they hadn't kissed in ten years, sloppy and hard. They were still kissing as he walked her backward out of the elevator on the twenty-first floor. She lost her bearings, and when she hit the wall opposite the elevator, the force knocked some of the breath from her lungs.

When she ripped away and he began to lick up her neck, she found the ability to say, "We're not doing this in the hallway."

"No." He raised his head to show her that wicked grin. "We're doing it in your apartment. Which one is it?"

She fumbled for her keys and stumbled on legs drunk more on lust than whiskey down to the end of the hall. It took three tries to get the key into the two locks because Leith was covering her from behind, one hand skimming over her chest, the other painting a light line up and down the front of her thigh.

At last she got the door open and they fell inside, tripping over each other's feet. He was trying to direct her deeper inside, but this was her place and she knew where she liked to have sex. She got him swung around, turning the tables, and pinned him between the small table where she usually dumped her keys and the beach prints she'd bought in Cabo San Lucas. His lips curved up in what she guessed to be surprise and amusement—and something else she couldn't quite name . . . a dare, maybe?—and then he buried his hands in the hair behind her ears and pulled her into him. She was practically climbing him already, so when he grabbed her legs and hoisted her body higher onto his, she felt like she was flying.

He peeled away from the entrance and lumbered into the living room at a speed that spelled disaster. He didn't know the layout of her apartment, couldn't see where the furniture was in the dark.

"Watch out for the—" she began. Too late.

He hit the low couch that was set near the floor-to-ceiling windows, lost his balance, and dropped her onto the firm black leather. As she bounced, he tripped and fell on top of her. Not the most graceful of entrances into sex.

"Thanks for the warning." He was laughing, but his hand found her face, searching.

He must have mistaken her squirming for discomfort, because he tried to shift his weight off her, but she wrapped one leg and one arm around him. "Don't go anywhere."

"Don't worry. I'm not." He hooked his hands under her arms and pushed her farther up the couch, moving her as easily as a pillow. Pausing, testing the leather with his palms, he frowned at the long, low couch with no sides or back. "What is this thing?"

"I have no idea. A really big ottoman? Leith, I don't care."

He pushed up on his elbows and angled his head so he could look at the thing under the city lights streaming in. "No sides. Close to the floor. I could get you in just about any position on this thing. And you, me. Jesus, Jen, it's a sex couch, is what it is."

She laughed. "It is not!"

He fell back on top of her, sweeping his tongue into her mouth and setting her on fire. "It is now."

"We've got all night to use it."

At that, he rose above her, huge and glorious in the city glow, his hair mussed. He didn't reach for her, just touched her with that eleven-ton stare.

"Yes," he said. "We do."

A few long, agonizing seconds later, he reached down and toyed with the hem of her dress, flipping back the flap to expose her parted thighs. He fingered the outer tie of the dress and set it free with a tug, then he released the inner clasp that held the whole thing together. With a gentle sweep, he opened the dress and bared her. She lay there, loving it.

He opened his mouth, took a short breath. Yeah, he wanted to say something, and it was troubling him, because his eyebrows pinched together and the finger running painfully slowly back and forth across the tendon in her upper thigh paused.

She refused to let him stop. She dug in her heels and arched her back, thrusting herself up into his touch. He caught his breath, shook his head as though coming back into himself.

His gaze wandered a path up her body. "God, you're sexy."

All she could think was: *God, I've missed you. I was such a fool to let you go.*

Where had that come from? It wasn't like she'd been sitting here in her apartment, pining for him these ten years and moaning, *If only, if only.* Except . . . she'd missed him. There'd been a hole in her life where he belonged, and she'd been stepping over and around it for so long that she'd completely forgotten how that negative space affected her life.

She needed to be naked. With him. She hooked thumbs under the straps of her thong and started to push it down, but his big hands clamped over hers, slowly plucking her fingers off.

"I'm going as fast as I want to," he murmured.

"But—"

She struggled, but even in his light grasp, she couldn't move her hands from the couch.

"Stop thinking," he said. "Stop trying to direct. Just . . . let me. Please."

Those were the last of his words. He dragged her underwear down her legs with one stroke, and then he was staring down at her spread legs with an open mouth and the return of that grave, passionate expression. He pulled off her high heels without looking away from the place she could feel getting more and more slippery by the second.

Quick as a flash, he shimmied backward off the couch to kneel at its edge, simultaneously dragging her with him. He pushed her legs apart. The angle was perfect, the position heavenly. Through her legs, he gave her the king of wicked looks, and they shared an unspoken moment. He licked his lips.

Long ago, they'd taken each other's virginity, green and

fumbling but still exciting. Many men had gone down on her
since then, and without a doubt Leith had done it to other
women, but it was new to the two of them and there were simply
no words to describe this excitement, heightened by maturity
and history and the blaze of emotions that roared through her.

He bent his head, his eyes the very last thing to turn down.
And then his mouth was on her. A wet, open kiss that sucked
in her clit and swirled it with his tongue at the same time. She
bowed off the couch, just her shoulders and heels digging into
the black leather. Her loud, surprised, fantastically aroused
shout filled her apartment and bounced from wall to wall.

Good Lord, the man knew how to use his mouth for something other than just grinning and flirting. His arms slid under
and around her thighs, his fingers digging into their upper
crease. He clasped her to him, held her in place, and *feasted*.
In between the sparkly bits of pleasure he fed her, she could
sense his greed and also how he restrained himself. The sounds
he was making, those tiny groans in the back of his throat—
fuck—they were the most erotic thing she'd ever heard.

And *she* was doing that to him.

He pulled everything from her. The orgasm was coming
fast, faster than she'd ever experienced, and she didn't know
why it was scaring her so much, why it was making her panic.
But she was shaking already, and he hadn't even made her
come yet.

"You . . . can . . . stop," she stuttered, frantically grabbing
for his head. Handy, that hair now.

He shook his head, refusing, and the motion had his lips
and tongue hitting all sorts of new spots, striking new chords.

He put two fingers inside her. Just slid them in, no resistance,
all soft and surrounding and beyond sensitized. Absolutely
ready. She'd never been so aware of herself before, and yet
completely out of her own head. Usually she went into things
like this with scenarios and fantasies at the ready, just in case
things didn't go like she wanted. Just in case she needed a little
mental push.

Stop thinking, he'd told her. And because he was doing such
an amazing job of convincing her, she did.

Suddenly he hit the perfect spot deep inside. A secret, mag-
nificent, hidden place that she suspected all her other partners

had never reached because she'd been so intent on steering them to her clit. Involuntarily, her legs clenched around his neck. He breathed harshly through his nose. The pressure from his fingers and tongue increased, turning much harder than she ever thought she'd like. But she did.

She loved it.

Tremors catapulted through her. There was no stopping them, no barricades they couldn't break through. All sorts of nerves and wirings and emotions were strung up to where his tongue circled and his lips sucked and his fingers stroked. She went stupid in the head and limp of body. Even when her orgasm finally crested, shaking her entire body like a leaf, pushing high, short gasps and cries up and out of her lungs, he never let up. Not until her body had calmed and her legs released his neck.

He lifted his head. Smiling, he breathed almost as hard as she did. "See?" He touched his shiny lips. "A sex couch."

She came up on her weak elbows, then reached out to tousle a wave of hair that had flopped over his forehead.

He gazed back at her quizzically, the pattern of city lights making him look exceptionally mysterious and sexy. "You actually wanted me to stop? Before you came?"

She didn't respond, because he already knew what she would say.

"Scared of not being in control?" The question wasn't accusatory or frustrated.

He pulled her up to sit. Sliding his arms under the dress that still dangled from her shoulders, he held her like a fragile thing.

"It's okay," he whispered into her neck. "I get you."

The strangest sensation filled her head, and she realized too late it was impending tears. She tried to turn her head away but he caught her mouth with his, and the feeling of being vanquished died with his taste and trust and understanding.

When he pulled back, he stared at her in a most incredible way, like she was The Answer. His massive erection grazed her inner thigh. She could definitely take care of that. Slowly, she peeled off the rest of the dress and then unhooked her bra. Naked, her chest rose and fell, but he looked only at her face.

"Protection?" he asked.

She nodded. "Condoms. In the drawer by the bed."

She started to rise, meaning to head for the darkened

bedroom, but he rocked to his feet with ridiculous power and told her, "I'll get them."

Them?

With a half smile and a jerk of his head toward the jagged city vista, he added, "When I come back, I'd really like to see you standing against that window."

As he turned for her bedroom, he unbuttoned and stripped off his shirt, the muscles in his back doing acrobatics underneath his skin. The *V* created by his wide shoulders and waist made her legs quiver all over again.

And because he'd proved to her that control wasn't always necessary for pleasure, she went over and stood by the window.

Chapter

16

*N*aked from the waist up, his jeans already unzipped, Leith hurried back to the living room from the bedroom, box of condoms in hand. One thought alone played on exuberant repeat in his mind: *I'm about to have sex with Jen Haverhurst.*

When he came out of the hall, he thought he knew what to expect. After all, he'd been the one to tell Jen he wanted her up against the window. But the truth was, no amount of preparation or fantasizing could have set him up well enough for the actual sight. Jen's curved silhouette cut an erotic shape against the rectangles of the city lights. Her hair swung at her shoulders and she stood with her legs apart, far enough that he could trace the lines of her inner thighs all the way up to the place he most wanted to be. Though he couldn't see her face in the shadows, he knew the moment she saw him, because she raised her arms and flattened her palms against the glass.

"Jesus Christ," he mumbled, hoping Da's ghost would forgive him for such a curse in these circumstances. "Look at you."

He sauntered toward her, forgetting he'd been in a rush only a minute ago. As he got closer, the city lights let him see her wide-eyed, openmouthed expression. The look of expectation and anticipation. Of lust. She breathed deep and even, her nipples rising and falling, the shadows shifting across her chest.

When he finally touched her, it was to take her cheek in his palm. There were too many words to say, so he kissed her. It was a slow, deliberate stroke of his mouth over hers. Her lips were so smooth and soft, and even though they'd kissed countless times in their lives, even though he'd just gone down on her for the very first time and had made her come in a way that still left him happy and dizzy, this kiss felt much, much different.

He inched closer. Close enough that her nipples grazed his bare chest. Just a brush, a tease, but it sent waves of sensation over his skin. God, she was so, so soft. She leaned back against the window, her warm hands sliding around his waist and dipping into the back of his loosened jeans, curving around his ass. Slowly, she pushed his jeans to the floor and the sound of the denim hitting the parquet heightened the kiss. The air-conditioning felt wonderful on his hot skin, but the cotton of his underwear weighed heavy as chain mail. When her fingers slipped beneath the top elastic, he sighed. When she shoved the underwear down to his ankles, he groaned.

With a long swipe of her tongue against his, she released his mouth from the kiss and trailed a slow, hot gaze down his bare body to his erection.

Stepping out of his jeans, he said, "Touch me."

Her lips quirked at the order because she was already halfway there. She wrapped her fingers around his dick—*sweet, sweet girl*—pushed them all the way to the root—*holy fucking God*—and gave an agonizingly slow, gentle pull all the way to the tip—*whatever you do, just keep doing that. Just like that.*

Darkness fell as he shut his eyes and concentrated on the way she stroked him, how she managed to build his need when he hadn't thought it could go any higher. He'd gone willfully blind, every stroke of her hand a torture. Her mouth found his chest, and he could feel her smiling against his skin.

He wasn't smiling, though. Hard, short breaths left his open lips. He had one fist planted on the glass, his forehead grinding into the curl of his fingers. At last he pushed away from the glass and encircled the wrist of her stroking hand. "Enough."

She stopped. He saw the little vibration of her pulse, the live beat dancing in her throat.

"I want in you," he said.

Without words, she slipped the box of condoms from his hand and took one out. Ripped open the packet. She lifted her face to him as if to question what they were about to do, just as she'd done all those years ago in the back of the Caddy. As if this were their first time or something.

It was, actually. It was their first time as the people they were now.

He thought about all she'd revealed to him earlier that evening and kicked himself over how his eighteen-year-old self should have guessed there was more beneath her surface. He cringed at how cock-blind he'd been. How he could have been helping her instead of trying to get in her pants all the time, and then getting pissed off that she left him.

He thought about how he'd done such a bang-up job at convincing himself he was steady and fulfilled these past three years, but how sad and alone he truly felt, thinking himself abandoned by the two people who'd meant the most to him.

He had to stop thinking like that. Like Da had died on purpose. Like Jen had been laughing as she'd gotten on that plane. Neither was true.

Though she stood gorgeously bared before him now, she'd never been as naked to him as she'd been in the lounge, her story on her lips. It made his heart hurt. After all this time, she still had the ability to do that.

She touched him again, bringing him back to the present, and a playful light came to her eyes as she rolled the condom down his cock with an efficiency and care he refused to think about.

As he slid his arms around her rib cage and lifted her up against the glass, an echo of his thought, and her words, in the lounge returned: *I really did love you. And if I'm not careful it'll happen again.*

Her legs folded around his waist, heels on his ass. Her narrow arms wrapped around his neck and he found her mouth again, holding her with shaking thighs in that position.

The tip of his cock nudged against her, and even that part of her felt different and exciting to him. A whole new woman, a whole new experience. She was trying to grind against him, trying to get him inside, but the position restricted her movement.

"Wait," he said against her lips. "Let me."

"Hurry," he thought he heard her say, the word shredded.

He flexed his arms and pushed back slightly, holding her body away from him. Together they looked down as he positioned her over his cock. Just the tip of him went in, a wet, tight pressure covering his most sensitive place. At the same time, their heads snapped up and they looked at one another. This moment was only the beginning of the most powerful physical and emotional connection in existence, and he was already lost.

Bending his legs and leaning her back against the glass, he got better leverage. He pushed in a little more, watched himself slip inside. He refused to let his eyes close. He wasn't missing a millisecond of this. He drank in her gasp as he slid in even further. He watched with awe the dilating of her pupils, the string of staccato, musical moans that punctuated each of his thrusts, until he was fully inside her.

She was everywhere, all around him. Her body surrounded his cock like a beautiful glove, her sounds filled his mind, and her being encased his heart.

"Leith," she said, shuddering, and there was too much to decipher in that word. A plea, a prayer, an expression of disbelief.

At last he got his bearings, found his strength. Muscles clenched, he started to move, a gentle pulse inside her. He wasn't capable of much more. Not in that position. Not with the way his chest felt like it was about to explode. He used the slow, clutching pump as long as possible, until it just simply wasn't enough.

"I want . . . I need more. I need to move faster," he whispered into her hair. "Can I get you back on the couch?"

Wordless, she nodded and his fingers dug into her thighs, pulling her off him to the soundtrack of their mutual groans. He lowered her to the ground, and he was filled with a caveman satisfaction that she wove on her feet, and that her nails clawed into his arms to steady herself.

He kissed the dreamy look on her face and slowly nudged her toward the low couch. She sat on its edge.

"Scoot back," he said. "This time I'm getting on with you."

"And getting on me?"

That unselfconscious giggle of hers sent him over the edge. What edge that was, he wasn't quite sure. All he knew was that she had all her weapons trained on him that night and he was going down, down, down.

"And getting in you." He prowled over her, pressing her body into the black leather. She lay down, arched her back and opened her legs. Jen, splayed out for him. No chance of Olsen showing up this time. This woman was all Leith's.

He wedged his knees between hers, spreading her out, his cock pounding with need between them, dying to get back in where it belonged. As he came down over her, he loved the way she sighed against his weight. He kissed her as he entered her again. He slid into her far too easily, and with so much power it shocked him. Instead of taking her sounds between his lips, he fed her his own—a long, low groan as she took him even deeper inside. A murmured curse as she tilted up her hips and wrapped her legs around him, one of her hands digging into his hair, the other scratching at his ass.

He fucked her with the depth of everything he felt. And yeah, even though his forehead was pressed against hers, their eyes locked in a dizzy haze, this was fucking. Fucking at its finest, its most intense.

Pleasure immediately raced for his groin. All sensation from every available nerve rushed to the center of his body, his world. That feeling built and grew, driving him deeper and harder into Jen. He was losing control, but he wanted this to last a hell of a lot longer than he feared it would. He'd bragged that he wasn't eighteen anymore, and he wanted to be inside her as long as possible, but the feeling of her wrapped around him was making that nearly impossible. Every stroke chiseled away at what he'd always considered to be spectacular control.

His head sagged to her neck as his hips did their thing, steered by the need for her, piloted by the emotions he never expected to feel again.

Her name unintentionally leaked from his mouth. He felt her palm on his neck, touching him with a gentleness that almost hurt. Lifting his head, still plunging into her with long, heavy movements, he watched the flicker of recognizable emotion in her eyes. She was struggling with the same things he was.

Withdrawing from her with a moan, he pushed back to his knees. She was reaching for him, trying to guide him back to where he'd been, but he loved taking her out of her control zone, and instead took her knees in the crooks of his elbows. Hoisting her hips off the couch, he penetrated her at a whole new angle that shot his eyeballs straight to the back of his head.

Then it was her turn to say his name, a million times, one after the other, at the peak of every one of his thrusts. She felt amazing. She *looked* amazing—small underneath him, her arms flung out and clinging to the edges of the couch.

He couldn't hold back any longer. Couldn't temper himself. His body just let go, and his crazy, Jen-addled brain lost what little control it had managed to cling to.

He came, the orgasm spiraling like a cyclone through his body. Everything tightened. Ten years' worth of desire that he hadn't known was building up inside all released at once. It was goddamn heaven. Nothing else to it.

Two minutes later his brain still hadn't come back to reality after being short-circuited. His whole body still tingled. Finally he realized he'd collapsed on top of her and she'd wrapped her limbs around him, the crush of her embrace nothing short of possessive. They stayed that way, entwined, for who knows how long.

"Wow," she whispered. "I loved watching that."

A wave of emotion crashed into him, took him under.

With a regretful wince, he pulled out of her and rolled to the edge of the couch. He tied off the condom and padded to the bathroom to get rid of it. When he came back, she was lying in the exact same position, legs and arms all loose and lovely, only her head had turned and she looked out at her city.

He stretched out naked beside her, the leather sticking to his damp skin, and draped an arm over her belly. She rolled her head back to meet his eyes.

"You didn't come again," he said, unable to keep the disappointment out of his voice. He knew very well what she felt like when she came, how her muscles got all tight inside, and how her whole body set off in a cascading series of quivers from head to toe. "My fault? Too fast?"

She gave a little shrug and ran light fingers across his collarbone. "I've turned into a clit girl. Doesn't mean I didn't love it."

He narrowed his eyes and gave her a doubtful grin. "I don't believe that."

She laughed once, loud and sharp. "Well, believe it. I think I know what I need."

"You didn't used to be like that."

"People change. People's bodies change."

He considered her as he widened his smile. "No, I think that's the control talking. For some reason you turned your mind off to anything else. You *think* you're only a clit girl, therefore you are." When he scraped a nail over her firm nipple, she hissed, her pupils dilating all over again. "I want to try to get that back. Can I? Please? With a little practice, I'm sure I could do it again."

She pushed at his chest in a feeble, adorable attempt to act pissed off. It would have helped if she wasn't smiling. "Oh, really? We haven't been together in ten years and you're an expert on my body?"

His palm made a slow trail down her belly. Her far knee came up, cradling the heel of his hand as it pressed against her pubic bone. He loved this part of her, how it surpassed the softness anywhere else on her body. As he touched her where she was still slippery, she went still.

"I am." He nosed the dark hair from her neck and said into her skin, "Remember that night when I taught you how to come? When I just kept touching you here and you exploded in the back of my da's Cadillac?"

She let out a sound that was part indignant, part disgust, and a whole lot of remembered ecstasy. "You did not teach me that."

"Sure I did."

"I was doing just fine on my own, thanks."

"Exactly. It was just a solo effort. But it's better when someone else does it for you, isn't it?"

"It is." She swallowed, and he licked up her moving throat. "And you've gotten even better at it."

"Well, I've learned a few new tricks."

She edged away, and he removed his hand from between her legs.

"I don't know how I feel hearing that," she said.

He shrugged and took to lightly rubbing her arm. "Sure you do. It's probably the exact same way I feel. Let me see if I get it right: You and I were each other's first sex all those years ago, and it was cool and exciting, but in that awkward teenage way. We got a little better at it and we thought it was the bomb. All that intense exploration that opened up a whole new world. Then we weren't together anymore and we slept with other people"—she winced—"and we learned what we like and how to please another person. Jen, I don't like knowing you've been with others either, but guess what, neither of us can change that. I can't get pissed about what's happened before this, not when it was never something I could control." Then he kissed her soundly and grinned. "I can only enjoy the benefits of a fine education."

She looked a little stunned at that, considering, then she nodded in the way that reminded him of when her spreadsheets all balanced up and her crazy world suddenly made sense.

"So." He ran a hand through his hair as silence settled between them. "You never answered me back in the bar. You just jumped me. It was so embarrassing."

She looked at him like she honestly had no idea what question he was talking about. It made his throat dry up, and not in a good way. No turning back now, though. "Are we going to try this again?" he asked. "You and me?"

The gentle movement of her hand on his chest paused. She rose up on one elbow so they were eye to eye. She looked terribly worried, like she'd already made up her mind to leave him here and now. Like it was ten years ago and they were on another picnic blanket. Then she kissed him, close-lipped but sweet and long. That hadn't happened a decade ago, and it sent his mind spinning toward hope.

"How?" she asked when she pulled away, and she looked genuinely confused. "How could we make that work?"

Tucking a piece of hair behind her ear, he replied, "We try."

"All right, then," she said seriously, and something sharp and sweet struck him in the heart. "We try."

Chapter

17

"*S*peaking of not answering questions, you *still* haven't answered mine from last night." Jen slid into the nook between the counter and the window overlooking Bleecker Street, marveling over the fact that Leith MacDougall was sitting at her tiny kitchen table, devouring a bowl of Frosted Mini-Wheats.

An impish look preceded his smart-ass comment. "Which question again? Was it: 'Do you like that?' or 'More?' Because the answer is 'yes.' To both."

Though she acknowledged him with a smile, she clutched her coffee mug in both hands and tried to look as earnest as possible. "No, the one about why you aren't staying in Gleann for the games. Or competing. The *real* reason. I know part of it, but I think there's more. And I'm here to listen, if you want."

He set down the cereal spoon so carefully it didn't make a ripple in the milk. "You do know part of it. Because I showed it to you."

She wanted to touch him but he'd gone shuttered, and he leaned so far back in his chair she couldn't easily reach him. "Your dad. The house. You haven't dealt with losing him yet, and going to the games, which was such a huge part of growing up—for both of you—would be too painful a reminder."

He coughed. "Put like that, it seems so easy to fix." The sun coming through the window turned his eyes the color of the whiskey they'd drunk last night.

"It's not. I know it isn't. But it's something you have to do on your own. No one can make you get over losing the most important person in your life." He nodded slowly, and she leaned over her mug. "But I can make you talk about the other reason you're not competing."

Narrowed, challenging eyes focused on her. The corners of his mouth drooped. "And what would that be?"

She'd thought about this for several days, ever since Olsen had told her about Leith's final games. "You won the all-around three years in a row, coming on the heels of the best high school football season the valley had ever known and two state track championships. You've never not won anything your whole life. You said it yourself the other night at the Stone, that you'd never really been given a challenge. But then you didn't win those final games, and then you stopped throwing."

She'd never seen him so still. He looked into his bowl. "That was the last time Da saw me throw."

"And I bet he loved it. I bet he cheered you the whole time. Didn't you see that photo he had hung in your old room? Those last games where he looked proudest of all?"

Leith squeezed his eyes shut.

"You didn't fail him," she said. "You didn't fail, period. Not winning doesn't mean failing."

Those whiskey eyes flew open. "Who said I thought that?"

"No one. No one had to. I know you, Mr. All-Star. I also know how Gleann worships you." He winced. "I know it bothers you, but now I know it's deeper than that. That it pressures you to not let them down. But since no one else will say it, it's fallen on me to tell you that no one except you expects you to win everything."

He opened his mouth and she sensed his protest. She held up a gentle hand.

"You think people love you because of the feats you've accomplished, but that's just stupid. I'm sorry, but it is. They love you because you're Leith, you're impossible not to love, and you're theirs. Do you think that if you go out on that field and throw shitty, Gleann will, I don't know, erase you from memory or take down the caber monument and that billboard—"

"I *want* them to take those things down."

"What I'm saying is, that because they are still up there, you feel responsible to uphold them, to keep them true. And because your dad taught you to throw, you think a bad day out will somehow sully his memory. Once upon a time you threw because you loved it."

With a great inhale, his chest expanded. "You're wrong. I'm fine with losing."

See? she wanted to say. *It's either "losing" or "winning" with you. No in-between.*

"Then prove it." She pushed her mug away. "Throw in the games next weekend. One last time before you leave for good."

He spread his palms over the table. "Can't. I'll be transporting a lot of big equipment down here and finally meeting with Hal Carriage to get his approval on his yard plans. It's a big weekend for me. A lot rides on it."

It was a good reason, one she could definitely relate to, and she nodded, her stomach suddenly pinching in hunger.

"Trying to fix me, too, Jen?" Suddenly he was smiling again, wiping away all that she'd just said. Just like he'd done with his father's house: ignoring it, pushing it to the side.

She wadded up a napkin and threw it at him. He snatched it out of the air and tossed it back onto the table.

"I'm not afraid of failure." He stood, taking her hand and drawing her to her feet and into his arms. Framing her face, he kissed her, and she couldn't deny that he tasted like the warm sunshine filling her apartment.

"What I am afraid of," he murmured during a break in the slow kiss, "is not seeing you naked again until after the games."

So she fixed that and, two hours later, they left her apartment separately.

*J*en had her hand on the gate latch, about to head up the flagstone path into the Thistle, when her phone chirped with a text message.

Back in Gleann tomorrow. Can't wait to see u.

Like a schoolgirl, she read Leith's words over and over again, hearing them in his voice. The drive back up north from the city had flown by, her little rental zooming over the highways on a warp speed that seemed fed by this crazy new energy zipping through her system.

Leith had returned to Connecticut to make sure his project was moving forward and to check out more locations for a permanent move of his business. It was an aspect of him she'd never witnessed before, this businessman who clearly knew what he was doing and whose love for the work transcended that knowledge. It made her exceedingly proud, and it endeared him to her even more.

Ugh, listen to her. Forget the flowery language. It made him hot as all hell.

For the second time, a very calm, very rational voice asked, *How on earth do you expect to make this work with your jobs, your lives in different states, your separate lifestyles?*

The first time it had happened was when they'd been lying naked, when he'd asked again if she wanted to try a relationship. Her immediate thought? *Yes. Hell yes.* The thought that came quickly afterward, however . . . So he moves to Connecticut. Still an hour by train, more with traffic if he drives in. She doesn't own a car. She works insane hours, often at night, plenty on the weekends, nothing that would fit neatly into a train schedule. He works weekends during every season but winter. When could they possibly see each other? Would phone calls and occasional visits work? Could that ever be enough?

And then there was the possibility of her partnership within Bauer Events. The very real chance she could be sent to London. More distance, more time away.

Yet she and Leith were adults, not kids with a world of unknown spread out at their feet. They were more grounded now, more passionate and reasonable. Maybe it would work. So she'd agreed to *try*, and told him so, and prayed that it would be enough.

The Thistle's front door opened and Ainsley bounced out, wearing a two-piece bathing suit covered in sequins over her flat chest. Denim shorts just barely covered her bottom and her flip-flops had even more sparkles on them. A beach towel swung over her shoulders.

"Hey, Aunt Jen."

"And where are you going, Sparkly McGee?"

"T and Lacey are working at the pool and I wanted to go say hi."

The local pool was still open? Ten years ago it had been nothing more than a concrete hole in the ground, and Jen doubted it had changed much in her absence. She pictured T and Lacey snapping gum behind the stainless steel counter of the snack stand.

It worried her that Ainsley was going to go see Owen and Melissa's girls when it sounded like she'd invited herself. It worried her that her niece was attaching herself to older girls whose connection to her could very well snap at any moment.

Jen tousled a wave of Ainsley's dark blond hair. "What happened to Bryan and his slingshot?"

Ainsley made a thoroughly confused face. "I'm not bringing Bryan to the *pool*."

Jen smiled, though it felt forced. "How silly of me."

Ainsley walked down the sidewalk, doing a little dance and snapping her fingers to some song Jen couldn't hear.

"You're back in town," came Aimee's voice from the front steps. "Looks like I'll win that bet."

Jen turned to her sister. "What bet?"

Aimee crossed her arms and wore an inscrutable expression. "Whether or not you'd come back again from New York. I knew you would. Vera wasn't so sure."

Jen pulled the gate shut and latched it behind her. "The trip to the city was worth it. Everything's falling into place for the games."

"Come on in and tell me about it."

As they entered the kitchen, which was filled with the sweet scent of vanilla French toast batter, Jen told Aimee about Shea Montgomery's whiskey tent and how Duncan had called earlier this morning to tell her more about the group of heavy athletes he'd rounded up at the last minute to compete this weekend. None of them were pros, but Jen didn't care. There would be enthusiastic bodies on the field, throwing heavy weights around, and that's all that mattered.

"There was a rumor that Chris's band wasn't going to play?"

Aimee dipped slabs of white bread into the egg batter and set them to sizzling on the hot skillet.

Jen frowned. "Where'd you hear that? I may have teased him a bit, but I'm not about to turn them down. I love their sound, they're local, Chris seems really excited. Man, he can play that fiddle, can't he?"

Aimee shrugged. "It's just what I heard. There was that fight over at their house a few months back, and then Chris moved out. The sheriff said there was trouble at his bandmates' place two nights back; I thought maybe they'd broken up. Guess not, though."

Jen vowed to look into it.

She turned in her chair and realized what was different about the Thistle. The plastic work drapes in the front sitting room had been taken down, and the new drywall was up and taped. The furniture was covered, the room ready for the paint cans stationed around the perimeter to be opened. The place would be finished by that weekend, just in time for the Scottish Society president to stay here.

"Wow," Jen said, impressed. "Owen works fast."

Aimee's voice pitched low. "Only when he has to."

Jen winced and turned back around, but said nothing. Sex had never been something the sisters talked about, not even in playful terms. Maybe because it had been such a big deal because of Frank's constant cheating. Maybe because it had gotten Aimee into such trouble when she was younger.

Aimee set the butter and powdered sugar on the table. No syrup on French toast in this house—a little quirk Aunt Bev had taught them that they'd both carried through to adulthood.

Jen changed the subject. "Oh, I have other good news." And she told Aimee all about Bobbie and the craft convention now set for March. Jen had called Bobbie on her way back from New York to tell her everything, and Jen could have sworn the older woman had gotten a little choked up. The thing was a go, and Jen couldn't have been more excited for her and for Gleann.

Aimee's spatula, piled with three slices of French toast, stopped halfway to Jen's plate. "All those people coming for it will need places to stay."

Jen grinned. "Exactly. They'll need lots of things. I was

going to talk to Sue about it later, after our games meeting. Lodging, food, transportation—"

"Let me do it."

The French toast plopped onto Jen's plate and she looked up from it into her sister's face.

"I want to do that," Aimee said. "I want to talk to Mayor Sue about bringing in or starting those kinds of businesses."

"But—"

"No 'buts,' Jen. I'll be here long after you're gone. I'm the one who could see that kind of thing through. I'm the one who wants to open up more B&Bs."

Jen felt horrible for thinking it, but . . . *Aimee*? A business owner of something other than the Thistle, which had been practically gift wrapped for her? "You do?"

Aimee straightened. "I do. I want to own something that's mine, that I created. I know how to run one B&B. I want to create another from my own vision."

Jen had never seen her sister look so sure, so confident. She opened her mouth but shock prevented anything from coming out.

Aimee rolled her eyes and sat. "I know that look. The one that thinks I can't do anything for myself."

"Please forgive me," Jen said, keeping calm and maintaining direct eye contact, "but experience is proof."

"I told you I'd prove it to you, that what happened with the burst pipe and Owen wasn't really me. That I've changed, that I'm a different person. This is it. My chance. Give it to me."

Jen sat back and folded her napkin. Folded it again. "Honestly, it's not my thing to grant or take away. I just thought that I could—"

"What? Do everything?"

Now Aimee was starting to sound like Mom. "Wait a minute. You called me here, remember?"

Aimee's voice gentled, her eyes closing for a long blink. "I did. For the games. I know it's in your nature; I should have seen this. But you swoop in, pick out all these other peripheral things that you think need fixing, and then take them on yourself, because you think you have all the answers."

"Maybe I like to help. Maybe I like to see good things grow out of bad things, or out of other good things."

The sigh Aimee let out was large enough for two people, and she lifted glistening eyes and a sad smile to the ceiling. "I know you do. I know you do."

Was that . . . envy?

Jen started to pick at her French toast. Aunt Bev's recipe, but somehow better because Aimee had made it, here in the kitchen that was now her own.

"Shouldn't you be focusing on keeping the Thistle up and running," Jen asked, "before even thinking about opening up something else?"

Aimee gave the kitchen a sweeping, loving look. "I have dreams now, too, you know."

They ate in silence for a bit, their forks clattering on the porcelain, as Jen turned over and over in her mind all the ideas she'd had during that long drive up from New York. All the potential changes that could be made to make the town more conducive for events and tourism and marketing . . .

"I know things," Jen said, unable to keep silent. "I know people. Let me—"

"Thank you." Aimee set down her fork rather deliberately. "And I will probably take you up on that, too."

Jen couldn't deny the itch that burned just underneath her skin, that feeling of starting something and not seeing it through. Not applying her ideas, not giving input. It was like leaving dirty dishes in the sink from now until the end of time, and it made her dig her fingernails into her palms.

Then Aimee's kind hand curled over hers. And suddenly Jen felt it: that feeling of being cared for, of being mothered. Of actually being the younger sister, and not having to act like the older one. This wasn't a gradual role reversal over the course of years, but a turn on a dime, one that had her tripping over her own choices and actions.

"You can't take on everything," Aimee said. "I know you like to tell yourself that, but you can't." She gave a little shake of her head. "I actually have no doubt that if I hadn't said anything today, you would've found a way to live and work in New York and also take on Gleann's transformation single-handedly."

Jen just sat there because she couldn't deny that truth. The thought of working with Gleann to turn it around to attract potential events, and then assist in putting on those events . . . it was incredibly exciting. And it shocked the hell out of her because it was something she'd never before considered. In her mind, bigger had always been better.

Aimee released her hand and rose. "You're my biggest influence, Jen. You always have been. You teach me, even when you aren't here, even when you don't know it. You saved my life."

Holy shit.

"But don't you get it?" Aimee continued. "Everything you've ever done is to get out from under Mom's shadow. Hers is dark and horrible, and I totally get that. But you throw a shadow over me, too, sis. It's a good shadow—it's always protected and directed me—but it's time I cast it aside."

Chapter

18

The bed in the 738 Maple house was way more comfortable than the one in 740. Leith should have tested each of them out before he'd dropped his bags in Mildred's Old Lady Museum. Or maybe this mattress was better simply because Jen was curled up next to him in it.

On cue, her eyes cracked open. Since the sun was just coming through the window, they were a sparkling, sleepy green. The color reminded him of dew on early morning grass as he arrived on site for a day's hard work. He could get used to waking up like this.

"Hey," she said, stretching. The sheet slipped just enough to show the outer curve of her breast. He tried not to touch and failed.

Arriving back in Gleann late last night, he hadn't even bothered pulling his truck into 740. He'd seen Jen's kitchen light on, her silhouette pacing behind the curtains, and swerved right into 738's driveway. She'd actually locked the door and he'd had to knock, but when she opened the door, the metal window blinds slapping against the wood, he'd immediately been on her. Pushed her against the bad wallpaper and kissed away all her excuses about having a million things to do. Turned out that he got rid of those pretty easily.

"What do you have to do today?" he asked, pulling the sheet down to give himself free access to her perfect nipple. It tasted just as amazing as it had last night, only for some reason her high-pitched sigh sounded even better.

"Everything." She pushed at his head. "Someone distracted me last night and I'm behind."

He came up on an elbow above her. "Sorry."

"No, you're not." She craned her neck to look at the clock, which showed six thirty, and winced. "I've got to get going. Tell me about Connecticut while I get ready."

He was struck momentarily speechless as she slid from the bed and bent over for her robe. Throwing his bare legs over the side of the bed, he pulled the sheet over his lap. "It was great. Put a deposit on a new storage facility and signed a lease for an apartment until I can find a house I love, made nice progress in the Carriage assessment and planning. Still need the official sign-off and contract, but that'll come this weekend when I go back."

She peeked her head out of the bathroom, toothbrush sticking out between her lips, her hair in that messy knot on the top of her head that, for some reason, drove him crazy. "So you came back to get the rest of your equipment? Start moving things down by the weekend?"

Though he responded with a "yes," the weird, uncomfortable twinge in his chest told him there was something else he had to do before that happened. He turned to look out the window toward town.

Jen finished brushing her teeth and came out to kiss him with a minty mouth. Then she took his hand and placed it high up on her inner thigh, where she knew he liked to touch. "Sure I can't convince you to stay for the games?"

"It doesn't have anything to do with being convinced."

Suddenly he remembered what she'd said to him the other morning in the kitchen of her city apartment: *Your dad. The house. You haven't dealt with losing him yet, and going to the games, which was such a huge part of growing up—for both of you—would be too painful a reminder.*

The house.

The tightness in his chest now had a name, a purpose. That house was why he'd truly come back. Because once he started transferring his big equipment and computers and supplies down to Connecticut, he would convince himself there would be no reason for him to come back to Gleann. Except that there was. Da's house was still sitting there, filled to the brim with things of a life gone, and it would sit there forever if Leith didn't do something about it.

"I know," Jen said softly, and moved to the closet to pull down one of the long sundresses he loved on her. He watched her dress, watched how the fabric flowed over her body.

She'd been inside Da's house, had seen how he'd left it, how he'd locked up his emotions. For a moment he was moved to ask her to come with him that day, but she was already starting to talk to herself, her lips moving through silent lists, her brow furrowed in a look of concentration, and he knew that her mind was already back at work. He'd already stolen a lot of her time last night.

Besides, he wanted to sort some shit out on his own before he talked to her about his mindset.

Before she left for a meeting with the caterer, he kissed her with resolution. He liked that, kissing her good-bye in the morning. He wanted that every day. But first there was something he needed to do.

After he made one phone call to an old contact who could help him out on short notice, he called Duncan and then Chris, asking them both the same thing: "Hey, man, you busy today? I kind of need your help."

Leith was standing on the flagstone path leading up to Da's house—the closest he'd gotten to the front door in three years—when Chris pulled up in his crappy Chevy two-door. Leith's lone remaining employee got out of his car, worry plastered on his face, his shoulder-length hair bed-messy.

"I just did the yard two days ago," Chris said. "Everything okay?"

"No, no, the yard looks great." The younger guy had taken too much off the euonymus shrub there in the corner, but it didn't matter now. "I need you for something else."

Duncan arrived then, heavy metal screeching out from behind the closed windows of his SUV. He parked crookedly in the grass on the opposite side of the road and crossed to the two men, his shaved head already shining in the hot summer sun. He slapped palms with Leith and gave a polite nod, hands on hips, to Chris as Leith introduced them. Duncan shaded his eyes with a hand as he took in the tiny, dark ranch house. "So what the hell is this place? What do you need help with?"

Chris gave Duncan a funny look, like he should have known this was the place where Leith had grown up, but Duncan was a throwing buddy, not a Gleann local, and Leith had already moved out of here by the time they'd become friends.

Just then came the rumble of a heavy truck at the top of the hill, then the shrill *beep beep beep* as it reversed down the slope. It took several attempts and lots of time between the three men to direct the truck down the curving road, but eventually it deposited its load in the MacDougall driveway.

As the disposal company truck struggled back up the hill, Leith surveyed the giant Dumpster now sitting in his driveway, the one his contact had pulled through at the very last minute. He took a deep breath. Words still wouldn't come out. He cleared his throat. "I need some help cleaning out my old man's house. Do you mind?"

And there it was.

Though he didn't look at his employee, he knew Chris's face would be twisted in a confusion he'd never voice to his boss. But Duncan, in his trademark "Fuck it. Whatever" attitude, just clapped his hands and said, "Let's do it."

Yes, Leith thought. *Let's.*

The keyhole was much stickier than he remembered, the doorway much tighter. He'd waved off the guys, telling them to wait in the driveway and give him a sec. If they saw his sorrow and his discomfort, so be it. It was time to stop hiding it anyway.

The door opened inward, throwing light into the tomb. He didn't smell the must and dust, as he knew he should. Instead he smelled Da's old pipe filtering in from the front stoop where he'd smoked every evening. He smelled Sunday morning bacon and the fresh Christmas tree they'd chopped themselves and that stood tilted in the corner every year. He heard Da's old folk albums, played on that turntable still sitting on the coffee table, and the yap of the small mutt they'd had when Leith was a boy—the best dog neither of them had been able to replace because there simply was no replacement.

The world shifted and Leith sagged against the big hutch, a few unknown items rattling around inside. Without realizing it, he'd moved deep inside the living room, the light from the front door like a faraway mouth to a cave. Nothing had been changed, nothing moved, yet everything seemed different. Felt different. He was a man separate from the one who'd buried his beloved father, literally and figuratively, and he hated that he'd allowed himself to split apart like that.

He hated what he'd allowed this house and his memories to become.

Pushing off the hutch, he skirted around the coffee table, and edged along the kitchen counter pass-through. To the left stood the door leading into the garage, and as he went toward it, his thigh brushed the folded afghan crocheted by his mother long before he'd been born. A plume of dust shot up, tickling his nose and settling into his eyes. He rubbed them. Damn, the dust was making him tear up.

The garage was pitch-black, so he left the house door open to guide him as he went to the single-car rolling door, bent down, and heaved it up manually. The screech of metal on metal made him cringe, but not as much as what filled the garage floor.

Growing up, he'd watched Da lean back on that workout bench and do reps using those ancient black weights on that tarnished bar. When Leith was little, he used to sit on his bike and count while Da used the big dumbbells to do curls. And when he was old enough, when Da finally gave him the okay and taught him proper technique, Leith had learned how to lift.

And then Da had taught him how to throw the traditional Scottish events.

The old hammer still leaned against the back wall. So did the weight used for the height throw—a round metal ball topped with an attached ring for your hand. The weight for distance—its ball on the end of a short chain—sat in the corner. The caber, the one they'd used to practice with, was sitting pretty in the town park.

He remembered Da perched on the edge of the bench, the weight-for-height on the floor between his feet.

"Come 'ere, boy. Pick it up."

So excited. At nine, Leith was so excited he didn't recognize the teasing gleam in Da's eyes as he braced his feet on either side of the weight and yanked. The ring didn't budge. Leith stumbled.

Da chuckled, slapping his knee. A good-natured laugh, though Leith didn't realize that at the time.

"Someday, boy. Someday, I can already tell, you'll be a better man at this than I."

Impossible, Leith had thought.

He still thought it.

Leith just stood there, looking at all the equipment. He could still feel the roughness of those bars in his palms, could still hear Da coaching him from the lawn chair when he'd gotten too weak to lift himself—though he often tried to lift anyway, covering up his disappointment over aging and illness with self-deprecating laughter.

"You ready for us?" Duncan called from where he'd taken to leaning against the landscaping truck.

"Not yet," Leith said over his shoulder. "Just give me another moment."

"Take your time."

He'd already taken three years, but he only had his friends for today, and he needed to determine what would go and what he'd keep this week, before it came time to move away for good. Passing back through the living room, he headed down the creaking, claustrophobic hallway to the bedrooms, thinking how much longer the hall had seemed when he'd been a teenager.

He knew what Da had turned Leith's old bedroom into after he'd moved out: a monument to their relationship. Documentation of pretty much every feat Leith had ever performed. That level of pride was still too much for now, so the door remained shut. Instead, Leith turned another doorknob and entered his father's bedroom.

He didn't remember making the bed the last time he'd been in here, but the blanket was pulled neat and tight over the mattress, the pillows still propped against the chipped headboard. If he'd sit down on the bed, he knew it would squeak something terrible, but that's not why he'd come in here.

Why had he come exactly? What did he want from this room? The hat on the dresser and the cane still leaning by the door? Yes, definitely. His father to still be sleeping in here? Absolutely.

But instead Leith headed for the closet. He was drawn to it without explanation. As he cracked open the door, the smell of old wool and leather leaked out. Leith flicked on a flashlight and peered inside. All the sweaters and pants and coats he remembered, still in a neat line, waiting to be worn by a man who'd never come back.

Oh God. Oh *God*.

The stale air in the room—the whole house—caved in on him. Three years of loss that he'd buried somewhere outside under the new viburnum and roses slammed into him, knocking out his knees and collapsing his body to the floor. He sat there at the bottom of Da's closet in a heap, gasping for breath and pounding a fist into the plaster. The loss was too great for tears. Crying simply wouldn't be enough, although if Da were here, he would have clapped Leith on the back and told him to let it out, and to take his time doing it, because that's what a real man did.

His eyes stung and burned, and his chest heaved with great effort, but the tears still wouldn't come. Leith pressed his back to the closet wall and lifted his head to look at each article of Da's clothing, recalling days and moments when the older MacDougall had worn them. Leith reached out and thumbed through them . . . until he got to one piece in particular, and stopped.

The MacDougall tartan, brought over from Scotland decades ago, the wool now thin and worn. It was a field of red crossed with thin white lines, thicker blue ones, and intermittent green and blue squares as accent.

And this was Da's kilt, the one he used to throw in. The old man had been in his formal Highland dress for his memorial, but this kilt, the one he wore all the time with great love before it no longer fit him, still dangled from a hanger.

That's when Leith cried, a slow leak of tears. He had no idea how long he sat there, a blurred tartan pattern dancing across his vision. Finally knuckling away the tears, he shoved to his feet and reached for the kilt. Unhooked it. This was why he'd come in here. Neatly draping the thing across his arm, he grabbed the hat and the cane and left.

Across the hall stood his old bedroom door, and he looked at it only for a moment before opening it and stepping inside. Jen had come in here. He could see a fresh set of footprints in the dust coating the carpet. She'd already known that Leith and his father were more brothers than father and son, and that Da had been Leith's hero, but her seeing this, finally realizing all that Leith had shut away, she would know how bad he'd been hurting in order to do that.

He needed to stop ignoring the hurt.

There was a laundry basket still sitting at the bottom of his old, empty closet. Dragging it out, he took down all the photos of him and Da and placed them carefully in the bottom. He laid the cane and hat and kilt on top, then went to the living room and took the afghan of his mother's. Then he carried it all out into the bright sunshine.

"Now?" Duncan asked.

Leith slid the basket onto the truck bed. "Leave the hutch in the living room, I still have to go through it. But everything else can go."

Chris slapped a pair of work gloves into Leith's hand. As he pulled them on, Duncan walked into the open garage and flipped on the old boom box Da had kept there to listen to baseball games, and that Leith had used when he worked out. How about that? The damn batteries still worked, as though Da had changed them yesterday. The blare of guitar-heavy rock filled the once silent house and yard. Duncan cracked some joke Leith couldn't hear and Chris laughed, and the whole place was washed in a light atmosphere Leith hadn't expected to feel here again.

Leith reached into his truck and pulled down the cooler. Snatching three beers from the pile of ice inside, he snapped off the caps and handed them to the other guys. They clinked bottle necks.

"Thanks," he told them.

"To old man MacDougall," said Duncan.

As the cold beer slid down his throat, Leith turned to look again at the house, its doors and windows thrown open, all saying good-bye.

To old man MacDougall indeed.

Eight hours later, the shitty furniture and worthless household goods mounded over the lip of the Dumpster. The garage was stacked with other things to be donated. The men lounged on lawn chairs in the gravel drive as the sun finally disappeared, the last of the beers in their hands.

Leith glanced up at Da's kilt peeking out of the laundry basket. He realized that none of this would have happened without Jen, if she hadn't come here, if she hadn't unknowingly given him this final push.

"Hey, Duncan?" he asked.

"Yeah?"

"You, ah, need an announcer for Saturday?"

Duncan finished his beer with a smack of his lips and grinned, showing a missing tooth on one side. "Fuck yeah, man."

Leith still wasn't sure he could throw—out of practice and still some lingering ghosts—but he could still participate in the games. Still honor Da's memory in that way and give one final good-bye to Gleann.

Leith whipped out his phone and dialed. She answered on the second ring. "Jen? I have some news I think you're going to like."

Chapter

19

Jen stood in the middle of heaven. The sun speared the last of its gold light through the trees on the western hills, a warm breeze blew across what used to be Hemmertex's side lawn, and everywhere mingled smiling, laughing people, come to enjoy Gleann's opening party before tomorrow's Highland Games.

The parking lot was already half-full, and couples and families were making their way up the Hemmertex drive from town, pulling their kids in wagons decorated with Scottish flags. The locals wore all kinds of tartans in all sorts of manners: full kilts, T-shirts declaring their clans, hats. Jen even saw a scarf, though it was pushing eighty degrees.

She had enhanced the long entrance from Route 6 by draping flags along the Highland cattle fence. The hairy beasts had eyed her and she'd tried to talk to them as she did it, assuring them the things would be gone in twenty-four hours and they could have their unobstructed view back. But they still didn't look too pleased over having so many people this close to their domain. Loughlin, the old farmer and landowner, had stood in the center of his field with his border collies, watching her the whole time in that hard, wordless way, looking like he shared his cattle's feelings.

None of them were used to crowds, after all.

From inside the giant music tent streamed the first low, sexy draws of Chris's fiddle. The rest of his band had yet to show up for sound check, but he'd arrived early and was going through his own practice with an admirable enthusiasm. His hair brushed and pulled back in a low, loose ponytail, he made the kind of music that no recording could capture. She guessed he'd be getting his pick of the girls that night.

A short bus rattled its way up the drive and into the staging area, the product of Jen's marketing the bus service in Westbury last week. Jen held her breath, watching to see how many people would get off. The tinted windows showed nothing. The doors opened. An older couple staggered to the ground, then no one else. Crap.

Wait. Another couple—this one in their midforties—got off, then another. The four were laughing together, looking around, and then the man with salt-and-pepper hair pointed at the warm, white tent decorated with the Amber Lounge logo. They'd come for Shea and they'd found her. Perfect.

More and more people streamed off the Westbury bus. The beautiful thing had been full. Some trailed the first four to the Amber tent, some families wandered toward the Highland dance exhibition set up in the Hemmertex amphitheater. Others trickled off toward the tug-of-war competition already underway.

Raised voices shot out from the music tent and Jen hurried over, in tune with the sound of panic and impending event trouble. Three more guys had joined Chris on stage, one shouldering a guitar, another with a set of bagpipes under his arm, and the last lazily twirling a drumstick. Chris was laying into the drummer, and as Jen drew closer, she noticed that the drummer didn't give a shit as he rolled his head in every direction but at the guy yelling at him.

She walked right up to them and tapped the stage with authority, silencing the fight. "Everything okay, guys?"

The drummer swung his head toward her, his eyes bloodshot, his body swaying. Chris stepped between her and the drummer and pushed a wan smile onto his face. "Everything's great, Jen. We're still on at nine, right?"

She laid a long, long stare on the drummer. "You better be. Pay depends on it."

Chris picked up his fiddle and said, "No worries. No worries at all." But as she turned away, she heard Chris hiss, "For fuck's sake, Scotty. Get it together."

As she exited the music tent, a chorus of sound erupted from the tug-of-war competition. She'd gotten the idea to organize one after looking at Mr. MacDougall's scrapbooks. Though other American Highland games had adopted the concept, she really wanted to make it into an *event*, a true competition with the prize of some pretty serious Scotch.

She'd pounded the pavement to recruit local businesses to field tugging teams, and when the response had been less than expected, she'd appealed to the rugby teams who would be competing in the tournament tomorrow. Another level of competition seemed to entice the baser instincts of the bruiser males who liked to shove each other around a field, and they'd jumped at the chance.

From what she heard, her idea was delivering.

An enthusiastic crowd had gathered in a long line down the rope. They cheered their friends or husbands or coworkers. Jen didn't care, as long as they were cheering. As she drew closer she could glimpse the teams through spaces in the crowd. They synchronized their grips and tugs, planted their boots hard into the dirt, and leaned back, almost horizontal to the ground. Their timed shouts and grunts rose and rose as one team made their move, giving the rope all they had, making their opponents fight for it. Finally the judge's whistle blew, and one half of the crowd whooped. The victors of this round, wearing purple rugby jerseys, jumped up, red-faced and beaming, clapping each other on their backs.

Jen gave herself an inward nod of approval and moved on.

On the other side of the heritage tent, where the historical society had set up information about Scottish genealogy and displayed a fine assortment of tartans, spread the heavy athletic field. Leith was over there with Duncan, looking things over for tomorrow's competition.

Leith had told everyone in Gleann that he'd decided to stay for the games as his final good-bye. But privately, he'd told her: "I'm staying for Da. And for you."

He wasn't throwing but he was acting as the announcer, describing each event as it came up, highlighting each competitor, and calling scores and placement. The crowd was going to love him.

"Aunt Jen!"

The little voice made Jen smile before she even turned. Ainsley was weaving through the dispersing tug-of-war watchers. "Hey, Tartan McGee." Jen went to touch Ainsley's plaid headband, but the girl ducked away and fluffed her hair. "Whose clan is that?"

Jen remembered that you didn't just choose a random tartan to wear when living in Gleann. Oh no. You may as well declare war for a side when you picked what colors and pattern to wear.

"T's family. Melissa is a Campbell."

"Oh." Jen struggled not to cringe, choosing to smile instead. "Where's your mom?"

"She said to come stand by you until I ran into T and Lacey. They said they'd watch the next round of tug-of-war with me, but I can't find them."

Of course they did. Teenage girls made all sorts of promises to tweens, who would hold their word as that of God and then be devastated when those words proved false. And what the hell was Aimee doing that she couldn't be with Ainsley tonight of all nights, when she'd been the one to beg Jen to come in the first place?

"You want to come and watch me order around a bunch of men?" Jen asked Ainsley. "Maybe you'll run into the older girls later."

Ainsley's nose crinkled, then she caught herself. "But I want to sit with T."

"Okay." Jen laughed. "Can't help feeling a bit rejected, but okay."

Suddenly Ainsley's whole face brightened and she thrust out a finger. "There they are!"

Jen turned. The two girls were ambling toward the tug-of-war field. The younger one, Lacey, was chewing gum and thumbing away on a phone. T had put blue streaks in her hair. Ainsley was touching her own hair, as though contemplating the color herself.

Ainsley called out to the girls just as a piper blasted a warm-up chord near the music tent. Ainsley called again. The girls didn't hear. Or didn't want to hear.

Jen turned to Ainsley. Oh, boy. Here comes the disappointment, the disillusionment. She prepared for the distraction, ready to sweep Ainsley off toward the tug-of-war. Damn Aimee for—

T swiveled then, seeing Ainsley. She swatted her sister, who slid the phone into a pocket. Shit, they were actually going to look right at Ainsley then walk the other way . . . no. Wait. They started to come over.

"Hey, squirt," T said to Ainsley with a genuine grin.

Lacey reached out to ruffle Ainsley's hair—with Ainsley actually letting her—then caught sight of the tartan wrapped around it. "Nice, kiddo." Lacey flashed a shiny set of braces, then wrapped her lips around them again.

Both girls were tall, taking after their dad, and Jen wanted to knuckle their backs to get them to stand up straighter. With a secret smile, she remembered that at one point, when she and Leith had been eleven, she'd been an inch taller than him.

"How's it going?" T said to Jen, knocking her out of her memories. "I mean, I can tell this was a lot of work. Seems like a pretty cool party so far."

Jen blinked at her. "Thanks."

Ainsley's big eyes danced between the two older girls like they wore halos. "Are we still going to watch the tug-of-war?"

"Absolutely, squirt." T patted the backpack dangling over one shoulder. "Got the blanket and everything."

Ainsley peered around Jen and called, "Hey, Mom, can I have some money?"

The piper chose that moment to start his set, marching around the grounds to heighten the atmosphere, as she'd hired him to do, so when Jen turned around to find Aimee, the piper blocked the person walking with her sister. A moment of panic set Jen's heart pounding. Yeah, the girls were being cool to Ainsley, but what if Aimee was walking arm in arm with Owen out where everyone could see? Right in front of their children?

She'd witnessed enough sidelong looks and heard enough whispers to know it wasn't something the town wanted to see. What if *this* was the start to the scene Jen feared from her own childhood? On tonight of all nights?

Jen glanced fearfully at T and Lacey, imprinting her and Aimee's faces onto theirs, remembering the day they'd had to intercept their mom in the grocery store when she'd clawed after some woman she'd caught sleeping with Frank.

The girls wore no similar look of disgust.

Even odder, when the piper moved on, his absence revealed that Aimee wasn't actually walking with Owen, but Melissa. They walked close enough to touch, their heads bent together, Melissa saying something with very fervent hand gestures. And they were *smiling.*

Aimee saw Jen and steered Melissa over to make introductions. Melissa had a strong, confident handshake and a raspy voice. "Great to finally meet you, Jen."

And it was Jen, for once, who had to struggle to find equilibrium in this strangest of strange situations, when usually she could fake it pretty well.

Then Melissa did the most surprising thing. *She* reached for Ainsley, giving her arm a quick, affectionate squeeze paired with a brilliant smile. It couldn't possibly mean anything other than *I like you, kid.*

"Mom," Ainsley said, eyes bright, "T just told me there's a whole 'nother town under the lake. That when they made the dam, they covered the first Gleann with water. Is that true?"

T and Lacey were giggling as Melissa rolled her eyes. "Stop telling people that, Tamara Jean. Especially the younger kids. You'll get one of them drowned when they go to swim for it. Your dad made that story up ages ago to get you to go to sleep."

"I'm not a kid. Lacey's only three years older than me," Ainsley protested to deaf ears.

"Oh, look, there's George," Melissa said, "getting ready for the tug-of-war. Team Highway Repair and Roadkill Pickup. Wouldn't want to miss them pulling against those massive rugby guys you had bussed in, Jen." With a wink, she turned back to Aimee. "So, we're meeting with Sue on Monday at ten? At the Kafe?"

"Yep." Aimee smiled. "Have you seen Owen?"

Melissa squinted at the whiskey tent. "In there. Trying to relive his youth. Don't let him drive home if that's the case. Girls, Ainsley is yours for the night. You understand?"

Solemn nods all around.

Jen watched Melissa approach a telephone pole of a man dressed in jeans and a plaid T-shirt—no discerning tartan— with *New Hampshire Department of Transportation* stamped on the back. Melissa melted into his arms, having to stand on her tippiest of toes as he gave her a deep, closed-mouth kiss.

T and Lacey made faces appropriate to seeing their mom kissing, and then turned away, but otherwise showed no disapproval. A small group of men and women nudged each other in speculation, but Melissa and George didn't care.

"Here's a twenty." Aimee passed the wrinkled bill to T. "Keep any change."

"The sign-up for tomorrow morning's foot races is over at the heritage tent," Jen said to Ainsley. "Didn't you say you wanted to do the Kid Sprint around the grounds?"

Lacey slapped her sister's arm. "Oh, let's do that. First prize is fifty bucks."

The girls wandered off, and Jen resisted jumping up and down over their enthusiasm and participation.

She and Aimee looked at each other, the pall of their tense, honest conversation back in the Thistle still hanging over them.

"Melissa and I are opening a B&B," Aimee said abruptly. "Together."

Jen boggled, her mouth hanging open.

"That's what the Monday meeting is about, because I know you're wondering. We've already approached one of the old Hemmertex families with a huge empty house up for sale about going in with us, joining as a part owner, letting us run it from here. Melissa's got the start-up money—her family is the oldest in the valley—and I've got the skills in running an inn. It's going to be the first of many, Jen. I thought you should be one of the first to know."

"Wow, I . . . I don't know what to say."

The piper had trailed back by the beer tent, bleating out an up-tempo song.

Aimee stepped closer. "Say you're proud of me."

"God, Aim. I am. I really am."

There was no *I told you so.* No *I don't need you.* Just absolute proof, exactly as Aimee said she'd give. The world suddenly felt a little bit lighter.

Aimee's gaze flicked over Jen's shoulder. She said, all casual, "Oh, I see Owen. Better go tend to the whiskey consumption. It's already a great night, Jen. Tomorrow's going to be even better. I know it will." She started to walk off, then stopped. "I also thought you'd like to know that Owen filed for divorce this morning. Melissa says the papers will be signed in record time."

Aimee had put a good twenty feet between them before Jen finally processed it all, gathered herself, and called after her sister, "You know what would be good?"

Aimee turned around. "What?"

"Starting an association of inn owners in the valley. There are some in Westbury, you know. Maybe you could band together, use each other to help market the area. Just a thought."

Aimee beamed. "And it's a great one. Thank you." She took a long, happy look around the grounds and came back to meet Jen's eyes. "For everything."

*A*t last the sun dipped behind the hills in a perfect New Hampshire sunset, the kind she remembered, the kind she occasionally, futilely wished for while in the city. The fairy lights kicked on, and all the tents became outlined in strings of white. The murmurs of approval made her glow.

Big pockets of people milled around the beer tent, and the whiskey tent was so full Shea had tied back the flaps to accommodate everyone. Drinkers spilled out onto the grass slope leading down to the parking lot. Chris's band was finally ready to go on, and it seemed like the tension that had cut through their earlier sound check had been smoothed over. Or at least shoved onto the back burner, which was all that Jen cared about at this point. In the meantime, the Scottish Highland dance exhibition was concluding, the last notes of the sole accompanying piper floating across the grounds.

The party would go on as long as it was successful and fun . . . or until eleven, according to Sue McCurdy. Whichever came first. For now, Jen stood in the shadows just outside the music tent, surveying her success, feeling proud but not remotely smug.

There was a silent tug on her awareness, something pulling at her from the side. It was a warm feeling in her heart, a little dance in her belly, and she knew its source before she turned.

Leith was crossing the grass beneath the strings of fairy lights connecting the tents. She hadn't seen him all evening, word being that Duncan had asked him to run back to Westbury for some needed equipment. The sight of him now, here at the games where she'd wanted him from the beginning, more than made up for his absence.

He smiled with only his eyes, but it was a potent look, enhanced by the glitter from the overhead lights. His chin was set in hard determination, and she realized, with a great shiver, that she was his focus. His goal.

He wore a black T-shirt with a beer logo. It clung to his chest and waist, and fit snugly around his great arms. And then there was the kilt.

Holy mother of God.

No photo could have done him justice, no memory strong enough. She let herself enjoy watching him approach, noting with pleasure the way his mighty thighs kicked out the kilt, the way his big boots struck the ground. Each step brought him closer. Each step got her a little hotter.

"Hi," he said when he reached her, and she loved how even if her eyes were closed, she would have been able to tell he was smiling.

"Hi, yourself. How's it going over there? Everything set and all right? Do I need to talk to Duncan?"

He shook his head at the ground, sweat-dampened shag drifting over his ears and eyes, but he was grinning. "Always work with you first, isn't it? I can't even get in a flirt edgewise."

She let out a huff of exasperation. "Leith, I—"

"I'm kidding." He slid both hands around the nape of her neck, thumbs resting gently on her throat. "Everything's great. Although Duncan's canceling the hammer. Not quite enough room, unless you want to chance a broken window in the Hemmertex building or a hammer landing in the middle of the rugby field."

"No, I trust you guys. Whatever you say will work." She exhaled. "Good, good."

"Dougall!" came some drunken bellow from outside the beer tent. "Just throw, damn it!" Sporadic laughter, followed by cheers.

Leith's hands slid from Jen's neck. He raised an arm toward the tent and gave the drunk a tight-lipped smile. When his head swiveled back to her, the heat had left his eyes, but not the easy joy she'd noticed in him since that evening a few days ago when he'd called her out of the blue to say he'd stay through the weekend. They stared at each other for who knows how long, their primal connection eviscerating the shadows between them.

"I just have to tell you," she finally said, "you look so hot I can't even stand it."

"Funny"—he dragged a long, slow appraisal over her white tank top, jeans, and riding boots—"was going to say the same about you." Then he gave her a confused look. "You've seen me in a kilt before."

A nervous laugh escaped and she held up a hand. "Yeah, teenage Leith. Not the same thing. Not by a long shot."

Hands coming to his hips, he turned solemn and said, "It was Da's."

She'd recognized the red MacDougall tartan of course, but she hadn't noticed the slightly ratty hems and dulled fabric until he mentioned it. Deep lines crossed his forehead, and his chin dipped low. She finally understood what he didn't say, and gasped. "You went inside."

He nodded. "Duncan and Chris helped me clear it out. I'm going to put it on the market when things get a little better around here. Mayor Sue says they will, and if you've had a hand in turning this place around, I'll believe it."

She reached up to brush a piece of hair off his temple. "If you'd called me, I would've gone in with you. I would've helped, too."

"I know. And I did call. Only after."

She touched her lips, comprehending. "So that's what changed your mind about staying."

He took a few huge gulps of air and still didn't meet her eyes. "Da is everywhere in the valley, in Gleann. He and I are . . . everywhere. I never let him go; I never let myself grieve. Always too much to do, always a million other ways to push aside what I didn't want to accept." His great shoulders hunched for his ears, stayed there. "It's why I need to leave, Jen. It's why I won't throw. Because the games—any games, not just these—have always been about him. I can't do it and not have him there where I can see him." Those shoulders fell. "I realized, as I was taking out his stuff, the things he really, truly loved, that I needed to say good-bye to him. And I needed to stay this weekend to do it. So I called Rory in Connecticut and told her I wouldn't make it back until next week."

Though it seemed there was something else he wasn't telling her—about the house or his dad or work, she couldn't be sure—he wasn't dwelling on it, and neither would she. This was a huge step, and an overwhelming sense of pride overtook her. That energy swept through her again, starting in her toes, climbing its way up her legs and making them tingle. It sent her body surging forward, her fingers grasping that beer T-shirt and balling it in tight fists. She yanked him down to her level, and if he was thrown off guard it was only for a moment, because she was distinctly aware of his lips parting before their mouths met in an unrelenting kiss that had her feet rising off the ground. No, it was him lifting her up, his arms wrapped tightly around her back in one of those grips that wordlessly said he owned her.

Because he did.

The thought, for once, didn't deter her. Didn't send her mind spinning away in panic. Didn't make her think she was losing ground—because now, she was most definitely gaining.

She'd also gone dizzy, her toes dragging in the dirt, her body swaying out of her control. Something hit her back, then there was faint laughter and a stranger said, "Hey, what's going on out there?" She opened her eyes to find Leith had backed her up against one of the tent poles, making the corner shake. The drunk, laughing man had peeked his head around the opening to watch them.

She struggled away from Leith even as he kept reaching for her. Her body called her a traitor, because it was absolutely on fire for him. She was ridiculously wet—she could feel it beneath her jeans, their tight fit driving her insane—but there was no time for sex, not with a couple of hours left on her clock. It made her want to cry.

He licked his lips. Stared at hers. "What do you want?"

She glanced down at his kilt, very nearly salivating. "I want that."

"Want what, exactly?" God, his voice was so deep, like fingers stroking her soul.

"Don't make me say it."

"Not making you say or do anything. But let me just tell you that I want you, too. Right now."

She released a groan of frustration to the sky. "Can't happen. Not now, anyway." Not for her, maybe. But there was something she wanted to do to him, and right now seemed a better time than any, given their circumstances.

Given what he was wearing.

"Come with me." She took his hand and dragged him away from the party, away from the strings of fairy lights and the stage, deep into the dark canyons of parked cars along the fairground edge. In the distance the charred skeleton of Loughlin's barn blocked out stripes of stars.

"I know where we could go," he offered, the suggestion mixing with the exquisite pressure of her jeans, rubbing her right between the legs.

She glanced playfully over her shoulder. "Do not say the back of your truck. I'm a classy New Yorker now. I only go down on guys in alleys and in the bathrooms of nightclubs."

She was kidding, of course, but he answered after a slight pause. "Oh, is that what's going to happen?"

When they'd gotten far enough away from the party, all the cars black and silent, the voices turned to a distant, dull hum, she finally stopped. Whirled around. He was grinning like a madman, but also a very turned-on madman. He reached for her, getting that openmouthed *I'm going to kiss the hell out of you* look.

She slammed a hand into his chest, stopping him. Because she knew if he did that, if he got her going in the way only his mouth could, they'd be out here all night. She'd be draped across the hood of that yellow hatchback over there, and she'd never go back to the party where she should be right now.

"Yeah," she said, her voice gone all throaty. "That's what's going to happen. And I'm adding parking lots to my repertoire."

She pushed him into the side of a conversion van, the closest vehicle that could take his height and build. A metallic boom rang down the line of cars, but no one was around to hear. She dropped to her knees, the asphalt and gravel biting. She'd worry about what her jeans might look like later. Or maybe not.

"Jesus, Jen. Is this you and your control issues?"

Leith's hand threaded through her hair and she flipped her eyes up to see that his grin had vanished, replaced by such a fierce expression of lust that it made her stop and stare, reveling in it. But only for a second.

"No." Okay, maybe it was, but she wasn't going to admit that. Not now. "This is me wanting you. Just like this."

One side of his mouth tilted up. "Another first for us."

Wow, she guessed it was.

Just as she shoved up his kilt, yanked down his underwear, and sucked him into her mouth, Chris's fiddle struck its first long notes on stage. The drums came in, nice and steady, followed by the pipes and guitar. Music filled the valley as she worked her way down Leith, tasting and licking him, dragging her tongue and the inside of her cheeks all over him. He was hers right then, and the whole valley belonged to them.

Leith's head fell back with a crack against the van, and it might have been one of the best sounds she'd ever heard.

Chapter

20

*I*n no way did Leith want to know where, when, or on whom Jen had learned to give head like this. He literally had to bite his tongue to not shout out. The sensations were plenty amazing—the hard suck and the stroke of her gentle hands drawing every drop of blood to where he needed it most—but it was the sight of her that shoved him hard against the wall of insanity.

He hadn't meant to look down. Hadn't meant to slit open his eyes to see her mouth surrounding him, her eyelids closed tightly over the green emeralds he adored. Hadn't meant to see how her thighs were spread, and how her hips undulated with every pull of her mouth on his dick.

The need for her would never go away. It would always be there, a constant thing, ready and waiting. She held his desire in her fists, and to release it all she had to do was open her fingers. It was that simple. It was that potent.

He forgot where he was—in what town, in which state, on what planet. His eyes rolled back in his head. She was picking up the pace, taking some sort of coaching advice he must have been wordlessly feeding her, because she was doing it absolutely perfectly. Hand still wrapped in the smooth silk of her hair, his thighs started to shake.

All the emotion he'd ever owned fled from every corner of his body, rushing, rushing toward his groin and pushing into his cock. The power of the pleasure stole his brain and sent him flying into the heavens. He came in her mouth, unable to hold back his sounds anymore. He couldn't hear himself, didn't know what sort of gibberish she'd reduced him to.

Then she pulled off him and sat back on her heels, and . . . smiled. Leith wasn't really capable of reaction just then. Even the feel of his kilt drifting down and touching him was too much, and he winced. But she somehow got him dressed again, T-shirt tucked back in and everything, and he could stand without having to lean against the stranger's van.

He touched her face. "Seems a bit uneven, wouldn't you say?"

Her smile was brilliant and confident, and he loved the knot he'd made in her hair by her ear.

"You'll get me later," she said.

He kissed her and said against her lips, "Yes. I will."

"But now I have to get back. Thanks for the cigarette break."

He barked out a laugh. "You're thanking *me*? I'm the one who needs the cigarette."

"Taste of whiskey instead? I need to check in on Shea."

This time it was he who reached for her hand and pulled her gently through the maze of cars. The band's music got louder and louder as they made their way back to the grounds. Chris sounded excellent on his fiddle, as usual. The kid really needed to play more solo, maybe even ditch the other guys. Scott, the drummer, didn't look so good, like maybe he'd fallen off the wagon, which might explain why Chris had been on edge the past couple of days. Jeremy, the piper, was giving the rest of his bandmates hard looks. There were people dancing though, and the beer and whiskey tents had turned raucous, so maybe no one else noticed.

Just hold it together for this weekend, guys, Leith thought. No bullshit tonight or tomorrow. For Jen. For Gleann.

As he and Jen ducked into the whiskey tent, Shea jumped up onto the bar to a chorus of whistles and cheers, which faded when she gave the offending whistlers a withering glare.

"Supposedly it's my duty," she called out over the heads, "to hand over this case of whiskey, handpicked by yours truly, to the winning tug-of-war team: Manhattan Rugby."

A great hoot went up from a mess of about ten guys wearing red and black striped T-shirts. One of them, a big guy with a haircut that had Manhattan written all over it, his body half-covered with mud, and already a little red-faced from drinking, came forward to accept the case. He took an awful long time sliding it from Shea's hands, staring at her with a look Leith knew all too well. The rugby player tried to chat her up, but she just gave him a polite nod and went back behind the bar.

"Dougall! Holy fuck, I thought that was you!"

Leith turned to find three of his old throwing buddies weaving around the crowded tables toward him. Damn but it was good to see them, a blast of the not-too-distant past that somehow felt forever ago.

"You just dropped off the face of the earth," Ward said with a sauced grin. "Not even on the online forums or anything anymore. What the hell have you been doing?"

"Throwing for a PR tomorrow?" Leith said, changing the subject with a laugh, and clapping Ward hard on the back. "Because there's no fucking way you're winning if Duncan's throwing. He's pretty sick right now."

Ward guffawed. "No shit. He twisted my arm into coming. Haven't been back here since I took second to your scrawny ass."

"Thanks for coming and competing on such short notice," Jen piped in, stepping to Leith's side. "It'll be a great day tomorrow. I promise."

Leith looked down at her with pride, loving how new people and situations didn't scare her at all. He introduced Jen to the athletes and they all shot the shit for a while, the old camaraderie coming back to him. Once Duncan found them, he did a couple of quick shots and the volume of the party jumped up several notches. Leith fell into the easy rhythm of competition talk, and found himself eager to know how all the other guys had been doing on the circuit.

He could admit it now. He missed this.

Jen touched his waist. "I think Shea is beckoning to me."

"I'll go with you," he said, wanting to say hi to her, too. To the guys he added, "I'm announcing tomorrow. See you then."

Ward threw a knowing look at Jen and nodded. Leith just smiled, not hiding a damn thing.

"I recognize a lot of the people in here. Not just the other athletes," Leith said to her as they made their way to the bar.

"You should," Jen said proudly. "Old Hemmertex employees. I marketed the new format of the games and Shea's presence in their new headquarters, gave them a good reason to come back for the weekend."

Leith rubbed his face. "Damn smart of you."

She batted her eyelashes and gave him a faux-coy look over her shoulder. "I know."

They passed by two tug-of-war teams who were reliving the tournament and making challenges for next year. Hearing that, Jen pressed her lips together in a small, confident smile.

"How's it going?" Jen asked Shea. "Need anything?"

Shea smoothed back her nearly white hair as she surveyed the stacks of empty boxes of whiskey bottles teetering behind her. "Yeah, cups and napkins, if tonight is any indication of what tomorrow will be like."

Jen had her phone in hand before Shea even finished. Even late on a Friday night, she could get stuff done. The woman pretty much blew his mind.

Shea pulled out two new tasting cups and set them in front of Leith and Jen. With a stone face, she dragged up a bottle of whiskey from underneath her makeshift bar, one that she hadn't been tilting for the masses.

"If you're pouring," said a man's voice on the other side of Jen, "I'm drinking."

Both Leith and Shea looked up to find the rugby player/ tug-of-war champ/hopeful flirter leaning both elbows on the bar, his plastic tasting glass extended toward her. Shea just glanced at his glass. He gave her the kind of smile that guys reserved for girls they wanted to see naked.

"This is a special bottle," Shea said in a tone that might have been taken for flirting if not for the severe arch of a single eyebrow, "reserved for the games organizer."

Then without breaking eye contact with the new guy, she splashed the whiskey into two glasses and pushed them across to Jen and Leith.

The guy straightened, his smile fading but not disappearing.

A new glimmer came to his eye though, and Leith knew full well that Rugby believed he'd just been given a challenge he was ready and willing to accept. Rugby turned away with a nod and a toast of his empty glass to the whiskey expert.

"Nice rejection," Jen said to Shea as she tapped off her phone. "You're quite the pro."

Shea shrugged and swiped a damp towel across the table. "When I'm on this side of the bar, I talk about the good stuff only. It's just my rule. If someone wants to chat me up, here isn't the place."

Leith hid a grin in his glass. Thank God Jen didn't have that rule.

He took a sniff and a sip. Damn. Shea really knew her stuff. She'd poured them a smooth, peaty mouthful that he savored.

Jen also drank and groaned in approval. "I don't know; it sounded to me like he wanted to talk whiskey."

"No, he didn't," Leith and Shea said at the same time.

Jen laughed. "Maybe you're right. He's standing over there now, trying to make it seem like he's not looking at you."

Sure as hell, that's exactly what the guy was doing. Only when Shea followed Jen's finger, Rugby turned and gave Shea a smile that said he didn't really care that she'd turned him down before. He was coming for her, and the both of them were going to enjoy the chase. Then he gave her his back, leaving her wide-eyed and, if Leith dared to say it, intrigued. *Well played, Rugby. Well played.*

Jen told Shea, "Well, when you're done here you should go for it. He's hot." She took Leith's hand. "Come with me to the beer tent and listen to some music."

"Yes ma'am."

They bid Shea good-bye; she was still blinking at Rugby as though she was equal parts offended and interested. Maybe she'd let her rule go lax tonight; maybe she wouldn't.

The band sounded like it had found its groove, and Leith breathed a sigh of relief to see that all four members had loosened up. Chris's fiddle transcended everything, and every time a solo of his came up, the crowd erupted in applause. He played with his eyes closed, one shoulder to the audience. He really didn't know how good he was.

As Jen texted someone, Leith went over to grab two beers.

Both hands holding cold plastic cups of the Stone's stout, he turned around to head back to Jen. In one eyeful, he took in all that she'd accomplished in such a short time . . . and froze.

The old Gleann Highland Games were gone, replaced by this fun, classy, but simple affair that seemed to have breathed new life into everyone. No more rickety, cheesy castle decorations. No more warm beer hand-pumped out of kegs by old ladies. No more terrible athletes who couldn't turn a caber.

Locals mingled with people from across the lake and, hell, rugby teams from New York. This was his town and he barely recognized it.

Correction: it *used* to be his town.

Gleann had exhaled, shaking off its bad times. Or maybe that was Jen. She'd succeeded where DeeDee and even Hemmertex hadn't. All this in two weeks. All this to help a town that had been left to rot. She hadn't been born here, but now that he knew her history, she considered this place home. She was part of Gleann.

She'd started something exciting here that he was positive would bloom even after the two of them were long gone.

The crowd parted and, for a split second, he thought he glimpsed an older man wearing the same kilt Leith wore, pipe clamped between his teeth, flat gray cap slightly crooked on his thinning hair, cane held between his legs, as he sat tapping his heel to the music.

But then the crowd shifted again and the man was gone.

Shaking off the moment, he started back for Jen.

It took a little while for him to recognize Mayor Sue. She wasn't wearing Syracuse regalia, but instead a blue long-sleeved T-shirt with *Edinburgh* done in some sort of stitching across her giant boobs, and she was making a beeline for Jen. A man with a scraggly, mostly white beard and the most impressive gut Leith had ever seen trailed the mayor.

Leith reached Jen just as the man was saying something to her about the Scottish Society board reconsidering withdrawing their funding of this event for next year. "If this is what you did with tonight," he told her, his whiskers dancing, "I can't wait to see what you do with tomorrow."

Leith all but whooped, but Jen's response was a modest smile and bow of the head. "I'm positive that when you do, you'll not only continue to fund the Gleann games, but also increase your investment for next year."

The man—the society president, Leith assumed—shook Jen's hand and moved on. Mayor Sue merely said to Jen, "We'll talk tomorrow. After the whole thing's over."

"Unbelievable," Jen muttered as the two of them left and Leith pressed the beer into her hand. "I don't know what I have to do to get that woman's approval. Turn lead into gold?"

Leith watched Sue go over to scratch the heads of her Yorkies, which had been tethered to one of the tent poles. "Why do you care so much?"

"I suppose I don't," Jen said at the end of a long swig of beer.

"Of course you do."

"Okay! I do! It's killing me! If you have to wake me up from the grave to get me to hear her tell me 'Good job,' do it. Please."

He chuckled.

"I'm serious, Leith. Not even in front of the society president could she say it. Not even in front of *you*."

He took a seat on a folding chair and pulled her between his legs, positioning her so her body fell back into his. The perfect little puzzle piece.

On stage, the band finished an upbeat folk song. As Jeremy, the piper, was saying something about how they'd updated the next song for modern times, Chris took a swig of water from a bottle. Scott reached for one of the cups of beer that had been set in a line next to his drum set and finished it in one long drink. Tossing the cup to the side, he pulled a cap from his back pocket and fixed it on his head.

Jen went still in his arms. "Is that—"

"Yeah. I think it is."

The red potato chip logo cap they'd seen in the hidden corner of Loughlin's barn before it had burned down.

She sagged against him. "Do you think he did it? Maybe on accident? There were cigarettes there and you need a lighter for those things."

"Maybe."

"We're going to have to tell Olsen about it."

"Okay."

She leaned back, settled in to him again. "But not now. The

barn's already burned and I'm not pulling the drummer off the stage when they're doing so well. As long as he can hold it together."

Come on, asshole, Leith thought. *Hold it together.*

The warm June breeze swept through the open tent, swirling her scent around him, and he briefly closed his eyes as his cheek rubbed her hair.

"You knew this would go off like fireworks," he said. "Didn't you."

"Fireworks . . ." She tried to pull away, to sit up. "That's an idea for next year."

He yanked her gently back against his chest. "Don't even think about going for your phone." She relaxed, but just slightly. Then he asked, "Would you do this again next year?"

It took her a while to answer. Her hand came to rest on his forearm, and she drew light lines up and down his skin with her fingernails. "I don't know if I can. The timing for this was . . . unique."

It was exactly the same kind of pause she'd given him when he'd asked if they could try to be together. He'd tried not to read too much into it. He had yet to hear her not speak the truth. Her word, even if he hadn't always agreed with it, was gold, as far as he was concerned.

"Ah, that's right," he said. "Your crazy job." He was joking, but his stomach felt strangely sour.

A silence fell between them as they rocked to the music, clasped together. Then he got up to get another beer, and by the time he got back, she was dancing with Bobbie and Rob and looking gorgeous doing it. Thoughts of crazy jobs and guesses over odd pauses vanished.

Chapter

21

Jen stayed at the games until Chris struck his last fiddle note and the applause died. The music tent had long since been cleared of families, and all that remained were drunken, happy adults. The buses fired up in the parking lot, ready to take the last people back to Westbury, and locals were stumbling home, shouting "See you tomorrow" across the fields.

"Look at that smile," Leith said, taking her hand and turning her toward him.

She hadn't been aware of what her face was doing, but now that he said it, she could feel the stretch of her cheeks and the satisfaction in her heart. "It was a good night. Now I think I'm ready for bed." Her free hand fumbled for her phone as she checked the time. She whistled. "A few hours of sleep before I have to be back here at six."

The fingers twining with hers tightened, pulling her closer. Shoving her phone back into her purse, she looked up at Leith. Heat sparked in his dark eyes. She knew that look. She knew it, and loved it.

"No sleep yet," he said. "Come with me."

As if she had a choice, or desire, not to.

She willingly let him lead her to the parking lot, where the remaining cars were humming to life and pulling away.

"Where's your truck?"

He looked sidelong at her with a shit-eating grin, eyebrows disappearing beneath the shag of hair. "No truck tonight."

Jen blinked, finally recognizing what vehicle sat directly in front of her.

"Wow, you still have it?"

"Yep. It's been sitting in Mildred's garage, the one at the Old Lady Museum. I couldn't let it stay down at Da's. Until the other day, it was the only thing I'd taken away from there."

Leith exhaled and reached out to run a hand over the gorgeous, low tail fin of Mr. MacDougall's 1969 Cadillac DeVille convertible. The robin's-egg blue was exactly as she remembered, as well as the gleam of the white leather seats. The car was as long as a boat and could easily fit three bodies in the trunk. Leith touched it with reverence. Unlike the day he'd dropped her off to look for his father's scrapbooks, there was no pain, no loss on his face. Only wistfulness. Only love.

Come to think of it, that's exactly what she'd sensed in him all night.

He walked slowly toward the driver's side door, hand trailing along the blue, those heated eyes lingering on Jen. She could feel them as strongly as she could feel the cool metal of the car beneath her fingertips.

He glanced pointedly at the backseat. "I want to have sex with you in my car."

Her first instinct was to laugh, but since he looked so serious, she didn't. Instead, she studied him. "Trying to relive the past?" Because if he was, this thing between them, whatever it was, wouldn't last.

He shook his head. "No, not trying to relive anything. You are you, and I am me, and I want us to make new memories. Tonight. Before we both leave Gleann for good. Look, I don't have a house of my own and the thought of spending our last night here with Mildred's ghost really doesn't appeal to me. I'm sure as hell not taking you back to Da's, and the Thistle is booked up. So can we please have sex in my car? Please?"

She licked her lips to keep from smiling. "Not behind the produce stand."

Finally he grinned. "Now *that* would be trying to relive the past. No, I've got a better place in mind."

While he drove he held her hand, and even though it could be labeled as a childish form of affection, right then it felt wonderfully adult and intimate. And, oddly, a little sad.

He brought her to the gravel ramp where day-trippers could back their boats into the lake. Trees and tall grass bent over them and the crescent moon dangled crookedly over the water. The stars were out again, Jen thought as he shut off the engine and turned his whole huge torso toward her, just as he'd done their first night together, here in this very car. New memories, she told herself. New memories.

You are you, and I am me.

Leith had one leg bent on the seat, the other thrust under the dashboard, his kilt draped between his knees. He looked like he wanted to devour her.

She pushed herself up and slipped through the opening between the front seats, plopping down in the familiar back. The smell of the leather chucked her into the past, but the sight of Leith, with his longer hair and more powerful body and incredibly masculine confidence, grounded her firmly in the present.

The backseat was wide and deep, and the leather creaked under his weight as he joined her. Expectant, she came to her knees beside him. A slow grin widened his mouth, and he reached around to grab the back of her neck and pull her into him. She took that smile, kissed it right off his face, and licked at the lust dripping off his tongue.

He groaned, his fingers tightening, pressing her mouth harder against his. Then he was grabbing her around her hips, lifting her like a toy, and settling her to straddle his lap like she'd done at the Amber Lounge. Subtle pressure on her hips told her how he wanted her to move, and she gave him a long, slow undulation. It shoved the kilt higher up his thighs. It rubbed her clit against him. She felt herself swell, tingle, go wet. Beneath her, he shuddered.

His abs contracted as he pushed up against her, hard-as-stone thighs flexing. His kiss was made of iron and silk, and it went on and on and on, until he finally broke it. She loved the sound of his ragged breath; she drank it like water.

"I don't want to lose this," he whispered in her ear. "I can't lose you again."

Pushing back, feeling the air struggle in her chest, she stared into his eyes. A powerful bolt, made of desire and dreams, ripped through her.

"You think I'm going to let you go? Sir, you don't know how wrong you are."

"Then show me." A flash of white teeth. "And I'll show you."

She rose up, reached between her legs and tugged up his kilt. She'd already had him, already knew what he tasted and looked and felt like, but for some reason, at that moment, it all seemed brand new. She stroked him over his underwear. "Show me what?"

"New things," he stuttered.

"Oh, reallllly?"

Then she was falling, tilting back and to the side under no power of her own. But she didn't worry, not in the slightest, because she was in the arms of a man who had pretty much carried an entire town, and cared for a dying father, and thrown giant tree trunks all over a field.

The white leather sighed against her back. It cradled her and gave her up to Leith, whose body blocked out the stars above, but whose face was half lit by the moon. He tugged on the underside of her knees, tucking them around his hips. Why wasn't he taking off her jeans? Her body was screaming for him, and it seemed like he just barely had his own under control. He settled himself between her legs, his kilt bunching up between them, his boots making hollow sounds as they struck the side of the interior.

Coming down to his elbows he took her in a tender cradle, his thumbs finding her face, his fingers wrapping around her scalp. Their eyes met, and she knew at that moment she'd never get enough of him, that she'd spoken the truth before. No way in hell was she letting this go. This—*he*—was hers. She'd earned it and he'd earned her. They'd met in a time of their lives when emotions were new and forming, and they'd barely known themselves. They'd had to separate and go make their own lives before finding each other again. She couldn't look at it as ten years wasted without him, but instead ten years of growth, ten years of learning.

But now he'd put her under siege. There was no hope but to throw up her hands and declare herself conquered.

By the shift in his expression—a sudden clearing of his eyes, the smoothing of the skin around them and his mouth—she dared to think he might have come to a similar conclusion.

"Take off my jeans," she said, toeing off one boot, but not being able to get enough leverage for both.

He kissed her, then pushed back with a mighty exhale. He yanked off her boots, tossed them into the front seat, and went to work on her jeans. With a rip of the snap and a furious yank on the zipper, his determination might have been comedic if her desperation didn't echo his. She lifted her hips and he shimmied down the denim, stripping it off her legs, then stared, openmouthed, at the stretch of thin lace between her hip bones.

"Those, too," she said stupidly, as if he needed direction.

He ran a slow finger just underneath the top edge of lace, back and forth, back and forth, teasing the hell out of her.

"Here's my new thing for tonight." His eyes flipped up to hers, and they looked gloriously depraved. "I would really love to try to make you come. Inside here."

In one motion, his hand dove beneath her underwear and two fingers slipped inside her. So fast, so incredibly easy. The way was slick and welcoming, and she cried out at the pressure, then asked for more when he didn't move at all. He just watched her, his fingers deep inside.

"You're asking for more because you know it's going to happen." Damn cocksure man with the evil villain grin.

"Give it up, Leith." She was having a hard time finding words that were true, because she sure as hell didn't *want* him to give up. "It won't. Or it'll take way too long. I know myself."

Hand still touching her intimately, he leaned down and kissed her.

"I love everything about you," he murmured. "There's no such thing as too long. You can take forever and I won't mind."

She snaked a hand underneath his kilt, this time not stopping at the barrier of his underwear. She dove inside it, sighing at the feel of steel and soft skin as it filled her palm.

Suddenly he froze, grimacing. "You've got something, right? I should've asked. Or I should've brought them myself."

She had to smile. "I wouldn't have gotten in the backseat if I didn't. My purse."

He delicately extricated himself from her grip, reached over the front seat, and rummaged around until he found the inner side pocket with the condoms. Shoving down his underwear, but keeping on his boots and kilt, he hurriedly put the thing on. The rush didn't bother her. She didn't care. She didn't want time; she just wanted him.

The moon gave her only one half of his lust-twisted face. The rest of his body was in dim outline, and she tugged at his T-shirt, pulling it free so that she could run her hands up his chest and feel all that power captured inside him.

Curling his fingers around her underwear, he pulled the lace down and snapped it off her leg, letting her go as wide as she needed to be for him. The feel of the kilt wool rasping against her inner thighs was exquisite . . . but not nearly as good as the feel of him inside her.

The entrance was slow and steady, a push that had them both gasping, their eyes locked on where they were joined. He started to move with deep, long motions that rocked the car. She clamped around him. She couldn't watch anymore, her head falling back to the seat. But he was so deep inside her, moving so well and so smoothly, that she couldn't stay blind for long. When she opened her eyes, he was staring into her face. There was such severity on his, a deep concentration.

And there was such deliberation with his body, that huge thing that he could use so gently. He was strong but also giving. He was two beings at once, and everything in between, and he was taking her completely out of her mind.

This wasn't fucking. It wasn't even sex. Somewhere, between blow jobs in the parking lot and here in the backseat, this whole act had transformed into—oh boy, she never thought she'd be able to even *think* the term without giggling—making love.

Thinking that, even though the term was antiquated and silly, sent a surge of emotion through her, enhancing the gift of his physical sensations. Something about his movement, his strokes, was different that night. Special. They were powerful and focused, and they were doing things to her she instinctively knew were right.

Still, she needed . . . she needed a hand between them, rubbing where she wanted, giving her that extra push, throwing her over the edge. She needed it now, now, now. But there was no space, and he wasn't giving her any time to think.

Leith touched his forehead to hers, his hair brushing her skin. He gave a mighty thrust, curling upward. It dragged something out from deep inside her, and she let out a ragged cry. He did it over and over, for more minutes than she could ever count. On and on, for forever and a day. Her hands scrabbled at the leather, looking for . . . what? Purchase? Something to hold on to and ride out this wave? Him?

His voice rumbled low. "I found it, didn't I?"

"Leith . . . oh, *God* . . ."

He pulled out again, thrust back in in that upward motion. *There.*

"Stop fighting it. Let go." Then against her ear: "Be mine."

This was her last stand, the last measure of control she had over herself when she was around him. But why was she clinging to it? Why wasn't she letting go? Was she every bit the control freak Aimee and Leith and so many others had made her out to be? If she was fighting it, it wasn't deliberate.

He pushed in again and again, finding and stroking that invisible spot inside, despite the fact she'd convinced her body it didn't exist or that it had somehow died or gone numb over the years. The rhythm changed, ramping up, his accompanying grunts turning to music in her ears. The motion pressed the top of her head against the side of the car, and she put her palms to the wall, pushing off. The resistance drove Leith in even deeper.

His knees were wedged under her legs, lifting up her body, crunching her into the tiny space, completely at his mercy. No room to twist away or do what she wanted. No room to be anything but his.

You are you, and I am me.

And I am yours, she thought.

Tremors started inside her vagina, and slowly, achingly radiated out through her body. She wanted to speak, to tell him what he was doing was magic, but she couldn't find her voice. It had flown straight up into the stars.

"Don't . . . stop," she finally got out.

"That's my girl."

"Don't stop," she said again. And again, and again.

He obeyed, timing his thrusts to her words, until a brand new kind of orgasm, born of a secret place, stole her body and replaced it with a quivering, hot mass of skin and bone. She could feel sweat break out all over her skin, the warm night air sweeping over it, and Leith touching her everywhere. She was flying, her body weightless and sensitive. When she came down, he was still holding her, still moving urgently inside her, and it created a new fear—that this night, what he'd made her feel, had splintered her veins with cracks, and any move away from him would make her shatter.

She was still pulsing when she opened her eyes. Leith was still looking at her, but he wasn't smiling. There was a beautiful animal inside him, a man of such strength whom she'd reduced to this driving need. Forget throwing giant weights around a field; *this* was power.

"Oh, my *God.*" He shuddered, grinding out her name between his teeth. Then he, too, disappeared into orgasm. She could feel him through the condom, and then his whole body turned shaky and unstable. She watched it all in a strange kind of wonder.

As he pulled out, wedged his arms underneath her back, and collapsed on top of her, she welcomed the weight. They clung so tightly to one another, she didn't know if she'd ever be able to unhook her legs from around his hips, or her arms from around his neck. He crushed her, combined with her, and it was the most sacred feeling.

She felt blindsided by her emotions. She'd driven up to Gleann two weeks ago to put on a good party to help her sister and to honor the memory of her aunt, and instead she'd found . . . him. Leith. Never in a million years had she expected this. It certainly wasn't something she'd been looking for. As Leith had put it, she had that "crazy job" that had long prevented her from even considering a relationship with serious undertones. Or maybe that had been her just making excuses.

The more she thought about it, the more she realized that how she felt now had everything to do with him. This never would have happened with another man, at any other time in her life. The timing, his presence, who they both were now—everything had aligned. It had nothing to do with orgasms and everything to do with her heart.

Ten years ago—or three years ago, or five and a half years ago—they might have tried to fit back together and found that the teeth and grooves in their respective gears didn't quite match up. But somehow, being the people they were today, and finding each other again under these specific circumstances, the machine snapped together and ran way too smoothly.

Leith drew a deep breath as if to say something, but Jen cut him off. "If you want to live, do not say 'I told you so.'"

As he lifted his head, the moonlight showed his feline grin. "I told you so."

"Argh!" She futilely pressed at his shoulders. "Get off."

"No." He kissed away her protest, and she tried to hate that it worked. "I believe you were the one who got off. With me inside you. Just like I said you would."

Involuntarily, her arms went around him again, the low rumble of his laugh against her chest.

He helped her dress in silence, passing her articles of clothing. All he had to do was pull up his underwear and smooth down his kilt. But she loved how it had gotten wrinkled, that his T-shirt was now crooked and untucked.

As he drove her back to Maple Avenue, she worried he might veer off the road, he kept looking over at her so much. He pulled the car into Mildred's garage and as they got out, the sound of the Cadillac's car door slamming brought back a forceful memory. Her, getting out of the Cadillac in front of the Thistle, then running around back to the garage apartment before Aunt Bev would wake up.

Jen turned to Leith, only to find he was already watching her from where he stood on the other side of the car, arms folded across his chest.

She knew full well what she'd told him back in New York, that they would try to make this work again, but was that a fantasy? A delusion? Had they been swept up by something way too quickly? They were two adults, standing in the small town in which they'd formed their friendship twenty years ago, so very far away from their current realities. The second they left this valley for good, would the glistening, sparkling bubble pop?

"Come on." He walked to the trunk of the big, beautiful car, holding out his hand to her. "Now you're allowed to sleep."

She went to him willingly, because that's what her heart demanded. As he folded her into his body in an embrace she could only describe as loving, she thought: *I am in deep, deep shit.*

Chapter

22

"If my event next March goes off as well as these games," Bobbie said to Jen at eight the next morning, "I'm going to owe you a whole hell of a lot."

The last of the 5k runners disappeared down the Hemmertex drive, the Highland cattle watching the group of fifty-four competitors stream by. Bobbie, Jen's race assistant, clutched her tablet computer in which she'd list the finishers after they wound through Gleann, struggled up the hill overlooking the lake, and then made their way back down to the games grounds. The Kid Sprint, which would circle the grounds once and award prizes in different age groups, would go off in a moment. Tons of excited kids and camera-wielding parents milled about in the sunshine.

"You won't owe me a thing," Jen told Bobbie. "It was my pleasure."

And it was. Perhaps more so than planning any number of city events for big-time clients who would never display such honest happiness or personal satisfaction. Besides, Bobbie's new convention would benefit people she cared about . . . and Gleann.

The games were such a small thing in the grand scheme of

this town. Sue McCurdy and Aimee and many others had wanted to believe that just putting on the games again this year—opening the gates to the same-old, same-old—would've magically saved the town from falling into ruin, but Jen knew better. This was one weekend out of the entire year. What Gleann had asked her for—without even really knowing it—was long-term help. And Jen was ecstatic that she'd been able to give it, especially now that her sister and Sue and, yes, even Melissa were moving forward on new business opportunities.

Change was in the air, and it smelled wonderful. It filled her with a new sense of accomplishment she couldn't recall ever experiencing before.

She skirted around the music pavilion—the garbage volunteers had done their job after last night, excellent—and passed the tent where the heritage researchers and kilt makers were rolling back the flaps and setting up their wares.

"Testing, testing." Leith's voice crackled across the athletics field, coming through the PA system she'd begged off the local high school. "What do you do with an elephant who has three balls?"

Jen cringed, throwing a wary glance at the families gathering for the foot races. She hurried for the field, intent on stopping Leith short of saying *penis*.

"Walk him," Leith mugged into the PA with an exaggerated flair, "and pitch to the giraffe. Ba dum dum."

Low, scattered laughter came from the corner of the field where a group of fourteen men in kilts were doing squats and lunges, or stretching themselves out on the ground. Leith pointed to them, clapped for himself, and set down the mike.

"Sounds good," she said, coming up to him. "Although I was a bit afraid where you were going to take that one. I never asked, but have you announced before?"

"Nah, but they love me. I'll just wing it." He winked.

They did love him, and she was positive his winging it for no charge would be far better than the drone who demanded money, whom Gleann had hired in the past.

He began to rotate his arms in big circles, mimicking what a few other guys were doing on the opposite end of the field.

Her eyes bulged. "Are you . . . warming up?"

He blinked at her, then turned in stupefication toward the

place where two bulked-up athletes were launching into a slow jog around the field. "Wow. Old habit coming back, I guess."

She didn't say anything more, just let him process whatever was going on in his mind. He gazed at the towers to be used for the sheaf toss and the weight throw for height—two tall poles with a horizontal crossbeam rigged on ropes, able to be raised and lowered for the different events. In the sheaf toss, throwers used a pitchfork to get a stuffed burlap sack up and over the bar. In weight for height, throwers used a single arm to get a fifty-six-pound weight over the bar.

His eyes then trailed off to the side where a long white board in the grass marked the "trig," or the front border of the throwing box for the weight for distance, and the open and Braemar stone puts. If Gleann was doing the hammer throw, they'd used that trig, too, but they weren't. They were throwing two weights for distance that day: the twenty-eight pound and the fifty-six. The open and Braemar stone puts both used a heavy river stone, the main difference being that throwers could use any style to throw the open stone—like the classic shot put—and had to stay in a standing position to throw the Braemar.

The cabers would be thrown last, once the field had been cleared of all other equipment, and since it seemed to be the biggest audience draw.

Fifty feet away, Duncan backed a large Suburban up to the edge of the field, three cabers roped to the roof. Six high school students came running over to help him take them down and also unload the sheaves and pitchforks from the back of the cab. Getting younger volunteers—especially interested athletes—had been Leith's idea, and it seemed to be working out splendidly.

"Duncan brought some great sticks," Leith said next to her, breaking out of his reverie. "Excellent shape, light enough to turn so the crowd'll be happy. None of these guys are pros, but if anyone does really well and wants to try a challenge caber, something longer and heavier, he's got a sick one."

She waved to Duncan, who was barking orders to the high school kids like a drill sergeant one second, then making them laugh the next.

"The guys are really excited for this," Leith added. "A lot of them haven't thrown together in a long time. Duncan did a great job, bringing them all together here on such short notice. Some old rivalries are heating up again. Lots of side bets. It's going to be a good day."

He was staring across the field, hands on his hips. Today he wore his own kilt and hose, the colors bright, the fit perfect. She gave him extra points for a clean, unstained T-shirt, too.

"It is." She took a deep inhale of the best air she'd ever breathed, feeling it trickle into her lungs.

"Dougall!" Duncan boomed. "Get over here!"

"The boss calls." A gorgeous smile spread across Leith's rugged face.

"I'll check in later," she said, having to look away before she jumped him right then and there.

"You got it."

She'd swiveled and was already heading to the whiskey tent to check on Shea, when she heard Leith call her name. She turned to find him jogging back up to her.

"Forgot to tell you something," he said.

"Oh? Problem?"

"No, not at all. I, uh, I just wanted to tell you that I love you."

Time stopped. So did the wind and the sounds of the awakening games. The thump of her heart picked up, though. Good and strong and fast.

"What?" she said.

She didn't think she'd ever seen him smile so widely, and that was saying something. "You heard me." He opened his arms then let them slap down at his sides. "But I'll say it again if you want. I love you." Duncan called him again. "And now I really have to go."

He held her gaping stare for as long as possible before finally turning and loping over to the AD.

So it was just like that, she thought with her own hidden smile. He loved her. Again.

She could say she loved him again, too, but the warmth that spread through her limbs was not something she'd ever felt before. It was not the same emotion that had existed in their previous lives, their earlier incarnation. It was not the love that she'd spoken over the phone all those years ago. It was something entirely and wonderfully new, and she embraced it with her whole being.

On her way over to the whiskey tent, lost in a delirious haze she didn't quite know how to navigate, she glimpsed a patch of the old fairgrounds between two cars. Not just any patch, but the center of the field, where the rugby teams were warming up in preparation for their first match. The very spot where, ten years ago, the declarative words Leith had meant as a beginning turned out to be an end.

Not this time, she told herself. Not if she could help it.

Shea came out of her tent to straighten the Amber Lounge signs that had gone crooked overnight. Jen went over to her. "How's it going?"

"The extra glasses and napkins arrived this morning," Shea said. "How'd you do that on such short notice and on a weekend?"

"New Hampshire Highland magic." She winked. "They were local, is all."

Shea surveyed the grounds in the direction of the athletics field, where a scattered few people had already set up chairs and blankets. Jen's attention was drawn back to the fairgrounds and that patch of grass, but then someone else caught her eye.

"Don't look now"—she nudged Shea—"but that hot rugby player from last night is staring at you."

Shea turned to follow Jen's line of sight to the dark-haired man who now wore shorts, cleats, and a clean, red rugby shirt. He was sitting on the grass, one well-muscled leg bent inward, the other straight out, as he stretched. But he was definitely looking up toward the whiskey tent on top of the small rise, and it definitely wasn't at Jen.

"That's nice," Shea said in a flat tone. But she looked at the guy for far too long before heading back into her tent. She'd better be careful, because her curiosity was showing.

Down by the ticket entrance, the families of the kids who were about to race had massed into a big group. Aimee was down there, along with Ainsley, the number three pinned on her chest.

In Loughlin's field, which bordered the games grounds, one of the shaggy orange Highland cattle started to cross the grass toward the crowd. Jen had no idea those things could move any faster than a lazy amble, let alone be capable of the slow jog the giant beast was doing now. It looked like curiosity had gotten the better of the animal, too, only it wasn't as determined to hide it as Shea. The cow wore a great, clanking bell around its neck, and as it came right up to the fence, the kids got really excited and started to mill around it. That seemed to excite the cow, and it paced back and forth, opening its huge pink mouth, probably looking for food. On the far side of the field, looking only like a black blur from this distance, one of Loughlin's border collies started to bark.

The parents tried to usher the racers back into position with one hand and take pictures with the other. Once the kids were lined up again, Bobbie shouted directions to them and pulled the trigger on the cheap plastic popgun Jen had picked up at the Gleann gas station. The kids took off in a squealing surge, no concept of pacing themselves, heading out and around the heritage tent, past the field and its lone cow, in a flat-out sprint. Jen watched with a smile as Leith and all the guys on the athletics field turned to applaud and cheer on the smaller ones, some of whom wore kilts as well.

The cow in the pasture let out a bellowing cry and tossed its horns, shaking the fringe from its eyes as it watched the kids run away. It looked like it wanted to run with them, dancing back and forth, getting closer to the fence, leaning into the posts that were already a little tilted and loose.

And then one post tilted too much, grinding up the dirt at its base. The cow hit it again as it strained to race with the kids. The post fell over in slow motion, dragging the connecting wires with it . . . and the next two posts on either side. The middle one landed completely flat, hollowing out a space in the fence big enough for even a great hairy cow with a four-foot horn span to get through. Which it did.

The freed cow trotted happily out of its field, its orange coat bouncing, heading for the route around the athletics field. Maybe it thought it was part of the kid herd. Maybe it wanted the candy and money first prize.

No no no no no, Jen screamed silently, already running down the hill, not really thinking how stupid it was to go charging *toward* an animal that had gotten loose from its pen. Then someone screamed for real—one of the moms standing at the finish line. As everyone finally realized what had happened, there started a chain reaction of panic. Even Jen, a country-turned-city girl, knew that shouting and running about with a loose animal was the wrong thing to do, but it didn't deter anyone.

A mass of parents, arms flailing, started to run for their kids, who were still gleefully and ignorantly chugging around the athletics field.

The cow got spooked and changed course, away from the crowd and in the opposite direction. Toward the tents.

Across the field, way back by Loughlin's house and barn, the barking of the border collie drew closer and closer. The dog was a black-and-white bullet, streaking across the scrubby grass. Out hobbled Loughlin from his barn, holding a whistle to his lips and then calling herding orders to his dog, but the smart little thing was well on it.

The cow wasn't running, not stampeding, but it was huge and loose and panicking, and in an unfamiliar setting. It hit the heritage tent, its hooves uprooting the ropes, its horn ripping at the sidewalls. The white tent came down. Tables collapsed inside. The proprietors had already left, thank God, having come out to see why forty adults were shouting as they ran for their kids.

The cow snorted, mooed, kept going farther into the grounds. The dog barreled down on it, leaping gracefully over the downed fence, yapping its head off. The cow recognized its herder, and turned its head as the dog circled around, crouching low, pushing it back the way it had come. The dog wove back and forth, keeping the cow on track, but in its rotating path stood Shea's whiskey tent. It went down, too, with a trip of rope and good sweep of massive orange hindquarters. From underneath the billowing pile of white came the distinct shatter of glass and a wet gurgle.

That's when Shea screamed, "No fucking *way*!" and Jen was glad all the kids had been safely gathered on the opposite side of the grounds.

As soon as the dog cleared the cow from the general area, Shea dove for her collapsing tent. A few more bottles tipped over underneath, and she whimpered.

"Save the whiskey!" cried a couple of the rugby players as they sprinted over from the field. They were smiling and laughing, damn them.

Hot Rugby Guy was the first on the scene, hurrying to Shea's side and shouldering a thick fold of tent before it fell on her. "Here," he said, his legs flexing under the sagging weight of the breaking tent. "Can you get under? Or see inside at least?"

Poles snapped and Jen's heart sank. As more rugby players dove for the tent and held up the white fabric, the sound of breaking glass tapered off.

She'd never felt such panic on-site before. Her events *never* went down in flames. Or got stampeded by cows. She never failed. Ever.

The cow stumbled back over the downed fence, the dog crouching and weaving at its heels. Loughlin finally made it over, his wrinkled face red and twisted from effort. He leaned against one of the still-standing fence posts, rubbing his knee, making no effort to call to his dog anymore or go to the broken section.

Turned out he didn't have to.

The heavy athletes came running over from the field, kilts and all, Leith at their head. He bent down, picked up the toppled center fence post, and walked it upright, sliding it into its old, ragged hole. The wires from the row of attached posts were dragging it down, pressing down on him. The cords in his neck popped out, the muscles in his chest and arms going tight as he motioned for the other guys to fan out.

"Hold the other posts up," he called out. "Duncan. In the back of my truck are some shovels. We'll sink these things deeper, then I'll send one of the kids over to Mildred's garage to get some Quikrete."

The disgusted look he threw at Loughlin was unmistakable and there for all to see. Leith MacDougall, actually showing his displeasure with one of Gleann's esteemed locals, and one of the biggest names in the valley, no less.

"You're welcome," Leith gritted out to the old farmer, as he shouldered the post.

Jen rushed over once the athletes had the fence upright and the cow had been herded by the dog well into the field. The stupid cow was looking over its shoulder at the kids, as if it still wanted to run with them.

"Thank you." Jen desperately tried to keep a handle on her voice.

"Hey, you," Leith replied. "Quite the morning."

She knew he was trying to pull a smile from her, but it wouldn't work. Not now. Her mind was racing.

Loughlin adjusted his pants as he turned and started to hobble back across his field. His insurance company would be getting a call from Sue McCurdy's office, that was for sure.

"You okay?" she asked Leith as he pressed his butt and lower back against the pole and stood half bent, hands on his thighs.

"Oh, sure. I'm Atlas, baby."

She'd never allowed any man to call her *baby*. He was mostly joking, but there was an easy warmth in his expression, and it didn't rankle her at all. In fact, it gave her a little island of peace in all this.

"Any reason why the competition can't go on?" he asked.

She looked around. Everyone was safe . . . but everything else was a disaster. The heritage tent—the tables, books, and photos, and all the kilts for display and sale were strewn everywhere. Shea and a bunch of men in shorts and cleats were burrowing under the remains of her tent and mourning the sad, sad death of some fine bottles of whiskey. Strings of fairy lights made a minefield of the lawn, and most of the tables in the eating area had been overturned or splintered. The athletics field—thank you, Spirit of Mr. MacDougall—was untouched. There really wasn't any reason the guys couldn't get to throw around the big stuff.

"No," she told Leith with a great sigh. "Keep it going. For the love of God, we've got to give these people *something* to do today."

Duncan came back with the shovels, passing them out, and Leith gave instructions on where to dig, how far down to go. Jen wandered away from the noise and pulled out her phone.

That early on a Saturday, it would be a miracle if her tent contact would be available. He wasn't. She left a frantic message, knowing there was very little he could do, being that he was located close to New York, but it was worth a try. In the meantime she could help the kilt makers and heritage people dig out their wares. Rolling up her sleeves, she waded into their tent and helped pull out some tartans and books from the dirt. Many were unsalvageable, stamped with massive hoofprints.

Aimee and Ainsley came over. "What can we do?" her sister asked.

Jen could hear Shea swearing up a colorful storm just as a lot of other locals and attendees were starting to mill about. She told her sister and niece, "You guys stay here and help the heritage people. Too much broken glass over by Shea. Don't want Ainsley to get hurt. I'll go to her."

By the looks of it, Shea didn't really need the help. Pretty much every rugby player had come over to sift through the broken tent and salvage what bottles were whole and unbroken. Whenever they found one, they raised it above their heads and bellowed like a pirate finding treasure. Hot Rugby Guy was still there, but instead of staring at Shea or attempting to flirt with her as some of the others were hopelessly doing, he was helping to methodically pick through the debris.

Someone tapped Jen's shoulder. She turned to find Chris holding his fiddle case under one arm. He looked *pissed*.

"We can't play today."

"What?"

He sneered at the dirt, kicked a chunk with his sneaker. "This morning the sheriff took Scott in for questioning about the Loughlin barn fire."

She clamped a hand over her mouth. Neither she nor Leith had had the chance to tell Olsen last night about Scott's potato chip hat, but when the sheriff's office had called her last week to inquire about what she'd seen in the back of the barn that first day, she'd told them about the items. Maybe Olsen had seen it last night and had put two and two together on his own. If Scott had caused the fire, he'd called himself out on stage.

"So unless you can find another drummer in the next couple of hours . . ." Chris said.

Fuck. She bit at the curse and it tasted nasty. "Maybe you can play solo? The crowd loved you last night. You were undeniably the star."

He paled. "I don't know. I've never done that. I sort of need the other guys."

"Please. I'm begging you."

"Let me think about it." He wandered off, already looking like that answer would be no.

Great. Absolutely great.

For the next half hour, Jen picked glass out of the grass. Her phone rang. Jogging away from the noise, anxious to hear what solution the tent company had for her, she picked up the call without checking to see who it was.

"Jen." Slight New York accent with a strong twinge of desperation and disappointment. She knew that voice like the sound of her own alarm clock.

"Tim, hi. Listen, can I call you back in, say, an hour?" Even that timeline was being hopeful.

Her boss cleared his throat. A different phone rang in the background and she recognized the tone as that from the Bauer Events office. "I really don't think you have an hour," he said. "The vacation's over a few days early. I need you back in New York. This afternoon."

Chapter

23

To say Jen's heart sank would have been an insult to gravity. The great muscle in her chest that had been treating her so well over the past two weeks plummeted with cheetah speed.

Out of the corner of her eye, she noticed Sue hurrying over, frantically waving her arms to get Jen's attention. Though it killed her, she held up a finger to the mayor and headed around Shea's tent, away from the athletics field, and into the parking lot.

"I'm in northern New Hampshire, Tim, working on some personal stuff. There's no way I can get back by tonight."

"Not tonight. This afternoon. And if you hit the road in the next hour, it should be plenty of time. Umberto Rollins goes off at eight and the thing is a giant clusterfuck. You need to come back to fix it, or we'll lose one of our biggest clients. And I might have to reconsider you for a partnership."

She sank onto the bumper of some stranger's car.

"What's happened?"

"I'll tell you what's happened. Rollins's assistant went to the site first thing this morning to check on setup for tonight's event. I thought you two were on the same page, that you were on board with what they wanted."

Jen gasped as a flash of red crossed her eyes. "I was. I mean, I am." She ground fingers into her eyelids. "Gretchen."

"Damn straight it was Gretchen. Changed pretty much everything they didn't want changed."

Save for her mother, Jen didn't think she'd ever been this furious with anyone. "I didn't pass the buck," she told her boss. "I've been keeping in touch with her, checking up on her almost daily."

"I know you didn't pass the buck. You did what good managers do; you managed. But now it's on your head to fix." He was an excellent businessman, a hard-ass when he needed to be, and her idol for a very long time. When she'd first met him, she'd had visions about the kind of worker she wanted to be and the heights she needed to reach.

His voice dipped low. "It's bigger than just the setup. Rollins said he's being courted by Morris Events, and he's threatened to walk if you personally don't come back and fix this."

The very first thing that came to her mind was: Did anyone die? Was this really *that* serious?

This world that Bauer described—the frantic city business life she'd been living for six years in which life or death seemed to hang on table seating or napkin selection or the guest list—had felt so distant while she'd been here in the mountains, even though it was a world she'd hunted with fervor, and then purposely built up all around her. Suddenly she was dunked back into it, and it felt bracing and unwelcome.

"I understand," she heard herself say, but it sounded so far away.

"And it goes without saying you need to fire Gretchen."

Why can't you just fire her now? Jen nearly asked, then realized that Tim was entirely correct. This was Jen's mistake, Jen's assistant, and it was her responsibility.

The little phone felt like a brick in her hand.

Leith's voice streamed out from the PA system. "Ladies and gentlemen, despite what has happened here today, these talented athletes are at your disposal. The throwing events will go on."

Enthusiastic applause followed. Some people who had started to fold up their blankets now snapped them out again. The light tone to Leith's voice was bittersweet, because his excitement was the people's, and even though he'd soon be gone from Gleann, the town would carry on without him. It would carry on without her, too.

She was exceedingly proud of what she'd done here—despite the cow disaster. It had started out as a favor—a bit of a concession, done out of a sense of responsibility and the desire to pay people back who deserved it. But it had since turned into much, much more—a large, warm presence in her heart, and she wasn't even talking about Leith. She couldn't give it a name, didn't know where it fit into her bigger life, but she knew she wasn't quite ready to walk out on it yet.

There *had* to be a way for her to straighten things out with Rollins remotely and stay in Gleann for the afternoon.

"Jen?" Tim demanded.

Her head dropped, her eyes closing tightly. On the back of her eyelids was imprinted the image of her mom throwing her college applications in the trash and dumping coffee grounds over them. Telling her there was no way she could afford to send Jen to college, not knowing how much Jen had secretly saved herself. Sneering as Jen lugged her sole suitcase out the front door for the last time. Saying to her, *You'll be back. You're just wasting your time. The world is made so people like us fail. You'll see. You think you're different, but you're not. You'll end up right where I am someday.*

Jen was so close to snatching the gold ring. She could not fail. She would not get fired. That was something that happened to her mother, not her. If she stayed in Gleann and got knocked back a notch in her upward climb, what would that say about her? Would that put her on the path to failure? Would staying here, in the very place she'd left ten years ago in order to begin that climb, start the transformation into someone who settled for the small instead of going for the big?

She broke out in an icy sweat. Oh, God, she felt sick. So conflicted. So unsure.

"Jen. Are you there?"

There was so much more she needed to do here. But her future—the big, bright one she'd been striving for—glowed from a city six hours to the south.

"Will I see you later today?" Tim was starting to get angry, and disappointment from her mentor felt like coffee grounds dumped over her dreams.

If she went back to New York, she'd let down Aimee and Sue and—oh God—Leith. She'd be leaving right in the middle of a crisis. But if she stayed, she'd be right back where she started, and that scared her more than anything.

She swallowed around a throat laced with needles. Pushing off the car, she gazed up at the games. At the mess.

"Apparently I am in demand as a stand-up," came Leith's chuckle over the PA, and Jen heard rousing, masculine shouts spring up from the athletes, "so here you go . . ."

She refused to crumple. This was a new beginning between her and Leith, she reminded herself. She'd agreed to give them another shot, and that would be relatively easy, what with him moving to Connecticut and her in the city. Look how well they'd done in their brief time in the city last week. They could exist outside of Gleann. Their magic wasn't limited to this little valley. It had broken free from the links of the past.

But it didn't mean he wouldn't be pissed off that she was abandoning the one thing she'd come here purposely to do. She just had to believe he'd understand.

"Yes," she told Tim, her voice dying. "Yes, I'll be there."

*S*ue had wandered over to Shea and stood frowning at the mess, her arms folded under those giant boobs wrapped in today's T-shirt that proclaimed her love for the Isle of Skye. Tomorrow it would be back to the wide range of Syracuse wear, Jen thought numbly. Sue's back was to her, so Jen skirted around, not ready to face her yet. Instead she headed for Aimee and Ainsley, who were helping the heritage people restack their books and rehang the kilts and scarves and such on the few unbroken racks. T and Lacey were also there, lending a hand.

"Check it out," Ainsley said with a toothy grin as Jen came up. "Clan Hamilton. Wasn't that who your Aunt Bev married?"

The Hamilton tartan was similar to MacDougall: lots of red, but a bit more blue and white.

"That's great, McGee." Jen's mind was too thin to think of a witty descriptor.

Aimee stood up, brushing her hands free of dirt and grass. She eyed Jen perceptively. "What's up?"

"Um . . ."

She idly noticed Leith and the guys had managed to get the fence posts into new holes, but the things were still listing.

"What is it?" Aimee's voice crossed over into worry.

A buzzing and jangling from Jen's pocket. The phone had become a fifth limb to her over the years, so why the feel and sound of it surprised her now was more than disconcerting.

Giving Aimee an apologetic look, she saw on the phone screen that it wasn't her tent contact or Tim again. An unfamiliar number.

Oh God, what? she wanted to scream into it. "Yes?"

"Is this Jen Haverhurst?"

"It is."

"This is Valley Transportation. I'm calling to tell you the bus you rented to bring in a—what is this? Oh, a bagpipe and drum band—from Mount Caleb has broken down on Route 6. The driver didn't have your number."

Great. Wonderful. Perfect. Exactly what today needed.

The pipe band from across the state should have been arriving right about now. She thought the grounds had been a little too quiet between the panic of a loose cow, a barking herding dog, and collapsing tents.

"So what are you going to do about it?" Jen demanded into the phone.

"Uh, well, all my other buses of that size are taken today, but a tow truck is on its way."

Shit shit shit. "Unless a tow truck is going to tow that thing and everyone inside all the way to Gleann, that doesn't do me or my musicians any good."

She ended the call with numb fingers, then turned back around to see that Owen and Melissa had arrived, each shouldering two folding lawn chairs. They and Aimee were staring at Jen.

"What happened?" Aimee asked. Jen told them about the broken-down bus.

Even if she couldn't stay, she could try to fix this one last thing. A Highland Games needed a pipe and drum band, damn it. "Owen, do you have a big car? Maybe a work truck?" The plumber nodded. "And friends who possibly own similar trucks?"

Owen slid his chairs to the ground. "I hear you and I'm on it. We'll bring them in, then figure out how the hell to get them back later."

"I'll take the Suburban," Melissa added, and the two of them marched back to the parking lot, phones at their ears.

Jen watched them go with a dull sense of satisfaction. The pipe band would get here, disjointed and very late, throwing off the whole day's schedule, but what the hell, it wasn't like the games she'd slaved over during the past two weeks hadn't already been thrown into a lidless blender and spun on *puree*.

Aimee narrowed her eyes and folded her arms. "That's not why you came over here. I know you. What's going on?"

Jen braced herself, opened her mouth. She'd never told Aimee about the potential promotion because she hadn't wanted her sister to feel like she was pulling Jen away from anything. She'd wanted Aimee, and Gleann, to feel important— because they were—but she had to bring it out now. She knew full well how it was going to sound, that she was dragging out an excuse to take off. To abandon Aimee for work again, at the worst possible time, when things between them were just starting to get better.

And that's when Sue walked up. Jen looked at the phone in her hand. It was one hell of a stone, and she was about to kill two birds with it.

When she was done telling them everything, Aimee just went over to Ainsley, told her to kiss her aunt good-bye, then wordlessly steered her daughter somewhere out of sight.

"I'm sorry," Jen told Sue, who'd been standing there with her head tilted and lemon-sour lips. Jen couldn't remain under the weight of that look anymore, so she turned away.

She couldn't put off telling Leith any longer. Knowing how fast word spread in this town, if she didn't get over to the athletic field right now, she'd miss her chance.

Ropes of colorful flapping flags divided the onlookers from the big men in the interior field. The athletes had returned to ribbing each other and warming up after their brief landscaping-and-fence-repair interlude. Leith included.

He and Duncan were taking turns jumping up onto a high

box. Leith claimed he wasn't in shape, that he was out of practice and couldn't do stuff like that anymore, but he looked better even than Duncan. The two stopped to share a laugh, Leith doubling over. As Jen neared, she could make out new lines of sweat trickling down the side of his face. He raised an arm to wipe one cheek against his short sleeve. It pulled the T-shirt free from his kilt, displaying a patch of hard skin. A patch she knew particularly well.

Duncan gave Leith a nudge and pointed to her. Leith's powerful torso twisted, and when he saw her, he flashed that thrilling grin, the one that said *Everything is right with the world*.

He met her halfway across the field, his eyes bright. "What's up? Wait, I know that look. Things aren't perfect, but everything'll be fine. No one here cares about the tents. The damn cow will have people talking for months. And I know Scott will probably go to jail and Chris's band won't play, but Chris just told me he's gonna go on solo later this afternoon. The crowd'll love him—" He stepped back, his face falling. "That's not it, is it?"

Just rip off the Band-Aid, Haverhurst. The longer she stalled, the worse it was going to be.

She licked her lips, feeling the hot morning sun on the part of her hair. "I have to go."

His eyebrows pinched together. "The pipe band truck thing? Yeah, I heard. T came over to flip that blue hair in front of one of the high school helpers and told him her parents had gone off on the rescue. You taking off to help them?"

"No. I'm . . . I have to go back to New York."

Now his eyebrows formed one long strip as he lowered his chin. "Right. Tomorrow. When we said we'd drive south together."

"I mean today."

He just stared. And stared. "After the closing ceremonies?"

"No. Now." She drew up her shoulders and held up her phone like it could magically provide proof. It might have been the wrong thing to do because he looked at the thing with immediate wariness. "My boss, my real boss, called. There's an emergency back in New York. If I don't get back tonight and fix it, I'll lose a really big client and possibly the promotion I've wanted since the day I started working there. I need to leave as soon as possible."

He wiped at the corners of his mouth with a forefinger and thumb. He took several breaths before finally getting out, "Now. You're leaving now. Before the games even get going."

She put her phone away and her hands felt terribly empty. "It's my actual job, Leith. My real one. The one that pays the bills."

Lips tight, he nodded. "I thought you had an assistant."

"She's the one who fucked everything up and now it's on my head."

"It's Saturday. Can't you fix it Monday? You know, during *normal* work hours?"

She breathed steadily through her nose. She'd expected this, she reminded herself. "I don't work normal hours. Neither do you, as I recall." As she stepped closer to him, he didn't reach for her. "I'm not a superhero. I can't be two places at once. I've been standing over there, wracking my brain trying to figure out how to do both, but I just can't. I have to choose. And, yes, my heart is telling me to stay, but my brain and my duty are pulling me back to the city."

Over Leith's shoulder she glimpsed one of the athletes starting toward him, until Duncan stopped him with a hand to his chest.

Leith's hands slid to his hips. "I was supposed to go back to Connecticut this weekend, you know."

"Yes. I do know."

"It was the only weekend Rory's husband was going to be in town to approve my plans. She moved up my complete date by three weeks. I can't really afford to be here either, but I am. I stayed. For them." He nudged his chin at the pockets of people he'd grown up with, and many more he hadn't. "For Da's memory."

"I understand what you've done," she said. "What it took to make you stay. But really, what made you stay—your past, your roots—is the very same reason why I have to go. There were things you needed to do and finish here. There are things I need to do and finish there."

He seemed to barely hear her. "I also stayed for you, remember."

She started to fidget, shifting from foot to foot. "I know. I don't want to go. I told you. I had to make a choice. But we'll see each other next week, when you get to Connecticut. Then we'll figure everything else out."

He shook his head in disbelief. "You really aren't seeing this? The similarities? How this looks to me? How it *feels*?"

"Similarities to—? Oh." She closed her eyes. "Shit. I'm sorry. I really am."

"I mean, I understand that what happened ten years ago was when we were kids, that you had legitimate reasons for not staying, but right over there"—he jabbed a finger toward the fairgrounds and his voice rose—"is where I told you how I felt, and then watched you walk away right after. And today I'm standing in almost the exact same spot, watching you leave again. After I told you *exactly* how I feel now. I fucking hate watching you walk away. I can't change that reaction, and I won't apologize for it."

"You shouldn't have to apologize. I should. And I am."

"I'm not pissed off because you're going after your dream. I told you I get you, and I do. What you told me in New York, about your mom and Iowa and coming here . . . it's powerful stuff that I totally understand. But if we're being honest, I'm pissed off because I sacrificed something big to be here for Gleann and for you, and you're turning away. I'm scared for what this could mean to us, that this is a sign of things to come."

His unspoken question: When will *you* sacrifice for *me*?

But she had, by pushing aside her larger goals for a time to be here in the first place. So in essence she already had sacrificed to be reunited with him. Why did she have to sacrifice more to keep his faith? It wasn't fucking fair. The whole thing was all too convoluted and didn't make any sense. This was supposed to end perfectly.

She reached up to take his face. He let her, but his reciprocal touch—light fingers at her waist—lacked his usual warmth.

"I told you we would try," she said. "I meant it."

"Don't go," he whispered, his frustration coming through loud and clear. His hands at her waist suddenly bit in.

"I have to," she whispered back, then tried to step out of his arms. He held fast. "I'm so sorry."

He kissed her, swift and light, like she'd already slipped away. Like it was their last time. Like he was saying good-bye. She forced herself to ignore the sense of foreboding it caused.

"Call me tomorrow from the road?" she said.

Leith did not look at her as he replied, "Why don't you call me? Hopefully it'll go better than the last long-distance phone call we had."

Ouch. "It will."

But he'd already turned, and right then she knew exactly what he'd meant about hating to watch her walk away. The sight of his stiff back and shoulders, and the heavy plod of his boots on the grass thundered through her body. It shouldn't have made her worry that this might indeed be the last time she'd see him . . . but it did.

Numb, she walked to the edge of the field and lifted the flag rope without feeling its plastic snap at her skin. She wove her way through the crowd without sensing the other bodies. She'd gotten halfway across the parking lot before she realized she'd left the Hemmertex grounds and the new world of the Gleann Highland Games she'd helped create. Blinking into the sunshine, she knew she had to do what she'd always done: Go forward. Not back.

Doing so had just never hurt this much before.

As she opened the unlocked door to 738 Maple, her phone rang again, jangling her from thoughts of Leith. The little black thing she practically slept with, the inanimate object she usually clung to, she now wanted to chuck across the driveway, like the athletes did with those massive weights.

With a roll of her eyes that felt a little wet, she picked up the call from the guy who'd loaned her the tents as a return favor. Of course they couldn't provide replacements within a timeframe that would do the Gleann Highland Games any good. And of course he wanted payment for any damages. That was to be expected; she'd demand the same thing if she were him.

Jen dug into her purse and pulled out her wallet. "After you come get the tents and inspect them, send me an itemized list of the damages, then charge them to my personal credit card." She read off the series of numbers on the piece of plastic in her hand. "I don't want you to charge Gleann a thing."

*L*eith knew the AD was staring at him.

"What was that about?" Duncan asked, and when Leith didn't answer, he added, "Everything okay with the athletic events?"

"Yeah," he mumbled. "Events are good."

"Ah." Duncan drew out the single word in a way that didn't need explanation.

After a few long moments of pretending to examine the sheaves Duncan had brought for the toss, Leith finally turned back to see Jen moving slowly away through the gathering crowd. Past her sister who just watched her go. Past Mayor Sue, who shook her head. Even past Shea, whose mess of a tent was nearly cleaned up thanks to the swarm of rugby players. Though Jen walked with her head high, she clutched her giant purse to her chest and Leith knew she was protecting herself using that green leather piece of armor which held her mighty weapons: the laptop and her phone.

That goddamn phone.

If she was so affected by her choice, if she questioned it so much—and she did; her excuses weren't fooling him—why the hell wasn't she staying? There were a million more things he'd wanted to say to her, but knew it would've done no good, and they might have sprung more from frustration than true reason. She didn't respond well to that. And besides, he'd made his argument.

She'd forgotten that he knew her, that he'd glimpsed what her life was like back in New York, what sort of world she'd built up around herself. Maybe the threads of that world had loosened since she'd come back to New Hampshire, but once she crossed the bridge back into Manhattan, she'd be swallowed so fast by those jaws of fast-talking, fast-moving events that meant nothing in the grand scheme of things, that she wouldn't even realize she'd shut him out again.

He didn't know if his heart could take that. Not twice.

He wasn't looking for a woman to stay back at home while he went out and worked to bring home the paycheck. Hell no. No, Jen was smart and driven and it wasn't his place to change that. Those were just two of the reasons why he loved her. He loved her for who she *was*, but he was worried about who she was striving, or even pretending, to be. Doing something to escape pain and heartache wasn't the same as doing something because it spoke to your heart.

He wanted to be assured she wouldn't disappear again. But most of all, he just wanted her.

*You want her because she was right, boy. Women usu-
ally are.*

Ah, Da. Leith could hear the old man's chuckle, the same
low, secretive laugh that always came out when he used to talk
about his beloved wife. Leith closed his eyes and bowed his
head. In the distance, beneath everything else, Chris struck some
warm-up notes on his fiddle. Though unamplified, the song
still traveled, and Leith wondered if he was hallucinating,
because it was Da's favorite folk tune, the one he used to play
over and over on the wobbly record player.

Right about what? Leigh almost asked. But he knew.

I know, I know, came Da's ethereal, accented voice. *The last
time you competed you threw like shite in front of me. I get it.
But if you really think that ever mattered to me or to anyone
else, you're a fool. You're also not a father yet. These things
are almost impossible to explain to a man who isn't.*

"It does matter," Leith mumbled. "It matters to me."

"Huh?" Duncan asked, looking up from his clipboard with
a frown.

Leith gave him an awkward smile and shook his head. Duncan ambled away with the clipboard to go check on the high
school volunteers.

She was right, Da whispered in Leith's ear, *what she said
to you about failure and what's holding you back. Failure's
only in your mind. To so many others, it's success.*

Jesus. Leith couldn't breathe. His head snapped up and he
scanned the crowd again, but Jen's dark hair and white dress
were long gone.

*Boy. Just get in there and throw already. You cleaned out
my house. Now clean out your own head.*

And just like what had happened in the music tent last night,
some people shifted on the other side of the flags—a dad trying
to wrangle his five wild kids—and there was Da, sitting on the
edge of the scrappy lawn chair, pipe between his teeth, cap on,
walking cane upright between his knees. He nodded once.
Leith blinked twice. When two of the kids started wrestling,
the image was obliterated.

Leith whirled toward the center of the field, where Duncan
was mingling with some of the competitors. A few handshakes
were going around, a few friendly challenges.

A Braemar stone sat all lonesome off to one side. Twenty-two pounds of black rock calling Leith's name. With a purpose he hadn't felt in at least four years, he stomped over to the stone. Picked it up. Rolled it between his hands. Warm and smooth, a little bit of home in his palms.

He could hear the murmurs starting, the building roar of the crowd, his name spoken in several voices he recognized and just as many he didn't. The sound followed him like he approached a waterfall, building and building the farther into the field he walked. Out of the corner of his eye he could see people hurrying over to the field, beckoned by family members or strangers. A few whistles and scattered applause filled the air.

"Do it, Dougall!" someone yelled.

But that wasn't why he took his place behind the trig, got his feet set into position. Wide. Steady. No, this didn't have to do with them. This was for the man and the woman who weren't even here. And for himself.

"What're you doing, Dougall?" Duncan this time, loud and clear, for all to hear.

Leith swung out his left arm, finding his balance, assuming the form Da had taught him. He raised the Braemar stone and tucked it between his chin and shoulder. A few deep breaths. A crouch. Then he launched that sucker up and into the field, not really caring where it landed. That wasn't the point.

All of Gleann seemed to erupt in cheers.

He walked away from the trig. Duncan's round face was split by a massive grin, that missing tooth making an appearance. His huge arms were thrown out wide and he was laughing. "What the hell are you doing?"

Leith stomped over and snatched Duncan's clipboard from his hands. "What's it look like?" Leith scrawled his name at the bottom of the list of competitors. "I'm fucking throwing."

Chapter

24

Leith sat on the edge of the motel bed, cheap polyester bed-spread sticking to his thighs, cold air rattling out from the window unit but just barely filling the room. The second floor window overlooked a parking lot near Stamford, Connecticut, off I-95.

Beyond that lay one hell of a challenge.

How much had changed in his life in the last twenty-four hours. Most of it not good.

His phone jumped from where it sat by his hip, buzzing and blaring Jen's name. He hated to admit he'd been waiting for her call all day, but the truth was, he had been. He'd left Gleann early that morning, heading south, high on how throwing in the games had made him feel, even if he hadn't thrown that well.

Now he looked down at her name and realized that if she'd stayed at the games, chances were he wouldn't have picked up the stone or the sheaf fork or the caber again. He wasn't quite sure how that made him feel.

He ran his thumb over her name then touched *Answer.* "Hey, you."

"Hi." It came out in a sigh, and he was thrown back two

nights, to the sounds she'd made in the back of Da's Caddy, her exhalations in his ear.

"How did it go last night?" he asked, because he felt like he should. "Everything squared away?"

"Um, yeah, pretty much. Saved the event. Retained the client."

"Your superhero cape looks good fluttering in the breeze." He'd meant it as a joke, of course, but she didn't laugh. Neither did he. He wondered if Jen had heard about him throwing. "Have you talked to Aimee today? Or anyone back in Gleann?"

"No, I haven't. She, ah, isn't picking up my calls or answering my texts. Listen, can I take the train out tonight? I need to see you."

He rose from the bed, his heart pounding with hope. "Absolutely. Hell yeah. I'm just in a shitty motel, but—"

"I don't care."

She was doing this, coming to him. She'd heard what he'd said about trying, about not running away. He started to pace, a strange brand of excitement pumping through him. On a day that had had such turbulent ups and downs, this was definitely an up.

"Can't wait to see you," he said. "I have a lot to tell you." So, so much.

There came one of those pauses that lasted a beat too long, but still he could have sworn she was smiling. "Good. So do I. Pick me up at the Stamford station at 6:44."

Two hours. He couldn't wait to tell her face-to-face about throwing, how incredible it had felt—how she'd been right. She wouldn't gloat. Not his Jen. She would look at him with those sparkling eyes and she would be happy for him. She would slide her arms around his neck and then they'd talk about his Da, how Leith had finally been able to let him go.

Then he would tell her that he'd lost the Carriage job.

*H*e parked his truck in the Stamford train station lot and got out, leaning against it, waiting, unsure if he should go inside to the platform like they did in the movies and immediately drag her into his arms. It seemed like a month since he'd seen her, not a day. In the end he chose to stay in the lot, his weight shifting from foot to foot. But when her familiar figure—*not* carrying that purse with the laptop—finally exited the building and crossed the street to him, he pushed away from the truck.

She looked incredible. Just . . . phenomenal. Black pants that fit her thighs and ass perfectly. Black high heels he'd never seen before but would kill to see on the ends of her bare legs right before she wrapped them around his neck. She wore a short-sleeved top that might have looked demure on anyone not as achingly sexual as her.

Turned out he didn't have to drag her into him. She came willingly, a great magnet pulling them together across the barren Sunday commuter parking lot. She wasn't smiling, but that was okay because her eyes were filled with an apology. He folded her into his arms and she gripped him tightly, her hands splayed on his back, reminding him of how she'd clung to him naked.

"I'm sorry," she said.

This time he was ready to hear it. Ready to accept it. "It's okay. It's okay," he whispered, and then he took her mouth in a kiss that burned with slow fire.

After he'd pulled his mouth away but kept his hands on her face, she didn't look so sure that he'd accepted her apology. Or maybe it was something else. He couldn't quite tell. But at that moment he didn't really care. She was here.

"So this is Connecticut." She smiled. "Your new home."

He coughed. "Never been here?"

"I have. Just not with you."

They got into his truck and he rumbled slowly out of the lot. "Are you hungry? Need a drink?"

"Sure, I guess." When he pulled in front of a little cafe on a busy street whose narrow outdoor patio was dotted with orange umbrellas, she peered out at it and asked, "What's wrong with your hotel?"

"Motel," he corrected with a grin. "It's a sad, sad place not fit for a superhero."

Plus, he knew she would likely head back to the city tonight, and if they went back to his motel he would, without a doubt, have her naked for the next few hours. Believe it or not, he couldn't afford that. He had things to tell her. Things he needed to say, to get out in the open, period.

She responded with the same weird pause he'd heard over the phone two hours earlier, only now he saw the accompanying facial expression. Jen, who always looked people in the eye with confidence, now turned her face to her lap, brow furrowed, that beautiful mouth drawn in a tight line.

"Superhero," she murmured with a little shake of her head.

His heart turned over. A sick feeling bubbled up in his throat.

"Oh, no." He wrenched off the ignition and turned in the seat toward her. "What."

She licked her lips and met his eyes. "Do you want to get out of the truck? Go sit down?"

"Something tells me I don't want to be in public for what you're about to say. We already did that once yesterday and I didn't really care for it. Just say it. That's why you came, right? To tell me to my face that you don't want to try after all?"

"No!" She stretched for him with both hands, placed them on his chest, and he was powerless against their pressure and heat. "That's not it at all. But I have some news that I know you won't like."

With the air off, the cab was starting to get stuffy, so he gave the truck half power to lower the automatic windows. Sweet summer air rushed in. It even smelled different than Gleann.

"What is it," he said.

Another lick of her lips. "I'm going to London."

That's it? Really? "London. Okay, when?"

"Tomorrow."

Ah, okay.

"And"—her hands pressed harder into his chest—"I'll probably be gone for a month. At least."

Ah, *shit*. "Let me guess. Work?"

Now her hands slid off him as she nodded. "Tim's co-owner, the guy who'd been running the London branch of the company, had a major heart attack early this morning. He survived, but he's old and Tim's pretty sure he'll want to retire after this. Tim wants me in London ASAP to oversee everything while they figure things out and find a replacement."

"And that replacement will be you."

She blinked. "Well. No. I'm temporary."

He scrubbed a hand over his cheek, unshaven since

yesterday morning. "You said you've been gunning for a big promotion, a partnership. An owner gets sick and retires. This is it. You can't see that? Tim will send you over there under the pretense of everything being temporary, on a 'trial basis' or some such, and then he'll spring the promotion on you. He'll want you to take over in London."

He really didn't know what he'd do if she tried to deny it again. She wasn't stupid; she was just being thickheaded and trying to soften things for him. He didn't need softening. He just wanted the truth. He wanted her to admit it.

"And then you'll accept it," he went on, "because that's what you do. That's what you've convinced yourself you want. This would put you at the top, and you'll proudly plant your flag up there and take a picture to send back to Iowa."

"I haven't accepted anything." She glanced away when she said it.

"Look." He stabbed fingers into his hair. "I'm not telling you not to take it. I'm not telling you to quit and buy a little Connecticut house with me and make dinner every night, or some other dumb idea that doesn't serve either of us well. All I'm asking you to do is reevaluate what you really want. Because sometimes what we've been *conditioned* to want isn't really what's best for us."

She looked at him askance but said nothing.

"I'm talking about your mom," he added. "I'm talking about Iowa."

"I heard you. I know what you meant. I think I need some air." She opened the door and swung her feet out. She was so composed he couldn't tell if she was angry or hurt or bothered. Or anything.

He jumped out from behind the wheel and jogged to catch up as she entered a little park bisected by defunct railroad tracks. She took a seat on a wooden bench.

"Can I finish?" He kept his tone even and low as he sprawled next to her. She just looked at him, her hair swinging next to one ear. "I'm telling you this because I don't want you to make the same mistake I did. I want you to be bigger than your childhood because you are utterly special in ways you haven't even defined for yourself. I'm telling you this because I . . . care about you."

She winced at that, at the fact he didn't use the *L* word, but since she hadn't said it to him, he wasn't even sure if it was the right word to use at all.

He leaned forward, elbows on his knees. "You think you've escaped Iowa, that you got away from your mom by getting to the top of your field, but she still rules you. In fact, I think she has a bigger power over you now than she did ten, fifteen years ago."

She made a pleading gesture to the sky. "That doesn't make sense."

Damp strands of hair tickled his forehead and neck. The evening was almost unbearably hot.

"I miss my da more than anything," he said, "and you were right, I never processed his death. Never said good-bye. Part of what made it so hard, the biggest part, was grief, but a much smaller part of it was resentment."

She let out a little gasp. "Resentment?"

He shrugged, then reached down to pluck a few blades of grass and roll them between his fingers. The scent of his future always made him feel better.

"He was my best friend. My hero. When he started to weaken when I was in high school, I had to do more and more for him. I didn't mind; I loved doing it. To carry him the way he'd carried me my whole life. But then you left and went to college and, even though I wanted to get out of Gleann, too, I had Da and he only had me. His health went downhill fast after you left, so I stayed. I had to make do."

"I don't understand. You love landscape design. You told me so yourself."

"I do. But even when I knew my business was dying in Gleann, I felt the compulsion to stay. For Da's memory and the roots he laid down. He always told me that home and family was the most important thing in the world, and to him, that family was me and Gleann. I felt like I had to stay for the people who cheered me on and looked up to me. I felt like I had to stay, even though I knew I should have ripped out those roots years ago."

He tossed down the now-shredded grass blades. When he turned his head to look at her, those green eyes were huge.

"So Da dies. I'm lost. The only thing I have left is my

business and the people who love me. Then Hemmertex closes, and I feel obligated to stick around as their billboard whatever and their replacement MacDougall. Meanwhile my business goes in the shitter."

She sat straight-backed, but he saw how her fingers dug into her thighs.

"Do you see what I'm saying? Do you get it?" He heard his voice rising but couldn't bring it down. "You're climbing and climbing, but for what? For who? Your mom, or for you? Honestly, I would love for you to say it's what you really, truly want, what really, truly fulfills you, but I just don't think that's the case. I've never heard you say you love your job, only that it drives you and that you're good at it. I *want* you to love what you do *and* the end product. I don't want you to get caught up in something you can't twist yourself out of down the road."

"You twisted yourself out of all that stuff you just told me about. You're starting over here."

He wasn't sure she was hearing him. Maybe she wouldn't; at least, not tonight. Not in front of him.

Their eyes met. Now would have been the perfect time to tell her how Hal Carriage had called him shortly after he'd left Gleann for Connecticut. How Hal had told him that because Leith hadn't come down that weekend—the only weekend he'd be in town for a long while—Hal had met with and hired another landscape company. A bigger one, an established one. One that could guarantee to have the work done by his daughter's September wedding.

Yep, now would have been perfect. Except that she'd take it that he was trying to guilt her into staying. She'd think he was trying to make her feel bad for asking him to stay for the games. So he kept his mouth shut and let his points about her mom and Iowa do their own work.

He wanted her to stay in the U.S. for herself. And, yes, he wanted her to stay for him—there was no denying that—but she had to come first.

"I'm not trying to talk you out of going to London—"

"Yes, you are." She stood up, and as she glared down at him, he knew the rational part of their conversation was over.

"I'm trying to talk you into doing something for *yourself.* If you decide it's London and your job, great. Then I'll know

you've embraced your dreams and I will have to live with that."
Hands on his knees, he pushed to his feet, towering over her.
"But I know what distance does to us. That's history. That's
fact. You have yet to prove me wrong." Maybe that was harsh,
but it was the truth. And she knew it, too. "Tell me you don't
feel what's between us. Tell me that it isn't worth fighting for,
that it's not twenty times as strong as it was a decade ago. Tell
me you no longer want to try. I'm sorry, but if you go to London
and take that promotion they're surely going to give you, that's
exactly what you're saying."

She swallowed. "You're not sorry."

No, he guessed he wasn't. "I'm not doing a long-distance
thing. I can't. I'm not built for it. Not with you, when I want all
of you. I guess I'm selfish like that."

"Take me back to the train station," she said, all warmth
gone.

"That's it?" he threw at her as she turned and headed to his
truck.

"I need to think," she fired back.

They said nothing more on the short ride back to the station,
Jen staring out the side window the whole time.

He didn't park, but instead just pulled up to the curb outside
the station steps and left the truck idling, the air-conditioning
blasting. He gripped the steering wheel and spoke to the space
between his hands. "I'm not saying it again, Jen. You know
how I feel about you."

When she inhaled, he could have sworn it was ragged. That
maybe she was dragging back her tears by their heels.

"If you want to hear those words," he said, "I need to hear
you say them first. And then I'll know for sure whether or not
you think we have a future."

She sat there for so long he lost track of the branches of his
thoughts. They raced away from him, splintering, turning into
so much doubt and dread.

"I need to think," she said again, only this time in a whisper
that filled the truck cabin. "And I'm trying really, really hard
not to be angry. I'll call you."

Then she did look at him. There was definitely anger in her.
But there was also sadness and attachment, and a powerful
amount of determination that he recognized as her brand. He

desperately hoped she'd figure out for herself what that brand meant.

She opened the door, the latch and squeak ringing in his ears. Once on the ground she looked back into the cab and said, simply, "Bye."

Then she was gone, moving slowly up the steps into the building.

He knew right then that she would be going to London, and that she wasn't coming back.

Chapter

25

*T*here were clouds over London. At least they made for a pretty sunset.

Jen stood in front of one of the three kitchen windows in Tim Bauer's spacious English apartment. The place was severe, like him, with everything in its place. A year ago—hell, a month ago—she would have been dancing through the halls, ecstatic to be put up here. She would have been taking notes on how he lived, how he organized himself. Mulling over ways to apply his work ethic to her own.

Now, having been here a full two weeks, all she did, every night, was stare at the phone in her hand and wonder whom she should call first.

This evening was no different. Below, the random angles of the narrow London streets made a dramatic triangular corner, and the blue-painted pub situated there was doing marvelous business. People spilled out onto the sidewalk, cigarettes and pints in hand. In the distance, above the silver rooftops, rose the imposing dome of St. Paul's Cathedral.

She'd been to London before, to work in Bauer's office here, but she'd never gotten up to Scotland. Odd, that. She'd escaped one life and found another one in a tiny, faux Scotland over in the States, but now that the Borders and Edinburgh and the Highlands were a quick flight or train ride from where she stood right now, she wouldn't get to see them. She would have loved to find Mr. MacDougall's childhood home.

Her palm grew sweaty as she clutched the phone. This was it. She was doing this tonight. Simply because she couldn't go another day without.

She dialed the number she still knew by heart. The phone rang and rang. She didn't ever remember being this nervous. Ever.

"Yeah?" came the throaty voice on the other end.

Jen swallowed. "Hi, Mom."

A long drag on a cigarette. "Aim? You sound different. And what kind of number are you calling from? It's coming through on the caller ID with a bunch of weird zeroes."

She couldn't get any moisture in her mouth. "It's not Aimee. It's Jen."

What followed was the longest pause in the world. "Jennifer." No inflection. No emotion.

"Yes, it's me."

How are you? would have been the dumbest thing in the world to ask, considering they hadn't spoken in ten years, so she didn't.

Another drag on the cigarette. "Are you still in Gleann?"

"No, I left over two weeks ago. I'm in London now."

"London." Mom grunted in the way Jen remembered so vividly—her sitting on the stained couch, a smoke in one hand, reacting to Jen's excellent report card.

She tried to conjure up this new image of Mom that Aimee had painted for her, but it was impossible. Was she gray-haired now? Had she gained or lost weight? Was she still sitting on that couch watching daytime TV?

"England," Jen added.

Mom sighed. "Yeah, I figured that. That where your work is taking you these days?"

Jen hadn't called to talk about London. "Mom, I didn't . . . I had no idea you and Aimee and Ainsley had been talking."

"Why would you? So why are you calling me now, after all this time? Did Aimee put you up to it?"

"No, not at all. This is me. Doing something I should have done a long time ago. I, uh, I'm calling because I just . . . well, I need to. I wanted to personally tell you some things. Is now okay?"

"Yeah." She heard the rattle of a glass ashtray as Mom poked out her smoke. "I don't have to leave for work for fifteen minutes."

Work? She had a job? Jen blinked back surprise. She drew a deep breath and said, "First, I wanted to call you and tell you that I did it. That I finally got to where I always wanted to be."

"You mean London." Mom didn't sound so impressed, but what else was new.

"No. I got a promotion. The big one. The one I've been want-ing since I took the job at Bauer Events after graduation."

Mom must have had a cold or smoker's phlegm or some-thing, because she blew her nose. When she finally spoke, her voice was a little muffled. "Good for you, Jennifer. You must think you're so much better than me."

Ten years of bitterness made the phone weigh a million pounds. Jen sank into a chair. "Um . . ." *Yes,* she wanted to say. *Yes, I do.*

"You *are* better than me, Jennifer," she said, so matter-of-factly that Jen was sure she hadn't heard right. "You always have been."

That's when Jen started to cry. They were silent tears, but they were fat and made big wet spots on her pants. "I have to ask. Are you drinking?"

"If you were seventeen I would've raked your eyes out for that." After a pause she added, "Because the guilty are usually the most defensive."

"So are you?"

"I'm almost two years sober."

Jen wanted to be angry for not knowing this, until she real-ized she had no one to be angry at. It wasn't Aimee's job to tell her. Mom wouldn't have called, considering Jen had made it clear she never wanted to talk to her again. And she couldn't blame Ainsley, who'd only ever wanted a grandma.

Mom said, "I used some of your money for rehab. Well, for a really long time I used it to get really fucking drunk.

Gambling. Some other stupid shit. It took me years to know what I had, to come to appreciate it."

Jen found the strength to stand and moved closer to the window. The lights were coming up over London and she'd never felt so far away from everything. "What changed?"

"Aimee reaching out, despite what I did to her and to you. Ainsley changed me, too. At first it was hard to talk to her, but now I sort of, I don't know, live for it." Mom blew her nose again. "And then there's the fact that your checks never stopped coming, even though I was sure you knew what I was using them for. I felt shame. For the first time in my life. Why'd you send me money, Jennifer?"

It took her a few minutes to answer, because suddenly she was consumed by the memory of Leith's voice. "Someone once told me I feel like I need to fix everyone, that I think I have all the answers. I guess I thought I could fix you like I tried to do with Aimee. I guess I wanted you to do what you just told me you did, about the rehab. And, yeah, I think part of me wanted to rub my success in your face."

"Points for honesty. One thing you've never lacked."

"Neither have you."

Down at the triangular pub, a fight broke out on the sidewalk between groups of guys dressed in different colors meant to represent sports teams she didn't recognize. "Mom, the other reason I'm calling is to tell you that I won't be able to send money for a while. I'm going to be a little short on cash, and I don't know for how long."

What came out of her mother's mouth shocked the hell out of her. "Are you in trouble?"

"No, not in trouble."

"I don't need it anymore, if that's what you're worried about. I have a job. It's just cleaning offices, but it's a job. I've been saving what you've been sending for a surprise trip to see Aimee and the little girl I've never met."

Through the phone, Jen heard the metallic strike of a lighter, the gentle hiss of a newly lit cigarette, and her mom's deep inhale. "Why are you gonna be short on cash? Thought you just told me you got this big promotion?"

"I did get the promotion." Jen placed her palm on the glass. "I just didn't accept it."

* * *

*L*eith had been right. About so much.

Tim had called from New York that morning to offer Jen the position of running the London office. On one hand she'd been expecting it; on the other she'd been in complete denial. She kept waiting for the relief and triumph to sweep through her, but it never came. After telling Tim she'd think about it and would get back to him, she went for a walk along the Thames. She stood on the Millennium Bridge for a long time, over one of the world's great rivers, in one of the world's most majestic cities, and all she could think about was the little creek running through Gleann.

That shouldn't have made any sense. But it did.

She had thought that making it to this point in her career would heal her, that it would take a needle and thread and stitch up what had been shredded during her childhood.

But it didn't actually *mean* anything to her, not inside at least. Not where it mattered most. This promotion was a title and something to tell people, but it was only window dressing.

That true healing she had to find elsewhere. And she already knew where to start looking.

She called Tim back right then and there, plugging one ear with a finger to drown out the sounds of everything she was turning down, and told him, "Thanks, but no." And then gave him her resignation.

The rest of the afternoon she'd hunched over her computer crunching numbers, researching, formulating business plans, consolidating files . . . and trying *not* to call Leith.

He'd made it pretty clear that if and when she came back to him, she had a lot of proving to do. She understood; her track record with taking off and leaving him high and dry wasn't so good. That's exactly what she intended—to give him proof— but she needed to get a lot of things squared away before she contacted him.

Two weeks away from him felt like an eternity, but she would have to force herself to wait just a little bit longer.

After the sun had gone down, and her eyes burned with computer strain, and her brain hurt from thinking, she'd finally sat back and surveyed what she'd created.

It was her dream, her needle and thread, right there in pixels and paragraphs, and she'd never even realized it until this very moment. She'd been dying to call Leith right then and there, but there'd been two other people she needed to talk to first. That's when she'd dialed her mom.

One more person to go.

As expected, voice mail picked up. Jen sighed. "Aimee, it's me. I know you've been getting all my messages these past two weeks and I don't blame you for ignoring them, but please call me back. I just talked to Mom and I want to tell you about it."

An hour and a half later, at nearly midnight London time with still no sleep in sight, the phone rang. And then Jen told Aimee every word she and their mom had shared, except the part about Mom wanting to visit. That little tidbit she'd let come out on its own; she'd let her mom have that.

"Your messages said you're in London. How the hell did *that* happen?"

Jen considered that. "Misguidedly. Anyway, it doesn't matter now. I'm coming home."

"Does Leith know that?"

"We, uh, haven't spoken since the day before I left. I told him I was going to England, he got angry, which made me angry, and then I left. It was stupid and I need to make it up to him. I want to get him back."

A long, pregnant pause. "I'll tell you what you should do. You should go surprise him at the Connecticut Highland Games this weekend."

Her heart started to pound in her ears. "The . . . why?"

"I guess he's throwing? Last I heard was that Duncan dragged him back into the circuit after how well he did in Gleann."

Jen pressed a straight arm to the counter edge and leaned in heavily. "He *threw*? After I left?"

"Yeah. You didn't know?" Aimee sounded genuinely surprised.

"Oh God. No. He didn't say anything."

And why would he have, given how she'd blindsided him with news of her leaving for London? He hadn't wanted to guilt her into staying, because he didn't work like that. He'd just wanted to make his points about her goals and her upbringing and her mom, and to keep himself out of it.

Damn selfless man . . . whom she wanted so much it made her chest ache.

She wished she could have seen him throw.

"So you're coming home?" Aimee cut in.

"I am. I quit my job and I'm going to start my own events company."

It felt incredible to say, the first poke of the needle through torn flesh and muscle.

"I'd say I'm impressed, but very little of what you do doesn't impress me."

Jen smiled into the phone. "You'll like this, then. I'm going to focus on smaller events put on by smaller clients like Gleann who maybe need overall help with organization. I'm a whiz with budgets and I really, really loved bringing the citizens together. You know, teaching them how to fish instead of casting the line out all by myself."

Aimee gasped. "You were really good at that. Maybe Bobbie would hire you. Melissa's underwriting the winter crafts convention, so there's no lack of money. And they trust you."

She couldn't deny it. Going back to teeny tiny Gleann and working on those events gave her a sense of hope, an undeniable exhilaration. "When I get my materials put together, I'll send them over." At last she yawned, the crazy, full day suddenly smacking her upside the head.

"I get the hint," Aimee said. "I'll tell Ainsley you called. She's over at Bryan's now."

"How is my Flirty McGee?"

"Ah, stop! Too young for flirting!"

Not if she kept hanging around T, she wouldn't be, but Jen didn't say that.

"So can I tell Sue what you're doing with your job and all?"

Jen rolled her eyes. "Sure. But don't tell me what she says. I don't want to know if she gives you those tight lips and looks at you over her glasses, and then maybe mentions how I didn't pick up her dog poop that one day fifteen years ago."

Aimee laughed. "Okay, but maybe she'll hire you back for the games next year and, I don't know, actually pay you."

"Love you." She couldn't remember the last time she'd said that to Aimee. Maybe never.

"Love you, too, sis. I was mad at you for leaving during the games, but I'm not anymore. We all came together after you took off. It turned out great. Well, as great as it could be. Everyone talked about what a wonderful job you did. Despite the cow."

"Maybe that could be my new tagline. '*Haverhurst Events. I do a great job. Despite the cow.*'"

Jen hung up with her sister and fell into bed with a smile, her hand stretching to the empty pillow beside her.

*T*hree days later, Jen was carrying a backpack filled with her stuff out of the office building where she'd worked under Tim Bauer for six years. It wasn't much, in the grand scheme of things. She hadn't brought much of herself in.

But that would change. She was going to put her heart and soul into her new venture, and each and every client would be able to see and feel it.

Her phone rang. It did that decidedly less these days, so when it happened it never failed to make her jump and then rush to answer, wondering who it could be. Hoping against hope that it would be a certain someone.

The number on the screen was unrecognizable, but it was an area code she knew to be upstate New York.

"This is Jen Haverhurst."

"Jen, hi, my name is Ann Wagner. I'm director of the Finger Lakes Tourism Bureau. I'm looking for assistance in setting up incentive packages in my area. I'm told this is an area of expertise for you?"

Suddenly Jen felt light as air, her sandals barely touching the concrete. "It is, and I'd love to talk to you about it."

Ann exhaled. "Fantastic!"

"May I ask how you got my name? My business cards aren't even printed yet."

"Oh. Sue McCurdy told me about you."

Jen stopped walking, right there in the middle of the crowded New York sidewalk. Someone crashed into her from the back and glared at her, and she shuffled off to stand in front of the window of a Greek restaurant. "Wait. Sue McCurdy. As in Mayor Sue?"

"I can't believe she wants people to call her that, but that's

Sue for you." Ann chuckled. "She and I were roommates at Syracuse way back when. She called me specifically to give me your name."

Jen slapped a hand over a blue-and-white-striped flag painted on the glass, in order to keep herself upright in the face of shock.

"She said you did a bang-up job up in Gleann for her Highland Games," Ann went on, "and that I couldn't go wrong in hiring you."

Chapter

26

While Gleann had the benefit of the northern New Hampshire mountains, an atmosphere that lent itself more to Scotland, at least the Connecticut Highland Games, held in a small town northeast of Stamford, didn't have a giant glass box of an abandoned corporation looming over it. These smallish games, where Jen had secretly confirmed Leith was throwing, were set in a beautiful park surrounded by thick stands of trees and pockets of shade and shadow. A building of pale stone overlooked the circle where pipe bands marched in to their competition. Little girls dressed in tartan and velvet, their hair pulled tightly back, giggled and stretched, preparing for their competition. The blare of perfectly timed drums and pipes sailed toward the athletics field, and it was there Jen headed.

Unsure of how Leith would take her sudden appearance, she timed her arrival toward the end of the athletics competition in the afternoon, desperately wanting to see him throw but also not wanting to distract him. After all, he'd thrown *after* she'd left Gleann, and apparently her absence had changed quite a bit in him.

The day was ridiculously hot, and people huddled under

portable canopies and umbrellas as they cheered on the ten or
so men and one woman, all kilted up, on the athletics field.

Still a good distance away, Jen immediately picked out Leith.
He'd cut off the sleeves to his T-shirt, and the navy blue thing
with the white *X* on the front to symbolize the Scottish flag
was nearly soaked through. He wore his father's kilt and one of
his giant smiles. The kind that lit up his whole body and envel-
oped anyone near him. God, she'd missed him.

"And now," the announcer said, his tinny old man's voice
sputtering through the bad speakers, "the final round of weight
for height." Applause circled the towers holding the crossbar.
"Competitors are Duncan Ferguson and Leith MacDougall."

Jen grew excited. She'd arrived just in time.

Leith gave a respectable nod to the audience, but Duncan
lifted both meaty arms and turned in a circle, mouth opened
in a roar, begging the audience to give it up for him. They did,
too. Leith just shook his grin at the ground, sweaty, shaggy
hair plastering itself to his cheeks and neck. He pushed it off
his face and went over to the towers and bar.

A few more onlookers straggled over to watch this event,
and Jen found a place in the shade of a big tree, behind an older
couple holding hands in their lawn chairs—just out of sight,
should Leith happen to look up.

He didn't, though. An intense look of concentration masked
his face as he went over to the weight—a great black orb with
a thick ring attached to its top—lying tilted in the grass
between the towers. She'd once picked up that same kind of
weight in the MacDougall garage, and had nearly toppled over
under its fifty-six pounds. She remembered how Leith had
laughed with her, but Mr. MacDougall had thrown out some
words of encouragement, wanting her to try the women's
twenty-eight pounder instead. She'd politely declined.

"The bar is at fifteen feet," said the announcer. "Each
thrower gets three attempts to get it over using any style necessary, as long as they use only one hand. The weight touching
the bar doesn't matter, as long as it ends up on the other side.
First to throw: Leith MacDougall. A fine Scottish lad."

Leith pointed at the announcer, grinning, then positioned
himself under the bar, looking up several times to get his placement just right. Giving his back to the tower, planting his feet

wide, tugging the bottom of his kilt up and over his knees, he reached down and wrapped one big hand around the ring of the weight. Any semblance of a grin died. His lips rolled inward with concentration.

Knees bent, torso forward, the great muscles in his gripping arm flexed, the ligaments popping out. She watched his neck and face flush. With a heave he pulled the weight from the ground, sending his body rocking, the weight sailing once between his legs, once along the side of his body, and a third time back between his legs. When the weight came forward, he pushed his legs to straighten, let out a shout of effort, and launched the weight high up into the air.

The hefty thing sailed upward, looking way too big and bulky to get anywhere near fifteen feet. Leith stepped away, whipped around . . . and watched, teeth clenched, as the curve of the ball hit the bar, then rolled over the back side to land with a *thunk* in the grass.

The crowd cheered, no one louder than Jen. Leith slapped his hands together once and then acknowledged the audience. Jen ducked behind the old couple in the off chance he'd see her, but he turned to Duncan, who was showing him a jovial double thumbs-down.

Duncan gave his competitor a hearty clap on the back, then assumed his own position under the bar. He used a little different method to throwing this event—a full-body pivot and spin, more like a classic shot put throw. To Jen, he didn't seem as graceful as Leith, being shorter and bulkier around the middle. Leith was more streamlined, a little more top-heavy, and at least five inches taller.

Duncan made fifteen feet, but missed sixteen all three times.

Leith got sixteen on the second attempt, and the crowd erupted. Duncan stood off to the side, shaking his head but grinning. When the cheering died down, Jen distinctly heard Duncan say, "Good to have you back."

She read Leith's lips: "Good to be back."

"And the Scottish lad wins the weight for height!" chimed the announcer to a terrific amount of applause, even though it was apparent Duncan had been the overall crowd favorite.

Leith took a seat on a stool and grabbed a water bottle, pouring some down his throat, then squirting a healthy dose over his head and on the back of his neck. It took all of Jen's strength not to go to him. Another competitor went over to talk to Leith. The other guy was older, clearly strong but in a softer, less defined way. It looked like he was asking Leith for advice on the weight, because Leith was showing the man a grip and gesturing to his back and legs.

This was how Leith had been his whole life. Giving. Accommodating. Generous sometimes to the point of forgoing what he wanted. When he'd revealed the bit of resentment he held for his father and for Gleann, it had shocked her at first, but now she understood. It was okay for someone like him to feel that.

"Next and final event, the heavy hammer," the announcer said. "And looking at the score sheets, ladies and gentlemen, this event will determine the overall winner of the heavy athletic events here in Connecticut. Duncan Ferguson and Leith Mac-Dougall vying for first place, Duncan with the slight edge. It is my understanding that Duncan won the Gleann games a few weeks ago, so MacDougall might have a score to settle here."

Leith and the older man looking for advice went over to the edge of the field and grabbed a foldable set of chain-link fence, like what you'd see behind home plate in Little League games. They set it up behind a log painted white that they were using as the trig. Duncan brought over the hammer—a large ball on the end of a long bar weighing twenty-two pounds—and set it by the trig.

The scene was so much like Gleann, with the cook smoke drifting through the air, the kids' area off to the side where the little ones were trying to throw minicabers, the same bagpipe song played over and over again with varying degrees of talent. And Leith, out in the athletic field, looking every bit at home as he did in his truck or . . . lying next to her. Or on top of her.

She wanted that back. She *needed* that back.

On the field, as though her desire had formed a whip and lashed out from her body, Leith looked up from where he was toeing the dirt behind the trig. It wasn't like his gaze had been wandering around the crowd and then he did a double take when his eyes mistakenly landed on her. No; he raised his head, his stare making a burning line across the grass, and found her instantly.

Jen startled, pushing away from the tree, her arms falling to her sides. Her first thought sent her back in time and space to how she might have acted in seventh grade when the boy she crushed on looked her way. For a moment, she considered ducking low and crawling away. But he'd seen her, recognized her, knew she was there—there was no denying it now. And really, she'd come here to talk to him anyway.

Leith froze and just stared. Then, shaking himself out of it, he excused himself from the other competitors and stalked toward her, kilt flapping about his legs, those powerful arms swinging. A few onlookers watched him pass, skittering out of his way as though he might mow them down.

Jen took a deep breath and left the shade of the tree, meeting him on the border of the field.

She smiled at him, because he was just too beautiful and it made her heart swell with equal parts pleasure and hurt. His eyes, however, were far too wide with confusion and, yes, a little anger. For showing up? For not calling first? She couldn't guess, but it actually made what she'd come here to do a little easier. She'd prepared for his doubt, and if there was one thing Jen Haverhurst excelled at, it was planning.

"Hi." His twinge of anger morphed into wonder and surprise. "What are you doing here?"

"I'm sorry," she replied, suddenly feeling the ninety-degree heat in triplicate. "I didn't mean for you to see me until after you'd thrown. I didn't want to distract you."

He ran a hand through his wet hair and swept a gaze around the grounds. "I should've known word would get out. Aimee?"

Jen nodded. She almost said, "I wish you'd told me you'd thrown in Gleann," but then realized that would have been the worst thing, considering how they'd parted. Instead she said, "When I heard you were throwing this close to New York, I had to come."

His eyebrows made a V. "What happened to London?"

That fed her a little more confidence. "That's one of the reasons why I came. I have a lot to tell you, a lot to say. Will you meet me tonight? After this is over?"

His face said that he was being cautious because she'd disappointed him twice before.

No more. I won't disappoint you anymore, she longed to

say right then and there, but knew he wouldn't buy it. She needed him to meet her later.

"It won't take long," she added hurriedly, "if you have plans with the guys or something."

He rotated each arm, signaling that his mind was divided between her and why he was here on this field. "We were all going to grab a beer in town later."

"Please. A few minutes, is all."

He considered her for more seconds than she thought herself capable of withstanding. "All right," he finally replied, and she exhaled. Then she gave him the address of where she wanted him to come.

He started to walk away and she got scared over his indifference. Then he stopped and turned back around. "The heavy hammer's not my best event. Just so you know."

These games were larger in attendance than Gleann's, but the grounds weren't that much more expansive, and the athletic field was ringed with trees. There was room enough to throw the heavy hammer without compromising safety, but the light hammer, with its sixteen-pound weight and the way it cut through the air much faster and farther, couldn't be thrown here due to space.

Out of all the heavy athletic events, to Jen the hammer was the craziest. The movement to throw it was incredibly primitive, and also looked beyond unnatural. Dangerous, even. Every time she watched this particular throw, someone's broken back or ripped muscle seemed imminent. As she recalled from Mr. MacDougall, form was paramount.

She worried terribly that she'd screwed this up for Leith. That he'd break form and then totally break his back.

The other competitors cycled through their first attempts, including the sole female thrower who had the raucous support from the gallery. As far as Jen could tell, she threw awesomely, using a smaller hammer than the guys. Good on her.

The announcer left Leith and Duncan for last.

When Leith's name was called, he raised an arm to the onlookers, his profile showing lips pressed tightly together. He approached the trig, divided from the audience by the fencing, his steps heavy and focused. For this event the throwers faced the audience, their backs to the open field, and loosed the hammer backward over one shoulder. They used the best of three throws.

She didn't know why she'd been so worried. Leith was nothing but centered.

Lifting the hammer up by the long end, the ball resting on the ground, he kicked his legs out, shifting to find the perfect stance. When he got it, he tilted the long hammer to one side and wrapped both hands around the end of the bar, pinky of one hand resting against the thumb of the other. He swung the ball out far to his right so his arms were angled low in front of him and the ball was in the grass. Knees slightly bent, he shifted his weight, heaved the hammer ball off the ground and swung the thing in a great arc in front of his body. It seemed to start slowly, almost too slowly, but using his tremendous power, the hammer looped once up and around his head. Momentum and strength brought it swooping back down in front. He kept it going, around and around and around his body. Faster and faster with every turn, every second. His face reddened, his features flat with exertion.

Each loop around was punched with a crazy power that pulled out every line in every muscle of his arms. Just when it seemed like the hammer movement would carry him off his feet, he brought it across his left shoulder and . . . released.

Leith roared, fists slapping to his sides.

Jen held her breath.

The ball sailed back and back over the empty space, looking far too heavy and strange to ever be airborne. It landed hard in the grass and a kilted judge jogged over to give it a measure, but it was clear to everyone in attendance that he'd blown away all the other competitors.

Only then did Leith swivel around, and it was to great applause, perhaps none louder than Duncan's masculine grunts of "Yeah! Yeah!"

The judge called out a distance to the announcer, who said into the microphone, "Seventy-three feet, one and a quarter inches." As a new round of cheers went up, Leith finally smiled, his shoulders dropping in obvious relief. In clear pride. He melted into his group, and the other throwers pounded fists on his back.

Duncan threw one foot shorter than Leith on his first attempt, then six inches longer on his second.

Leith never beat his first hammer throw, but he also never stopped smiling or laughing. And Jen thought that the only time she'd ever seen him look happier was the night they'd first kissed, all those years and miles away.

Chapter

27

Leith wheeled his truck into the parking lot of the address Jen had thrown at him back at the games. It was a small, well-kept strip mall on the outskirts of the seaside community of Norwalk. He sat behind the wheel in the lot, staring at the suite number she'd indicated, confused by the dark windows with the drawn shades. A sign was taped to the glass—*For Rent. Call Sheryl.* And then Sheryl's number—but Leith double-checked the address and, yep, this was where Jen had told him to go.

He got out of the truck. Even though the sun was setting, the day was finally cooling off, and he'd showered back at his motel, he started to sweat.

Seeing Jen across the field like that . . . He'd written her off weeks earlier. She'd gone to London, just as he'd predicted. She hadn't called before leaving, just as he'd predicted. She never came back, *exactly* as he'd predicted.

So he'd done what any lovesick, pissed-off, heartbroken American male would do. He punched a hole in the wall of his motel and had to pay damages, then he'd gone out and gotten drunk. And then he'd tried like hell to get over her. Again.

To do that, he knew he couldn't go back to Gleann. At least, not to live. He'd keep what few accounts he had left there, with Chris on staff. Maybe if things picked up in the town as Mayor Sue hoped, he could expand and open a full branch, with Chris in charge. While he had no set jobs to speak of in Connecticut, he did have his talent and determination. And even though Hal Carriage had nixed Leith's best start, Leith still had Rory's support, and she'd given him some serious leads, talking up his name in her new circle of friends. He'd made a few contacts at the games today, too, and he'd follow up with them this week. He was hopeful.

So he was staying in Connecticut. Starting over. And he was throwing again, which sent him flying high in a way he'd nearly forgotten. How could he have done that? How could he have ever turned his back on something that fed both his competitive nature and his spirit?

In a way, Jen had been right all those weeks ago. He *had* been afraid of not winning, thinking that second place would never fill him up like first. What a fucking moron. He'd held his own against Duncan and it had felt so, so amazing. He would make time to train now. No more excuses.

No more worrying that he'd let his father down.

But then there was the matter of Jen Haverhurst. He couldn't describe how exhilarated he'd felt seeing her face in the crowd that afternoon. She was so damn good at that: disappearing then reappearing in shocking, dramatic ways that had his heart pummeling his ribs and his head telling him to not fall for her again.

Only he had. And this was the second time she'd come back. What was that old saying? Fool me once, shame on you. Fool me twice, shame on me? Yeah, no matter what she was going to say to him in there, he had to remember who she was, her MO. He had to protect himself a hell of a lot better this time.

He crossed the short lot and tried the door. Locked. *What the—*

The latch clicked and the door opened inward. Jen stood before him.

"Hey—whoa." He couldn't hold back his verbal reaction as he eyed her strict black skirt and fitted black short-sleeved sweater with the severe V-neck that did killer things for her tits. Her hair was pulled into a ponytail and she wore those glasses, the ones he'd first seen on her through Mildred's kitchen window.

She cleared her throat and extended her hand, not an ounce of emotion on her face. "I'm so glad you could make it, Mr. MacDougall. Come in."

He let out an uncomfortable laugh. "Okaaaay." As he took her hand, he noted absently that she had a great, firm handshake. But of course she did.

She widened the door to let him enter, then locked it behind him. Inside it was strangely dark, and it took his eyes a few moments to adjust. Only three pieces of furniture—two cushioned chairs facing a long, narrow table—were set right in the center of the room. On the table was Jen's fifth limb, her open laptop, connected to a small projector. A square of bright, white light streamed from the lens and struck the empty, back office wall.

"What is this place?" he asked.

But she just gave him a polite smile and said, "Please have a seat." She gestured to one of the chairs facing the lit wall.

As he lowered himself to the chair that smelled and felt brand new, she walked around the table. It was impossible not to notice her legs in that skirt, how they ended in towering black heels with red soles, a delicate strap wrapped around her ankle.

Focus, Dougall. Keep your head.

"So what's up?" Anticipation mixed with frustration, and that wasn't the best combination. Especially since lurking just underneath it, ready to stab its way through to the surface, was base lust and . . . hope.

Why are you here, Jen? Why are you back? Why?

Jen picked up a small remote from the table and stood just to one side of the square of light. "I am a businesswoman. I love staying busy. I love making clients happy. I love laying out a plan and carrying it out."

He opened his hands. "Yes. I know."

"And I love my phone and this computer, as you can attest to." He had to crack a smile at that. "But what I don't love— something I've come to realize over the past weeks and months—is working for someone else. I thought once that dragging as many pretty, vapid models to a product rollout actually fulfilled me, that it would be what set me on top."

Leith held his breath and straightened in his chair.

"But I was wrong." Jen clicked a button on the remote and the screen burst with understated, simple color.

Jen Haverhurst. Strategic Planning and Events.

"You're sitting in my new world headquarters," she said with a smile. "Here. In Connecticut. Not New York."

Holy shit.

"My new company will focus on bringing suburban and rural communities, small businesses, and entrepreneurs together to put on fantastic events within their budget. I will meet with clients to strategically plan functions that enhance their brand, expand their influence, and are just plain fun."

She spun through a series of slides, going through her marketing plan and potential clients, like he was some sort of investor. Maybe he was. Because every sentence, every word she said drove into his brain, slowly making him realize that she *wasn't* running away. She wasn't leaving him this time; she was *joining* him. This place was only half an hour from where he'd chosen to base his own new company.

"You were right. I didn't love my job before. Working in Gleann, I discovered what I do love, and it's this."

"Wow." He just sat there, stunned into silence, surely looking like a fool with his mouth hanging open. "I—"

"I'm not finished." She held up a teasingly prim hand, then walked across the projector beam to the other side. As she did, the light cast her figure in silhouette—the gentle swing of her ponytail, the curve of her ass, the proud lift of her chin—and it mesmerized him.

She extended out a slim metal pointer with a balled tip.

"This"—she advanced a slide and slapped the pointer with gusto to the wall—"is why we belong together."

On the wall, in bright rectangles of color, was one of her famous charts. He ground his molars into his cheek to keep from smiling.

On scales of one to one hundred, she'd bar-graphed the following categories: Sense of Humor, Mutual Respect, Future Goals, Sexual Compatibility, and Physical Proximity.

"Sense of Humor," she began in that same businesslike tone. "You and I are at one hundred. It's why we became friends in the first place, right? We laugh at the same things, make jokes no one else gets—"

"Relocate Mayor Sue's outdoor doghouses to the lawn of Town Hall."

"Ahhh, now there's an idea to file away for later. Put that on our Action Item list."

"Will do." He leaned forward, rubbing his hands together. "Go on."

"Mutual Respect. As you can see, I've divided this column into two. One for you, one for me." She turned serious, the pointer dropping as she faced him. The light from the projector reflected off her glasses. "My respect for you is one hundred, as high as it can possibly get. I want you to know that. I *need* you to know that."

He couldn't talk around the pressure in his chest.

"But I only gave myself a fifty from your point of view, because of what you told me earlier. How you thought I was compromising myself for revenge or for some reason other than what was in my heart. You were right, you know. It took me going away to see that, to know what I lost, what I wanted back, and where I want to be for good. I know it all now. It's very, very clear to me."

He pumped a thumb a couple of times toward the ceiling. "My number needs to go up a few notches. Like, say, fifty."

She drew a deep breath. "Well. Then, that brings me to my next point. We have similar goals. We want our own businesses to be successful. We have dreams and I know we would support each other in those dreams."

He nodded, completely agreeing. "What about family?" The question surprised them both. He held on to it though, grinding his teeth. He wouldn't take it back. "I mean, you have Aimee and Ainsley, but that's about it. I don't have anyone." He cleared his throat. "Would you want family? With me?"

She looked at him for a long moment. "I think we need to get our careers going first, make sure they're nice and established." Her expression turned wonderfully warm. "But, yes. I think I might."

"Action Item list?"

"Given that our Sexual Compatibility score is closer to two hundred"—a slap of the pointer—"I'd say that 'action' is a good word for it. But I don't even want to think about it for a couple of years. That okay?"

Pressing his lips together, he nodded. "A sound plan, boss."

"Which brings us to the final point: Physical Proximity. As you can see, the score is at zero, but I want to fix that. All the rest doesn't matter if I don't, and I know your coming to New York just won't work for your business. Once my lease runs out in the city, I do not plan on renewing it. I want my own place. Here. With an easy commute to my new work and a bed big enough for you. Maybe someplace like this. Or this. Or this." She flashed a series of photos of homes for sale in the area.

Leaning an elbow on the armrest, he scratched at his face and then covered his mouth with his hand. If she could see how much he was enjoying this, how much he never wanted her to stop, how hard it was to hold himself back from jumping up from the chair and pinning her against that lit wall, he feared it might scare her off again.

Except nothing about her looked scared right now. She was courageous and gorgeous and brilliant, and he could not stop staring.

"Oh!" she said, setting down the pointer. "One last thing, but perhaps the most important."

She slid right in front of the projector beam at the same moment she clicked the remote, her body bathed in light. And then her fingers rose to the buttons of her sweater. Starting at the top, between her breasts, she unfastened the first one.

A peek of a nude lace bra had him involuntarily scooting forward on the chair, his mouth first drying up, then watering.

Another button. Her lips quirked. The smooth patch of skin below her bra looked delicious. He wanted to run his tongue up and down the vertical divot between her stomach muscles.

Was that . . .? There were lines on her stomach that he thought could be letters, but were too difficult to make out. Things that hadn't been there last time she'd undressed for him. Did she get a tattoo over there in London? He squinted.

Another button came undone. The black fabric parted even more, exposing her breasts and coming apart all the way to her bellybutton. Now he was sure. They were definitely letters on her midsection. Not tattooed, not painted, but coming from the projector.

The final button. The sweater halves separated, and then

came fully off. She let it drop to the ground. Then she reached around and unzipped her skirt. Shimmied out of the tight thing and then let that fall, too. She stood there, perfectly still, with her perfect body in that perfect lace bra and underwear almost the exact shade of her skin, and he had to concentrate to absorb what he was looking at.

There, in black computerized script, written across the smooth skin of her belly, were the words, "I love you."

He blinked at them several times.

"So that's it," she said, and her voice sounded shaky. "That's my presentation."

He ripped his gaze from her beautiful body to her even more beautiful face. "Can you say it?"

"Yes. I can now." He loved how her body moved, unclothed, when she breathed. "I'm in love with you. I always have been, even when I wasn't fully aware of it, even over all these years. It's why coming back to you felt so easy, so natural. I'm not saying that we were meant to be together or destined or anything as new-agey as that, but I do think we had to grow up, that we had to figure things out on our own in order to find our way back to each other. I know that I will always love you, even if . . . even if you give me a taste of my own medicine by walking away right now."

"Fuck." He got to his feet. "No way I'm walking out. You did one hell of a job here."

Now she smiled, and it was shining with relief and happiness. Her eyes were huge and glorious. She started toward him but he threw out a hand. "Don't. Stay right there."

He went to her, skirting around the desk to take in the whole sight of her, that gorgeous declaration written across her body just for him. Spoken just for him. He reached out and removed her glasses.

"Look at you," he whispered, and he went to his knees.

Then he was touching those projected words, throwing them across his own fingers, mixing them together. He leaned forward to press a kiss to her skin and the words disappeared.

"I'm sorry you didn't win today." Her hands in his hair now. "Was it because of me?"

He laughed. "What? Didn't you see that first hammer throw? That was a personal record. I kicked ass." He rocked to his feet, and then walked her backward until she hit the wall, his hand behind her head. He settled into her body. "I was shit before you showed up."

Maybe that was true in more ways than just today.

"But you won the weight for height and you didn't know I was there watching."

He thought about that. "Maybe some part of me knew."

He kissed her smile, wrapping himself around her. The projector light fell across his back, and every now and then his eyelids would flicker open to see the tangle of shadows their bodies made. He was almost painfully hard and she was mostly naked, and he prayed she still had that stash of condoms in her giant purse.

Pulling her away from the wall, he spun her, turning, then pressed her onto the brand new table, shoving aside the laptop and projector. To her credit, she didn't protest. He hoped this would be her desk someday. Every time she'd sit down at it to work, she'd remember exactly what he was about to do to her on it.

He kissed her for what seemed like forever, stopping only to whip off his shirt.

"So what exactly are we doing?" She was breathless, eyes wild, lips smudged.

He came down on top of her, skin on skin, folding her into an embrace. "We're starting over," he whispered into her ear. "Together."

Author's Note

The New Hampshire Highland Games exist, but all other games and societies mentioned in *Long Shot* are fictional. Real Highland Games take place all over the world. There's a very good chance there are games near you. If you're interested in seeing what they're all about, do an Internet search, pack a lawn chair, bring your family, and enjoy a bit of history.

TURN THE PAGE FOR A SPECIAL PREVIEW OF

THE NEXT HIGHLAND GAMES NOVEL

BY HANNA MARTINE

Coming in Fall 2014 from

Berkley Sensation!

*W*hiskey shouldn't be untouchable, relegated only to a certain social level of drinker, but that's exactly what Shea and her bottles were today, hidden away in a too-fancy tent on a small rise overlooking the heavy athletic field. An actual velvet rope kept most attendees away from the fine brown whiskey she served, and no one could enter who wasn't wearing a one-hundred-dollar yellow wristband. Ridiculous for this kind of festival, but that's what the organizers of this Highland Games wanted: a special place to send their VIPs, and any other attendee willing to pay for the "privilege."

Shea just wanted to talk whiskey. Just wanted to serve what she loved.

Two couples ducked out of the bright sun and came in laughing. The taller husband, the one in a plaid, short-sleeved button-down shirt, was holding a set of stacked, empty beer cups. A Drinker, Shea pegged him, come in here chasing the buzz. The other man, the one in a blue T-shirt, headed right for Shea, nodding as though they already knew each other. He was either an Assumer—someone who thought he knew a lot about the good stuff—or a Brown Vein—someone who really did know.

Of the women, one wore a red visor that parked itself around her ears and extended far over her face. The other had a short blond ponytail. Neither looked particularly interested in why they'd come in here, though all four sported wristbands.

Shea spread her arms across the table and gave them all a welcoming smile. Didn't matter why they came in. They were giving the drink a chance, and educating newcomers was one of her favorite parts of her job. Sometimes it was the best kind of challenge, to win over someone who'd been skeptical—a Doubter—or who had cut their teeth at age fourteen on ten-dollar bodega whiskey they'd snuck from their parents' liquor cabinets.

"So what do these get us?" Drinker waved his yellow wrist.

Always genial, always polite. "Tastes of three amazing whiskeys and a walk-through of each, by yours truly."

"That's a big deal, my friend," added the other man. To Shea he gave a small nod. "Saw you on the History Channel the other night." He didn't mention which special.

"Yeah? That's always great to hear. Glad you came by." She turned to her artful setup of bottles and swung back around holding a tray of glasses, flipping each over to slide across the white tablecloth with practiced ease. One, two, three, four—

A fifth yellow wristband appeared at the elbow of the man she was leaning toward pegging as a Brown Vein. This new wristband wrapped around an arm that was crusty with caked mud at the elbow, the fingers and palm looking like they'd tried to be wiped clean, but black still clung under the nails. Shea followed that arm, which widened out significantly at the biceps, upward to take in the newcomer's red-and-black-striped rugby jersey. His short dark hair was sweat-damp and stuck out all over the place, his cheeks sunburned.

"Hi," he said. "Do you remember me?"

She blinked at him. Out of the corner of her eye, she saw one of the wives nudge the other.

Shea remembered regular faces, especially those who repeatedly came in to the Amber Lounge in Manhattan, but with so many tastings and events and interviews these days, transient people tended to dissipate from her memory.

Yet there was . . . something . . . familiar about him. Something about the off-center, bright-white smile against the tanned skin layered with sweat and specks of dirt. But she couldn't place it right away, and there were four other customers who needed her attention.

"I'm sorry, I don't." She was careful to hold on to the genial smile.

"I'm Byrne."

A little cocky of him, but not quite obnoxious, to assume that she'd remember him based on one name. She didn't.

"Shea Montgomery," she replied, using the moment to swivel back around, reset the tray, and grab the first bottle.

"Yes, I know."

The sound of his laugh, soft and low, slid an invisible hand around the nape of her neck, took a light hold, then dragged itself down her back. A delicious shiver. This did not happen to her while she was pouring.

People laughed in her bar every day, in tones exactly like Byrne's, and it never gave her that reaction. She shook it off and faced her tasters, holding the eighteen-year-old blend. She poured a shallow tasting amount in each glass, starting with Drinker and ending with Byrne, who pushed his glass a few inches closer.

"Last summer?" he prompted.

She made the mistake of looking up, of getting a good, long look at his eyes. An almost-powder-blue with a dark blue ring around the edges.

"Up in Gleann, New Hampshire," he continued. "That cow took down your tent. Me and my team helped you clean it up."

The bottle slipped from her fingers. Just a few inches, but it made a graceless clink on the table.

He had a crooked smile that layered a boyish tint over his confident, intense focus on her, and softened the way he pressed his hipbones right up against the bar.

And that was far longer a personal assessment of any taster she ever allowed herself. Time to move on.

"Oh, yeah. Now I remember." Cool as the breeze, that was Shea.

She purposely left Byrne, stepped to the middle of her set of tasters, and poured herself her own tiny glass. "Are we ready, folks?"

Drinker held up the small, squat stemmed glass. "Why not the flat-bottom glasses? What do you call those again?"

"These are better for nosing the whiskey. Here, hold the base like—" She didn't mean to look over. Habit, really, to take in everyone at the tasting table, to make sure she had their attention and that they knew they were important to her.

Assumer—for that's what she knew the second husband to be now—was grasping the glass underneath, holding it in his palm like a bowl. But Byrne already had the base balanced lightly in his fingertips. Correctly. As he set his elbow on the bar, the whiskey in his glass was as still as a windless hidden lake.

She ripped her gaze from him and focused on the couples. "Hold it like this." She showed them how to hold the base of the glass and not grip the bowl like a Viking. "What we're going to do first is nose the whiskey three times, each time slightly longer than the last. One second, two seconds, three seconds. I'm going to count. Why don't you all watch me."

The women shared a glance and laughed, and Shea wondered how many of those empty plastic beer cups were theirs.

"One."

Shea lifted the glass to her face, inserted her nose, and inhaled.

The couples followed suit, and displayed pretty much the range of reaction she'd expected. Everything from I Don't Give A Shit Let's Drink, to Ew This Is Disgusting, to dramatic, chest-pounding coughing thanks to inhaling too deeply and too long. Assumer's expression said that this was nothing he hadn't already known.

And then there was Byrne. Nose in his glass for about a quarter second longer than was necessary. Powder-blue eyes lifted just over the rim. Set solely on her. He was feeding her some serious energy. Shouldn't a rugby player have released all that on the field? And shouldn't a rugby player be able to read the defense correctly? Who did he think she was? That she'd ever been affected by flirting from the other side of the bar? This flat surface in front of her where she daily poured out her heart was No Man's Land. Quite literally.

"Should be different the second time, now that you've got the shock of the alcohol out of the way," she heard herself saying. "It should be sweeter."

The corner of Byrne's mouth twitched, a hint of that crooked smile, then he buried his nose in the glass again, following her movements to the letter. Concentrating. Not looking at her. Black lines of dirt settled into the deep grooves of concentration along his forehead.

On cue, Assumer started spouting off to his companions a list of all the things he smelled in the whiskey, and while there were never any right or wrong suggestions as to specific scents—it was an entirely personal experience—he was messing with her rhythm.

"And the third?" Byrne asked Shea, cutting into Assumer's thesaurus recitation. Assumer shut up, throwing a glance over his shoulder at the rugby player.

"On the third nose," Shea said, "you should smell some fruit, going deeper into the intricacies of the glass."

Her tasters followed her movements.

"Byrne! You done in there yet? Come on, let's go!"

Byrne turned to the sound of the chorus of male voices. Outside in the sun, the rest of his team, muddy and disheveled in red-and-black, beckoned to him, laughing. No other rugby players wore yellow wristbands.

Byrne acknowledged them with his glass, then tasted what Shea had poured.

The brown liquid disappeared slowly into his mouth. His jaw worked it over for a good four or five seconds. Biting it, chewing it. Savoring it, as it should be done. Then he swallowed it back, his throat working.

Exactly the way she was about to instruct her newbies.

Byrne lifted his eyes to Shea without a hint of pretentiousness or flirting. "Excellent, thank you." Then, with a nod to the other four people, he swiveled and left her tent.

He had a long stride, masculine but oddly graceful. A leisurely confidence to his gait. He also had ridiculous legs, and she was annoyed with herself for noticing. They were tanned and thick and strong, a distinct pronunciation to his quads. Goddamn it.

Outside, she watched him wiggle off the yellow wristband in a way that would have the organizers rethinking their purchase next year, should they have seen that. Byrne went over to a group of middle-aged adults spreading out a blanket next to the flag rope surrounding the athletic field. He tapped a woman on the shoulder, said something to her, then when she smiled and nodded, he offered her his hundred-dollar wristband.

Then he pulled three more brand-new ones out of his shorts pocket and passed them out to the others. As one of the men reached for his wallet, Byrne waved off any sort of compensation.

The four recipients of the new wristbands slapped them on, and Byrne headed back to his team.

As he passed by the roped-off outdoor seating of the whiskey tent, he turned his head and immediately, instantly found Shea. Found her staring.

She quickly ducked her head and wiped off an already-clean section of her serving table. But not before she caught a final glimpse of that crooked smile, far too bright in the sunshine.

That crooked smile promised a lot. Things she hadn't allowed herself, or been afforded, to think about in a long, long time. Things that hit her right where she hadn't been touched in an embarrassing number of months.

It disturbed her, to become disarmed while in uniform, so to speak. It disturbed her more that the man who'd done it was a taster, and quite possibly a Brown Vein. An absolute no-no. He wouldn't win, though. She wasn't one to ever back down from a good challenge. He had to know that even though he'd caught her staring, and even though she'd looked away like a virgin schoolgirl, it didn't mean he'd won, or that he'd gained any sort of ground with her. She had rules to uphold, a business reputation to maintain.

But when she looked up to tell him all that with her cool expression and Stay Back eyes, Byrne was gone.

Discover Romance

berkleyjoveauthors.com

See what's coming up next from your
favorite romance authors and explore all
the latest Berkley, Jove, and Sensation
selections.

See what's new

~

Find author appearances

~

Win fantastic prizes

~

Get reading recommendations

~

Chat with authors and other fans

~

Read interviews with authors you love

Penguin Group (USA) Online

What will you be reading tomorrow?

Patricia Cornwell, Nora Roberts, Catherine Coulter,
Ken Follett, John Sandford, Clive Cussler,
Tom Clancy, Laurell K. Hamilton, Charlaine Harris,
J. R. Ward, W.E.B. Griffin, William Gibson,
Robin Cook, Brian Jacques, Stephen King,
Dean Koontz, Eric Jerome Dickey, Terry McMillan,
Sue Monk Kidd, Amy Tan, Jayne Ann Krentz,
Daniel Silva, Kate Jacobs...

You'll find them all at
penguin.com

Read excerpts and newsletters,
find tour schedules and reading group guides,
and enter contests.

Subscribe to Penguin Group (USA) newsletters
and get an exclusive inside look
at exciting new titles and the authors you love
long before everyone else does.

PENGUIN GROUP (USA)
penguin.com